Praise for *Lady in the Lake*

"The closest writer America has to Ruth Rendell. . . . What makes this book special, even extraordinary, is that the crossword puzzle aspect is secondary. . . . [*Lady in the Lake*] reflects the gulf which then existed between what women were expected to be and what they aspired to be."
—Stephen King

"Don't miss this novel."
—Anna Quindlen, *New York Times* bestselling author

"A cavalcade of narrators—including Cleo's ghost, who wants Maddie to stop poking into her world—and Lippman's expert storytelling bring the city's tensions wondrously to life."
—*People*

"[Lippman] tells a classic mystery through the prism of many characters, all feeling the reverberations of dawning feminism and racial tension in civil-rights-era Baltimore. . . . *Lady in the Lake* is aching, thoughtful, and compulsively readable."
—*Vanity Fair*

"Baltimore in the mid-1960s is the setting of *Lady in the Lake*, the latest novel from the ever impressive Laura Lippman. . . . Lippman's book is revelatory, too, in showing the personal and professional costs to others—friends, loved ones, sources, witnesses—of Maddie's single-minded quest for achievement and recognition."
—*Wall Street Journal*

LADY IN THE LAKE

LADY IN THE LAKE

A NOVEL

LAURA
LIPPMAN

wm
WILLIAM MORROW
An Imprint of HarperCollins*Publishers*

P.S.™ is a trademark of HarperCollins Publishers.

LADY IN THE LAKE. Copyright © 2019 by Laura Lippman. Excerpt from DREAM GIRL © 2021 by Laura Lippman. All rights reserved. Printed in the United States of America. No part of this book may be used or reproduced in any manner whatsoever without written permission except in the case of brief quotations embodied in critical articles and reviews. For information, address HarperCollins Publishers, 195 Broadway, New York, NY 10007.

HarperCollins books may be purchased for educational, business, or sales promotional use. For information, please email the Special Markets Department at SPsales@harpercollins.com.

A hardcover edition of this book was published in 2019 by William Morrow, an imprint of HarperCollins Publishers.

FIRST WILLIAM MORROW PAPERBACK EDITION PUBLISHED 2020.

Designed by Fritz Metsch

The Library of Congress has catalogued a previous edition as follows:
Names: Lippman, Laura, 1959– author.
Title: Lady in the lake : a novel / Laura Lippman.
Description: First edition. | New York, NY : William Morrow, 2019.
Identifiers: LCCN 2018058807| ISBN 9780062390011 (hardback) |
    ISBN 0062390015 (hardcover) | ISBN 9780062390028 (paperback)
Subjects: | BISAC: FICTION / Suspense. | FICTION / Mystery &
    Detective / Women Sleuths. | FICTION / Mystery & Detective /
    Historical. | GSAFD: Suspense fiction. | Mystery fiction.
Classification: LCC PS3562.I586 L33 2019 | DDC 813/.54—dc23
LC record available at https://lccn.loc.gov/2018058807

ISBN 978-0-06-239002-8 (pbk.)

20 21 22 23 24 LSC 10 9 8 7 6 5 4 3 2 1

In memory of:

Rob Hiaasen
Gerald Fischman
John McNamara
Rebecca Smith
Wendi Winters

PART I

I SAW YOU once. I saw you and you noticed me because you caught me looking at you, seeing you. Back and forth, back and forth. Good-looking women do that. Lock eyes, then look one another up and down. I could tell at a glance you've never doubted you're good-looking and you still had the habit of checking a room to make sure you were the best-looking. You scanned the crowd of people on the sidewalk and your eyes caught mine, if only for a moment, then dropped away. You saw me, you tallied up the points. Who won? My hunch is that you gave yourself the crown because you saw a Negro woman, a poor one at that. In the animal kingdom, the male performs for the woman, woos her with his beautiful feathers or flowing mane, is always trying to out-strut the other men. Why do humans do it the other way? It doesn't make sense. Men need us more than we need them.

You were in the minority that day, you were in our neighborhood and almost everyone else there would have picked me. Younger, taller, shapelier me. Maybe even your husband, Milton. Part of the reason I first noticed you was because you were next to him. He now looked exactly like his father, a man I remembered with some affection. I can't say the same about Milton. I guessed, from the way people gathered around him on the temple steps, patted his back, clasped his hands in theirs, that it must have been his father who had died. And I could tell from the way that people waited to comfort him that Milton was a big shot.

The temple was a block from the park. The park and the lake and the fountain. Isn't that interesting? I was probably taking a roundabout way to Druid Hill that afternoon, a book in my purse. Not that I liked the outdoors that much, but there were eight people—my father and mother, my sister and two brothers, my two boys and me—living in our apartment and there was never a moment's peace, to use my father's phrase. I would slip a book into my purse—Jean Plaidy or Victoria Holt—and say, "I'm going to the library," and Mama didn't have the heart to say no. She never faulted me for picking two good-for-nothing men and turning up back home like a bad penny. I was her first and I was her favorite. But not so favored that I could get away with a third mistake. Mama was on me to go back to school, become a nurse. A nurse. I couldn't imagine taking a job where you had to touch people you didn't want to touch.

When things got too much at home, when there were too many bodies and voices, I'd go to the park and walk the paths, drink up the silence, drop to a bench, and lose myself in ye olden days of England. Later, people said I was a terrible person, moving out on my own, leaving my babies behind with their grandparents, but I was thinking of them. I needed a man, and not just any old man. My boys' fathers had proved that much to me. I had to find the kind of man who would provide for us, all of us. To do that, I needed to be on my own for a little while, even if it meant living with my friend Latetia, who basically ran a one-woman school on how to get men to pay for everything. My mama believed that when you put the cheese out for the mouse, you have to make it look at least a little appetizing. Cut the mold off or place it in the trap so the mold is on the side that doesn't show. I had to look good and I had to look as if I didn't have a care in the world, and I couldn't manage that in my family's crowded apartment on Auchentoroly Terrace.

Okay, so maybe I could imagine taking a job where you had to touch people you didn't want to touch.

But what woman doesn't do that? You did it yourself, I'm guessing, when you married Milton Schwartz. Because no one could fall in fairy-tale love with the Milton Schwartz I once knew.

It was—I can remember if I figure out how old my babies were— 1964, late fall, the faintest chill in the air. You had a plain black pillbox hat, no veil. I bet people told you that you looked like Jackie Kennedy. I bet you liked it, even as you denied it with a Who, me? laugh. The wind ruffled your hair, but only a little; you had that 'do shellacked. You wore a black coat with fur at the throat and cuffs. Believe me, I remember that coat. And, boy, Milton looked so much like his father and it was only then that I realized that old Mr. Schwartz had been kinda young and kinda handsome when I was a kid. When I was a little girl, buying candy in his store, I thought he was old. He wasn't even forty. Now I was twenty-six and Milton had to be almost forty and there you were next to him, and I could not get over what a fine woman he had gotten for himself. Maybe he was nicer now, I thought. People change, they do, they do. I did. It's just that no one will ever know.

What did you see? I can't remember what I was wearing, but I can guess. A coat, too thin even for that mild day. Probably came from a church box, so it was pilled and limp, saggy at the hem. Scuffed shoes, run-down heels. Your shoes were black and shiny. My legs were bare. You had the kind of stockings that almost shimmered.

Looking at you, I saw the trick to it: to get a man with money, I would need to look as if I didn't need money. I was going to have to find a job in a place where the tips came in folding money, not change thrown on the table. Problem was, those kinds of places didn't hire Negroes, not as waitresses. The one time I got a restaurant gig, I was a dishwasher, stuck in the back, cut off from the tips. The best restaurants didn't hire women to wait tables even if they were white.

I was going to have to be creative, find a job somewhere that I could meet the kind of men who bought a girl things, which would make me more desirable to the men who played for bigger stakes, allow me to trade up and up and up. I knew what that meant, what I would have to exchange for those things. I wasn't a girl anymore. I had two sons to prove it.

So when you saw me—and you did, I'm sure of it, our eyes caught, held one another's—you saw my ratty clothes, but you also saw my green eyes, my straight nose. The face that gave me my nickname, although later I would meet a man who said I reminded him of a duchess, not an empress, that I should be called Helen. He said it was because I was beautiful enough to start a war. And didn't I just? I don't know what else you would call it. Maybe not a big war, but a war all the same, in which men turned on one another, allies became enemies. All because of me.

In a flash, you showed me where I wanted to go and how to get there. I had one more chance. One more man.

I did not imagine that day that our paths would ever cross again, *small as Baltimore can be. You were just the woman who married the nasty teenager who used to torment me, and now the nasty boy was a nice-looking man who was burying his father.* I need a husband like that, *I thought.* Not a white man, of course, but a man who could buy me a coat with fur at the neck and the cuffs, a man who would command everyone's respect. A woman is only as good as the man at her side. *My father would have slapped me if he heard such words come out of my mouth, make me find and memorize all the Bible verses about vanity and pride. But it wasn't vanity on my part. I needed a man to help care for my boys. A well-to-do man needs a beautiful woman. That's what I figured out that day. You were there to comfort Milton, to help him bury his father, but you were also an advertisement for his work and success. I can't believe you left him a year later, but death has a way of changing people.*

God knows, my death has changed me.

Alive, I was Cleo Sherwood. Dead, I became the Lady in the Lake, a nasty broken thing, dragged from the fountain after steeping there for months, through the cold winter, then that fitful, bratty spring, almost into summer proper. Face gone, much of my flesh gone.

And no one cared until you came along, gave me that stupid nickname, began rattling doorknobs and pestering people, going places you weren't supposed to go. No one outside my family was supposed to care. I was a careless girl who went out on a date with the wrong person and was never seen again. You came in at the end of my story and turned it into your beginning. Why'd you have to go and do that, Madeline Schwartz? Why couldn't you stay in your beautiful house and your good-enough marriage, and let me be at the bottom of the fountain? I was safe there.

Everybody was safer when I was there.

October 1965

"**WHAT DO YOU** mean you've invited Wallace Wright to dinner?"

Maddie Schwartz longed to take the question back the second it was out of her mouth. Maddie Schwartz did not act like women in television variety shows and songs. She neither nagged nor schemed. She did not need to hear a Jack Jones song to remind her to fix her hair and makeup before her husband came through the door at day's end. Maddie Schwartz prided herself on being unflappable. Invite the boss home at the last minute? Surface with two never-before-mentioned cousins from Toledo, show up with an old high school friend? Maddie was always ready for the challenge. She ran her household much as her mother had run hers, with a sly wit and effortless—effortless-*seeming*—organization.

Unlike her mother, she accomplished these domestic miracles by spending freely. Milton's shirts went to the best laundry in North

Baltimore, although it was miles from her usual routes. (She dropped off, he picked up.) A cleaning girl came twice a week. Maddie's "famous" yeast rolls were out of a can, her freezer full of staples. She used caterers for the Schwartzes' most ambitious parties, the New Year's Day open house for Milton's colleagues from the law firm and the spontaneous spring party that was such a success that they felt obliged to keep having it. People really loved that party, spoke about it throughout the year with sincere anticipation.

Yes, Maddie Schwartz was good at entertaining and therefore happy to do it. She took particular pride in her ability to throw together a dinner party with almost no warning. Even when she wasn't enthusiastic about a certain guest, she never kvetched. So Milton was within his rights to be surprised by her peevish tone on this afternoon.

"I thought you'd be excited," Milton said. "He is a little, well, famous."

Maddie regrouped quickly. "Don't mind me, I'm just worried that he's used to dining in a grander style than I can manage on short notice. But maybe he would be charmed by meatloaf and scalloped potatoes? I guess life is all lobster thermidor and steak Diane when you're Wallace Wright."

"He says he knew you a little? Back in school."

"Oh we were *years* apart," Maddie said, knowing her generous husband would infer that Wallace Wright was the older one. He was, in fact, two years younger, a grade behind her at The Park School—and many rungs down the high school social ladder.

He had been Wally Weiss then. Today, one could barely turn on WOLD-TV without being subjected to Wallace Wright. He hosted the noon news show, where he interviewed celebrities passing through Baltimore, and also did "Wright Makes Right," a relatively new evening segment that took on consumer complaints. Lately, when the beloved WOLD anchor Harvey Patterson enjoyed the rare evening off, Wallace filled in for him.

And, although it was supposed to be a closely held secret at WOLD, Wally also was the voiceless tramp who hosted *Donadio,* the taped cartoon show that aired on Saturdays. Baltimore's un-imaginative answer to Bozo, Donadio never spoke and his face was hidden beneath layers of makeup. But Maddie had seen through the ruse when Seth watched the show as a child.

Seth was a junior in high school now. It had been years since she'd watched *Donadio,* or even WOLD. She preferred WBAL, the number one station.

"He's a nice guy, this Wallace Wright," Milton continued. "Not full of himself at all. I told you, we've been playing singles at that new tennis barn in Cross Keys."

Milton was a bit of a name-dropper and just silly enough to be impressed by playing tennis with a television personality, even one known as the Midday Fog because of his distinctive baritone. Sweet, starstruck Milton. Maddie could not begrudge his tendency toward hero worship, given how much she had benefited from it. Eighteen years into their marriage, he still had unguarded moments in which he gazed at her as if unsure how he had ever won such a prize.

She loved him, she really did, they had a harmonious life together and while she publicly made the right lamentations about their only child's heading to college in two years, she actually couldn't wait. She felt as if she had been living in one of those shoebox dioramas Seth had built—*she* had built, let's be honest—in grade school, and now the lid was coming off, the walls breaking down. Milton had started taking flying lessons recently, asking how she felt about a second home in Florida. Did she like the Atlantic side or the gulf? Boca or Naples?

Are those the only choices? Maddie had found herself wondering. *The two sides of Florida? Certainly the world is bigger than that.* But she had only said that she thought she would like Naples.

"See you soon, darling." She hung up the phone, allowed herself the sigh she had kept at bay. It was late October, the High Holy Days finally over. She was tired of entertaining, exasperated by disruptions to her routines. Rosh Hashanah and Yom Kippur were supposed to be a time to reflect, take stock, but Maddie couldn't remember the last time she had been able to go pray before breaking the fast. The house had finally returned to normal and now Milton wanted to bring a guest home, Wally Weiss of all people.

Yet it was essential to impress *Wallace Wright* with dinner. The chicken breasts thawing in the fridge would keep another day. And meatloaf, even with scalloped potatoes, wasn't the note she wanted to hit. Maddie knew a clever way to make a beef casserole that everyone loved; maybe it wasn't Julia Child, but there were never leftovers. No one guessed that the key ingredient was two cans of Campbell's cream of mushroom soup, plus several generous splashes of wine. The trick was to surround such a casserole with things that suggested elegance, planning—biscuits from Hutzler's bakery, which Maddie kept in the freezer for just this reason; a cheeseless Caesar salad that Milton would dress at the table, then chop using the same technique as the waiters at Marconi's. She would send Seth to Goldman's for a cake. It was a chance to practice his driving, after all. She would tell him that he could have whatever fast food he wanted, too. He would choose *trayf,* no doubt, but Milton asked only that they keep a kosher home.

Maddie checked the bar, but they were always well stocked.

There would be two rounds of cocktails before dinner—oh, she would do something clever with nuts, or maybe serve pâté on toast points—wine flowing through dinner, brandy and cognac after. She didn't remember Wally drinking much, but then she hadn't spoken to him since the summer she was seventeen. Nobody drank then. Everybody in Maddie's crowd drank now.

He would be different, of course. Everyone changes, but pimply teenage boys especially so. They say it's a man's world, but you'll never hear anyone claim it's a *boy's* world. That realization had been brought literally home to Maddie when Seth entered high school. She had told him to be patient, that he would sprout to his father's height, that his face would be smooth and handsome, and her prophecies had already come to pass.

She could never have said the same thing to Wally. Sad little Wally, how he had yearned for her. She had used that yearning, when it was to her advantage. But then, that's what girls do, that's the power available to them. Who was he kidding? He may have been taller, the pimples gone, the hair tamed, but everyone in Northwest Baltimore knew he was a Jew. *Wallace Wright!*

Was Wally married? Maddie recalled a wife, possibly a divorce. The wife wasn't Jewish, she was pretty sure of that. She decided to balance the table with another couple, the Rosengrens, who would provide the wide-eyed wonder that Maddie would have a hard time faking. She could never see Wallace without seeing Wally. Would it be the same for him? Would he see the Maddie Morgenstern that lurked inside Maddie Schwartz? And would he consider the new version an improvement? She had been a beautiful girl, there was no use pretending otherwise, but terribly, almost tragically naive. In her twenties, she had lost herself to raising a baby, risked frumpiness.

At thirty-six, she had the best of both worlds. She saw a beautiful woman in her mirror, still youthful, but able to afford the things that kept you looking that way. She had one streak of silvery hair, which she had decided to consider incongruous, dashing. She plucked the rest.

When she opened the door to Wally that evening, his open admiration was delightful to see.

"Young lady, is your mother at home?"

That irritated her. It was such obvious flattery, something one would say to a simpering grandmother who wore too much rouge. Did Wally think she required that kind of buildup? She tried to hide her frostiness as she served the first round of drinks and snacks.

"So," Eleanor Rosengren said after gulping her first highball, "did you really know each other at Park?" The Rosengrens, like Milton, had gone to public high school.

"A little," Maddie admitted with a laugh, a laugh meant to signal: *It was so long ago, let's not bore the others.*

"I was in love with her," Wally said.

"You were *not*." Laughing, flustered, and—again—not complimented. She felt mocked, as if he were setting up a joke for which she would be the punch line.

"Of course I was. Don't you remember—I took you to the prom when—what was his name—stood you up."

A curious glance from Milton.

"Oh, not stood up, Wally. Sorry, *Wallace*. We broke up two weeks before prom. That's very different from being stood up." She wouldn't have cared about going at all if it weren't for the new dress. It had cost $39.95—her father would have been scandalized if it had gone to waste after all the begging she had done.

She did not provide the name for which Wally had fumbled. Allan. Allan Durst Junior. When they had first started dating, the name had sounded Jewish enough to placate her mother. His father *was* Jewish, sort of. But Mrs. Morgenstern was not fooled once she saw him. "That's not someone to be serious about," her mother had said, and Maddie had not argued. She was becoming serious about someone else, someone even less likely to win her mother's approval.

"Should we go into the dining room?" Maddie asked, although people were still in the middle of their cocktails.

Wally—Wallace—was the youngest of the five at the table, but he had clearly grown used to people wanting his opinions. The obliging Rosengrens pelted him with questions over dinner. Who would be running for governor? What did he think about Agnew's latest gaffe? Baltimore's crime rate? What was Gypsy Rose Lee really like? (She had recently been in Baltimore to promote her own syndicated talk show.)

For someone who did interviews for a living, Wallace was not much on asking questions. When the men offered their opinions on current events, he listened with patient condescension, then contradicted them. Maddie tried to steer the conversation toward a novel she had read, *The Keepers of the House,* which made some excellent points about the race problem in the South, but Eleanor said she couldn't get through it and the men had never heard of it.

Yet it was a successful dinner party, Maddie supposed. Milton was delighted that he had a famous friend; the Rosengrens were charmed by Wallace. He seemed to genuinely like them, too. Late in the evening, deep into his brandy, the lights dimmed so that the burning ends of their cigarettes looked like slow-moving fireflies in the living room, Wallace said, "You've done okay for yourself, Maddie."

Okay? *Okay?*

"Imagine," he continued, "if you had ended up with that fellow. Durst, that was it. He's a copywriter. An adman."

She said she hadn't seen Allan Durst since high school, which was true. Then she said she knew about his job from The Park School alumni bulletin, which was not.

"I never heard there was a big high school love," Milton said.

"That's because there wasn't," Maddie said, more sharply than she meant to.

By eleven P.M. they had sent everyone home weaving, insisting they do it again. Milton toppled into bed, felled by drink and excitement. Maddie normally would have left the heavy cleaning to her Friday girl. There was no crime in letting dishes sit overnight as long as you rinsed them. Though Tattie Morgenstern had never left so much as a fork in her sink.

But Maddie decided to stay up and put things to rights.

The kitchen had been redone last year. Maddie had been so proud of the project when it was completed, so happy with her new appliances, yet the pleasure had burned off quickly. Now the remodel seemed silly, even pointless. What did it matter, having the latest appliances, all these sleek built-ins? No time was actually saved, although the reconfigured cabinets did make it easier to maintain two sets of dishes.

Wally had expressed surprise when he realized, during the salad course, that the Schwartzes kept a kosher household, but that was a nod to Milton's upbringing. Two sets of dishes, never mixing meat and dairy, avoiding pork and shellfish—it wasn't that hard and it made Milton happy. She deserved his devotion, she told herself as she soaped and rinsed the crystal, dried the good china by hand.

Turning to leave the kitchen, she caught a wineglass drying on the drain board with the tip of her elbow. It plummeted to the floor, where it shattered.

We're supposed to break a glass.

What are you talking about?

Never mind. I always forget what a heathen you are.

The broken glass meant five more minutes with dustpan and broom, ferreting out every sliver. By the time she finished it was almost two and yet Maddie still had trouble falling asleep. Her mind raced, going over lists of things undone and overlooked. There was nothing here in the present. The things she had failed to do were twenty years behind her, when she had first known Wally—and her first love, the one her mother never suspected. She had sworn she would be—what, exactly? Someone creative and original, someone who cared not at all about public opinion. She—*they*—were going to live in New York City, in Greenwich Village. He had promised. He was going to take her away from stodgy Baltimore, they were going to live a passionate life devoted to art and adventure.

She had kept him out of her mind for all these years. Now he was back, Elijah showing up for his Passover wine.

Maddie fell asleep paging through an imaginary calendar, trying to calculate the best time to leave her marriage. Her birthday was next month. December? No, not over the holidays, unimportant as Hanukah was. February seemed too late, January a cliché, a mockery of New Year's resolutions. November 30, she decided. She would leave November 30, twenty days after her thirty-seventh birthday.

We're supposed to break a glass.

What are you talking about?

Never mind.

The Classmate

I GRIP THE steering wheel of my new Cadillac, talking my way through the drive from Maddie's house to mine, short as it is, a dog's leg down Greenspring, past The Park School—our alma mater, although Park was in a different location in our day—then a right turn on Falls Road, and finally up the hill into Mount Washington. I talk to myself like a coach, not that I ever played for any team. Couldn't even make water boy. *Focus, Wally, focus.*

In my head, I'm always Wally. Everyone looks up to Wallace Wright, including me. I wouldn't dare try to talk to him the way I talk to Wally.

I'm terrified that I'm going to cross the center line, hit another car, maybe worse. *WOLD anchorman Wallace Wright was arrested for vehicular manslaughter near his Northwest Baltimore home.*

"The newsman can't end up as the headline, Wally," I tell myself. "Focus."

A cop stop would be almost as bad. *WOLD anchorman arrested for drunk driving.* News only because it involves a newsman. Who doesn't drive a little tipsy from time to time? But a cop also might wave me off, even ask for an autograph.

Where did Maddie learn to drink like that? I guess it's like the old joke about Carnegie Hall, *practice, practice, practice.* I've never had a chance to develop the cocktail habit because I'm seldom home before eight, have to be at work the next day by nine, on air by noon. That routine doesn't lend itself to liquor. Or marriage.

Mount Washington is so dark at midnight, so hushed. How have I never noticed that before? The only sound is the crunch of the fall leaves beneath my tires. By the time I creep up South Road, it seems the better part of valor to park by the curb, not attempting the driveway, much less the garage.

Why did I stay so late? It certainly wasn't the scintillating conversation. *Because it's not every day you get to show your first love what a mistake she made.*

If you had asked me even this morning—and people ask me many things, you'd be amazed what an oracle I am—I would have told you with all sincerity that I never thought about Maddie Morgenstern.

But the moment I saw her on her own threshold, I realized she had always been with me, my audience of one. She was there Monday through Friday, when I faced the cameras between noon and twelve thirty on the midday news show. On Wednesday nights, when I did "Wright Makes Right." Whenever I was lucky enough to substitute for Harvey Patterson, whose job I will take one day. Maddie somehow managed the trick of being a seventeen-year-old girl *and* a suburban matron, sitting at home with a cup of coffee, the morning housework finished, watching channel 6 and thinking: *I could have been Mrs. Wallace Wright if I played my cards right.*

She's even there when I put on makeup and play Donadio, the sad, silent clown that was my fluke entree at WOLD-TV.

I had been working in radio, prized for my voice, but not considered camera ready. The Donadio gig meant an extra twenty-five dollars a week. The only stipulation was that I must never tell anyone, and I was more than happy to keep that promise.

One Saturday, as I was removing my makeup, a cop killing came over the scanner. I was the only reporter available. Somehow, during the fourteen months I had been masquerading as Donadio, I had gotten taller, my hair smoother, my complexion paradoxically clearer. Maybe I did a better job cleaning my face once I started wearing clown makeup. At any rate, my face and body finally fit my booming baritone. I went to the scene, I gathered the facts, a star was born. Not Maddie, not that putz she dated in high school, not her perfectly nice lawyer husband. Me, Wally Weiss. I'm the star.

We met in, of all the unlikely places, our school's ham radio club. We quickly established that we shared an intense admiration for Edward R. Murrow, whose London reports during the war had made a big impression on us. I had never met any girl who wanted to talk about Murrow and journalism before, much less a pretty one. It was like that first great work of art that transfixes you, that novel that stays with you the rest of your life, even if you go on to read much better ones. It was all I could do not to stare at her, mouth hanging open.

Maddie's appearance at the ham radio club turned out to be a one-off; she had thought it was a *radio* club, for people interested in writing and performing, not a room full of losers who liked to tinker. She switched to the school newspaper, quickly landed a column and started running with a very fast, goyish crowd, including Allan Durst. Obviously, Maddie Morgenstern could never be serious about him, but her parents were shrewd enough not to fight a high school romance. I heard they had even invited the Durst parents to their home for Shabbos. The mother was a famous artist, painting huge abstracts that hung in museums, the father a competent painter of portraits, specializing in Baltimore dowagers.

Allan dropped Maddie right before prom. I found her weeping in an empty classroom. It was an honor to have her confide in me. I suggested she take me as her date.

"What could be a greater insult?" I said, patting her back with a flat up-and-down motion, almost as if burping a child. My hand brushed what felt like the clasp of a bra, my most erotic experience to date.

She agreed to my plan with an almost painful alacrity.

I bought her a wrist corsage with the most expensive orchid to be had in Baltimore. She did her part, ignoring Allan, who had come stag, and laughing at my jokes as if I were Jack Benny. Allan approached her at one point and asked for a dance "for old times' sake." Maddie cocked her head to the side as if she were trying to remember exactly what old times they had shared, then said, "No, no, I'm very happy to spend the evening with my *date*."

I whirled her away, feeling every inch the young Fred Astaire. If you think about it, Astaire wasn't conventionally handsome. He was never the tallest guy in the room, he wasn't an athlete. But he was *Astaire*.

As I drove her home after the dance, she slid across the seat of my father's Buick and rested her head on my shoulder. She confided in me that she wanted to write, really write, poetry and fiction, which was almost more exciting than her very real kiss at the front door. Back in the car, I discovered that the flower had fallen from its ribbon. Maybe its fragrance was nothing more than the usual orchid smell, but to me it carried Maddie's distinctive scent, as singular as her voice, subdued and husky for a teenage girl. Maddie never squealed, she was no bobby-soxer. She was dignified, regal, the girl who always played Queen Esther in the Purim play.

I called her three days later to ask for a movie date, a proper date, having calculated that three days was the right amount of time. Not too eager, not too detached. Very Astaire.

Her tone was puzzled, polite. "You're a sweet kid, Wally, to worry about me," she said. "But I'm fine."

Within a year, she was engaged to Milton Schwartz, big and hairy and older, twenty-two to her eighteen, his first year of law school already behind him. I went to their wedding. It was like watching Alice Faye run away with King Kong.

I had not thought of Milton Schwartz again for almost twenty years when I ran into him in the locker room at the new tennis barn, the only convenient place for me to exercise before work, given its proximity to Television Hill. We were well matched at singles and Milton clearly enjoyed having a famous friend. It was only a matter of time before he asked me if I would like to have dinner at his house. "No big deal," he said. "Just the wife, maybe our neighbors, anyone you want to bring."

Bettina and I have been apart almost two years and although I date, there's no one serious. I decided to go stag, like Allan at the senior prom. Milton knew that I had attended the same high school as Mrs. Schwartz but said his wife had never spoken of me. Rather than feeling demoralized that Maddie didn't brag about our ac-quaintanceship, I saw it as a compliment. If she hadn't mentioned to her husband that she knew Baltimore's Midday Fog, it must be *because* she had the occasional fantasy, a what-might-have-been moment. At her kitchen table, with her coffee, a cigarette burning between her fingers, she relived that prom night and my phone call three days later, kicked herself for not saying yes. Her dark hair would be prematurely gray, her hourglass figure dumpy and plump. Neither of those things were true, as it turned out, but that's how I imagined her.

I was surprised to discover they kept a kosher house. I never set out to distance myself from Judaism, but a television personality such as myself has to connect with his audience, and my audience is mostly Christian. That's the cost of being an oracle. Then again, there is Orthodox and there's *Orthodox,* and the refusal to mix meat and dairy was the Schwartz household's only concession to Judaism I could see. I was a little shocked by the things they said about the changing neighborhoods to the south, the more religious Jews who lived along Park Heights Avenue, to whom they clearly felt superior. If you ask me, there's no one more anti-Semitic than a middle-class Jew.

But we did not spend that much time talking about Judaism. We discussed politics, with the Schwartzes and their guests deferring to me, as people tend to do. We laughed about Spiro Agnew's most recent blunder, the speech at Gettysburg where he was clearly confused about which side had prevailed on that battlefield. By the after-dinner drinks, everyone felt warm and familiar. I thought it was safe to bring up the prom—and Maddie's subsequent refusal to go on another date with me.

And she denied it. She insisted I had never asked her out at all.

Yes, she agreed, we had gone to the prom, but she was adamant that I never called her again, when I know I did.

"Because of course I would have gone out with you!" she said, by way of argument for her memory over mine. But she couldn't help undercutting it: "If only to be polite."

Still, her heat on this topic was disproportionate. There was no reason to get so angry about it.

Safe on my own doorstep, I drop my keys two, three times before I stumble into my house, still baffled by Maddie's hostility. Is it because she could tell I saw through her? I may have been the one with a goyish name, but I was still a Jewish boy in my heart, whereas the Schwartzes, with their two sets of dishes, were ersatz. Everything in their house was for show.

My house is so quiet—and so dusty—since Bettina moved out. I thought she would fight to keep it. The house had been her chief preoccupation for our six years together. But, by the end, Bettina wanted no part of it or me. We didn't have kids. I still don't know how I feel about that. A child would have been delighted to have Donadio for his dad.

Although exhausted and stumbling drunk, I go to the "study" that Bettina made for me, in our marriage's first, hopeful year. It is all leather and mahogany, with English horse-racing prints that embarrass me, although I suppose the proximity of Pimlico justifies such airs. Bettina arranged the books for visual appeal, which drives me mad, but I finally find the one I want: my old battered copy of *Arch of Triumph,* relegated to an upper shelf with the other paperbacks. When I first read it, it made me want to write, make other people feel as novels made me feel. Instead, I tell them the headlines and the weather, raise an occasional eyebrow at a celebrity.

And there it is, between pages 242 and 243, Maddie's orchid, brown and brittle.

Of course, the flower's existence proves nothing; we are agreed that we attended the prom. Yet to me it is the smoking gun, irrefutable evidence—but of what? That everything happened as I said. Why did she deny it? My story is a testament to her power, the glory of her youth.

Anyway, it's a good thing that nothing came of our date. At thirty-five, I am still young, my life nothing but possibility. I might be interviewing second-raters now, but one day I will talk to presidents and kings, maybe work for one of the networks. Whereas Maddie Schwartz, pushing forty, has nothing to look forward to.

January 1966

IT WAS ONLY when the jeweler put the loupe to his eye that Maddie realized she had already mentally spent the money from selling her engagement ring. What would he pay her? A thousand? Maybe even two thousand?

She needed so much. The new apartment was a two-bedroom, sparse on furnishings. She had assumed Seth would be living with her. But he refused, said he would rather stay with his father in the Pikesville house, near his friends and his school. Even after she offered to drive him to school, he refused to move. Milton's meddling, Maddie suspected. She comforted herself with the knowledge that Seth had only two years left at home.

But she would have chosen a one-bedroom in a better neighborhood if she had anticipated Seth's resistance. And then she might actually have a phone, although not having a phone wasn't completely tragic. It meant her mother couldn't call her every day to discuss Maddie's future and what Tattie Morgenstern unfailingly called her *reduced circumstances.*

Now that you are living in reduced circumstances, Madeline, you might want to clip coupons. I saw that Hochschild's was having a good sale—you'll have to get used to shopping sales and cutting coupons, Madeline, because of your reduced circumstances. With your reduced circumstances, it might make sense not to have a car at all.

The infuriating thing was that her mother was right. Everything about Maddie's post-Milton life was smaller, shabbier. The apartment was pretty enough, but Gist Avenue, while on the right side of Northern Parkway, was *not* nice, it turned out. The landlord had persuaded her to meet in the afternoon, when the neighborhood was empty and quiet. At that time of day, the apartment reminded Maddie of a 3-D Paul Klee painting, with the warm winter sunlight creating golden squares on empty wood floors, glinting on the tiny pink-and-blue tiles in the bath. All she saw were shapes and light, space and possibility.

It was only when she started moving her things in that she realized while the apartment was charming, the neighborhood was decidedly *mixed.* Mixed on its way to being not so mixed. Maddie wasn't prejudiced, of course. If she had been younger, without a child, she would have gone south to join the voter registration project a few years back. She was almost sure of this. But she didn't like being so *visible* in her new neighborhood, a solitary white woman who happened to own a fur coat. Only beaver, but a fur nonetheless. She was wearing it now. Maybe the jeweler would pay more if she didn't look like someone who needed the money.

When Milton had learned her new address, he said Seth couldn't visit at all, not overnight. He said that she could spend her weekends with Seth at the old house if she liked, that Milton would vacate the premises so mother and son could be together. A kind act, a gracious act, but Maddie wondered if Milton had already started seeing someone. The idea annoyed her, but she consoled herself that a new lady was probably the only thing that could persuade Milton to stop fighting the divorce.

She had leaned farther over the counter than she realized, close enough that her breath was forming little clouds on the glass.

"You didn't buy this here?" The jeweler made it sound like a question, but she had already provided that information.

"No, it was from a place downtown. I don't think it's there anymore—Steiner's."

"Yes, I remember. Very fancy place. Put a lot of money in the fixtures. We keep things simple here. I always tell my employees: In a jewelry store, it's the jewels that should shine. You don't need to arrange them on velvet if they're of good quality. You don't need to be downtown, where the rents are high and there's no parking. Weinstein's may not be fashionable, but we're still in business and that's good enough for me."

"So my ring . . ."

He looked sad, but it was a polite, fake sad, as if an unlikable acquaintance had died and he was pretending to care more than he did.

"I couldn't do more than five hundred dollars."

It was like a gut punch, not that Maddie had ever been punched or hit in any way.

"But my husband paid a thousand dollars and that was almost

twenty years ago." Aging herself a little, for she was only thirty-seven and had married at nineteen. But two decades had more gravitas than eighteen years.

"Ah, people were giddy in the forties, weren't they?"

Were they? She had been a teenager, a pretty girl; giddy had been her natural state. But Milton was a practical young man, careful about debt, smart about investments. He would not have chosen a ring without resale value.

Except—Milton never expected this ring to be sold. The most cynical man in the world didn't expect his engagement ring to be sold; even the men who courted Elizabeth Taylor thought they would be with her forever.

"I don't understand how a ring that cost a thousand dollars in 1946 could be worth half that amount today." Even as she spoke, she was aware how quickly she had moved from an exaggeration to a lie, how "almost twenty," which was essentially correct, had *become* twenty.

"If you really want to know, I could bore you with a lecture on the used diamond market and profit margins. I could tell you about clarity and cut, how the fashions change. I'm happy to explain all those things, but the bottom line is, I can't do better than five hundred dollars."

"We had it insured for two thousand dollars," she said. Did they? It sounded right. Or maybe it was that she had hoped to get as much as two thousand dollars.

Milton had been giving her an allowance since she left, but it wasn't quite enough and it was fitful, with no fixed date or amount. Because she had assumed that Seth would come with her, she had expected a more generous stipend. Milton would never deny his only son. But with Seth's remaining in the house in Pikesville, she had no such leverage. She needed money. Milton was trying to starve her out, force her to come back to him by being stingy.

"He's not kidding about the boring part," said a young woman with reddish hair, polishing the top of the case. Maddie was surprised that an employee would dare to speak so impudently to her boss, but Jack Weinstein only laughed.

"That's enough out of you, Judith. Tell you what, Mrs. Schwartz—leave your number with us and if a customer comes in looking for a ring like this, maybe we can work something out. It's not the style—"

"It's a classic solitaire."

"Exactly. The young girls getting married today, they have interesting ideas. Some don't want stones at all." Now he looked genuinely sad.

"I don't have a phone yet. I'm waiting for it to be installed. C & P says there's a terrible backlog."

He put away his loupe and handed the ring back to Maddie. She was loath to put it on. That would feel as defeating as moving back to Pikesville. The young woman, Judith, understood immediately what was bothering Maddie. She pulled out an envelope and said: "For safekeeping. I'd give you a box, but I can't endure the lecture that my brother would give me on how much everything costs."

"Your brother? That explains a lot."

"You have no idea."

The young woman was more handsome than pretty. But her expressions were droll and her clothes went together in a way that came only with hours in one's room trying things on, creating combinations, pressing and mending, shining and brushing. Maddie knew because Maddie had always been the same kind of woman. This young woman's style was almost *too* matchy, which aged her a little.

But her kindness was overwhelming, as kindness sometimes is, and it took enormous self-control for Maddie to not burst into tears.

She made it to the driver's seat of her car, only barely, before her sobs started.

She had expected that money. She had imagined a new bed, something sleek and modern. A phone on the wall in the kitchen, maybe an extension in the bedroom, too. It was so terribly inconvenient not to have a phone.

However, she was crying not for the things she might have had, but for the embarrassment of being found out, of being caught yearning. It had been a very long time since Maddie had let anyone see her dare to want something. She knew how dangerous it was to let one's desire be glimpsed, even for a moment.

A tap on the window; the droll girl's face—Judith, her brother had called her—filled the frame. Maddie fumbled for her dark glasses, rolled down the window.

"So bright today," Judith said, politely offering an excuse.

"I know. I don't really believe it's going to snow later this week. If we can believe what the weathermen say."

"A big if. Look, we don't really know each other, but I know who you are. Of course."

Of course? Why of course? For a confused second, Maddie thought she was the woman she almost became, a seventeen-year-old girl embroiled in a scandal. But, no, she had avoided that fate. The problem was all the other fates she had avoided as well, the lies she had told herself, which she had come to believe. When Judith said she knew who Maddie was, it was probably because of gossip at the club, that terrible nouveau clique run by Bambi Brewer, with her airs and her Salems and her acolytes. The Morgensterns were old money relative to that crowd.

"Is there something you need from me?"

As if anyone wanted advice from a middle-aged woman trying to sell her engagement ring. The world was so different now. This young woman crouching by Maddie's car couldn't possibly have had the same problems Maddie had known twenty years ago. Today, young women could have sex worry-free by taking a daily pill. Of course, most probably still pretended to be virgins when they found the men they wanted to marry, but that was as much for their mothers as for the husbands.

"I thought you might be interested in attending a meeting at the Stonewall Democratic Club. There's an open governor's race this year. It's a good way to meet people. My brother—not Jack, Donald, Jack's a bit of a jerk, but Donald is a sweetheart—he's very active in politics."

"Is this a fix-up?"

This question seemed to amuse Judith. "No, no, Donald's not—in the market, best I can tell. He's a bachelor, and content to be one. When I say 'meet people,' I mean just that—people. Some are men. Some are single. For me, it's a way to get out of my parents' house without so many questions. And if I started going with a nice lady from Northwest Baltimore, they might not worry so much about what time I come home."

Maddie risked a tremulous smile. Kindness could be so much more painful than cruelty. She scrambled for a piece of paper from her purse, wrote her mother's number on the back of a cash register receipt from Rexall, checking first to make sure there was nothing embarrassing on it, like feminine products.

She drove home, although it was hard to think of the apartment on Gist Avenue as home. No Seth, so little furniture, and the neighbors snubbed her, as if *she* were the undesirable one in this

neighborhood of maids and laundresses, milkmen and streetcar con-
ductors. Once inside, she felt strangely warm; the landlord, usually
so stingy with heat, had the radiators set too high. She opened the
sliding door to the little patio off her bedroom. Then, on what she
wanted to believe was an impulse, she took her engagement ring
and shoved it deep into the dirt of a potted African violet she kept
on a rickety table near the patio door. She pulled the sliding door so
only a faint wisp of winter air sneaked through. Methodically, she
created the appearance of chaos by opening drawers in the kitchen
and bedroom, tossing some of her clothes to the floor.

She then took a deep breath and ran into the street, screaming
for help. Within a block, a patrolman, a Negro, rushed toward her.

"I've been robbed," she said. Her breathlessness made it easy to
sound frightened.

"Here on the street?" he asked, looking at the purse in her hands.

"My apartment," she said. "Jewelry—mostly costume stuff, but I
had a diamond ring and that's gone."

Ferdie Platt, for that was his name—"Short for Ferdinand? Like
the bull?" she asked, but he didn't answer—walked her back to
the apartment. His eyes studied the not-quite-closed patio door, the
apartment in disarray. Did his keen brown eyes also sweep across
the African violet, taking its measure? It suddenly seemed to Maddie that the impressions of her fingertips were visible in the soil. She
checked her nails surreptitiously for signs of dirt. He was one of
those men who seemed particularly spick-and-span, always smelling
of soap. Not aftershave or cologne, just soap. He wasn't particularly
tall, but he had broad shoulders and moved like an athlete. He was
too young to have to worry about getting exercise, maybe ten years
younger than she was.

"Let's call the burglary detectives," he said.

"I don't have a phone. That's part of the reason I ran into the street, calling for help. But also—I was worried that the burglar might still be here."

Her fear was almost real. She was beginning to believe that she had been burglarized, that a stranger had done these things. She could have been a very good actress if only she had pursued it.

Patrolman Platt said: "And I don't have a radio because—well, I don't have a radio. But I have a key to the call box, which is close to a drugstore. I'll put in the call and we'll wait there. We don't want to risk disturbing anything here."

At the drugstore, his call made, he bought her a soda. Maddie sat at the counter, sipping it, wishing it were a cocktail. Wishing, too, that he would sit down instead of standing over her, arms folded, watching her like a sentry.

"I don't see you in this neighborhood," he said.

"I've lived here only a few weeks."

"I don't mean it that way. I mean—this isn't the right area for you. I don't see you living here."

"Because I'm white?" She felt pert. She felt things she hadn't felt in years, maybe ever.

"Not exactly. You need to be in a place where you don't stick out quite so much. A place where you'd have privacy. Maybe more downtown, you know?"

"I signed a lease. I paid a deposit."

"Leases can be broken. For cause."

Two weeks later, Ferdie Platt did just that. Convinced the landlord to break her lease without penalty, even got her deposit back. Maddie thought it better not to ask how he had accomplished that.

Then he inspected the apartment she found near the downtown library, a location he decided was at once safe and private. "Your comings and goings won't be *notable* here."

A week after that, he helped her break in her new bed, the one she bought with part of the insurance. She had the money for selling her car, too, although that had required Milton's permission, of all things. So infuriating. But she had a new phone on the bedside table, in a delicious shade of bright red. Next to it, the African violet stood guard, serene and silent.

The Clerk

I HAVE ALWAYS been preternaturally patient. Everyone says
so. Well—everyone says I am patient; only Donald, my favorite
brother, uses words like *preternatural*. When I want something, I
can plot and plan for months to make it happen. Possibly years if
it comes to that. From the moment I sized up Madeline Morgenstern Schwartz, trying to sell her engagement ring as if she couldn't
care less how much money she got for it, I saw a means to an end.
Maddie Schwartz is my best chance to get out of the house without
marrying first.

I am the youngest of five children and the only girl. My brothers
were not forced to live at home until marriage, but they are men.
My mother, who rules the household, has decreed that I must stay
here until I marry, something I am not keen to do. I wasn't a wild

child, quite the opposite, and I'm not a wild girl. But I am increasingly sure of what I do *not* want. I do not want to teach school or go into nursing, the kind of stable jobs that would free me from my parents' home. I do not want to date men like my brothers or my father. I don't really want to marry, not yet.

But because I am a nice Jewish girl, I have to live at home until I marry. My parents are old-fashioned that way. "We would be comfortable letting you live with another girl, if we approved of her, but your friends are so flighty," my mother said. Are they? It doesn't matter. My mother has spoken. The only tactic available to me is to tease out information about what actions might merit my mother's rare approval.

That's how I managed to attend college. My parents were not going to let me go away, even if I received a scholarship that covered everything. They didn't trust me to be out of their sight. Besides, money was too tight after my father's bankruptcy, no matter how much my brothers kicked in. College Park was impossible for a commuter without a car.

So I got a scholarship to UB, then worked all summer to earn money that would cover my other costs—books, bus fare, clothes. They could muster no objection to this plan and I graduated last year with a degree in political science. Now I have to apply the same line of thinking to the problem of moving out. What are my parents' objections? *Cost.* (So I took the job, working at Jack's jewelry store, although I have no affinity for retail—all that lying and persuasion.) *Safety.* A roommate, then. *Morals.* Not just any roommate. Someone reliable, grounded. And, it goes almost without saying, Jewish.

Maddie Schwartz might be just the ticket. If she needs to sell her ring, she should welcome a roommate to share her bills. True, everyone is saying it's odd that she didn't take her son when she left Milton, but it must be Milton's fault. Everyone in Northwest Baltimore is just waiting for the day that Milton shows up with a secretary or a nurse on his arm. Whoever it is, it will be a comedown from Maddie.

It's been years since my family could afford the country club, but I remember stories about Maddie Schwartz when she was Maddie Morgenstern. I think it was my brother Nathan who had a crush on her. He's the one who told me what a sensation she caused the day she wore a flesh-pink suit. And smart, too—graduated high school at age seventeen, did two years of college before she married. Of course, she's almost old enough to be my mother, but why draw attention to that? My oldest brother could be my father if it came to that. Age-wise, I mean.

Besides, Maddie is nothing like my mother. My mother was born old. In photographs from the 1920s, Papa has the look of a dandy about him, someone who enjoys himself; Mama looks stern and unhappy, even as a child. But then, Papa was second generation, whereas Mama was three when her family came over. It makes a difference, all the difference sometimes. We never speak about the family members who didn't get out in time. "What is there to say," Mama said when I asked.

No, Maddie is my best shot. But I didn't know how to get in touch with her. She'd given me her mother's number; I suspected she didn't have a phone. (More evidence that she was living hand to mouth.) I would have to bide my time.

Then, just last week, I ran into Maddie's mother, Mrs. Morgenstern, at the deli counter at Seven Locks. (That's another thing I want to escape. My mother makes me do most of the shopping, saying it's good training for when I keep my own house.)

"Mrs. Morgenstern," I said shyly. "It's Judith, Judith Weinstein? From the club?"

She inspected me over the rims of her glasses. "It's been *years*."

It was hard to decode that innocuous statement, to know whether Mrs. Morgenstern was commenting on the passage of time or the scandal of bankruptcy that took the Weinsteins out of elite circles when I was still a child. I guess the fact that I can't figure out her intent proves what a lady she is.

"I was wondering if you knew how I could get in touch with Maddie? She was in the store the other day and"—I reached for a plausible reason—"something's come in that's closer to what she was looking for."

"Really? I can't see how Madeline would be in the position to *buy* anything. But she always was impractical that way. At any rate, she has a phone now. She moved downtown."

She took out a tiny notebook and wrote down the seven digits. Three three two—not an exchange I know. Mrs. Morgenstern's handwriting was remarkably like the woman herself, very straight up and down, pretty yet intimidating. I didn't think a mother could be more domineering than my own, but Mrs. Morgenstern seemed to have her own way of getting what she wanted.

That was Friday. I waited until today to telephone. I figured Mrs. Morgenstern must have shared the encounter by now, so Maddie won't be too surprised by my call. And I had mentioned the Stonewall Democratic Club meeting.

I phone at eight, figuring that's civilized. A woman living alone should have finished dinner and the dishes by then, would be preparing to sit down and watch the evening shows. *The Big Valley* comes on at nine. I like to watch that myself, although my mother's run-on commentary—"Barbara Stanwyck looks younger than that man playing her son, she's right, you know, women do have to take responsibility for leading men on, even if they're crazy like that, what do they call those pants, gauchos?"—makes me want to scream.

The phone rings and rings. I let it go five, eight, twelve times—a person could be in the bathroom. Or maybe I dialed wrong. I try again, just to be sure.

Maddie answers on the second ring, breathless.

"Maddie? It's Judith, Judith Weinstein."

"Oh my—I mean, was that you before? Letting it ring and ring? I couldn't get to the phone and I thought, no big deal, but when it started again, I was worried it was something to do with my son—" Her words seem to be tumbling through all sorts of emotions, relief and irritation and something I can't pinpoint.

"I'm so sorry. I only dialed again because I thought I dialed wrong the first time."

"What do you want?" Her tone borders on rudeness. But she was worried.

"Just to follow up on what I mentioned. About going to the Stonewall Democratic Club. I really think you might like it. I can even pick you up if I borrow my parents' car." Obviously, I want to check out the apartment, see if it is big enough. If not, I'll have to persuade Maddie to take a two-bedroom.

"Oh." It's as if she has no memory of our conversation. She seems vague. If I didn't know better, I would think she's a little drunk. But nice Jewish ladies don't get drunk on a Wednesday night.

"There's a meeting next week. It's interesting. I know, it seems like it's not important, supporting Democrats in a state like Maryland, but you can't take things for granted. The primary matters and there are so many ways to get involved."

"Can I call you back? Not tonight, but—later this week?"

"Sure, I'll give you my number."

Maddie must have put the phone down. I hear the kinds of sounds one makes when trying to find paper and pencil, but also—something else. A rumble, a sharp little yelp from Maddie—"No! I mean—no!" As if she has banged her hip into a drawer, but also, it seems to me, as if she enjoys the sensation.

"I'm ready," she says, and I rattle off my parents' number, although by now I never expect to hear from Maddie Schwartz. Maddie Schwartz, I'm pretty sure, does not spend her Wednesday nights watching *The Big Valley*. I am surer still she does not want a roommate.

Settling in with my parents in front of the television, I try not to sigh as my mother talks on and on, sharing her every thought, some of them even related to the program we're watching. My father is silent, as usual. He never really came back from losing Weinstein's Drugs. I always thought that part of the problem was that his name was intertwined with the store, that seeing the business fall apart and the signs come down was like watching his own body dismantled and sold for pennies on the dollar.

Tonight, he allows himself one comment and it's about the actress playing Audra. "She's really striking." Mama takes great offense. "Oh, so now you like *blondes*. That's a nice change of pace for you."

I have to find a way out of this house.

February 1966

MADDIE LAID HER head on the gingham cloth, marveling at what she was about to do. It seemed so unlikely—dangerous, even. But Ferdie wanted her to do it. Not that he had said as much, not in so many words. He hadn't really said anything at all, just tried to run his fingers through her hair, only to have them repelled by the hairspray she needed to keep her longish bouffant in shape.

"I know a woman—" he'd begun.

"I assume you know a lot of women," Maddie had teased. She did assume that. Ferdie might even have been married for all she knew. What did it matter? There was no way they were going to go any place outside her apartment, not with her divorce pending and not with—it just wasn't a good idea, the world being the world, Baltimore being Baltimore.

"A woman for hair," he'd said. "What they call a kitchen magician. She'd do it cheap."

"Do what?"

"Iron it." The word had come out as one syllable, *arn*. Ferdie was fourth-generation Baltimore, his roots deeper than Maddie's. The Platt family had come north from the Carolinas after the Civil War, and thanks to a lawsuit in the early fifties, he had been able to attend Poly, a fact he had managed to drop into conversation early on. One had to be an outstanding student to go to Polytechnic, the all-boys public high school for those with an engineering bent, yet Ferdie was mysterious about the gap between his high school graduation and his decision to join BPD. To Maddie's ear, he sounded like any working-class Baltimorean, with his long O's and extra R's. The first few times he had called her, on the phone he had insisted *they* needed, she had thought it was some strange white man. Although he was far from a stranger by the time she moved to the corner of Mulberry and Cathedral Street.

He had come by the apartment on Gist Avenue two days after the "burglary." The matter had been turned over to two detectives, who took a report and told Maddie they would check with the pawnshops, but she shouldn't expect much. Because she knew there was no ring to be found, she put the matter out of her head, so she was surprised—and a little fearful—when Ferdie Platt dropped by.

"Just checking on you," he'd said. Every word seemed layered with irony and innuendo. Did his all-seeing eyes stop on the African violet as he scanned the apartment? Did he know its secret? Was it racist to think that a Negro cop suspected her when she hadn't worried about the white detectives who took the official report?

Then he had stared at her, really stared at her, held her gaze and—*oh*. She had forgotten about that kind of look.

"I want to check that sliding door."

"The one in my bedroom?" Her voice squeaked on the last word.

"The one where the burglar entered."

"The one in my bedroom."

"Right."

She led him there, but they'd never made it to the sliding door. As soon as he had her over the threshold, he snaked his arms about her waist, turned her around, and started kissing her. In some part of her mind, she was offended by his presumption, but the rest of her body shouted down that remnant of Mrs. Milton Schwartz. She *had* been flirting with him in the drugstore that day, and if it had been an empty exercise at the time, she was glad to have her bluff called. She hadn't felt like this—well, she wouldn't say Milton never had made her feel this way, but she had been married a long time.

He didn't even bother to take off her clothes or his, just pushed her down on the bed, her skirt flipped up so it almost covered her face. *He's probably not circumcised,* Mrs. Milton Schwartz fretted, but Maddie didn't care. *And what about pregnancy?*

He'll do the right thing, she told her former self.

Then *she* was moaning, making sounds she barely recognized. Maddie had always enjoyed sex with Milton, but Ferdie was forcing her to consider the idea that maybe she just enjoyed sex.

Her real worry was that this would be all he wanted, this one time.

"We had to get that out of the way," he said when he was done. He kissed her, grabbed tissues from the bedside table to clean himself and dab at the sheet. "The next time will be slow and pretty. But I haven't been able to think about anything else since I met you."

Even in her haze, Maddie assumed this was a lie. He was too sharp, too focused, to lose himself to a daydream. Still, there was nothing wrong with this brand of flattery. How she had missed it. Oh, sometimes a husband got drunk over the years, cornered her at a party, and swore he was obsessed with her, but Maddie had always ducked those sloppy, unpromising embraces with practiced good humor.

This was something different.

"The next time—" she began, although she wasn't sure what she was going to say. That there would be no next time? That she couldn't wait for it?

"Don't worry," he said. "I've got no place to be."

Later, under the sheets, they inspected each other's naked bodies, satisfied customers. He was circumcised, after all—"Jew doctor," he said, when her hand lingered. The biggest surprise on his compact, athletic body was his navel, an outie, very large and bumpy. For his part, he seemed most interested in her breasts and her hair. She wanted to ask if she was the first white woman he had been with, but the question seemed rude. It was easier to make love a third time.

His suggestion that she "arn" her hair did not come up for several weeks, after she had moved and they had established a pattern. He would call, ask if she was free. She always was, for him. He would show up with Chinese takeout or pizza. They ended up eating the food cold, often in bed, between slugs of foamy beer. He liked Ballantine's Ale, so she kept that on hand and drank it with him, although she preferred wine or vermouth.

He called before he came so she could sneak down and leave the lower door unlocked. He arrived after dark and disappeared in the early morning hours. He always wore his uniform. Inevitably, people saw him—and her next-door neighbor did more than *see* him, Maddie knew. Funny, she had not been loud before. But she wanted someone to hear, to know that she was having sex two, three times a night, even if it was just her motley assortment of neighbors. Sometimes, Ferdie liked to bend her over the sink in her bathroom, and while he kept his eyes tightly shut, she was mesmerized by their images in the mirror. She had never looked so pale and tiny. Before Ferdie, she had thought of herself as dark.

And somehow this had led her to a stranger's home not that far from that apartment on Gist Avenue, Maddie's cheek pressed against the gingham cover of an ironing board, waiting for the kitchen magician to straighten her hair. The woman was tall and broad, wearing a shapeless dress and slippers. Her own hair was covered by a kerchief.

"How'd you hear about me?" she asked.

Ferdie had coached Maddie on what to say. "My mother's cleaning lady."

"You can get the same style putting your hair up on orange juice cans." She pronounced it *urnge*. "But this will last a little longer, if there's not too much dampness in the air."

When it was done, Maddie wasn't sure how she felt. Beautiful, yes, not unlike an actress she had seen on several television shows as of late, with big brown eyes and long, glossy hair. But she also felt as if she had surrendered part of herself, especially when she went to pick up Seth and he said: "What have you done?"

For a second, she didn't realize he meant the hair.

She touched her straight, shining locks, imagined Ferdie's fingers in it, hoped he would call before it began to frizz again. "Just wanted to try something different."

"Haven't you tried enough different things this year?"

Could he know? Maddie had noticed that the more sex she had with Ferdie, the more men seemed to notice her on the street, almost as if she were giving off some animalistic scent. But Seth was just a sullen teenager, doing what sullen teenagers do, torturing his mother. He was angry with her. Of course he was. She should have waited to leave, she supposed, until he was out of high school.

Her midweek "dates" with Seth were always awkward. She'd tell him to choose the restaurant, he'd say he didn't care, she would pick the Suburban House or the chop suey place on Reisterstown Road, and then he would complain about her selection. She asked him questions, he grunted one-syllable answers. They were both relieved when it was over.

Tonight, however, she tried to press him. "Seth—if you're angry with me, that's okay."

"Well, *thanks.*" They were at the Suburban House, where he had ordered a grilled cheese sandwich and fries, and she had let it pass, not bothering to lecture him about his complexion, with which he had just recently won a delicate truce. He ate with his mouth open. She didn't have the energy to correct that, either.

"I'm really sorry that your father and I are getting a divorce."

He shrugged, dragged a French fry through ketchup. "No skin off my butt."

"*Seth.* You don't even know what that means, not really."

He stopped to think. "Sure I do. It means—"

"Well, it's not nice. And it's not how you speak to your mother."

"You left. You're not my mom."

"I'll always be your mother. I just didn't want to be your father's wife anymore."

She could see him trying to feign nonchalance. But he couldn't help himself. "Why? You don't fight. Well, you do now, but you didn't before. I don't *get* it."

"I'm not sure I can put it into words. It's as if I had a glimpse of—

like in the poem, the road not taken. I don't think I'm the person I was meant to be." She added hastily, "I was meant to be your mother. You had to exist, the world needs you, Seth. That was part of my destiny. But not all of it. You're almost grown. I want to do something with my life."

"Like a job? But you've never worked. What would you do?"

Maddie did not fault Seth for not realizing that *he* had been her work. She hadn't seen it that way either. Running a household, raising a good if somewhat sullen boy, being a devoted wife—up until she left—these things were not work. Your children gave you cards on Mother's Day. Your husband, if he was prosperous enough, gave you jewelry on your birthday. Every culture was full of folk songs lauding mothers. But it wasn't *a job*.

As a boy, Seth had read biographies about the childhoods of great Americans—presidents, sports figures. The series included a few girls and some were outstanding—Jane Addams, Amelia Earhart, Betsy Ross. But one of the chosen women was Juliette Low, the founder of the Girl Scouts, a pretty minor accomplishment, in Maddie's eyes. How brilliant did one have to be to come up with a female version of the Boy Scouts? The series was so desperate for females to include that they even devoted one volume to Nancy Hanks, whose only role in history was to give birth to Abraham Lincoln.

"I know I have only two years of college, but there's a lot I could do."

"Like what?"

"I could—work at a museum. Or maybe get a job at the radio station." Wally Weiss owed her that much, she thought wryly, although she could not imagine calling on him for help.

Sensing weakness, Seth asked if he could have a second Coke.

"Sure," Maddie said, defeated. It was folly to expect a child to care about a parent's dreams and desires.

When she got home, she stared at the phone, willing it to ring. Ferdie almost never called on Wednesdays. Not because he knew of her standing dinner with Seth, but because—well, he never said and she didn't want to ask. There was a wife, there had to be a wife. That Maddie could endure. But she was pretty sure there were other women, too, and she was wild with curiosity about them. She stared at the phone, all too aware that she was living that Dorothy Parker story, the one about the girl's plaintive prayer to God to make the phone ring. Maddie had loved Dorothy Parker as a teenager but never worried about boys calling her. Everything had gone according to her plans until the summer after high school, when she tried to reel in a fish that was much too big for her inexpert hands. She was self-aware enough to realize that the relationship with Ferdie brought back that outlaw time, that it made her feel young, having to pursue another relationship in secret.

The phone didn't ring.

But there was another sound, like sleet against her window. She went to the bedroom and there was Ferdie on her fire escape.

"I was driving by," he said, "and I saw the light on."

"You shouldn't be out there," she said, "someone will call the cops."

"Luckily, the cops are already here." He swung a uniformed leg over her windowsill.

She was between his legs when the phone started to ring. He placed a firm hand on her head and she found herself working to the phone's rhythm. It kept ringing and ringing. Who let a phone ring twenty times? Ferdie and the phone finally gave way and she fell back, pleased with herself, when it started to ring again. It had to be Milton, and if it was Milton, then it had to be about Seth. What could have happened in the two hours since she saw him last?

She picked up the phone, but it was just the girl from the jewelry store, asking if she wanted to go to that political meeting. Sure, why not, sometime, depending on her schedule? She would have said anything to get off the call and back to Ferdie.

Later, as Ferdie napped beside her, Maddie wondered how she could keep her promise to her son. She had to do something with her life.

She had to matter.

MY FAMILY ATE *black-eyed peas for the New Year. Do you know the custom? It's supposed to bring luck. My father didn't like it. He didn't like anything that had the faintest shade of hoodoo to it. If you spilled salt at the table, he thought it better to just let it lie. He would walk under ladders, cross any black cat's path. To my father, superstitions were godless. Live right, follow the Ten Commandments, and you wouldn't have to worry about ladders or cats or the number thirteen. But he let my mama make black-eyed peas on New Year's Day, as long as we didn't talk about it, and I believed in those peas.*

But when I didn't show up on January first to eat with my family, no one paid any mind. They knew the life I was living. "Flighty," my father would say to my mother. "She is a flighty girl and I have to blame you for that, Merva." Even on a humdrum Saturday night, I would have worked or had a date. Sometimes I worked and had a date. No crime in that. Obviously, I would have gone out on New Year's Eve, no matter how late I worked. It had been an unusually fine day for December, a finer one still for January, topping sixty degrees.

It was, as it turned out, excellent dying weather.

When did my family think to ask after me? I had been there two days earlier, to see the boys. And although I had showered them with gifts at Christmas—because I could now, I had resources—I brought them more toys on the twenty-ninth. I never came to that house empty-handed. Toys for the boys, food for Mama—hams and roasts, things she seldom allowed herself, shopping the bargains at the no-name grocery store in our neighborhood. That night, I brought her a jacket of mine I knew she liked. I would have given her cash money, too. But my father wouldn't allow that. He said my money was dirty, that he didn't want it. He said that I should be saving it, so I could take my boys back.

He wasn't wrong. But it's a temptation, being paid in cash. It doesn't feel real, exactly, especially if one's other bills are taken care of. Except for my share of rent to Latetia, of course, and I never worried too much about that. If I ran short, all I had to do was cry a few pretty tears. And, sure, I spent a little on myself. Not as much as people think—my nicest clothes weren't new, but good as. Better, I think, because the beautiful clothes in my closet arrived with histories. Any man can buy a woman clothes. My main man was taking a risk when he gave me something.

Are you really missing if almost nobody misses you? I was dead, but being a ghost comes with fewer privileges than you might expect. I couldn't see my family, couldn't linger in their rooms, much as I yearned to. Besides, if I had been given the right to haunt someone, I wouldn't have chosen my family. They deserved better than my sad little ghost, hanging around, full of self-pity.

The mild weather quickly ended, the weather turned bitter, fol-lowed by that blizzard at month's end. It was only then that any-one began to take my mama seriously. There had been rumors that I had gone to Florida, along with Latetia, who ran away to Elkton and eloped on New Year's Eve. She cabled me that she was moving to Flor-ida with her new man, but the cable sat, unread, in a pile of bills and junk shoved under the door of our place on Druid Hill Avenue. The landlord discovered it when he came by on January 15, to complain about not being paid. He was ready to put all our stuff on the street, but my mama made good on my portion, ransomed my possessions, the ones worth keeping. She bundled up my beautiful clothes and took them back to my family's place. She wanted so to believe that I would wear them again.

The Afro-American ran the first piece about me on February 14. Happy Valentine's Day to me; my mother loved me enough to convince people that I hadn't just walked away on my own. The police began to ask questions, if only out of respect. The last anyone had seen me for sure was heading out on December 31—early January 1, actually—for what I told everyone was going to be a big, big night.

Tommy, who worked the bar at the Flamingo, even remembered my last words: "They say whatever you're doing on January first is what you'll do all year. I don't need to eat any black-eyed peas to know that 1966 is going to be a great year."

You could have read all of this in the Afro-American, Maddie Schwartz, but I'm guessing that you don't make a habit of reading the Afro.

March came in like a lion, they still hadn't found me, and the daily newspapers still hadn't written a word about me.

Tessie Fine—she was missed right away. I know, I know: she was only eleven. And white. Still, it did not escape my attention that her disappearance was noted almost immediately. You certainly noticed. That was your first taste, the little girl. You're a morbid one, Maddie Schwartz.

Again, I have to ask: are you really missing if nobody misses you?

The Schoolgirl

I CAN'T BELIEVE I end up fighting with the principal on my eleventh birthday, but I am one of the best students at Bais Yaakov and I like to argue. I'm good at debating. I'm good at everything. I am *furious* that I will not be publicly called to the Torah in front of my friends and family. I want a bat mitzvah, but modern Orthodox families like mine only allow boys that. Some of the Conservative families will throw parties for the girls, as for Reform—no one cares what the Reform families do. My parents say the Reform aren't really Jewish.

"This is pride," Rabbi tells me. "This has nothing to do with your life as a Jew. You yearn to show off. That is not the point of a bar mitzvah."

It isn't the first time I've been warned about pride, so I have an argument ready. "I am proud of being a Jew, yes. And the boys are proud, too. Even though most of them do not read Hebrew as well as I do."

"You need to cultivate modesty, Tessie."

"Why?" I stamp my feet, enjoying the hard sound of the taps that my mother puts on the heels so they'll last longer.

"The Torah tells us . . ." I'm not really listening to Rabbi. I am readying my own argument. The beauty of the Torah is that you can always find what you need to win an argument.

I toss my hair so my curls bounce on my shoulder, shiny as a shampoo commercial. My hair is just like my aunt's and she calls it my crowning glory. When I read *Anne of Green Gables,* I never understood why Anne wasn't delighted to be a redhead. I love being the only redhead in my class. "A cardinal among the wrens," people say. They think they're saying it out of my hearing. I am the tallest, too, and the first to start getting a shape. It's my plan to take my birthday money from my grandmother and buy a bra.

It's a secret mission, of course. My mother would never approve. But once I smuggle the bra into the house, what can she do? A bra can't be returned to the store after you wear it and my mother would never throw away a piece of clothing. We have lots of money, but my mother is frugal. She makes homemade brandy from cherries, darns our socks. I'm more like my aunt, the one they call the spendthrift.

Rabbi drones on and on about modesty, *tzniut.* "We must always remember that while the pursuit of knowledge is laudable, it is not to be used for show. Or as a weapon to make others do what we want."

Hmmm. I have noticed that while boys are praised for using their knowledge exactly like a weapon, girls are not. I am always being told to listen, not to interrupt. Two years ago, assigned an essay on my future life, I wrote that I wanted to be an opera singer or a rabbi. They told me a girl can never be a rabbi, or even a cantor. They gave me the same speech about modesty, *tzniut*. If I had a dollar for every time someone quoted "All is vanity" to me, I could buy five new bras, one for each school day. Modesty is for people who aren't lucky enough to have things about which to be conceited.

I can't wait to come to school in my white blouse, sheer enough that the other girls will see I have proper straps, not an undershirt. I'm going to buy a Vassarette bra because they're the best, I saw the ads when I sneak-read *Seventeen* magazine at the drugstore. I'll button my cardigan over my shirt so my mother doesn't know what I'm doing.

I have been planning this shopping trip for days. First, I tell a convincing lie to the mother who drives carpool this afternoon. The underwear store is next to a pet store, so I tell Mrs. Finkelstein that my brother's fish needs fish food and she can let me off there. She frets—she is supposed to take me to the door—but my house is only two blocks away and we are within the *eruv*. The days are getting longer, but it's still cold and today is particularly nasty, with a wet rain, hard as pebbles. She wants to get home, too, and I'm the last girl to be dropped off. There is no parking space—there are never parking spaces along this block—so she makes me promise to go straight home.

I make that pledge easily, no need to cross my fingers. What is "straight home," after all? I can't get home without walking past the lingerie store.

Aware that Mrs. Finkelstein is watching, I push my way into the pet store, which smells horrible. It is the most boring kind of pet store, all fish and turtles and snakes, nothing with fur. *Fur.* I'm going to get a fur coat when I turn eighteen. My grandparents, who own a fur store, have promised me this. But I want it sooner, maybe at age sixteen. That's still five years away, a whole new decade. I want a fur. I want a ring like my mother's, with a big green stone that my mother says isn't an emerald, but I think it must be. I want glittery earrings. I want to marry a rich man or make a lot of money on my own so I can have whatever I want, when I want it.

But, right now, I want a Vassarette bra, preferably in pink.

"Can I help you?" A man's voice, coming from the back of the pet shop. I am pretending to inspect the snakes in the glass boxes in the front of the store, but I am really trying to keep watch through the dusty window, making sure that Mrs. Finkelstein's car has pulled away and gone through the light.

"No," I say, using what my family calls my duchess airs. "I'm just *looking.*"

The man is skinny and pale, with orange hair and red-rimmed eyes. If a cold could be a person, it would look like this man. His eyes remind me of white mice, not that this shop sells anything as cuddly as mice. He has a sniffle and poor posture.

"You're a redhead," he says. "Like me."

No, I'm not. No, he's not. He's an orange head. I turn my back to him.

"Do you want a snake? Or maybe a pair of little turtles?"

"I'll tell you if I see anything I want. A person can walk around a store and look at things."

"But some of our fish require special tanks, and you can't put just any two fish together—"

"I'll tell you if I need you," I say. I don't want to talk to a man who works in a dirty, smelly store. An orange-headed man who thinks he can tell me, Tessie Fine, with ten dollars in my pocket, what I am allowed to do. My aunt doesn't let shopkeepers speak to her this way.

I've seen her in Hutzler's, when the salesladies try to spray her with perfume. "Darling," she says, drawing out the r-sound, "I wear only Joy." The customer is always right.

"Okay, but you can't go around just touching things . . ."

I don't want to touch anything here, but he can't tell me what to do.

"It's a free country." I stamp my foot. I like the sound of my metal-capped heels on the wood floor.

"Don't do that," the man says, making a face as if the sound is painful to him.

"You can't tell me what to do." I stamp my foot. It is a glorious sound. I stamp and I stamp and I stamp and I—

March 1966

"IS THERE ANYTHING more annoying than not getting to do something you never wanted to do in the first place?"

Maddie was trying to make a joke on herself, an observation about the eternal push-and-pull between mothers and daughters.

But Judith Weinstein must have thought this a profound inquiry, worthy of a thoughtful answer, for she did not reply right away. Maddie could not see Judith's face—they were working their way down a narrow path, with Maddie leading the way—but Judith, when she finally answered, sounded like someone who yearned to be agreeable, even if she didn't quite agree.

"It is frustrating that we made the effort and they wouldn't let us help. But they didn't stop us, did they?"

Her voice was as wobbly as their footing. Judith probably thought

Maddie was insane, following these old trails through the arbore-tum, darkness encroaching. How had they ended up here?

Because her mother had called her that morning, as she had ev-ery morning at nine since Maddie's phone was installed, and it never occurred to Maddie not to pick up. It was the one thing that was the same about her old and new lives, the daily call from her mother.

"Maddie, have you heard about Tessie Fine?"

"Of course, Mother. I'm on Cathedral Street, not in Siberia. We get the same newspapers. I listen to WBAL."

Maddie's mother had made a small but distinct "Pffft." This meant she disagreed with Maddie's facts but couldn't be bothered to argue. She also seemed to shudder reflexively at the mere mention of "Cathedral," as if the street name was an affront. She'd have been more horrified if she realized that Maddie's apartment, while on the Mulberry side of the building, actually overlooked the cathedral.

"It's been two days. Our synagogue has been sending volunteers. You meet up at the parking lot, then go in pairs . . ."

The "you" was specific, not general. Maddie's mother, Tattie Morgenstern—some strange childhood bastardization of *Harriet* that she refused to stop using—was telling Maddie that *she* would go to the parking lot, *she* would be paired up, *she* would walk an assigned route in the ever-expanding perimeter around the tropical fish store where Tessie Fine was last seen.

Baltimore had been aflame with the story. Tessie Fine, so pretty, so young. She had told the mother who dropped her off that she was going to buy food for her brother's fish. But her brother had no fish. The man in the store said she had walked in but left five minutes later without buying anything. He said she had been rude to him. Family and friends said, with evident admiration, "Yes, that's our Tessie."

Maddie's mother knew Tessie's grandmother. She didn't like her, but she knew her. They had been children together, classmates at The Park School when it was still on Auchentoroly Terrace. Park, although nonsectarian, was the preferred school for the German Jewish families, whose children had not been welcome at the city's older private schools at the time. As the neighborhood around Druid Hill Park "changed"—the preferred euphemism for integration— the families and the school migrated to the northwest. Maddie had attended Park at its Liberty Heights location; now it was in Brooklandville, almost all the way to the Beltway, and Seth was a third-generation student. Maddie had even had a date or two with Tessie's father, when they were young teens.

Tessie's father, Bobby Fine, was more conservative than his parents. He chose to live within the *eruv* in Park Heights. According to Tattie, his mother blamed Bobby's wife for this unseemly embrace of Orthodoxy. It was one thing to have two sets of dishes and eschew shellfish and pork. But Bobby's wife took Judaism *too far*. It seemed to Maddie that there was no end to Tattie Morgenstern's opinions about religion, about which was the correct one (Conservative Judaism), how much was the right amount. She also used "Presbyterian" as a pejorative for all things Protestant.

Over the years, Maddie had seen Tessie's mother here and there, registering her as a mousey thing, albeit well-dressed. But the Fine and Schwartz social circles did not overlap and it seemed vulgar to encroach on the Fine family tragedy. If they had been true friends, Maddie would have gladly assisted. But they had not even attended each other's weddings and—

Maddie didn't want to follow her own chain of thought, about the next Fine family ritual that she would not be attending.

"So awful," Tattie said. "I don't know how any parent could survive this."

"She could be alive," Maddie said. A happy resolution to the case was still possible, wasn't it? A little girl could wander away, get lost, maybe bump her head and not know who she was? But Ferdie had said much the same thing as Tattie just last night: Tessie Fine was almost certainly dead and the homicide detectives who had caught the case were under pressure to make some kind of progress as quickly as possible.

"When they find her—" Maddie tried again.

"*If*," corrected her mother. "When I was a girl, I remember hearing about a pervert who raped little girls and then killed them. It was where you live now, which was a ghetto then. A ghetto now, really. Anyway, he attacked one little girl and her mother had a gun and shot him, so that was the end of that."

Maddie's neighborhood was not a ghetto and her mother's story was lifted almost verbatim from the pages of *A Tree Grows in Brooklyn,* a book beloved by mother and daughter. But there was no point in calling her on it. Tattie Morgenstern believed everything she said.

"I hope they do find her, and soon," Maddie had said, surprised by her own fervency.

She'd told her mother she had to go, although she didn't have to do anything. She had the insurance money for her "stolen" ring and the proceeds from her car sale to tide her over until Milton was forced to pay alimony. Her lawyer was confident that Maddie soon would have her half of the house, her half of almost everything, including Seth. Until then, she could live off her savings, if she was careful.

She'd put on her coat and headed out for a walk. Her neighborhood wasn't *that* bad. She had a strange fantasy, strange even to her. She imagined one of the men she saw on the street grabbing her, trying to drag her into an alley. He would be foreign, spewing unintelligible syllables, pawing at her. It would be terrifying, yet also exciting, proof of how desirable she was, even at her age. With her straightened hair and tight sweaters, she looked younger than thirty-seven. The man would try to force his mouth on hers, then somehow—she didn't have to explain it, dreams had their own logic—Ferdie would be there, he would save her and they would both be so overwhelmed that they would find someplace nearby—a bathroom, a car—to make love. Risking exposure in every sense of the word.

It was a strange fantasy, but fantasies were never wrong, or so Maddie had read somewhere.

Lost in those thoughts, Maddie had walked farther than she'd planned. What should she do today? The giddy freedom of her early weeks, of having no one to care for, had ebbed and the affair—was that the right word?—heightened the do-nothingness of the rest of life. She was trying not to be *too* available to Ferdie. Sometimes, she forced herself to go out for dinner around the time he usually called, just to keep him on his toes. She still had the instincts that had made her one of the most sought-after girls in Baltimore, in her day. Back then, she'd even kept a little notebook, with a code, that allowed her to remember how far she had progressed with each boy she dated. K (obvious), SK ("soul kiss," which she thought a much nicer term than "French kissing"), OC, OB, UB ("over clothes," "over bra," "under bra"). Only two boys had gone US ("under skirt") and she had married the second one.

Wally Weiss had not merited a mention in her notebook. He had received only one kiss, one time, and it was sisterly, more of a promise that one day he would find a girl to K, SK.

Yet she had not been physically coy with Ferdie. She blushed with the memory of how quickly they had progressed. The first time he had grabbed her and kissed her, she had assumed it was because he knew. She was lying about the ring and this was the price she had to pay. She was a bad girl and he had this over her. But since that first encounter, she had come to realize that Ferdie had no idea she was, in fact, a criminal. She had found a pawnshop that wasn't fussy about paperwork, easy to do in her neighborhood, and it paid her half of what Weinstein's had offered, but it was all profit at this point. Maddie had used the cash to buy things for the apartment—bistro chairs and a marble-topped table, velvet throw pillows, a pretty rug.

She had stopped at the Beehive for a to-go cup of its strong, scorched coffee. Lying on her bed—so decadent, to be on a bed in the daytime, if one wasn't sick—she had tried to focus on her library book, *Herzog*. The poetry she had loved and tried to write as a teenager no longer affected her, but the recommended novels at the Pratt didn't move her, either. She had chosen *Herzog* because someone from Hadassah said it was anti-Semitic and she liked to make up her own mind about these things. Maddie was not persuaded, not so far, that Bellow was a "self-loathing Jew," but she squirmed uncomfortably at the coincidence of the titular character's second wife's name, Madeleine, so close to hers. She was an awful person, this Madeleine. It was hard not to take it personally.

Maddie wondered if she would ever be someone's second wife. She wanted to live passionately, fully. Is that possible in a marriage of long standing? She and Milton had been very amorous in their early years. She was almost *too* amorous. She still blushed at the memory, the two of them a week out from their wedding, parked in a popular spot near Cylburn Arboretum, so close to doing the deed.

He'd said no.

He'd said no.

She'd had her hand on him, something she did for him and just one other man, something else she never wrote down. Her diary was like a general's campaign, noting only what territory had been seized from her. It did not occur to her to document her own sorties. And there had come a time when she wrote nothing at all, when it was unthinkable to admit what she was doing—and with whom.

She parted her legs and tried to guide Milton inside her; she thought it was the greatest gift she could bestow. They were betrothed, almost married. What could be the harm?

"I don't want to lie before God," Milton said. For a second, she thought he meant lying down.

"Of course," she said, her always reliable instincts guiding her to what was necessary to rescue her dignity, her reputation. "I was just so carried away by you, Miltie."

On her wedding night, she remembered to mimic the pain she had experienced her true first time. If Milton ever suspected his bride was not a virgin, he was polite enough—or disappointed enough—not to let on. It was an important first lesson in a young marriage. Let some lies lie.

At noon, Maddie had put away her book and poked around the icebox for something to eat. Her practice for the past few years had been to lunch on things like melba toast and cottage cheese. Yet Ferdie wanted her to put on weight, was forever urging food on her. "Someone needs to take care of you, baby," he said, clearly having decided that her thinness was a by-product of her caring for others, not a rigidly achieved state. Maddie, who had always followed fashion, couldn't help noticing that a girl named Twiggy was suddenly everywhere. The new styles favored thin women. Of course, she was too old for such clothes. Or was she? No matter how thin she got, her breasts never seemed to shrink. She thought of how many boys had begged, *begged,* to progress from OC to OB to UB, how the discovery of her breasts took their breaths away, like they were men seeing land after a long time at sea.

Cylburn Arboretum. It wasn't that far from where Tessie Fine had last been seen, no more than a mile, a bit of wildness in the heart of the city. If one were to dump a body somewhere—

She'd checked the clock. Maybe she *should* go help look for Tessie Fine. Not doing something just because her mother had suggested it was sullen, the kind of behavior one would expect from an adolescent. Maddie would call that girl, the one from the jewelry store, and ask her to go along. She didn't know why she wanted a companion, but it seemed more respectable somehow.

Judith, clearly excited to hear from Maddie, had said her brother would let her leave work given the gravity of the mission. They'd taken buses to the synagogue parking lot, arriving just as the volunteers were about to set out.

"Men only," said the synagogue president, who had organized the search parties.

"That's ridiculous," Maddie said.

"This is no job for women." He looked at their clothes, as if he could eliminate them on that basis alone, but their shoes were sensible, their coats suitable to combing alleys and vacant lots.

"Then we'll do our own search," Maddie said. "It's not as if we need your permission to walk around Baltimore."

The arboretum was farther down Northern Parkway than she recalled, the grounds larger and more heavily wooded. The day, which had started with promises of spring, had aged into something raw and punishing. They walked the trails systematically, aware that they needed to leave by five, the closing time during winter. The trails went deep, all the way down to Cylburn Avenue. With their deadline approaching, Maddie said to Judith: "Let's walk this last one all the way to the fence."

Later, when she was asked, *How did you think to look there?* Maddie would be nonplussed. She couldn't say, *I remembered parking there with all the boys I dated,* much less, *I tried to get my future husband to make love to me there, but he wanted to wait because he thought I was a virgin.*

So she would say: *Just a hunch.*

On that hunch, they walked down the final trail, to the fence line along the avenue. The land dipped here, creating a gully. The fence was broken, torn open, but you couldn't see the bottom of the gully from the street, you had to be on the hill, above it, to see what Maddie saw.

She caught a glimpse of something shiny, too shiny, in the gray-green wintry underbrush. It was a bright silver crescent on the heel of a shoe. The shoe was attached to a leg, the leg to the body, the body to a head, a face. A face that was too composed, too still. No child's face was ever this still.

With her loden-green coat and brown tights, Tessie Fine had almost disappeared into the landscape. But her red tresses flamed like out-of-season wildflowers, and her shoes shined on, catching the last rays of light.

The Patrolman

WHEN THE CALL comes in, my first thought is, *Thank God, I don't have to go to Burger Chef.* Every night, my partner, Paul, and I argue about dinner and he won tonight. I prefer Gino's. Maybe that sounds callous, thinking about dinner when a call comes in about a body, maybe the body that everyone's looking for, but you have to understand I'm thinking it's going to be a big fat nothing. In fact, somehow I get it in my head that they are teenagers, a boy and a girl, doing something they weren't supposed to be doing. They looked at the clock, realized they were supposed to be home for supper, had no shot, so they had to have a reason.

At any rate, we're on Northern Parkway, headed west, the closest patrol to the arboretum, so we take the call. Usually, the place would be closed by now, but the staff stayed and kept the gates open.

The first thing I notice is that the couple aren't boy-girl and they aren't teenagers. It's two women, one in her twenties and one in her thirties, clearly not related. And although the older one has at least ten years on me, she's the looker of the two. The younger one is presentable, don't get me wrong, with shiny hair and a nice face. But the older one has dark hair and light eyes and a tiny waist—she's wearing a trench coat, belted tight—and it's hard not to think, *Wow*. I'm married and I don't whore around like some of my colleagues, but I'm not blind.

Still, I don't believe they've found the girl, especially when they lead us out and around the arboretum, down to Cylburn Avenue. It's not a busy street, but it gets enough traffic so that someone, somehow, would have spotted a body over the past two days. We leave the patrol car in the parking lot and walk, two by two, like the worst double date ever. I'm next to the dark-haired one, who's leading the way.

She's been crying. "I have a son," she says. "A teenager." I tell her that I haven't been married long enough to have any kids, which is more or less true. I've been married three years and we've had two miscarriages. The doctor says there's no reason we won't have healthy kids one day. Sons, I hope, to follow me into the line of duty. My father was a police and I'm a police. My grandfather arrived from Poland in 1912 and his English was never really that good, or else he might have been a police, too. People today are always talking about prejudice and stuff, like the rest of us never knew it. When my family came to America, to Baltimore, the Irish ran it and they took care of their own. Then the Italians ran it and they took care of their own. Then us bohunks finally got a turn. On and on, that's the way things have always been and always will be. You just have to wait your turn.

I ask what her husband does and she starts as if the question surprised her, but if you have a kid, you have a husband, right? She says: "Attorney," then adds quickly: "Not crime. Civil. Real estate law."

"I bet he makes a good living," I say, just to say something. The night is so quiet. You can hear the traffic noises not far away— Northern Parkway, the steady swish of cars on the new expressway, the Jones Falls, visible through the trees this time of year—yet it still feels hushed, like church. We keep our voices low out of respect.

Speaking only for myself—I don't know what goes on in Paul's head most of the time, if anything, other than a desire to eat at Burger Chef and chase tramps—I want these women to be wrong. Not because it will make for a late night. We've just come on, we have nothing better to do. But I don't want anything to do with a dead kid. It feels like bad luck. Two miscarriages, that's enough death for me. I wonder sometimes if the miscarriages are a punishment, but for what? I'm a good man. I had some wildness when I was younger, which is natural and right. In a man. My wife, Sophia, is six years younger than me, very pure. She deserves to have her babies. If God feels He needs to punish me for some reason, that's one thing, but Sophia doesn't deserve that. And if He would just give us children, we would raise such good citizens, boys who would follow me into the department and girls who would learn to make all the wonderful things Sophia can make, cabbage rolls and brisket and pierogies.

We reach Cylburn Avenue, and at first, it looks as if I'm going to get my wish. There's no body to be seen.

"Where is—?" The dark-haired one frets. "I thought she was right here." The younger one, she's barely spoken up 'til now, Paul has been nattering to her all the way down the hill. He's single, techni- cally, has a pretty steady girl, although I guess that isn't my business. Before marriage, whatever you do, that's your own business.

The younger one says: "No, go a little farther." Night has fallen, thick and fast, and we get out our flashlights. I'm trying to make them feel better: "You'd be surprised how often people make this kind of mistake"—and then Paul's light catches a flash of something and there she is. Tessie Fine, her neck snapped like a chicken's. You don't need to be a coroner to figure that out.

We call it in. Paul offers to walk the women back up to the arboretum parking lot, but they say they don't have a car up there, they walked here from the synagogue.

"We can call you a cab," I say.

The older one protests. "No, no. I—I have to stay. I'm a mother. If something happened to my boy and another mother found him, I'd want her to stay." I don't get this, but I have to respect it. I bet Sophia would do the same.

With the sun down, the cold begins creeping into our bones, that March dampness that's worse than dead-of-winter in some ways. I feel bad, not having something to drape over the ladies' shoulders, but if I take off my jacket, I'll be in shirtsleeves, and they've both got coats. The homicide detectives show up, but Paul and I have to keep the street clear and the women won't go, not until that little body is taken away, the head hanging at that horrible angle. You don't have to be strong to do that to a little girl. You do have to be awfully angry. Who could be that angry at a little girl? I hope it's not a sex crime. I think that would drive me crazy, if a child of mine died that way.

I can tell it hits her hard, the dark-haired one. It's more personal to her somehow because she has a kid. Or because it was her idea to search here. *How did you know to look here?* we ask her, but she doesn't say anything, just hugs herself.

The news people finally get wind of it. We've been careful on the radios, but we are less than a mile from Television Hill and the road has been blocked. On a clear late-winter night like this, the red-and-blues can be seen for miles. Some concerned citizen probably began making calls. The reporters are kept at the end of the street, sometimes yelling out questions, but mostly quiet. At some point, I see the *Star's* cop reporter, Jack Diller, walking down the street. Diller has been covering the beat so long he's more cop than reporter and when we tell him to get back, he's amiable. "But is it Tessie Fine? Just tell me that," he says. Somehow, he gets confirmation, but not from me.

We drive the women home, of course. Never occurred to me that they live in opposite directions. I wonder how they know each other, how they ended up paired off for the search. The older one gets in the front seat and we let it go. Paul takes the backseat and talks a blue streak. He's flirting, the bum. We drive up to Pikesville, which I expected, it's where all the Jews live. But then the other one, the lady with the lawyer husband, tells us: "I live downtown. I'm sorry—I know it's pretty far out of your way."

We tell her we don't mind.

On the drive downtown, I give her some advice: "You don't have to talk to the press. It's better if you don't."

"Why?"

"There's a killer out there. The less he knows about what we know, the better. And in the meantime, until there's an arrest, you're the story."

This seems to give her pause. "Is that a bad thing?"

"Not good or bad. But you can't undo it, once it's done. That's all. They're like dogs, reporters. They'll scramble for any scrap they can get. And because there are so many of them, they'll all want a different angle. The one who gets to you first, he'll build you up. So the others will have to tear you down."

"Tear me down? What have I done?" She seems really rattled now and I feel bad.

"Nothing. I'm just warning you—the reporters can make a good thing into a bad thing. That's how they do." A reporter did my dad dirty once. It didn't come to anything in the end, but I learned a lesson from it.

We let her out at this old dump of an apartment building near the cathedral. I want to walk her upstairs, but she's really firm. Almost too firm, like she thinks I'm going to try something, which is insulting. I'm just trying to fit together the pieces of her story. A son, so there was a husband at some point. Is the son grown? Could be, if she got a real early start. I can't imagine a kid living in that apartment house. My wife and I, we live in a rowhouse near Patterson Park, but once the kids start coming—and they will, I know they will, we've just had bad luck—and I start moving up in the ranks, we'll find a house farther out, with at least a little lawn. Kids need a yard, not that I ever had one. Anyway, what am I going to do, with Paul in the backseat, the patrol car due back at district before I can go home and get into bed next to my wife, who will be asleep, or pretending to be. She's going through a phase where she doesn't like to be touched. Her body has let her down and she thinks she's let me down, but I don't blame her, not a bit.

I grab a beer with Paul and some other guys, maybe play up our role in the discovery of Tessie Fine a little, which means downplaying what that Maddie lady and her friend did, but it was Paul's flashlight that caught that piece of shoe, we were the professionals on the scene. Anyway, after I finish my one beer, it makes sense to go home by way of her apartment building, just because—I don't know. I'm worried about her. That's no place for a nice lady to live.

When I get there, a patrol car is parked out front. Now I'm really worried. Has something happened? Finding a body can do things to you, or so I've heard. It was my first, too. Anyway, I'm about to cross the street and go upstairs when I see a uniform, alone, come out the building—and get into that patrol car. And there's no way, just no way, that guy can be legit.

Because he's blacker than ink and the coloreds don't get to use cars.

I make note of the license and the number. It's from my district, Northwest. Tomorrow, I'll start asking around, try to figure out why a car from Northwest District was parked outside Maddie Schwartz's apartment at three in the morning.

And why some colored cop was coming from there in the middle of the night.

March 1966

IT WAS STRANGE, moving through the world with a secret. Not Ferdie—Maddie thought of Ferdie as an *arrangement,* something she was obliged to keep to herself because of others' prejudices. But only a handful of people—Judith, the police officers—knew she was the one who had found Tessie Fine. "Discovered by two passersby" was the way the newspapers framed it, while on television, the hosts, including Wallace Wright, said it was a "young couple." Not wrong, yet not correct, either. And it wasn't only that "young couple" led people to infer it was some boy-girl pair. Everything said made Maddie's role in the discovery seem incidental. She had chosen the spot, it was her idea to head down that last trail, but you'd never have known that, reading and watching the news.

There had been no arrest yet, although Ferdie told her that there was a strong suspect, a clerk in the fish store. The clerk said the girl had been in his store and left immediately, but no one believed him.

And Maddie learned from Ferdie that she and Judith, if only briefly, had been "persons of interest."

"What do you mean?" she asked as they drank beer in bed two days after the discovery of Tessie Fine's body.

"First of all, homicide cops are always going to pay attention to people who find bodies. That's just how they do their jobs. So here are these two women, walking down Cylburn Avenue coming on toward dusk—they thought you might be lesbians. Probably still think that."

"I told them we were turned away from the search party and decided to go out on our own," Maddie said. How could anyone think she was a lesbian? If she were, she would be like Lakey in *The Group*.

"Honey, if detectives believed everything people told them, they wouldn't be very good at their jobs." A beat. "I'd like to be a detective."

"I'm sure you can do whatever you set your mind to."

"The department's segregated, Maddie. Negro cops walk patrols, maybe do undercover in narcotics. We can't use cars. I don't even have a radio, just a call-box key. Remember how we met?"

She glanced at the African violet. "I'm not likely to forget."

"Anyway, so you have these two women walking down a quiet street after dusk, far from where either one lives. I bet they asked you if you knew the girl."

They had, in fact. But to Maddie, it was almost like a social conversation, goyim trying to understand the connectedness of the Jewish community. Oh, how she had chattered away. *Her grandmother and my mother knew each other—I suppose almost any woman in Northwest Baltimore who owns a fur knows the Fines. And I went to school with her father, years ago. He took me to a dance once.* She was embarrassed, in retrospect, how easily she had shared her stories with them, wondered if they had found her tiny details portentous, at least briefly. It also had not occurred to her to wonder why she and Judith were questioned separately the next day.

"Not that you would ever be a serious suspect," Ferdie added. Somehow that was more insulting still. How had she become a bit player in a story that wouldn't even have happened were it not for her? Obviously, she didn't want to be in the newspaper or on television because then she would have to be defined as—what? A woman who was separated, the former wife of, the estranged (not by choice) mother of. Who was Madeline Schwartz? She could not lay claim to the discovery of Tessie Fine without having that question asked.

She realized that she should have been content with that trade-off when she came home from a walk the next day and found a portly man in a trench coat and hat perched on her stoop.

"Bob Bauer," he said, extending his hand.

"I know who you are," she said. He had a popular column in the *Star*. It ran with a winsome pen-and-ink sketch.

"And you are . . ."

"Madeline Schwartz."

"Just the woman I've come to see," he said.

"May I ask why?"

"I think you know—look, can we go inside? I walked here and it's uphill. That's hard on a fat man such as myself."

"I wouldn't call you fat," she said.

"Well, I don't know what else you would call it."

Charmed, aware that she was being charmed, she let him in and offered him water. He was practically wheezing after the climb to her third-floor apartment.

"Nice place," he said. "I almost went to the other address by mistake, but my source set me straight."

"The other . . . ?"

"Where you lived before."

For a moment, she thought he meant Gist Avenue. Then she realized he had almost visited the house where Milton and Seth still lived. A catastrophe averted, she thought, then wondered why she felt that way. She hadn't done anything wrong. It would be nice if Seth at least knew his mother had found Tessie Fine.

"My husband and I are divorcing," she said.

"Happens in the best of families. Anyway, I thought it was quite a human-interest story, you and your friend finding Tessie Fine. A story worth telling, don't you think?"

Part of her longed to say yes. But it meant laying too much bare. Not just her current stature, but also the chain of thought that had led her to the arboretum. It suddenly seemed impossible to explain her line of thinking if she didn't mention the fearsome necking she had done in that location. She worried if she offered even a sanitized version of that story, she would end up telling everything. Ferdie, how she had pretended to be a virgin on her wedding night, maybe even the identity of the man who had made that pretense necessary, a secret she had safeguarded all these years.

"I'm not interested in publicity," she said.

"We could use just your first name," he said. His manner was kind, polite, yet there was a coiled tenacity about him. He wasn't going to move from her kitchen chair, even if he did have his hat and coat still on. "Obscure some details."

"I'm not obligated to talk to you. I know that. My husband is a lawyer."

He smiled. "Of course you're not obligated. Not legally. But it's a story people want to know and it's yours. Don't you want to share it?"

She allowed herself to live the moment in her imagination. All eyes on her. What would that feel like? And why was she so keen to know? But no, not this way, she decided. She remembered the patrolman's warnings.

Yet she felt she had to give this man something. Why? She couldn't have said. All she knew was that when a man showed up and needed something from her, she felt obligated to help him. But it was like raising children. You could divert them. You substituted the healthy food for the lolly or sweet they wanted, making them think it was their idea all along.

"I'm not the story," she said. "The man from the pet shop—he is."

"How do you know that? They haven't arrested him."

She could not say, *I know because my lover told me.* Instead: "There's something about the body that the police haven't shared yet. Something they found on it. They're waiting to get some kind of report back. When they do, they'll probably arrest the clerk."

He was impressed. More important, he was, in fact, no longer interested in her. "I hate to ask—it's not something that could ever be in the paper—but do they think it's a sex crime?"

She didn't know the answer, yet she felt some weird desire to protect Tessie Fine. "No," she said. "But he's the one. Watch."

He doffed his hat. "Mrs. Schwartz, you have been extremely helpful."

"You won't mention my name, right?"

He smiled. "No, I can't even call you a 'source.' But when I chat up my friends at headquarters, I can tell them that I have firsthand information. It is firsthand, right?"

She wasn't completely sure what firsthand meant in this situation, but she nodded.

The Columnist

I'M A COLUMNIST. I don't have to break stories, worry about
getting beat. I don't really do that much news anymore. It's supposed
to be a badge of honor, reaching the point where you're above the
fray, allowed to pontificate, or just write these little sketches about
your own life. That's my gig, most of the time. I write about life in
suburbia—my wife, my kids. Then, sometimes, I get to thinking I
need to horn in on a story. H. L. Mencken didn't get his own room
at the Pratt library by writing funny stories about his wife. If you're
a Baltimore reporter, Mencken's the standard-bearer. Mencken, Jim
Bready, maybe Russell Baker, although I remember when he started
on night cops and he was no great shakes.

But Tessie Fine—I had to write about her. I had to know. The
obvious thing would have been to go talk to the parents. They would
have opened their door to me. Almost everyone does. There's some-

thing about being a cartoon that makes people more susceptible to trusting you. What could be the harm in talking to me? I'm just that funny drawing come to life.

I think about that a lot. How I'm an actual cartoon.

Anyway, I was chatting up Diller, our nighttime cop reporter, been on the job so long that he's more cop than reporter. About as incurious a guy as I've ever known. There are more of those types in newspapers than you might think. If you could teach a dog to put on a fedora and carry a notepad, he would do his job the way Diller does, barking out facts to night rewrite. *Girl, dead. Found alongside Cylburn Avenue. No arrests at this time. Sources confirm it's Tessie Fine.* But sometimes Diller knows stuff without knowing what he knows and he's the one who described to me the two women at the scene. I still have enough sources down at the cop shop that I was able to unearth the one's name.

I walk to her place over on Cathedral Street because I always forget how hilly the city is as you head north from the harbor, where the *Star* offices are. It isn't a bad neighborhood, but it isn't a good one. *What's a nice girl doing in a place like this?* I want to say when I see her coming up the street. She looks young, in her beatnik clothes. Okay, maybe not that young when she gets closer, but still pert and fresh, like the very breeze on this day, which feels more like early autumn than late winter. She reminds me of my wife, my real wife, not the woman I'm married to now. I mean, I'm married to the same woman, going on twenty-seven years, but she's not the woman I met back in Quincy, Pennsylvania, when we were in high school. And I'm not the same man. I can't blame her. Not even Job himself would have survived what we've been through.

I am shocked when this lady doesn't want to talk to me. Everybody wants to talk to Bob Bauer. But, fair play, she gives me something better. I assume it's because she was eavesdropping at the scene, or some patrolman was indiscreet. A pretty woman like that—you might be tempted to blow and brag a little bit. Anyway, I call a detective I know, someone who's always been kind to me. Out of pity, probably, but that's okay. I'll take it. I've earned it. I ask him to meet me at a bar where we wouldn't see other cops and reporters, so we end up at Alonso's on Cold Spring Lane.

And go figure, the lady was right. The clerk is the primary suspect.

"They found something under the fingernails," my detective friend says. "And in her hair. Mainly."

"Somebody else's blood?" Thinking: *She promised me it wasn't sexual.*

My friend shakes his head. "This weird dirt, more like sand. It wasn't like anything you'd find in that park. You don't find it in all of Maryland."

"How can that be?"

"Aquarium sand!" the guy says. "But you can't write that until they serve the warrant tomorrow. They're going to arrest him at home. He lives with his mother."

We both snort, knowing what a loser that makes him, although my heart would soar and burst like fireworks if my grown son wanted to be in our house.

"Might be good if one reporter had the inside track on this," I say. "Someone you could trust to emphasize how smart you guys are."

The flattery works. It usually does. I don't accompany the cops to the actual arrest, but I'm at headquarters when they bring the guy in. He tries to say he's crazy, but the crazy ones never say that.

If only his cleaning skills had been better. The basement of that pet store is lousy with evidence. And why is the evidence in the basement? She wouldn't have had any reason to go down there unless he promised her something. Medical examiner said he hit her first, hard, but not enough to kill her, then broke her neck. No, I'm pretty sure the guy didn't snap. He had probably just seen the movie *Psycho,* thought he had a surefire defense.

My scoop is a sensation. I knew it would be. All the other papers have to chase it. The young cop reporters, even the ones on my own paper, are pissed. (Except for Diller, whose only concern is figuring out my source.) Who am I to be poaching one of the biggest stories out of the cop shop? I'll tell you who I am. I'm Bob Bauer. I served in World War II, came home and married my high school sweetheart, started at the bottom and wrote my way to the top. I can do anything—features, hard news, political analysis. I'm the two-thousand-pound gorilla who sits wherever I want. In the newsroom, the day my story runs, I sit at my desk in the corner of the Sunday office and the other reporters come by to pay homage, congratulate me, ask me how I did it. I cock a finger at them and smile. "Trade secret, men. Trade secret."

No one asks me out after work. I'm not sure I could have gone if they had. But it would have been nice if someone had asked. I stopped going out with the guys a long time ago and they stopped asking.

So I go home, to the sad, dark house in Northwood, where the woman who inspired "Betty" in my columns, the Lucille Ball to my Ricky Ricardo, sits in a wheelchair, her body riddled with MS. She drinks all day, and who can blame her? In my columns, "Betty" goes to dances, runs around the neighborhood making good-natured mayhem, cooks and cleans. She can't really clean anymore, much less cook. I do the best I can, which isn't much. But I don't want to hire anyone because that means letting someone inside, exposing the lie of the fantasy life I've created for the paper, about the jolly house where the wife does scatterbrained things and the husband is a foil and the son and the daughter just laugh and laugh and laugh at it all.

The son lives in California. The daughter died of leukemia when she was three.

That's what I should have told Maddie Schwartz: *Everyone has secrets. I have secrets. I'll find a way to write around yours. I won't tell the world that you're separated. I don't need to know how you knew they were looking at the fish store clerk. But your source was a man, wasn't it, Maddie Schwartz? A woman like you—there's always going to be a man.*

My wife and I eat in front of the TV. My story is all over the news. She tries to rally to cheer me on, but she knows and I know how hollow my victories are. A fish store clerk, leukemia—at least, with a fish store clerk, you can imagine closing your hands around his throat, or seeing him go to the gas chamber. I'm not saying I envy the Fines. I never want to see anyone admitted to this horrible club. But they had eleven years, I had only three.

Three years. A thousand days and change.

My column's due tomorrow. I'm going to write about the time my daughter thought the devil lived in our garage. Did it happen? What does it matter? I don't have to be accurate about my own life. Who's going to complain if I get it wrong?

WHEN I WAS *eleven years old, our social studies class had to do reports on the ten largest US cities. Baltimore was number six, but the thing I noticed was the steep drop-off from five to six, Detroit, almost two million people, to Baltimore, which didn't even have a million. New York, at the top of the list, had almost eight million. Chicago, Los Angeles, Philadelphia—those were cities. Baltimore was a village. The other kids wanted Baltimore, maybe out of hometown pride, maybe out of the belief that it would be easier. I wanted nothing but New York. The teacher put me on Saint Louis's team, number ten at the time. Do I look like a Saint Louis girl? I was furious. Stupid Saint Louis, with nothing but the Mississippi River and its shoe manufacturing factories. Saint Louis was small-time and I knew I was destined for the big time.*

I mention this only to remind you, Maddie, that Baltimore is small, smaller still within its tribes. Everybody in my part of town knew about

Ferdie Platt, his eye for women, his fondness for Ballantine's. He never tried to get with me, but that's because I was already with someone, someone substantial, and Ferdie was no fool. Besides, he chose women he wouldn't have to squire, which saved him money. Ferdie Platt was tight with a dollar, as I'm sure you found out. And what kind of woman doesn't expect her man to take her places, spend on her? Women who can't go out in public, married women and white women. He really hit the Daily Double with you, Maddie Schwartz.

But Ferdie used to come by the club, my club, the Flamingo. People assumed he was on the take. He was chummy with Mr. Gordon and some other men of that ilk. I dared to ask him about it just the once, when he was drinking at the bar. Maybe I was flirting, I don't know. It would have been dangerous for us to have a thing, that's for sure. But I ended up dead, so maybe I should have gone for it, just the once.

I said, sassy as you please: "Just because you drink for free here doesn't mean you shouldn't tip."

"I tip."

"Not enough."

Look, he was a good-looking man. If I had realized I had the luxury of choosing men strictly for pleasure, I would have considered him. I bet that never occurred to you, did it, Maddie Schwartz? Choosing the men you sleep with based on your own pleasure is what makes a woman really rich.

I leaned on the bar, which lifted my breasts, already on display in the skimpy costume even I had to wear. He barely gave me a glance.

"I'll try to do better by you. Didn't realize my weekly stop-by was creating a grievance."

"Why do you come by here? It's not on your beat."

"Why do you think, Miss Sherwood?"

I said, bold as brass, because being bold was something that had always worked for me: "Because you're on the take."

It was funny how he handled that. He didn't get mad. He didn't jump to deny it. He just patted his pockets thoughtfully and said: "I think if I were on the take, I would tip much better."

"That's not a no," I pointed out.

"He didn't say yes, he didn't say no." He sang the words, but I wasn't sure if it was a real song or one he was making up on the spot.

"Is that a real song? It sounds like a real song. Even in your off-key voice." His voice was fine, actually, but he didn't need to hear that from me.

"Ah, young people today," he said.

"You've got five years on me at the most."

"I've also got every album Ella Fitzgerald ever recorded. 'She Didn't Say Yes.' The Jerome Kern Song Book. Released in 1963. I have a nice stereo." He paused and I held my breath. He was going to ask me over, which was crazy, dangerous. But brave. I had to admire it. By then, the men in the Flamingo left me alone. Mr. Gordon saw to that. A man crazy enough to risk such a thing—maybe he had feelings for me after all.

He said: "You can probably get a copy at Korvette's, or Harmony Hut. I'd lend you mine, but I don't like to lend my records. I'm too punctilious about their care."

There he went again, with the big words. I was pretty sure it meant being on time, but I wasn't going to ask and let him show me up.

"That's okay," I said. "I don't like that old-people music. I like the Supremes."

"Of course you do," he said.

He left me a five-dollar bill that night. I never saw him again. But that's because I died two weeks later. If I'd wanted Ferdie Platt, I'd have had him. Just so you know, Maddie Schwartz. I could have had him.

April 1966

SPRING FELT TENTATIVE that year, unsure of its welcome. But even on the coolest days, Maddie took to her fire escape to smoke. She had quit two years ago, very easily, when the surgeon general's report came out, and she had never been a true fiend. Smoking was an ancillary activity for her, something to do with a cup of coffee, or when waiting for Milton in a public place and feeling self-conscious.

Yet recently she had found herself yearning for cigarettes. They soothed her nerves, allowed her to think. Freedom was dizzying, paralyzing. People used the phrase "like a kid in a candy store" to denote crazed pleasure-seeking, but Maddie's hunch was that most children, after an initial dive into whatever sweet they liked best, wouldn't know what to do next. Should they focus on quantity or quality? Eat now or commit themselves to gathering as much as possible for later? There was a newish game show, *Supermarket Sweep,* in which women answered questions about how much things cost, earning their husbands time to "shop," the point being to grab the priciest things. Even if she were still with Milton, Maddie could not imagine playing such a game, and not just because Milton would refuse to grab the lobster tails on principle. Milton didn't know what anything at the supermarket cost. For that matter, she had stopped paying attention to prices years ago. Maddie was proud that she had reached a station in life—"a station in life," the phrase suddenly seemed new to her—where she didn't have to cut coupons or shop specials. Such thrift had been essential in the early years of their marriage. But it was more fun to have money than not.

She studied the ads under "Help Wanted, Female." Nurses, cashiers, waitresses, secretaries, office girls. Nothing seemed suitable. But wait—there was one job, a clerical one, at the *Star*. Would that nice Bob Bauer help her? She had helped him, hadn't she? He had written a big front-page story about the man who killed Tessie Fine. In the end, the whole thing had seemed strangely anticlimactic, so cut-and-dried. A little girl walks into a store and stamps her feet, and a man simply "snaps." Ferdie had told Maddie that the detectives didn't believe the man, that one doesn't snap, hit someone on the side of the head, then have the presence of mind to drag the victim to the basement to finish the job by breaking her neck. They believed the man had—what was the word Ferdie used? "Proclivities."

Maddie smiled at the memory. Ferdie liked big words, although he didn't always use them precisely. But in this case, he was close enough, although it sounded too genteel for such an awful thing. The police didn't think Stephen Corwin had killed before, but they suspected he had touched other children. He had probably been luckier with his previous victims, working in what was, after all, a very tempting place for a child, and doing things that the children didn't register as too odd. Guiding a small hand into his trousers, asking for no more than a touch or two. Tessie Fine, self-possessed and confident, probably fought back when he tried something with her. But, so far, they hadn't been able to find any other child who had visited the pet shop basement and the evidence they had wasn't going to allow them to pursue the death penalty.

"It's not like you can go on TV and say, 'Hey, mamas of Northwest Baltimore, do you think this pervert touched your kid?' We've got women working the schools, making inquiries, talking to ER nurses. But if he was just a toucher—or smart enough to make sure they touched him, without him so much as undoing a hair bow—we're not going to find anything."

Maddie had noted the *we're*. Ferdie yearned to be a homicide detective. He had charmed a few detectives, treating them as gods on an unreachable Olympus, and they confided in him.

She and Ferdie had been smoking in bed when Ferdie shared that particular confidence about Tessie Fine. Maybe it was Ferdie who had brought cigarettes back into her life, come to think of it. Married to Milton, Maddie had long been past the stage of wanting to talk and gossip when sex was over. But with Ferdie, a smoke break was a way to keep him there a little longer. She didn't want him to stay all night. (Good thing, because he never did.) But she always wanted him to stay a little longer than he was inclined to. So she asked him questions, teased out more answers about his work. In this way, she had learned a little about his boyhood. *Youngest of seven children, played baseball at Poly.* But he quickly shut down almost every other line of personal inquiry.

He wanted to be a cipher, Maddie realized. He was going to disappear from her life as suddenly and immediately as he had appeared in it. Sometimes, it seemed to her as if they were like one of those math problems from Seth's homework: *A westbound train leaves Baltimore at 6 P.M., traveling 100 mph, while an eastbound train departs Chicago at 8 P.M. Chicago time, traveling 120 mph. If there are 720 miles between those two cities, when will they pass each other?*

What happens if those trains park on a siding for a while? Who will notice, who will know? Will the trains be different when their journeys resume?

Ferdie wanted to move up. He wanted to be a detective, and not in narcotics, as an undercover. The department, segregated for so long, was rumored to be on the verge of changing. There would be opportunities soon.

"You're good," she had said. "I'm sure you'll make it."

He'd laughed. "It's not just about being good. They're going to be plugging people in, try to improve the numbers fast. Being good won't be enough. I have to be lucky."

So Ferdie was barreling into Baltimore's Penn Station at the fastest speed possible, whatever that was. Whereas Maddie was moseying along, unsure of where she wanted to go. Right now, she couldn't even decide if she wanted to buy some fabric for summer dresses, these gorgeous Marimekko prints she had seen at a boutique. Very cutting-edge for Baltimore, although Jackie Kennedy had been photographed wearing the label's clothes years ago, early in her husband's presidency. But the new patterns were bolder, bigger. Maddie had been studying them wistfully at a place called the Store Ltd., at Cross Keys, the new gated community on the North Side, sort of a village within Baltimore. Maddie liked Cross Keys. Maybe she would live there when she and Milton finally settled everything.

The fabric wasn't the only thing to covet at the Store Ltd. The owner made amazing jewelry. So simple—deft curves of silver, striking shapes, gems used sparingly, if at all. And yet so expensive. This was the future, sleek and streamlined. Looking at that jewelry, Maddie wanted to cut her hair as short as possible, but Ferdie would have objected. Ah well, there would be time enough to cut her hair. And he couldn't object to her getting her ears pierced, could he?

Sitting on her fire escape, she fingered her lobes, stretched thin from years of heavy clip-ons, some probably valuable. She had left most of her jewelry at the house, in what she believed was a show of good faith. But perhaps that had misled Milton and Seth, perhaps they were angry at her because they believed she would quickly tire of this odd experiment and return to them. She had never meant to leave Seth, of course. She had thought he would want to join this new life, too. Given her experience trying to sell her engagement ring, she wouldn't bother to see what she could get for those old things. But she wanted to get her ears pierced. She pulled out the yellow pages and found a jeweler up in Pikesville that would do it for the price of the fourteen-karat earrings she would have to wear until her ears healed.

She went straight from Pikesville to the Store, to stare lovingly at the Betty Cooke creations she could not afford. The saleslady, recognizing her from the previous visit, brought out new bolts of Marimekko.

"I shouldn't, I really shouldn't," Maddie said. There was a blue floral with black tones, perfect for her coloring. And spring was coming. She took six yards, then found a pattern for a simple halter dress, so simple she probably could have run it up herself if she had a machine. But that, too, was back at Milton's. She hated to ask him for it. She didn't want anything from him, except money.

She bought an apple at the little grocery across from the Store, walked the curving pathways of Cross Keys, studied the apartments and town houses. Eventually, she found herself near the tennis barn. What would have happened if Milton hadn't taken up tennis, brought Wally Weiss to their home? Maddie probably would not have moved out, not when she did. And if she hadn't moved out, she wouldn't have been harangued by her mother that day and she wouldn't have found the body of Tessie Fine. She knew it was a logical fallacy to think that meant Tessie never would have been found, but she would not have been found *that* day, the search had not yet gone that far afield. Maddie had done something important; Maddie was important. Even if no one knew it.

And having been important, even if no one knew it, created a taste. She wanted to matter. She wanted the world to be different because she had been born. Being Seth's mother wasn't enough. Even if he went on to be the first Jewish president of the United States or a doctor who cured cancer, his accomplishments wouldn't address this terrible yearning. She needed something for herself, beyond Ferdie and her bedroom overlooking the cathedral.

She wished she could talk to the man who had done it. She would have liked to understand him in a way that she didn't think was important to the police. They didn't care *why* he had killed, only that he would be behind bars, incapable of hurting other children. But if Maddie were Tessie Fine's mother, she would want to know more. It all felt so unfinished.

Maybe she could talk to the man who had done it. Not talk—correspond. Write him a letter, encourage him to confide, reveal to him the bond they shared, the body of Tessie Fine.

On her way back to her apartment, she got off the bus two stops early and visited a stationer's on Charles Street.

She took the box of stationery to the fire escape, despite the anemic light and cool breeze. Simple cream vellum, no time for monograms. Besides, what initials would she use? She went through several drafts in a notebook, then committed to the page in front of her, covering it with her fine, bold handwriting.

> *Dear Mr. Corwin,*
> *I am Madeline Schwartz, the woman who found the body of Tessie Fine. As a result, I feel connected to you, for better or worse. You were the last person to see her alive, I was the first person to see her dead . . .*

She walked to the main post office to make sure it would be delivered as soon as possible.

It never occurred to her that he might not write her back because men almost always did what Maddie wanted them to do. Almost.

The Suspect

THE FIRST LETTER comes with a photograph of her. She looks
like a nice lady. She wants to know my side of the story. She's interested in me. *In me.*

I didn't really confess, you know. I just stopped talking after
they arrested me. What was I going to say? The aquarium sand,
the fact that people knew she had gone into the store—what could
I say? I said I was done, refused to talk anymore, and when they
finally let me make a phone call, I didn't waste it on a lawyer. I
called my ma, knowing she would make the arrangements, that
she would want to take care of everything. She told me I was stupid, but I'm used to that. The morning of that day that everything
happened, she had told me I was stupid. She told me I was stupid
almost every day.

But she doesn't mean it. She just gets easily frustrated, my ma. She's high-strung. She has to take pills. It was a hard life, my father being gone and her having to raise a kid like me. I wasn't good at much. I wish I could tell you that I loved my job at the store, that I was one of those people who liked fish and snakes, because that seems like something a smart guy would say. I was a guy who needed a job. The man who owned the store needed someone who could work Saturdays because they did good business on Saturdays. Jews aren't the only people who buy fish and snakes, he said. I can't keep my doors open if I don't open Saturdays. And everyone will know *you're* not a Jew.

I don't know what it means not to look like a Jew. I have red hair and blue eyes and very pale skin, although no freckles. If you had to guess, you'd probably say I'm Irish, but our name is actually from Spanish, although we're not Spaniards, obviously. My ma says that there really aren't that many red-haired Irish people, that it's just that Irish people tend to be redheaded more than other people. My ma is smart. That's why she gets frustrated with me. I can't blame her.

I'm not slow, though, or retarded. I'm just not as smart as my ma, but she's *very* smart. She could have been anything she wanted to be, if she had been a man. Instead, she married a man who wasn't really good enough, a bum who ran out when I was little. Anyway, that's another reason I think I wrote to the lady who wrote me. I wanted to show that I wasn't a retard. And it was just a lady, writing me. I didn't know she would show my letter to anybody.

Plus, I didn't really tell her *anything*. In fact, I told her that I couldn't talk to her or anybody, that my lawyer was very firm on that. Yes, it looked bad that the girl had been in the shop, but that didn't prove I did it. I locked up at five. Anything could have happened after I left. The back door had been jimmied.

All I tell her is that I met the girl and she was rude to me. I was having a bad day. My ma and I had a fight that morning. It was so stupid. Our fights are always stupid. That day, I think she was mad at me for leaving only two eggs. She said you couldn't really get a good scramble from two eggs and I said, I'll make you two fried, and she said she didn't want fried or poached, she wanted scrambled and two didn't fluff up enough. Next thing you know, we were screaming our heads off at each other. That's how we fought. Like cats and dogs, like Andy Capp and Flo, we screamed at each other and she said I couldn't have the car to get to work that day, I'd have to walk in the rain.

Trudging to work, I knew she would feel bad when I got home. She would apologize, bring me a towel for my hair, dry my shoes so they wouldn't end up stiff and out of shape from the long walk. She would make me tea and we would eat our dinner on trays together. We fought a lot, but we always made up. But until we make up, I always feel out of sorts, as if the world isn't quite right. That's why I yelled at the girl, told her to get out of the store. She must have come back, later. Maybe she broke in, up to some mischief, and someone followed her. That's what I think happened, and that's all I told the lady who wrote me. Okay, I told her about the army, too, the things they did to me there.

Like I said, I'm not as smart as my ma. That lady used me. A pretty lady put her picture inside a letter, said we had something in common, that I was the last person to see Tessie Fine alive and she was the first person to see her dead, and that bonded us. I wasn't so dumb that I fell for that. I wrote, *No, the last person to see Tessie*

Fine alive was the person who killed her and that wasn't me. But I still said too much, and none of it privileged, as my lawyer and Ma kept yelling at me when it came out.

But then the lawyer calmed down and said, *Maybe it's a gift, after all. Maybe I can use this.* Ma was mad at first. She said, "No one's going to say my Stephen is crazy." But the lawyer changed Ma's mind pretty fast.

May 1966

MADDIE DRESSED CAREFULLY for her visit to the *Star*. Her instincts told her that this was an occasion to present as her old self. Gloves and a hat, even though the weather was finally warm. How odd she looked this way, how unlike the person she knew she was now. But her shorter skirts and dresses, the bright colors she had taken to wearing—these would not make her look serious. She had to convey seriousness, a sense of purpose.

It was an easy thing to walk down the hill to the newspaper building, not even a mile from where she lived. How simple it would be, if she got a job, to make that walk Monday through Friday, how satisfying to return home, up the hill, tired after a long day. She wondered if people at the newspaper socialized, if she would be invited out.

She also wondered how Ferdie would feel if she were no longer at his beck and call. Would he care? Or would he be relieved? It could create the pretext for a graceful ending, assuming that was what he wanted.

But just crossing the threshold into the building undermined her confidence. She had to approach a huge desk, where a woman sat at a phone bank, elevated, like a judge.

"Who are you here to see?" she demanded.

"Mr. Bauer?" Maddie said, hating the way her voice scaled up, as if she had no right to be in this holy place, asking for the well-known man who had sat in her apartment and pleaded to tell her story.

"Is he expecting you?"

"No."

"What's your name?"

She provided it in a whisper, almost as if she were afraid to be overheard, then waited, at the switchboard operator's instruction, on a wooden bench. After much muttering and sighing, the woman said: "Fifth floor."

"What?"

"Fifth floor, fifth floor. He's in the Sunday office on the fifth floor."

Maddie's first impression of the newsroom was that it was, well, filthy. Filthy and loud. So many newspapers, piled everywhere. People shouting, typewriters clacking, a bell ringing somewhere. And so many men. But there were women working here, she reminded herself. She had read their bylines, seen their stories. Women could be reporters, too.

Mr. Bauer had a desk in the corner of the room where the Sunday staff worked. Its windows faced south, toward the water, and the view would have been bright and expansive if the windows had not been caked with dust and dirt. Someone had written in the grime:

The Star, One of the World's Newspapers. It took Maddie a moment to get the joke. The *Beacon,* the more sober morning newspaper, with foreign bureaus and a large staff in Washington, called itself "One of the World's Best Newspapers."

"I'm surprised to see you here," he said, leaning back in his chair. He seemed different at first and Maddie realized the man she had met had been playing a part of sorts. Pretending interest in her, pretending empathy, pretending whatever he needed to pretend to get what he wanted. Now he didn't need anything from her—or so he thought.

"I want a job here."

He smiled. "I'm not the editor, Ms. Schwartz. I don't do the hiring. If I did, I'm not sure I'd stump for a woman with no experience."

"But you can help me."

"Maybe. Only why would I? This is a serious place, for serious people. You just don't walk in off the street and start doing it."

"I helped you get"—she debated with herself whether to use the word, whether it would make her sound ridiculous. "I helped you get a scoop."

Another smile. Yet it didn't cow her. She did not feel ridiculous. She knew what she had, in her purse.

"You deflected me. You were lucky that the deflection worked."

"I offered you something better than what you were seeking. I wouldn't call that deflection."

"And now you think you want to work at the newspaper? What could you possibly bring to this job?"

She pulled out a sheaf of papers, tied with string. "These are letters. From Stephen Corwin. I wrote him about the murder of Tessie Fine and he wrote me back. Twice."

The room did not go quiet—it was a place that was never quiet,

Maddie sensed. But something shifted. Other people were listening to them now, or trying to. Perhaps Mr. Bauer noticed as well because he said: "Take a walk with me."

She assumed he meant outside, but he took her to the corridor, then down a back staircase. "May I see them?"

"I'll show you the first one," she said.

Mr. Bauer could read very quickly. "So what?" he said. "He doesn't admit anything. He just repeats this cockamamie story that the girl came back and he was gone. No one believes it."

"I don't either," Maddie says. "But there's a detail that suggests he has an accomplice."

He raised his eyebrows. "I've heard of reading between the lines, but you've all but moved in between them and built a house. That's a lot to infer. So he made up a story about someone else doing it. How do you get accomplice from that?"

"Not from there," Maddie said. "Go back to the earlier part of the letter, about how he fought with his mother that day."

"That drivel with the eggs. Not even I could make it interesting."

"No, the part about how he walked to work."

"Right. So?"

"Tessie Fine's body was found almost two miles from the pet shop. How did it get there? Whose car did he use? I went back and read all the articles about him at the Enoch Pratt." How purposeful she had felt, going to the central branch, just steps from her front door, and requesting the long wooden rods of the daily newspapers. She had seldom used the Pratt. It felt castle-like compared to the modern blandness that was the Randallstown branch where she had checked out popular novels.

"He probably hid the body overnight, took it out the next day."

"Maybe. Or maybe he realized that he slipped, telling that part, which suggests there's an accomplice, or someone with knowledge of what he's done. That's why he wrote me the second letter, about his time at Fort Detrick."

"What about it?"

"Stephen Corwin was drafted five years ago. He claimed conscientious objector status as a Seventh-Day Adventist. He was sent to Fort Detrick and was part of an experiment known as Operation Whitecoat."

"That's ridiculous," Mr. Bauer said. "The army doesn't run tests that turn men into killers of little girls."

"It sounds ridiculous to me, too," Maddie said. "As if he's grasping at straws. But it's *interesting,* isn't it? Something that hasn't been published yet. I'd like to write the account of our correspondence."

"Won't that expose you to all the things you feared when I first visited you? Revelations about your personal life? Embarrassment to your son?"

"Not if it's under my name. If I'm the author."

He needed a few seconds to process what she was requesting. "Byline," he said. "You want a byline. You want us to hire you and then your first piece will be this page one scoop. But that's not how it works, Lois Lane. What are you going to do, insert yourself into every big murder? Dress up like a wino and go out and find the Tic-Tac-Toe Killer who's terrorizing Baltimore's drunks? Find the guy on the grassy knoll? That's not reporting. That makes you more like a stuntwoman, some second-rate Nellie Bly."

Another mask had slipped. She had offended him. And Maddie, whose instincts for what men need were unerring, knew immediately how to make it right.

"Would it be so wrong if I wrote this, with your help, and that would be my tryout? I'm happy to start at the bottom, to work my way up. I'm not asking for special treatment."

"Oh, Maddie, newspaper work coarsens women. You should see the battle-axe who covers labor."

"I'd like to think that, whatever I do, I'll always be a woman first."

"I bet you will," he said. "Look, this would be easier if I could have the letters, show them to my bosses—"

She slipped the one back into her purse. "I don't actually have the second one with me. I came here first. I came to *you* first. But there are two other newspapers in town, the *Beacon* and the *Light*. Maybe I should visit them, see what they offer."

TWO DAYS LATER—TWO days of sitting by Mr. Bauer's side, sometimes typing, sometimes talking, letting him rewrite her, but also insisting, at certain moments, on having her way with the words that were forming on the copy paper in his cantankerous typewriter—Maddie's piece appeared on the front page. A KILLER UNBURDENS HIMSELF. Mr. Bauer had the byline, but her name appeared in italicized print: *Based on a correspondence with Madeline Schwartz, part of the search party that discovered Tessie Fine's body.*

Her correspondence was woven into a larger story, augmented by Mr. Bauer's reporting. An army spokesman said staunchly that the "treatments" Stephen Corwin had been subjected to would not, could not, induce psychosis. His mother said Stephen was an unhappy person and had always been a disappointment to her, that everything he said was a lie, even the story about the eggs. He had shifty friends, men of whom she did not approve.

Finally, his attorney tried to subpoena Maddie, only to be told that her notes were protected by Maryland's shield law because she was a contractual employee at the *Star*. And if the newspaper's lawyer implied that contract predated her correspondence with Corwin, as opposed to being drawn up hastily in the wake of the request, he never said as much in so many words and the inexperienced public defender gave up that line of attack, deciding to focus on the idea that Corwin wasn't competent to stand trial.

The story was a sensation, dominating the news for several days. In part, Maddie was the story—attractive not-quite-divorcée tricks kid-killer into revealing he had an accomplice—but she never lost sight of the fact that she had *made* the story and, with Mr. Bauer's help, written the story. After all, although she had the good sense not to mention it to Mr. Bauer or anyone else at the *Star,* she had once yearned to write poetry and fiction, had worked at the high school newspaper. Which was where she had met Allan Durst, which had indirectly almost destroyed her life.

Now, perhaps, writing would indirectly help her reinvent her life.

Maddie's reward for her scoop was a job as an assistant to the man who ran the *Star*'s "Helpline" column, Don Heath, who was highly skeptical. "I've never had an assistant, why do they think I need an assistant all of a sudden," Mr. Heath fretted. "I guess you can open the mail. When you get the hang of things, I'll let you tackle some of the easier questions, the ones we don't write up for the paper."

Given the mundane inquiries that did make it into the paper, Maddie wondered just how fatuous the others could be. But it didn't matter. She had a desk. She had a job. As she sliced open the envelopes that arrived daily, a Sisyphean array of petty complaints, she imagined a future self explaining to someone young, someone worshipful, how it all began. Maybe to Seth, maybe a roomful of college girls. "They say a journey of a thousand miles begins with a single step. Well my journey of not even fifty steps, from the 'Helpline' desk to the real newsroom, began with a thousand paper cuts."

At night, Ferdie rubbed cream into her hands and worried over the damage she was doing to her lovely nails. Maddie told him, with a confidence that felt different from her old confidence: "I won't be opening the mail forever."

Mr. Helpline

I NEVER ASKED for an assistant and it scares me when they suddenly announce I need one. They put me in the "Helpline" job four years ago when I started making—let's call them mistakes. Nothing fatal or libelous. I got confused one day, said that a local banker who was getting an award had gone to Crown University in Long Island. No, I had never heard of such a place, but that's what it sounded like to me. Damn young people mutter and mumble so much these days. Okay, so it was Brown University in Rhode Island. They caught it before it went into the paper. Isn't that what the copy desk is for, to spot that kind of error? They sent me to an audiologist, but my hearing checked out fine. I told them that I had a couple of drinks at lunch that day. It's not like other reporters didn't do it. We're an evening paper. Final street deadline was two P.M. You filed, allowed the editor his tinkers, fought the good fight, then went to lunch. I like Connolly's, practically across the street. Decent fish sandwich. Came back, did the interview. It could happen to anyone. I promised I wouldn't drink anymore. I didn't tell them that I hadn't had a drink that day.

They bought it. But they eased me out of the column, gave it to that snake in the grass Bauer. Oh, such a nice man, with his nice stories about his nice family. I'd rather gouge my eyes out than write that sentimental crap. They gave me the "Helpline" column and a good editor and, from time to time, took surreptitious (or so they thought) sniffs at my breath.

If only there were something there to smell. I'd rather have gin or vodka on my lips. But I guess when the brain starts to go, it doesn't rot in a way that creates an odor.

My doctor says there's no sign of dementia. He forgets—ha, ha, the doctor I asked to diagnose my dementia, he forgets things—that I've been there, I've seen it close up. It took my mom, and don't tell me these things don't run in families. She started just the way I did. A mental slip here, a mental slip there. My doctor says forgetting things isn't the real issue. He asks me if I recognize the people in my life, if I ever forget basic words. So far, so good. But if that's the case, why did they give me an assistant? Train her, they said. She's eager. Not young, but eager. They can't fool me. She's almost forty, who starts working at a newspaper at that age? I wonder if she's a nurse, or someone hired to spy on me. It's not paranoia if they're really out to get you. The union makes it hard for them to fire me, but the union can't protect me if I make a big mistake, if I'm really sick. You can drink yourself to death in a corner of the newsroom, Ned Brown is doing it as we speak. That's okay. But if I show up here without my pants on one day, I'm out. Luckily, it's hard to make a big mistake running "Helpline." A monkey could do it. As long as he wasn't getting senile.

The assistant's first week, I can't figure out what to do with her. I'm in a corner of the office, the better to be forgotten. They manage to carve out a little spot for her, which irritates me. I am used to my privacy, to speaking on the phone without being overheard. I send her to fetch coffee, which takes up, oh, maybe ten minutes total every day. Finally, I turn the mail over to her, tell her to screen it. I say: "That will give me that much more time to work on my immortal prose." She laughs. She's the kind of woman who laughs at men's jokes even when they're not funny.

The real joke is, I have the stupidest column in the paper, but it's also the most popular. You can't believe the mail it generates, and yeah, I confess—I wasn't getting to all of it. I read until I had enough problems to fill the space. Four columns a week, I need at least twelve good questions. And they have to be consumer complaints, things I can *do* something about. I'm not Dear Abby, but you wouldn't know it by my mail.

I don't think anyone lives long enough to imagine his next decade accurately. You get to thirty and you think you know what forty will be like, but you don't, then comes fifty and boy does forty look good. I'm fifty-eight right now and I'm not going to pretend I have a clue what my seventh decade will be, other than disappointing. Because every decade so far has been less than I hoped; why should the next one be different?

I'll confess this, too: I have a system for culling my mail. Type-written over handwritten, masculine handwriting over feminine handwriting, cursive only, no jailbirds, I don't care if they have photographic evidence of the cops framing them. I'm here to fix traffic lights and find out why you can't return a pair of shearling gloves to Hutzler's if the tags are still attached. (The store agreed finally to take them back for store credit. I guess Hutzler's thought the gloves were shoplifted, and yeah, they probably were. Mr. Helpline isn't here to make moral judgments.)

So I give the eager beaver the mail. She does a good job, maybe too good. She catches on quickly, this one. She gets what makes a good question, learns to recognize the duds. She works the phones before she shows me the letters, making sure there are answers. She creates a whole new category—easy problems that don't rate a column mention but can be addressed by a quick phone call. I don't like that at first, but then I decide—why not? I still follow up, I still write the column, and it's my style that makes it popular. My style and the fact that it's one of two things in the papers that's actually trying to help people. The other is obits. You won't catch me saying this around the newsroom, but people are right that newspapers prefer bad news to good most of the time. Bad news sells papers. There is no *Happy Valley Gazette*.

Ambition comes off this one like heat. *Where did you come from? I want to ask. Didn't you have a husband, pretty as you are? Is Bob Bauer trying to get into your panties? You wouldn't be the first, the way I hear it. Mr. Family Man, Professional Nice Guy. There are no nice guys in this business, but you'll learn that soon enough.*

I make her start bringing me my lunch.

June 1966

"OKAY, SCOOP—WE'RE GOING to let you try out your training wheels."

Calvin Weeks, the assistant city editor, loomed over Maddie, an ominous piece of copy paper in his hands. Only two weeks into her job, Maddie already knew the legend of Calvin Weeks and his "black beans," which he usually shoved into reporters' mail cubbyholes at the end of his shift. He typed these missives on carbon paper, keeping the originals for himself and bestowing the smudgy duplicates on the reporters. Perhaps those smudges were why they were called black beans, but no one really knew. Calvin Weeks had been an assistant city editor for almost twenty years and he had been dispensing black beans for nineteen of them.

"There's a reason he's been in that job for so long," Bob Bauer had told Maddie. "You've heard of the Peter Principle. This is the Cal

Corollary, the newspaper's version of the Hippocratic Oath. First, do the least harm. That's why he's on the three-to-eleven shift. If a big story happens late, the overnight editor takes over. If news breaks during the day, the big bosses are here. Weeks is a traffic cop at best, directing the flow of copy."

It was three thirty P.M. Maddie's workday ended in ninety minutes. That should have been all the excuse she needed not to slip her neck into the noose that Cal was holding. "I'm off at five."

"I'm sure Don won't mind if I borrow you."

Mr. Heath nodded, a master surrendering his servant. Did he have the power to do that? Who was her true boss? Maddie should probably figure that out.

"There's a little party this afternoon," Cal continued. "Normally, we'd just send a photog. But with all the Negroes being so upset these days, the big boss thought it was a good opportunity to generate a little goodwill, show that we don't only write about the riots and muggings."

He handed her the piece of paper, the black bean, reciting its contents as she scanned it: "Violet Wilson Whyte is celebrating her twenty-ninth year on the police force today. Isn't that something? The first Negro cop was a woman. So there's a little party for her, at headquarters. You go by, get a few quotes—how she got started, how honored she is, rutabaga, rutabaga—and file six inches. We'll use it inside tomorrow."

Rutabaga, rutabaga was another Cal tic, his version of *et cetera, et cetera, et cetera.* Again, no one had a clue how this had come to be. He reminded Maddie of an actor she had seen in *The King and I* at Painters Mill, a mediocre one who was nevertheless extraordinarily pleased with himself as he strutted the stage in that dusty tent theater. He had entered for one scene by marching up the aisle alongside Maddie's seat, his cape flying behind him, although Maddie did not believe capes were worn by Siamese royalty. The cape's hem, flowing behind him on eddies of summer heat, had whipped the corner of her eye. It hadn't hurt, but the unexpected contact was startling and Maddie gave a little yelp. The actor had looked back, smiling as if he had bestowed a gift, then continued steaming toward the stage, where he proceeded to destroy Oscar Hammerstein's lyrics with a performance that appeared to be modeled on Marlon Brando in *A Streetcar Named Desire*.

She tried again. "I'm off at five."

"Then you better get going."

She understood, or was pretty sure that she did. The press release had come in late, but some higher-up was demanding it be done and Cal was carrying the bigger boss's water. The year was shaping up to be one of unrest throughout the United States, riots breaking out in various cities. Baltimore had been spared so far. Maddie was being given this "big chance" because Cal assumed she was too timid to file for overtime, or she was hungry enough for a byline to forgo her right to extra pay.

He was right on both counts.

She walked up to police HQ, showed her *Star* ID. "That's not a press pass," she was told.

"I know," she said. She didn't. "But I work there. They sent me here because Mr. Diller is busy."

Yet Diller, the police reporter, was in the room. Why couldn't he write the story? But Maddie, again courtesy of Bob Bauer, knew why. Diller couldn't write *anything*. He called in his facts, then the rewrite man shaped them into a publishable article. It was a beginner's job and most men angled to leave the police beat as soon as possible, eager to write the words that appeared beneath their bylines. Diller had no desire to move on. Diller could dictate the facts about a Negro woman if she were dead; he could do that in his sleep. But faced with a story without a crime, he wouldn't have a clue where to begin.

Maddie took out her thrillingly fresh reporter's notebook and tried to keep up with the police commissioner's rote, banal compliments. She had never learned shorthand and she wasn't sure how one was supposed to get quotes exactly right without it, but she did the best she could on the fly, creating her own set of abbreviations. The room was crowded, but the cake, not Violet Wilson Whyte, seemed to be the star attraction. When the commissioner insisted the guest of honor say a few words, she kept her comments short and spoke softly, but with a notable confidence and authority.

"Thank you," she said. "I'm just glad to be here, twenty-nine years later. But my work is not done, not yet." She leaned hard on that last word.

"Here's to twenty-nine years more," someone shouted from the back of the room. Inane, Maddie thought. Rude, even. It sounded sarcastic, as if the man who had spoken was mocking Mrs. Whyte. She wondered if Ferdie was here. Certainly, other Negro officers should have been called downtown for this particular celebration. But the crowd was very sparse, and very white.

She asked Diller as much. Not about Ferdie, but the lack of Negroes in general.

"It's a dog-and-pony show for the press," he said. "Who gets a party for her twenty-ninth year? They threw it together at the last minute. Straight-up public relations ploy to remind everyone that they do more with Negroes than bust their heads open."

"Then why are we covering it?"

He gave her an odd look: "Wait, are you with the *Star*?"

"I am, I'm Maddie—"

But he had already moved away, having secured his slice of cake, a brick of a corner piece. He was with a group of men. Reporters like him, probably. What did one call a group of reporters? A gaggle would be good, Maddie thought. A murder of crows, a gaggle of reporters.

She approached the guest of honor, notebook out, and introduced herself as a reporter. She was doing a reporter's job, was she not?

Mrs. Whyte demurred. "I've had many opportunities to talk about myself. If you checked the files before you came here—and, of course, I'm sure you did—you must know everything about me."

A veiled rebuke and a fair one. Maddie should have pulled the clips from the library. Her face flamed, but she was not going to go back to the newsroom without a story. She was being tested, and Maddie had always aced her tests.

"What's it like, being a first?"

"Not that different from being the second or the third or the thousandth."

"But the department still doesn't have that many Negroes. And they're not allowed to do as much as their white counterparts." Ferdie had told her that, of course. Negroes could be patrols or vice cops and that was pretty much it. No cars, no radios. Maddie had chosen not to ask Ferdie how he wrangled a patrol car for his late-night visits to her.

Mrs. Whyte, clearly surprised by Maddie's knowledge, softened a little. "Well, I'm an old hand at making more out of less. I walked a beat on Pennsylvania Avenue when I was younger. I felt like I did more for the children of that neighborhood in that job than I did as a teacher. I'm not criticizing teachers. I was one and my husband has spent his entire career in the school system. But there were plenty of women teaching. The children saw them every day. When I walked down the street, in my uniform, I showed them that there were other things to be. We cannot imagine what we cannot see."

Maddie scribbled furiously. She was so taken by Mrs. Whyte's fierce pride in her job that she almost forgot the basic questions—her age, her husband's name. She then asked a little about where she had grown up, how her parents had felt about their daughter's vocation, what she did to relax at day's end.

The last question amused Mrs. Whyte. "Watch a little television," she said. "Read the newspaper. I tried knitting, but all I could make were scarves and even then, the shapes were all over the place. My sister said I was loose with my needles."

Maddie was back at the paper by four thirty. She was a fast typist, but not a fast writer, and she labored over her copy. But she was enjoying herself; it was like working on her column back in high school, coming up with witticisms, bestowing nicknames on the other popular kids. It was almost eight by the time she turned in the requested four hundred words. She was too shy to call out "copy" as the other reporters did, so she walked the pages to Cal herself.

"Too long," he said, without even reading the copy, and promptly crossed out the final paragraph with a red X.

"But that's the best part," Maddie said. "That was her quote about how she hoped she inspired the children she saw every day." *We cannot imagine what we cannot see.*

"You're not supposed to put the best stuff at the end."

Since starting at the *Star*, Maddie had been reading the newspaper with an attention and focus that her previous self had never mustered. She had noticed what made some stories sing, while others were Dragnet-style: all we want are the facts, ma'am.

"It's a feature, right? Features can have . . ." She paused, unsure of the word and her right to use it. "Features can have kickers. Can't they?"

"It's supposed to be six inches about a Negro who's not rioting or stealing."

"But she's interesting," Maddie said. "I think there's more there."

"We've written about her plenty. Be glad that there's even a story— we could have done this with a photo and a cutline. But if you're good, maybe I'll throw some more stories your way."

If you're good. Maddie was not fooled. Cal was going to try to use her for future late-afternoon assignments, counting on her ambition and decorum to accept them. Counting on her to be too meek to push for what she was owed.

"It's past eight," she said. "I've worked three hours overtime. How do I enter that on my pay card at week's end?"

"Take comp time," he said airily. "I'll tell Don. You can take an hour a day over three days."

"Comp time?"

"Compensatory time. It's okay as long as everyone agrees to it. Oh, strictly, it has to be taken that week, to keep you below forty hours, but nobody worries about those technicalities."

Maddie was pretty sure that it was management that didn't worry about such technicalities.

"Overtime is paid at one point five. So shouldn't I get four point five hours? Otherwise, comp time sounds like a bad deal to me."

His eyes went cold and what little friendliness he had been able to fake vanished from his face. With his overly sharp incisors, too-white skin, and too-red eyes, Cal looked like a vampire or an albino cat. He was a man of no true authority, Maddie saw. How it must have grated on him.

"Very well, then," he said. "You've earned four point five hours.

To be taken by mutual consent. What are you going to do? Enjoy a longer lunch hour? Go shopping?"

"I'll bank the time for now. One never knows when one might need time. Will you explain the situation to Don? That you asked me to do this for you and I earned comp time?"

"To be taken by mutual consent," Cal said. "You can't just announce that you're leaving early. You'll have to clear it with Don."

"Of course."

She walked away, well aware that she had not answered his intrusive questions about what she intended to do with her time. She had no intention of telling him that she planned to find another way to get into the paper. A real story.

When the *Star* was published the next day, her piece had been cut to five paragraphs. There was no trace of Maddie's name and everything she had thought lively or good about the writing, the quotes, had been excised. She didn't care. She cut it out and put it in a manila folder in her desk, which she titled, after some thought, "Morgenstern, Madeline." When she did get a byline, maybe that should be the name she used.

She opened the letters she had left when Cal had sent her to the police station. Two of them had potential and she put them to the side to give to Mr. Heath. One was something she could handle. A passerby had noticed that the lights were no longer working at the fountain in Druid Hill Park. She would call the Department of Public Works tomorrow and report the outage. It wasn't worth space in the column. She had learned to make such distinctions by now and was proud of the initiative she showed. Bob Bauer had warned her that Heath was worried that Maddie was gunning for his job.

Maddie had her sights set much higher, so high that she could not yet see exactly what she wanted. She cosseted and spoiled

Mr. Heath, bringing him Entenmann's cookies or a slice of Sara Lee swirl cake with his afternoon cup of coffee. Soon enough, she was back in his good graces. Four point five hours, hers to use as she wished. But how did she wish to use them? What could one do with four point five hours?

An electrician in a rowboat was about to provide the answer.

Lady Law

I DID NOT want the party. Who has a party in one's twenty-ninth
year of employment? I'm not leaving until I make captain, as I have
told my superiors numerous times. *Numerous* times.

But I understood what was going on, why the department wanted
to celebrate me, why there were photographers, even a reporter, although she seemed very green to me, despite her age. I thought,
She's going to need more confidence to do that job, that's for sure. I
have been interviewed quite a bit, for much more in-depth pieces. I
did not need to be photographed holding a cake knife.

Confidence is something I have never lacked. My father taught
me not to fear death and that is why I have been able to do the
work that I do. Not fearing death is not the same as being fearless.
It means that I am not worried about where I'm headed, the conse-
quences of death. I have not led a blameless life. But I am a Christian

woman who prays to my Lord to lead me through my hard times, to forgive me when I slip from the path, to extend a hand and help me back onto the straight and narrow.

I often don't like things people think I should like. I don't like parties. I don't like being photographed. I don't like attention. I didn't really like being on that television show, *To Tell the Truth*, but at least I was the one telling the truth. Still, there was something undignified about it. The whole point of the show is that one is somehow odd, maybe even freakish. I am not freakish. I am a college-educated woman who cared about children, my own—I have four, two that I birthed and two that I adopted—and all the children of the neighborhoods I patrolled. I was, in some ways, more social worker than police officer. I think, though, I have made more of a difference than social workers. When a social worker comes to a house, she's the enemy, a meddler. When I visited—usually because of reports of drunken or loutish behavior—the mothers welcomed me, secretly. They knew I understood, that I cared. But I had to put their children first, always.

They called me "Lady Law." I did like that, especially the first part. I pride myself on my manners, my gentility. In the 1950s, when I supervised several younger women, I stressed the importance of good manners, a civilized appearance. There was no reason that our work had to make us masculine or rough. Sometimes, I had to be the strict schoolmarm, if you will. I would catch the young boys sneaking into the movies, cutting school. I'd tell them that I could take them home or to Cheltenham, it was their choice. They always chose home.

I suppose they think that I should be considering retirement. I will be sixty-nine this fall. Perhaps this party was a hint. But I don't take hints, don't worry about odd looks, muttered criticisms that

I may or may not be meant to hear. If someone has something to say to me, he can say it to my face. I am not ready to go. I have not planned my funeral. Not even staring into the barrel of a gun, as I did with that man who pretended to be a messenger of God but was just a procurer of young women—not even that moment prompted me to plan for my funeral. Why would I do it now? I intend to live a good long while. My legacy will be much more than simply being first.

That's what I was trying to explain to that reporter, so very tentative for someone well into her thirties. (One thing about white people, it's very easy to fix their ages. Their skin tells their age as surely as a tree's rings reveal its age.) Ah, well, I was new on this job when I was forty. I suppose it's never too late to start a career. Maybe I'll start a third one when I leave here. I would be a good preacher, I think. But I prefer *doing,* as opposed to exhorting others to do. Maybe there's a business or a charity I can start, based on my annual practice of assembling holiday baskets. But I won't use the Lady Law name. That would be undignified. The name will retire with me.

The next day, when the afternoon paper comes out, my photo is inside, only a few paragraphs attached, and the girl has misquoted me in spots. But one of the Northwest patrol officers, Ferdinand Platt, stops me in the hall, asks me questions, rather frivolous ones to my mind. *What did I think of the article? Was I pleased with it?* I told him the truth, that I was not much interested in articles about myself, that there had been many over the years. Why, my name was appearing in print long before I was a police officer, for my work with Woman's Christian Temperance Union chapters nationwide. In my opinion, alcohol is one of the great evils of our age. Drugs, too, of course, but alcohol is legal. When I drive past the Carling plant on the Beltway, I smell more than scorched hops. That is the

odor of destroyed, broken families. I have testified before the Ke-
fauver Committee about the danger of narcotics, but alcohol is even
worse, in terms of the costs it exacts. Yes, I understand the paradox
of prohibition. I was an adult woman then. I saw what happened.
But I'm not sure making it legal was the solution.

That young Ferdinand probably thinks it a grand thing to be in
a newspaper. He is a handsome man, a little too handsome for his
own good. According to talk, he also is too cozy with certain men
in our community, a particular bad man who tries to hide behind
good men. Shell Gordon is a disgrace. He owns the place on Pennsylvania Avenue, the second-rate establishment where the girls are
forced to wear those terrible outfits. Ferdie Platt goes there, according to the talk I hear, knows the people who frequent it. A small
vice, relative to the other sins of this department.

Besides, it might even be the mark of a good policeman. The
Shell Gordons of the world, criminals though they may be, have a
rooting interest in maintaining order. Mayhem and criminality are
their purview, theirs to pursue and organize, and they will not tolerate freelancers. I know the people at the club tried, in the early days
of the investigation, to help police figure out what happened to Cleo
Sherwood. Her parents are good people. I don't know how the girl
turned out the way she did. It's my understanding that she began
running wild when she was a teenager. Some girls are simply too
pretty for their own good and they don't know what to do with it. I
was never a pretty woman, but I do not think it is vanity to say that
I am attractive enough. Well turned out, with a good complexion.
Mr. Whyte has never complained.

It's a shame I never met young Cleo. I'm sure I could have helped
her find the right path.

SO YOU MET *Lady Law, Maddie Schwartz. I knew her, when I was a child. Everyone in that neighborhood knew her. She was the one who comforted me when your future husband made me cry. Milton made lots of children cry. Did you know that? He was a miserable fat boy, sitting in his family's corner grocery, studying his books. I was only six years old, a first grader, and this college boy decided to taunt me because he heard another child use my nickname, Cleo. My real name is Eunetta. Can you blame me for preferring Cleo?*

The nickname had been bestowed by other children, as nicknames usually are. I suppose some people anoint themselves, but that's a little sad, isn't it? We were studying the ancient Egyptians and there was a drawing of Cleopatra, in profile. A boy, thinking he was mocking me, said, "Miz Henderson, this looks like Cleo, her with her nose always up in the air." My nose is—was—beautiful. Straight, delicate, perfectly formed. It was like walking around with a ten-carat diamond, only no one could take it from me. So people tried to make me feel bad about it, tried to pretend that my beauty was ugliness, that up was down, black was white. But their teasing couldn't get to me because they couldn't mask their envy. I had light eyes and a pretty mouth and slanting cheekbones. But, really, it was my nose that organized everything, made me beautiful. I never had an awkward phase, conceited as that might sound. Maybe I should have. Men started coming around way too early, when I was fourteen, fifteen, and by the time I was twenty-one, I was tired of fighting them off. That's how I ended up with two babies and no husbands.

Soon I simply was Cleo; no one remembered "Eunetta," and no one realized they had saved me from the one ugly thing about me. I didn't think about it twice until the day that Milton heard my cousin use my name in his parents' store: "Whatcha gonna get with your pennies, Cleo?" Uncle Box had been to visit. He wasn't our uncle and I don't know why he was called Box and I don't know what ever happened to him. All we knew at the time was that he came and he went, and when he came, it was like a party, a party for no reason, the best kind of party. The children got money while my father glowered in the corner. My father hated parties, fun, anything that suggested that we might enjoy our time on this earth.

"Probably some Now and Laters," I said to Cousin Walker.

"Cleo?" Milton asked as I pushed my money toward him. "What kind of name is that?"

"It's short for Cleopatra," I said. "People say I look like her."

He laughed. "Like some dumb colored kid could ever look like Cleopatra. That's the stupidest thing I've ever heard. She was royalty. You're just a poor jig."

"Jig." That was most definitely the word he used. "Jig," short for "jigaboo." The other children laughed at me, as if they were somehow not implicated by Milton's disdain. I was alone, mocked. I burst into tears and ran from the store, forgetting my candy and my money.

"Why are you crying, little girl? Are you lost? Is there trouble at home?"

I raised my face, holding my arm across the bridge of my nose, my beautiful straight nose, ashamed of my tears. I would pay for those tears with my schoolmates. They would want to see them again. They would try to see if they could break me as that horrible fat Milton Schwartz had. I looked up, up, up, into the face of Lady Law. Everyone knew Miz Whyte. She was police, but she was okay. She didn't want to lock people up if she didn't have to, but lord help you if you tried to walk down the street with a bottle in a brown bag when Miz Whyte was out and about.

I stammered out my story in a jumble of hot, humiliated words, but somehow she followed every detail.

"There are people, scholars, who believe that Cleopatra was Nubian," she told me. "Now, let's go back to that store and get your money back."

She escorted me into the grocery. I got my candy and my money, which astonished me. Was that justice, was that the law? Did Milton owe me candy for free because he had tried to take something from me? When someone tried to hurt you, did they owe you more than you deserved? Who owes you, Maddie Schwartz, and who do you owe?

At any rate, I promised myself at age six that the one thing that nobody would take from me again was my dignity. But the promises we make to our young selves are hard to keep, as you have learned, Maddie Schwartz. For twenty years, however, I did keep my dignity. I cried over no man, not even the two who left me with two little boys and no wedding rings. I held my head high even when I had to wear clothes from the church box. I was Cleopatra, a Nubian queen in hiding.

And then I met a man, the king I always wanted, and that was the end of me.

Now it was five, almost six months later. The water in the lake was warming, shifting. Tiny creatures nibbled at what was left of my clothes. Rays of light pierced the murk at midday, but it couldn't reach me. Somehow that thing that had become me, that inconsiderate, restless rag of a body that had replaced my beautiful one—it moved, blocking or disconnecting a wire. A man heading to a rendezvous at the reptile house one night noticed the lights at the fountain had gone out. At least, I've decided that's who it must have been, what he was up to. Someone with a secret life, his heart racing, his senses at full alert. Everybody in the neighborhood knew what kind of men hung around the reptile house at night. Like calls to like. A man with a hidden life could feel a secret at the heart of something ordinary, sense that the dead lights were part of something larger. Something deader. He wrote a letter to Mr. Helpline, wondering why this bit of civic beauty had been allowed to go dark. He sent me to you; you sent a man to the fountain, rowing across the lake that was like the river outside of hell in the myths they taught us in school.

May you all rot in hell.

What was the verse they taught us in school? "For want of a nail . . ." Well, for want of a lightbulb, I was about to be found, and yes, a kingdom of sorts would be lost. Lives would be ruined, a king would be toppled, hearts would be broken.

And all that's on you, Maddie Schwartz. I had the good sense, the dignity, to stay silent.

PART II

June 1966

WHEN MADDIE STEPPED off the elevator, cardboard box from the luncheonette in hand, she immediately registered what she could only describe as an absence in the newsroom, a place already familiar and dear to her. A layer of sound had been stripped away. The wire machines still clacked and caroled and the phones rang, but the conversations were muted. No shouts, no laughter. Only essential murmurs, the bare minimum of words required as the newspaper steamrolled toward its final edition, the 8-star.

The features editor, a deep-bosomed, red-faced woman named Honor Livingston, was waiting in the "Helpline" cubbyhole with the paper's top editor, Mr. Marshall. It was like finding God loitering by your mailbox. Maddie put down the cardboard box of sandwich and coffee with trembling hands. Something terrible had happened, that was the only explanation. Seth? Milton?

"Madeline Schwartz," Mr. Marshall began.

"Yes," she said, although he had not been asking a question. It was disturbing that he knew her name. Was she in trouble? What could she have done? Had there been a mistake in her story about Mrs. Whyte? How bad could it be? She was still on probation, she could be let go without cause. Maybe Cal had accused her of something awful because she had stood up for herself over the overtime issue.

"There are two police detectives in my office, waiting to speak to you."

Her knees buckled and she bolstered herself, palms flat to her desk. *Seth,* one part of her mind screamed, even as another part whispered: *Ferdie.* But no one knew about Ferdie. She was in trouble. Something terrible had happened.

"We don't have much time," Mr. Marshall said, his voice low and swift. "It was a lucky thing you were at lunch when they arrived." Maddie registered the inaccuracy of this; she was *fetching* lunch, not taking it for herself. She brought her lunches from home most days. "The police are here because, Mr. Heath tells us, you called DPW about the lights at Druid Hill Park."

"Yes, I do that sometimes. Handle smaller problems. Did I make a mistake?"

"A worker has found a body there, a Negro woman. They want to know why you called, what you can tell them about the person who inquired about the lights."

"There was a letter." She tried to remember every detail she could. Handwritten, a masculine hand. Had there been a name? She thought so, but she also remembered that the name had struck her as false. Not John Smith, but similarly generic. She hadn't checked the name because the letter wasn't running in the paper, so there was no need to verify the sender. (Once, Mr. Heath had published a letter signed "Seymour Butts," and now Maddie was required to go behind him.)

"And you got rid of it," Mr. Marshall said.

She started to say no, that she kept a file of the answers she handled on her own, until the issues were resolved. But his deep-set brown eyes held hers and she knew, as she so often knew, what a man wanted to hear.

"We don't *retain* the queries that don't make the paper," she said slowly and deliberately. "That wouldn't make any sense."

"Good." Mr. Marshall nodded. "The newspaper's legal counsel is in my office. Why don't I take you there and let you explain to the detectives that we don't keep—retain—the queries that don't make the paper."

Hearing her words in Mr. Marshall's mouth was glorious. She must have chosen the right ones. Truthful, but deceptive. The letter about the fountain would have been tossed by week's end. But, for now, it was still in her files.

The waiting police officers were homicide detectives, men who didn't look much different from the city desk reporters. Only in their forties, aged by their jobs and the bad habits those jobs encouraged. They were disappointed to hear that it was policy to throw out un-published letters and they pushed Maddie to remember whatever details she could. She said that she did not remember the sender's name, only that he was a man. He said he had been passing the fountain late at night. No one was sure how long the lights had been out at that point, but DPW was dubious that the problem was one of long standing. She had been told that only a few days could have gone by before someone noticed the dark fountain.

"Any idea whose body it is?" Mr. Marshall asked the detectives. "The cause of death? How it even got there?"

It.

"The body's in pretty bad shape." The detectives seemed to watch Maddie's face, to see if that detail would rattle her. "A Negro woman. We—well, we won't say more for now."

You aren't telling us everything you know so we're not telling you everything we know. How childish grown men could be, in a way women never were, not in Maddie's experience. Sullen and grumpy, still playing by the sandlot rules, obsessed with fairness and stature. Of course women cared about stature, too, but they learned early to surrender any idea that life was a series of fair exchanges. A girl discovered almost in the cradle that things would never be fair.

As if to prove that point, Mr. Marshall dismissed her, as if she were of no importance to the meeting. She was an instrument, no different from a typewriter or her telephone headset. She conveyed information, but she couldn't tell you *how* she did it. Maddie sliced open that day's mail, seething. How many larger crimes lurked in the city's petty complaints?

But an hour later, when the detectives were gone, she was summoned back and asked to bring any files that she "thought might be relevant."

The editor in chief had a sumptuous office, which she had been too overwhelmed to notice on her first visit. An immense desk, possibly mahogany; a leather chair; a green-shaded lamp. Guests sat in upholstered wing chairs. It was a stark contrast to the newsroom's dingy chaos.

"I want to be clear about what just happened," Mr. Marshall said, hunched forward over his clasped hands. "We are good citizens. We cooperate with the police as necessary. But we want to know what we have before we share it. Once the police saw your files, we might not ever have seen them again. They could have been seized as evidence."

"I don't think there's much here," she said, handing him the manila folder where she kept "her" problems, the letters that she took on and solved, the invisible Mrs. Helpline. Or was she a "Miss" again? Neither honorific seemed right for her. Mrs. was Mrs. Milton Schwartz, who had run her household with ruthless ease. "Miss" was a seventeen-year-old girl.

"Why don't you take the letter out and read it to us?" he suggested. "After all, your fingerprints would already be on it. We can't keep the evidence pristine, but we can try to avoid contaminating it further."

She located the letter easily, its envelope stapled to it, although the only information that provided was the postmark, establishing it had been mailed in Baltimore last week. The inquiry was straightforward. The name, Bob Jones, sounded even phonier now.

"We don't check people's identities if we're not using the letter in the column," she explained. She realized that Mr. Heath had not been invited to the meeting, and this made her feel proud, although she couldn't have said why.

"Not much there," Mr. Marshall said. "I confess, I was hoping it would give us a little lead, something we could get out in front with."

"Dead Negro woman in fountain," said the city editor, Harper. "I wouldn't even lead the metro section with it. Diller says he hears that it's probably a woman who disappeared earlier this year, a cocktail waitress from the Flamingo, Shell Gordon's joint. The *Afro's* been all over it, but there doesn't seem to be any real news there."

The newspaper's lawyer was staring at Maddie. "You're the woman who tricked Stephen Corwin."

She blushed. "I wouldn't say *tricked*. I simply asked him to write to me."

Mr. Marshall picked up the thread. "And now here you are, making a random call to DPW and a body comes up."

She felt as if she were being accused of something. Meddling? Dishonesty? Neither characterization was entirely off base, but shouldn't she be praised as a go-getter, an employee with instinct and promise? She decided to say nothing. The moment was pregnant. Something was going to happen. She was going to be rewarded or singled out. At the very least, they were going to tell Mr. Heath that she was not his personal secretary.

Instead, she was dismissed for the second time that day. "Thank you for your help, Madeline."

She had not walked ten feet before she heard boisterous laughter from the editor's office. She did not believe that the laughter was at her expense, but it did not make her feel any better to realize how quickly they had moved on to some private hilarity. Miserable, she went to the ladies' room to splash cold water on her face, hoping to erase the high color in her cheeks.

The ladies' room was one of the few calm and relatively clean places on the entire floor. It even had a tiny anteroom with a Naugahyde love seat, although the only woman who ever lingered there was Edna Sperry, the labor reporter. She parked herself on the love seat with her copy, coffee, and cigarettes, emerging at the last possible moment to file, preemptively cursing the changes she anticipated to her prose.

"Mrs. Sperry . . . ," Maddie ventured after washing her hands and splashing water on her face.

"Yes?"

"I'm Madeline Schwartz, I work on the 'Helpline' column. But

I'd like to be a reporter here. I know I'm starting late—I'm just past thirty-five." After all, thirty-seven was only two notches past thirty-five, whereas "almost forty" sounded like death. "May I ask you—"

The older woman flicked her eyes across Maddie, flicked her cigarette ash into the brimming ashtray at her side, and made a sound that could have been a laugh.

Maddie refused to be intimidated.

"May I ask how you became a newspaperwoman?"

Edna definitely laughed then.

"What's so funny?"

"The minute you begin 'May I ask,' you've lost any edge you have," she said.

"I didn't know I needed an 'edge.'" Edna was no different from one of the old battle-axes she'd had to charm at the synagogue and Hadassah back in the day, when she had been a young bride, just beginning to serve on committees.

"You need authority, confidence. Do you know how I got into this business?" Maddie, thinking the question rhetorical, did not answer. "Well, you should. If you want to be a reporter, the first step is to prepare for every interview, to go in knowing as much as possible about your subject."

Maddie was thrown, but she didn't want to show it. "I didn't think of you as a subject. More of a colleague."

"That was your first mistake," Edna said.

It was a moment, that make-or-break second in which one's entire future depends on reacting the right way. Maddie had experience with such moments. Just like when she was not quite eighteen, standing expressionless in a Northwest Baltimore driveway, watching movers carry furniture, stowing her dreams away in the back of a truck as certainly as they loaded a yellow silk sofa. Just as when, a month later, she met Milton at a dance, and realized he was at once worldly and naive, a man she could fool.

"Thank you for your time," she said sweetly. She was thinking: *No, my first mistake was trying to get a woman to help me. I do better with men. I always do better with men.*

THAT NIGHT, FERDIE laughed at her, too. "Because she's a Negro, Maddie. That's why it wasn't a big deal when she went missing."

"I know that," she said. "I'm not naive."

But she was hurt. She had thought her anger over the callousness of the men at the *Star* was a kind of tribute to her lover. So what if they could never go out in public—it wasn't because of race. It had more to do with her marital status. And maybe his, although she remained unclear what that status was.

"There was a time when the death of a Negro woman didn't make the local papers," Ferdie said. "I don't blame your bosses for not caring until Cleo Sherwood was found. A girl like her—she got around. The *Afro* only made a big deal of it because the mother was so upset—and because Cleo worked at Shell Gordon's place. He's waist-high in a lot of stuff."

"Did you know her?"

Again, that laugh. "We don't all know each other, Maddie. It's a big town."

She was drifting off to sleep before she realized he had not answered her question. And by then it seemed too—*wife*like to follow up. What was it to her whom Ferdie knew or had known?

Yet Maddie couldn't let the subject drop. So much about the discovery of Cleo Sherwood seemed to parallel the death of Tessie Fine, but in a through-the-looking-glass way. No search parties, no attention. No official cause of death, not yet. No swift arrest, no outrage.

The one thing the two deaths had in common was Maddie.

A coincidence, but when one *is* the coincidence, it's hard not to find the fact momentous. There would be justice for Tessie, even if Corwin never revealed the identity of his accomplice. But what would there be for Cleo? How had she gotten there? Why had she gone there? Was she alive when she arrived at the fountain?

"Where did you say that Cleo Sherwood worked?" That seemed a fair question, a safe question.

"The Flamingo Club," Ferdie said. "Maddie, *don't.*"

"Don't what?"

"Don't get involved in this."

"How would I get involved?" Even she could hear the false notes in her voice.

"Let's see, how would Madeline Schwartz insert herself into a murder case? Well, she might join a search party. She might give an interview to a newspaperman—"

"I *didn't.*"

"—she might write a letter to some pervert who's going to end up on death row, then finagle her way into writing about *that* for the newspaper. There's something about you and that newspaper, Maddie. Moth to a flame, if you ask me."

"I work there now. It's my job. I'm trying to get ahead. How does that make me any different from you?"

Ferdie did not speak for a while after that and in the silence, Maddie's question took on more layers and meanings than she had intended. They were in bed. They were always in bed. Sometimes, they got up and drank beer and ate meals, but they never seemed to get dressed all the way. Once or twice, they had tried sitting on the sofa to watch a television show, but it had felt unnatural, upright and side by side, their clothes on. Ferdie lugged her television into the bedroom and propped it on the bureau, where they sometimes watched the Moonlight Movie on channel 11. This bedroom was their entire world.

Ferdie said: "I think you—" then stopped. Maddie was thrilled and terrified. Few things were as provocative as a lover telling you who you were.

"Go on."

"I don't have the words, exactly. I think you felt, I don't know, kind of hidden from the world. Or stuck between two worlds. You're not Mrs. Schwartz no more. But you're not *not* her, either. You liked it, when your name was in the newspaper. You want it to be there again. Not in a story, on top of a story."

"A byline." It was exactly what she wanted. When she had given Bob Bauer the story about Corwin, *her* story, they had printed her name at the top of the article, in italicized type: *Based on a correspondence with Madeline Schwartz, part of the search party that discovered Tessie Fine's body.* But she knew now that this did not count as a byline. It was not, in some ways, even her name. But then, what woman actually had her own name? Maddie's "maiden" name was her mother's married one.

Had she chosen Ferdie because marriage was literally forbidden to them, against the law in Maryland? Could she even claim she had chosen him? They were living in a bubble, in this room, hiding out—from what, she wasn't sure. She wasn't afraid of Milton. In fact she liked to fantasize about Milton's discovering that she had a *lover,* especially this one. Ferdie didn't have to run around chasing tennis balls lobbed by Wally Weiss to stay firm.

But Seth could never know. A teenage boy could not cope with his mother's romances, nor should he be expected to. What would happen when she was divorced at last, when she reentered the real world, whatever the real world was at this point? Would she marry again? Did she want to marry again? Maybe, probably. But for now, she wanted only *this,* whatever it was. This, and the newsroom. There were other women there, women who wrote about the port, the world, Washington.

Edna. Her cheeks flamed at how easily the woman had dismissed her.

In bed with Ferdie that night, she didn't tell him any of these things. Not the encounter with Edna, which she found shameful. Or that she planned to cultivate men for her ambitions, though he would be jealous, flatteringly so, she was sure. If Ferdie were her endgame, she would have desired this jealousy, required it. Like with Milton.

Only Ferdie was not, could not, be her endgame. Even if it were legal—but it wasn't legal, not in Maryland. That wasn't her fault and it wasn't something she could change, even if she wanted to.

They made love again. Sometime around three A.M., she became aware of his creeping away. He stroked her hair, kissed her one more time.

She thought: *Maybe I should change back to my old style.* Shorter, more bouffant. Edna wore her hair that way. Most of the women at the newspaper did, come to think of it.

No, no, Maddie reminded herself. She was going to cultivate the men.

The Battle-Axe

I STAB OUT my cigarette in the standing metal ashtray provided in the ladies' room. Most of the butts are mine. The other women on staff long ago conceded that this women's bathroom, one of only two on the floor, is my private lair. It is small and mean and utilitarian. Like me, some would say. But never to my face.

I go to my desk and start working the phones for a story I plan to file later this evening. The bosses hate how I schedule my day, but I'm too good at what I do for them to make me change. Still, they complain. *It's an afternoon paper, Edna. What if there are developments overnight or in the morning? What if we have to chase something in the morning papers?* As if anyone in town has ever scooped me. I come in when I please, make notes on how today's copy was butchered, scream at Cal, then start writing tomorrow's copy. I file about eight or nine, so Cal has to move my stories. I like working with Cal. He's a little scared of me, as he should be. But, still, he tinkers.

Today, he has all but tinkered his way into a correction box and you better believe it will say *Due to an editing error,* something they are loath to admit, but I make 'em say it. I will talk to Cal about this later and scare him sufficiently so he won't try it again for several months. He's like a dog, a dumb one, who has to be trained over and over again. Frankly, I should be allowed to hit him with a rolled-up newspaper when he misbehaves. There are plenty at hand and I think my lessons would stick better.

My desk looks like a fortress, one of those children's castles made with large, lightweight blocks, only the blocks are my files, stored in cardboard boxes. I wasn't trying to wall myself off from the newsroom, not at first. I simply wanted my files nearby and I ran out of space in the drawers. I know where everything is, can find anything I need in less than ten minutes, much faster than anyone in the library pulling clips. But no one else would be able to locate a specific file in my little warren. Perhaps that is by design.

I have a highly specialized beat, one I practically invented at the *Star.* They call me the "labor" reporter, which means I track the city's various unions. Inevitably, I am often the secondary on big stories coming out of the port or Beth Steel. Cops and firefighters and teachers. Labor touches everything in Baltimore. The only union about which I have never filed a story is the Newspaper Guild, which might end up striking by year's end. If it does, I will not join my colleagues on the picket lines. I will claim that would make me appear biased. I wouldn't cross a picket line—that would be foolhardy, make for hard feelings once the strike is resolved, and strikes are always resolved—but I won't march in one, either.

The truth is, I hate unions and negotiated for one of the so-called exempt slots when I joined the *Star*, so I'm not a dues-paying member of the guild. Marching is for children; strikes are games that distract the workers from the singular fact that no one is on their side. Not management, not their own leadership.

Some of my colleagues have tried to argue that it's biased for me not to be in the union, but I think it makes me more objective. My stories, my relationships with Baltimore's union leaders, speak for themselves. The fact is, the various union bosses prefer to talk to me because I don't cut them any slack. My questions—direct, skeptical, even adversarial—often help them see the defects in their strategies.

I have been the labor reporter eleven years, at the *Star* for nineteen years, a newspaper reporter for twenty-four years, twenty-eight if you count my years on the school paper at Northwestern. (I do.) Add the two years I spent stringing for the paper in my hometown of Aspen, Colorado, in high school and that puts me at three decades of newspaper work. I was never the *first* woman in the newsroom, but there were only a few of us, and fewer still who wanted to do the hard, masculine beats.

It helped, of course, that I am homely as a mud fence. Oh, I know some people would say I'm unfair to myself, but I was small and thin as a teenager, coming of age at a time when the hourglass figure was worshipped. And my nose, while not unsightly, is too big for my face. Other women dealt this hand might have gone the Diana Vreeland route, or emulated Martha Graham. I can't be bothered. At my first two jobs, in Lexington, Kentucky, and then in Atlanta, I ignored men completely, confident that I would be moving on very quickly. What was the point of romance in places I would never deign to linger?

But I am, despite what some of my colleagues say behind my

back, a woman with a woman's needs, and when I landed in Balti-more, I considered the men available to me. Colleagues, cops, assis-tant state's attorneys, labor bosses. Those were the sort of men that a female reporter met. None were to my liking. I found a gentle young man, a junior high school English teacher, drinking coffee at Pete's Diner and fixed my sights on him. Shy and inexperienced, he was so grateful for my romantic interest that it never occurred to him that he wasn't obligated to propose. We have two children now, well into their teens, and if the early years were hell—they were—the good news is that I no longer remember all the particulars of how we sur-vived it. We did, that's all that matters.

And now here comes this *housewife,* who has decided she can waltz into the *Star* and become a reporter, just like that. Certainly, many people on staff have made similar journeys, rising from clerical jobs, even the switchboard, but they started young and humble. This one—she doesn't burn to know things, I am sure of it. She wants the *accessories* of a newspaperwoman's life—a byline, a chance to perch on a man's desk and swing her pretty legs while bumming a smoke. One of the reasons that I seldom smoke at my desk is because it's a fire hazard. But also, by meting cigarettes out to myself—rewards for stories filed, phone calls made—I make myself efficient. I call it my three C's—copy, then cig and coffee. I proof the pages in the ladies' room and most of the women on staff have learned not to bother me.

Everyone knows that the pretty girl only got the job as Heath's as-sistant because she is pretty. But that post is a dead end. She should have tried for a job in the Sunday section; she would have been a natural writing up brides and engagements. Not that many Jewish weddings are featured in the paper, but there's always a Meyerhoff, the occasional Herschel.

I'm often mistaken for a Jewess, but my family were Scots, tough and durable, as hard as the marble they quarried. Again, people think this means I should have sympathy for unions, and again, it is quite the opposite. Unions work for average people and they are a godsend for the incompetent. If you are very good at what you do, a union holds you back.

I wonder what my own colleagues would think if they knew I've been contacted by Agnew, who's running for governor this year, not that it will be an easy road for a Republican. He offered me the press secretary's job, said it could lead to something in his administration. I countered that I want to be in his cabinet, preferably Commerce. Then I reached out to Congressman Sickles, who has the best shot of taking the Democratic nomination, and told him that Agnew wants me. Come November, I'm in a win-win. My agreements with the two camps prove that I'm unbiased, right?

I've had enough of newspaper life. Too many of these pretty girls, trip-trapping through the newsroom in their high heels, thinking it's fun and exciting. They even want to *date* newspapermen. I've made a lot of mistakes in my time, but that's not one of them.

June 1966

AFTER HER DISASTROUS conversation with Edna—and Maddie was no fool, she knew she had fumbled it badly—she took quick and quiet stock of what she had, what she wanted, and what she needed. She made subtle changes to her appearance, toning down her almost too-fashionable clothing, putting her iron-straightened hair up into a chignon. (She couldn't stop straightening it, Ferdie would be upset.) She looked at what she thought of as her "successes" so far—stumbling on Tessie's body near the arboretum, throwing Mr. Bauer a shred of knowledge to divert him from focusing on her, calling the city public works department about the fountain. Coincidences, yes, but what was the one common element? *Maddie.*

She decided not to emphasize the role of luck when she asked Mr. Bauer if he would go to lunch with her and advise her about her career.

He squinted at her, perplexed. "Where?"

"Here, at the paper."

"No, I mean where do you want to eat?"

"The New Orleans Diner?" It was a few blocks away, a place where clerks and secretaries grabbed lunches on the go, although Maddie almost always brown-bagged it to save money. Some reporters ate there, too, but not many. The reporters preferred the seafood restaurant on the nearby pier or, if senior, indulgent two-hour, three-martini meals at dark, hushed places after the final deadline. They bobbled back to the office on wavelets of gin, but that didn't matter so much with their daily deadlines behind them. They had all afternoon and into the evening to catch a second wind. Maddie would have loved to go to such a place for lunch, but if she suggested it, Mr. Bauer might think she had something else in mind.

Besides, she wanted to pick up the check.

Over their lunches—tuna salad and a Tab for her, a deviled ham sandwich and coffee for him—she said: "I know I'm not a reporter. But I think I could be a good one if they would let me. And I don't mean those silly things that Cal tries to give me."

"*Let* you," Mr. Bauer said. "No one's going to let you do anything. You have to make things happen for yourself."

"What if I found a story, a good one, that I reported on my own time?"

"You'd probably be poaching on someone else's beat," he said. "That's not going to fly."

"If the story is being ignored, I'm not really poaching, am I?"

"You sound like a kid with your hand in the cookie jar, trying to get off on some technicality." But he was amused by her doggedness, she could tell. He had a little crush on her. That was okay. Maddie was used to it. All her life, men had been getting crushes on her. The trick was to maintain this delicate emotion, to keep it from tilting into something serious, something with hurt feelings and wounded pride.

"So you think there's some story that's going to be missed if you don't follow up on it?"

"That girl—the woman—in the lake."

He shook his head. "That's not a story."

"Why not?"

"She was in her twenties, not taking care of her own kids, out for a good time. Wasn't even married to her kids' fathers. She goes out on a date with some strange guy. A chop suey date. He kills her. So what?"

"You know, if I were found dead in my apartment tomorrow, some-one could say similar things about me." Maddie did not really believe this, but she thought it a good argument. "I'm just a woman who left my husband. My own son doesn't want to live with me. That's why I didn't want to talk to you that day. Because you would have had to tell that part and my son, Seth, would have been so embarrassed."

Bob Bauer thwacked the ketchup bottle ineffectively. Maddie was about to take it from him but the waitress intervened, swift and familiar. She appeared to know him well, had joked with him about his order. *Deviled ham, you devil.*

"Why are you trying so hard to get a job as a reporter, Maddie? Most of the women in this business, they get in young, or they marry into it. And most of them are battle-axes, in my opinion."

"The world is changing," she said.

"Not for the better, I'm afraid."

"What about Margaret Bourke-White?" Even Maddie realized she was grasping. Why was she talking about a photographer? Who were the famous women journalists?

"The exception that tests the rule. There will be exceptions, always. Do you believe yourself to be exceptional?"

She took the daintiest bite possible from the messy sandwich, chewed more thoroughly than necessary. "As a matter of fact, I do. And Martha Gellhorn. I meant to say Martha Gellhorn."

"Then maybe you can turn this story into something. Tell you what, tomorrow on your lunch break, let's walk down to the cop shop, I'll introduce you to John Diller, and he can run you through some basics. How to pull a police report, for starters."

"I met him briefly at headquarters the other day, but I don't think I've ever seen him in the newsroom."

"You probably never will. He calls his information in to rewrite, couldn't write a note to his mother or even a grocery list without a rewrite man on the other end of the phone. Other reporters call him Deputy Diller or Deputy Dawg behind his back. We'll tell him that this is—kind of a training mission. That way, he won't get spooked about some gal he's never heard of making phone calls on his beat. Like I said, he's more cop than reporter. Blood runs blue. He knows everything that happens at the PD."

Not everything, Maddie thought, blood rushing to her cheeks.

The Waitress

THEY'RE TALKING ABOUT Cleo, Mr. B and the woman with him. I almost lean in and say, *I knew her,* but that throws people, being reminded that the waitress ain't deaf and dumb. It's a guaranteed way to get stiffed on the tip, let me tell you.

I'm surprised when the woman with Mr. B picks up the check at lunch, more surprised that she leaves a good tip. Not that all women are bad tippers, but this woman doesn't look as if she knows much about hard work, and that's what makes the difference in tips. Lawyers are the worst, very stingy. But housewives, who've never held down a job, they can be just as bad.

Maybe she's trying to impress Mr. B. I've been waiting on Mr. B for almost ten years now. I remember when he was younger, thinner. He says he's trying to reduce, then orders deviled ham. I know him well enough that I'll give him a playful tap when he reaches for someone else's French fries.

Of course, this woman doesn't order French fries.

Why would a woman pick up the check for Mr. B? That isn't allowed. He told me once he has to pay for himself, always. That if I see him with a stranger, I should make sure he gets the check. But he lets this woman pay. How odd. She clearly isn't a romantic interest, because then she definitely wouldn't have paid. Besides, he's married. He says "happily" but I'm not convinced the word *happily* can be applied to any part of Mr. B's life, except maybe the newspaper. He likes his job. He doesn't want to go home. I know because sometimes he comes in right before closing and drinks a very slow cup of coffee while I count my tips, talks to me about where he grew up, a town a lot like the one I come from, back in West Virginia.

None of my business. My business is to get the food on the table, fast and hot.

I've been waiting tables since I was thirteen, a leggy thirteen who could pass for sixteen. My parents brought the family to Baltimore during the war, for that Glenn Martin money. That didn't work out. Nothing worked out for them. They drank, they divorced, they got back together, which was worse than the drinking or the divorce. I had to find a way to escape, even if I was just thirteen, so I got a job at a place called Stacey's. Then I went to Werner's and now I'm at the New Orleans Diner. The NOD, as we call it, is long and skinny. It has defeated many a waitress. I've seen a lot of young ones come and go because they weren't efficient. Too much trot, not enough glide. But I know how to cover the maximum ground with the minimum steps.

Not that I was much smarter when I was a young pup. Turns out having cash money at the end of the day isn't the best thing for a teenage girl on her own. There were a couple of dark years where I almost became my mom. That's basically the story of every woman's life, right? You become your mother or you don't. Of course, every woman says she doesn't want to be her mother, but that's foolish. For a lot of women, becoming their mothers simply means growing up, taking on responsibility, acting like an adult is supposed to act. I hear the young women talking over their coffees, complaining about their mothers' opinions, their rules. I'm on the mothers' side. Especially now, with the young people starting to act so odd, dress so odd, listening to crazier and crazier music.

Still, I can sympathize with the girls, too. I remember being young, loving Elvis. I wish there had been a mother at home who railed at me a little, instead of a ghost in a bathrobe with a gin bottle who sneaked into my room while I was out and stole my tip money.

Anyway, one day, I woke up pregnant and that was that. The guy married me, but it was the only correct thing he ever did and pretty soon I was nineteen, with a baby, all alone.

Now that baby, Sammy, is fourteen years old, an honor student. I don't drink and our house is neat as a pin. A rental, but neat as a pin, whatever that means. How are pins neat? I go home every day and spend an hour with my feet up on the ottoman, a glass of Pepsi at my side. Because I do that, my legs are still worth a whistle, not a trace of a varicose vein. Less trot, more glide. Elevate. Those are the secrets I would share with the younger girls if they asked. But they never ask. They think they have all the answers, even the ones who manage to survive at the New Orleans Diner.

That name creates a lot of confusion, let me tell you. Some people think it's supposed to be New Orleans food, whatever that is. But it's just a joint that used to be on Orleans Street, then the owner moved it to Lombard, so he decided to call it the New Orleans Street Diner to keep his trade, but he screwed up and left the word "street" off the menus and was too cheap to fix it. He's a Greek, good with money and cooking, dumb about everything else.

The woman at lunch with Mr. B—she asks him lots of questions. But not in a get-to-know-you way. Not in a date way. I don't even need to hear the words to know that. This woman is like a dog stalking a squirrel, her body all a-quiver. Whenever I see a dog like that, I wonder: *What do you want with a squirrel? You're well-fed, it's not going to taste that good.* Whatever that woman wants from Mr. B, it can't be as important as she thinks. Nothing is. I have learned that lesson over and over again. Nothing you want matters as much as you think it does.

It's when I'm pouring Mr. B his third or fourth coffee that I hear her name, Cleo Sherwood. She worked in the kitchen at Werner's, although not very long. She wanted to be a waitress, but the bosses weren't having it. You had to be white to wait tables, they said it was what the customers wanted. Cleo was too pretty to be hidden away in the kitchen, in her opinion. She was right. Now she's dead. I saw it in the *Star* the other day. She's the first dead person I know, outside, you know, the kind of people who are supposed to die, grandparents and such. It was weird, reading in the paper that Cleo was dead. In the lake yet. How does a girl end up in a fountain? Had to be man trouble. A woman dies young, it's man trouble.

Thinking about Cleo makes me realize how short life is, how a person needs to live a little. When I count up my tips that afternoon and see that I've had an unusually good day, I find myself walking the opposite direction from my bus stop, over to the center of downtown where the big department stores cluster. Hutzler's is too much, I could never imagine myself shopping at Hutzler's. It's ten stories tall, there's so much to buy there that it runs over into another building. But Hochschild Kohn isn't as scary. I push through the revolving doors and march over to the perfume counter because it's the first thing I see.

Perfume is wasted on me. I pretty much smell like bacon and French fries all the time, no matter how often I wash my hair. Not that anyone's around to notice. When Sammy started school, I decided to forget about men. I'll be all of thirty-five when he goes to college. That's not too old to have some fun. The woman at lunch, she smelled good. I'd like to smell like that.

"May I show you something?" asks a salesgirl. Pretty dress, nice hair, gorgeous hands that make me want to thrust my own into my pockets.

Instead, I ask to try a sample of Joy, but only because I remember the ads that say it's the costliest perfume in the world. The salesgirl grudgingly hands me a piece of scented paper, won't even give me so much as a dab on my wrist. I sniff it. No, that wasn't the scent on the woman at lunch with Mr. B. Guessing wildly, I point at a bottle with a dove on top of it. L'Air du Temps. I don't dare say the name. Even if I could speak French, my accent would make it sound ridiculous. Until two years ago, I didn't even know I have an accent, then Sammy brought a friend home and I heard them talking in the kitchen. "Why does your mom talk like that?" "Like what?" asked Sammy, my good boy, my darling boy. "Like she's one of the Beverly Hillbillies." Unfair, because I don't sound like them at all. My West Virginia drawl has been eaten up by the Baltimore accents around me. My accent's kind of like Sammy, a nice result from an ill-advised collision. People like my voice. They like *me,* my regulars, their faces light up when I come to take their order. I am loved and beloved. I'm sure not going to try to say L'Air du Temps in front of some salesgirl just so she can mock me.

"The cologne is cheaper," the girl says. "But the bottle isn't as grand."

"I wouldn't buy perfume for the bottle," I assure her. I want her to know I'm no rube.

But the cost—jeez, Louise. Who could pay that just to smell good? Why not just dab some vanilla extract behind your ears and call it a day?

Yet I am sure, when I inhale it, that this is the scent on the woman at lunch with Mr. B. And I know this is something I can never afford, no matter how many miles I glide up and down the New Orleans Diner, no matter how many times newcomers look at the menu and make the joke, "What, no gumbo?" I always laugh as if I've never heard that one before, no sirree. I am as pretty as that woman, or could be. I'm prettier than the girl at the perfume counter, with her pointy nose practically touching the ceiling. My legs are shapely, my skin has good color. I have a great kid, we're doing okay. But I'll never have a bottle of perfume with a dove on top and it is probably just one of many bottles on that woman's bureau, sitting on one of those mirrored trays that fancy women have for their perfume.

"I'm afraid it's not my style," I say. "It's too—fruity."

She smiles as if she's caught me out at something.

I go home, I put my feet up for an hour, drink Pepsi, and watch *Bowling for Dollars*. It always makes me happy, that show. I don't know why. Sometimes I see ladies I know from around the neighborhood. I take my stockings off, rub cocoa butter into my legs. They look good. Less trot, more glide. I would have been a good carhop, the kind on roller skates, but you don't see those types of places in Maryland. I think they're a California thing, or wherever the weather is good more often than not.

Sammy comes in, fourteen years old, already four inches taller than I am, kisses me on the cheek without being asked. Last Mother's Day, he gave me lily of the valley perfume from Rite Aid and you know what? That's better than Joy, or some bottle with an angel on top. L'Air du Temps. What does that even mean? Air something? I'll ask Sammy later. He's getting straight A's at Hamilton Junior High, even in French. He's going to set the world on fire, my boy. He's all I need, the best thing I'll ever do.

I read the *Star* during commercials. Cleo Sherwood is truly yesterday's news, already gone from the paper. She told me once she was going to be famous and I guess she is, in a way. Or was, for a day.

I should have leaned in, told that lady: "I knew her, Cleo Sherwood. Ask me some questions." Wouldn't that have been something? But you never want the customers to know how much you hear. They think their conversations are private. I've waited on secret lovers, people breaking up, men clearly doing stuff they're not supposed to be doing. I bring them their food, flirt with my regulars, otherwise pretend I'm deaf and practically blind.

I move across the buckling linoleum floors of the New Orleans Diner like a skater, the best at what I do, all glide, no trot.

June 1966

MR. BAUER DROPPED Maddie at the press room in police headquarters like a careless parent taking his child to the first day of kindergarten. He got her as far as the door, but it was on her to march in and claim her place.

Even the *Star*'s newsroom, messy and chaotic as it was, had not prepared Maddie for the dingy corner of the police headquarters that had been set aside for the men of the press. And they were all men, although John Diller insisted there was one female cop reporter, Phyllis Basquette, who worked for the other afternoon paper, the *Light*.

"Where is she?" Maddie asked skeptically.

"Driving around the Beltway, trying to get her mileage to match her expense account," Diller said.

Maddie suspected she was being played, but she nodded. If there were such a woman, Maddie could understand why she would want to avoid this room. The room, the whole building, in fact, was one of the most masculine places into which she had ever ventured, and not in a good way like, say, the bar at Haussner's. (Or how she imagined the bar at Haussner's to be; women still were not allowed in, a strange rule at a popular restaurant where reservations were not accepted. Then again, the line for tables was always down the block, so it wasn't hurting business.) Yes, there were some female police officers and secretaries, this legendary Phyllis Basquette. But it smelled of men—of their sweat, their tobacco, of Brylcreem and aftershave. Cheap, bad aftershave.

Diller took her on a tour, first showing her how to pull a report. She read the brief details about Cleo Sherwood's disappearance, which had gone weeks without being noted. A bartender, Thomas Ludlow, said she had been picked up for a late date in the early morning hours of January 1. The man was tall, slender, thirtyish, with a turtleneck under his black leather jacket. Cleo did not introduce him and he was not someone the bartender had seen before. She wore a green blouse, leopard-print slacks, a red car coat, and red leather driving gloves. Maddie wrote all these details down in her notebook, if only for the sake of doing something.

"What's a number one female?" she asked Diller.

"A colored," he said. "Whites are number two, coloreds are number ones."

Diller led her from department to department, introducing the various sergeants. They perked up when she entered the room, but their faces fell as soon as Diller said she was his colleague. Her usual advantages with men did not seem to be working here. And when she tried to engage the captain in Homicide on the matter of Cleo Sherwood, he was taciturn to the point of brusqueness. "Not officially a homicide yet," he said. "Still waiting on the ME."

Throughout all this, Diller, a small, dapper man, was impossible to read. Maddie assumed he was enjoying her discomfiture, that he was trying to haze her so she would go away and leave him be. But he was the one who suggested, when their tour was done: "Do you want to go to the morgue and see if they've made any headway on this Sherwood case?"

She wasn't sure and her very lack of conviction told her she had to say yes.

"Is her body still there?"

"I don't think they've released it to the family yet. Even if they have, it won't be a wasted trip. If you want to write about police matters, you should get to know the fellas over there."

Oh, good—more *fellas*.

The morgue was a shortish walk from the *Star*, a slightly longer one from police HQ. Along the way, Diller talked about the Tic-Tac-Toe Killer, who preyed on the barflies along the waterfront, and pointed out an alley where one victim had been found. He also cheerfully detailed the wounds that the newspaper had hid behind the nickname, allowing readers to infer exactly what had happened to the bodies. "Normally, I wouldn't tell such stories to a lady, but you're a reporter."

The Inner Harbor was a grimy place. The McCormick spice factory on the western edge filled the air with cinnamon, an odd contrast to the landscape. Maddie had seldom ventured as far south as the waterfront, although she had passed through on field trips to Fort McHenry when Seth was a child. She tried to imagine the sad, sick men who were being lured from bars and then left dead in vacant lots and alleys. But even they were treated with more respect than Cleo Sherwood. Their killer had been named, personified, and their deaths linked.

"How can Cleo Sherwood's death be anything but a homicide?" she asked Diller. "How does a body get into the fountain in January?"

"Those are good questions," Diller said. But he didn't try to answer them.

The office of the medical examiner was a bright, sterile place. As Diller and Maddie entered, the men gathered at a gurney opened their tight circle, providing her an unobstructed view of the dead body lying there. It was a large man, his skin verging on purple. The body was positioned in such a way that she was staring straight at his crotch.

"This is Marjorie Schwartz," Diller said.

"Madeline," she said. She thought about offering her hand, decided it was unsterile. "I had hoped to talk to you about Cleo Sherwood."

"Oh right, the Lady in the Lake," the medical examiner said. Maddie made a mental note. She liked the nickname. Maybe using the term would humanize Cleo Sherwood's story the way "Tic-Tac-Toe Killer" granted some dignity to his victims.

The ME took her to the bank of drawers, began banging them open haphazardly as if he didn't know where Cleo Sherwood's corpse might be. Maddie saw a man with stab wounds, several unremarkable corpses, and, finally, the one she had come for. Her stomach churned, but she maintained her composure.

"Her . . . face," she said. It was barely a face and the color was neither white nor brown, more of a mottled gray.

"Did her mother have to see this?"

"Sister identified her."

How, Maddie wondered. Instead she asked, "What caused this?"

"Water, five months of exposure—it's not optimal. We have been able to establish that she didn't drown and there's no sign of trauma to the skeleton."

"No, I mean, how can it be anything but a homicide? How would a body even get in that fountain?"

"That's not our job," the medical examiner said. "We look for cause of death. So far, we can't find one."

"What are the possibilities?"

"Exposure, hypothermia. Maybe she got stuck in the fountain— January first, the last day she was seen by anyone, was a mild day."

"You think she swam to the fountain, fully clothed—she was fully clothed, right?—and crawled into the fountain?"

He read from a report: "'Subject was wearing leopard-print slacks, a red wool coat, and a green blouse.'" Looking up: "You'd be amazed at what drunk people do. People on drugs, they're even crazier."

"You mean like LSD?" Maddie had read scary things about the drug in *Time* magazine.

"In Baltimore? Her? More like heroin."

"Cleo Sherwood was a heroin addict?"

"I didn't say that. It's not something we can know."

The men were watching her, gauging her, waiting for her to break. Maddie turned to Diller: "It's almost noon. Do you want to go to lunch? I'm *famished*."

He took her to a tavern across the street. "Babe Ruth's father once owned this joint," he said. Maddie's stomach roiled when she saw some of the menu items—*scrapple, shaved meats, piled high*— but she was determined to eat heartily, or at least make a show of eating heartily. She was used to pretending to be the fun female who indulged in greasy, fattening foods. She ordered a club sandwich and French fries, knowing she would simply nibble at the sandwich, then push it around her plate, breaking it into ever smaller pieces. When Diller requested a beer, she did the same.

She had thought him unobservant, but he noticed how little food was making it to her mouth.

"Feeling off?"

"Trying to reduce," she said. "Some women eat cottage cheese. I get exactly what I want, then eat only a few bites."

They ate—*he* ate—in silence.

"Have you talked to her family?"

He seemed mystified by the question. "Whose?"

"Cleo Sherwood. The Lady in the Lake." Trying out the phrase, making it hers.

"Why would I do that?"

"Why wouldn't you? Isn't that something you normally do when people die?"

He finished the last bite of his burger, dabbed his mouth with a napkin. He was not a coarse man. His manners were as good as Maddie's, possibly better. His shirt was snowy white, his shave barbershop close, his seersucker jacket crisp.

"She's colored."

"So?"

He seemed to take the question seriously, if only because it was novel to him.

"They're not big stories, the colored dying. I mean, it happens all the time. It's the opposite of news. Dog bites man. Plus, you heard the ME. Probably drugs. She got high and decided she could swim to the fountain."

"But her death was so public. And so mysterious."

"That's why it got attention when she was found. But the *Afro* explored most of the avenues we might have gone down. She's just a girl who went out on a date with a bad guy. There's no story to that. She went out with a lot of guys, from what I hear."

"What's a lot?"

"I don't know. I'm—" He was struggling to be proper. "I'm just saying what I heard. There are women, good-time girls. It's how they pay the rent. And she worked at that club, the Flamingo. It's sort of a Playboy Club for people who can't afford the real thing. Girls in skimpy outfits slinging watered-down drinks, second-rate bands. The guy who owns it, he runs whores, everybody knows that."

Maddie thought about what she had seen, the degradation of the body that had once been Cleo Sherwood. Nature was vicious. When Marilyn Monroe had died four years ago, people had said she was undone by her age, her fading looks, that she wanted to leave a beautiful corpse. No one leaves a beautiful corpse. Even if the death is free of trauma, only the embalmer's skill can make the body presentable once a few hours have passed. Every day, Maddie was a little less beautiful than she had been the day before. Every moment she lived, she also was dying.

Monroe had been thirty-six when she died. Maddie had been just a few weeks shy of her thirty-seventh birthday when she decided to live.

"What if I went to talk to the parents?"

He shrugged. "Kind of ghoulish, especially if you don't get a story out of it, but I guess you can do whatever you like as long as Mr. Helpline is happy. But if you're looking for a feature story, why don't you visit the medium?"

"Medium what?"

"The medium. The psycho or psychic, whatever you call it. Parents went to her to try to figure out where their daughter was. You could use that to do a piece on her, kind of a profile. She said she saw green and yellow, but there's no yellow in that fountain and the only green is algae, which wouldn't have been there the night she disappeared. And the bartender had already told police she was wearing a green blouse, so that wasn't new. I bet if you ask her today to explain that, she'll say the face was turned toward the sun—only it wasn't—or that there were daffodils along the lake, but there weren't, not in January." He laughed and his laugh took over until he could barely speak; he had amused himself. "Don't call first because, because"—literally slapping his own knee now—"because I bet she'll never see you coming."

The Cop Reporter

I KNOW WHAT my coworkers say behind my back. They call me
Deputy Dawg. They say I've gone native, that I'm more cop than
reporter. That I can't write my way out of a paper bag, which is why
I'm still on the cop beat after thirty years. No one serious about
his newspaper career stays on the cop beat. Look at this little filly,
thinking she's going to make a career writing about some dead Negro. She doesn't get it. Even at the *Star,* which doesn't try to be like
the fancy-pants *Beacon,* with its foreign bureaus and eight-man staff
in DC, the cop beat is supposed to be a way station, a place you pass
through.

A fifty-two-year-old cop reporter is unusual. To my face, the other
cop reporters call me the "dean." They pretend to look up to me.
They try to steal my sources, certain they can do better by them.

But I have these sources because I'm not going anywhere. These young guys would betray someone in a flash. I socialize with the men on my beat. I go to their kids' christenings, attend the occasional FOP bull roast, buy rounds at the bar the cops favor.

I'm happy at HQ. My stomach drops to my ankles when I have to show up at the newsroom, unless it's to pick up my paycheck or cash out my expenses. Those are the only good reasons to walk into the *Star*.

My father was a newspaperman in Philadelphia, a columnist, a legend. Jonny Diller. He was Jonathan, I'm John, a mistake on the birth certificate that stuck, so I'm no junior and I don't let anyone call me Johnny. Of course I wanted to do what my old man did. It looked fun. People acted as if he was special because his name was on the front page of the paper on a regular basis. I ended up at the *Star* because I went to Hopkins, edited the *News-Letter*. I always imagined I'd make the hundred-mile journey back home someday, maybe as a columnist or a political writer.

There was only one problem: I couldn't write. I mean, yes, I can put sentences together in the right order, but I lost any flair I once had. I don't know how to explain it. The way they structure things at newspapers is that you don't write at first. You go to a crime scene, you find a pay phone, you call the facts in to rewrite. In an afternoon paper, there's no time to get back to the office and file. You know where every pay phone in the city is, that's your desk.

When I caught my first murder, my third day of work, I laboriously wrote the story in my notebook, thinking I would dictate it to the rewrite guy, saving him the work. He chewed me out. I wasn't saving him time, I was wasting time because what I had written was no good. "This is what I need and this is the order I need it in," he barked at me. And when I would try to add a bit of color, or a detail I found interesting, he would say, "Answer only the questions I ask, son."

I thought to myself: *I'll show them.* I began working on a novel at night. I poured everything I had into a story about a boy growing up in Philadelphia, one who lived on the right side of the tracks but was drawn to the wrong side, befriended a boy there. Classic stuff, Dead End Kids, one grows up to be a priest, the other a criminal, only not quite as stark as that. In my book, one boy was going to grow up to be a reporter, the other one was going to be a cop, and they would end up at cross-purposes, the reporter insisting on printing something that undercut a major murder case, gave the killer a chance to go free. The cop does what he feels he has to do, kills the killer, and he's arrested.

I thought I was hot stuff.

One night, I was sitting at my typewriter, looking at what I had written so far. By writing two pages a day, I had amassed three hundred pages midway into the year, almost a full novel. I began reading back through what I had accomplished and I was struck by two things.

One, I really hated the reporter in my own story. All my sympathies were with the cop, although the reporter was the autobiographical character.

Two, I couldn't write. I couldn't write for sour apples.

Don't get me wrong. It wasn't *bad.* It just wasn't good. I swear I was good once. I had filled notebooks with poetry and short stories, won contests in high school and college. But the *Star*, that rewrite man, had destroyed something in me and I couldn't get it back. I felt like a god stripped of his powers, forced to wander the earth in his reduced state as punishment. Only, punishment for what? As long as I kept calling my stories in to rewrite, my writing skills were going to diminish, diminish, diminish. The *Star's* narrow-minded view of what made a story was destroying my own.

But what if I moved up, got a new beat—and I still couldn't write. What then?

At that moment—I can still see myself at the desk in the living room, my young (then) wife gone to bed long ago, my shirtsleeves rolled up, and it's like seeing a man who thinks he can fly, only to wake from a dream and find himself standing on a ledge. I froze. I don't think I could have pressed a key on my typewriter with a gun to my head. I developed writer's block. I have it to this day. I can't write sentences, only words. I jot down facts in my notebook, but that doesn't count as writing, that's stenography. I actually know steno, which is why my notes are so good, so reliable, my quotes never questioned. No one has ever accused me of getting so much as a word wrong. When all the papers cover the same story and there's a discrepancy in a quote or a fact, I'm the one who got it right. I haven't had a single correction in almost thirty years on the job. Do you know how unusual that is?

At lunch, I ask the lady, Maddie-Marjorie, to cover her half. She seems a little surprised, but she gives me her share, as she should. This isn't a date. I pocket the check and go back to the office, fill out my expenses—including the one for the lunch I just had, writing "Sgt. Patrick Mahoney" on the back of the slip—and walk away with a nice fistful of cash. After work, I head to the cops' favorite bar, where I use my expense money to buy everyone a round, then grab the check so I can submit that expense later. All legitimate. If buying a cop a beer isn't part of doing my job, I don't know what is.

I see the patrolman from the Tessie Fine case, the one who was first on the scene, a young Polack with a reputation for being too good for his own good. He never stays for more than one beer and he has a sanctimonious puss on him, talks a little too much about his wife and not in the way most of the guys do, with good-natured jokes and complaints. No, this guy's wife is a saint, an angel. The man doth protest too much if you ask me.

"Did you know that that nice lady, the one who found Tessie Fine's body and became the killer's pen pal, is working at the paper now?" See, I give a little, then maybe I get a little.

He frowns. "I'm not sure she's a nice lady."

"What makes you say that?"

"I don't want to gossip."

Which is, of course, the first thing someone says right before he gossips. This one in particular likes to gossip, although he doesn't call it that. Men never do.

I prime the pump. "She's decided she wants to look into the Cleo Sherwood case. The barmaid from the Flamingo, the round-heels."

"Who cares about that?"

"Nobody cares, so why not let her have a crack at it."

"She sure does like 'em dark," he says.

I lean in, slide my pack of cigarettes across the bar to him. I know him. He won't stay for another beer, but he might nurse the one beer through a smoke.

"Not sure I catch your drift."

"You ever meet a patrol named Ferdie Platt? Northwest, blacker than ink. She *knows* him." He leans hard on that word, *knows,* makes sure I understand the implications.

"Yeah?"

"I've been looking into him. He's cozy with Shell Gordon, who owns the Flamingo. I don't think she's trying to get a story out of Cleo Sherwood. I think she's fishing to take information back to Platt. I think he told her some stuff about the Tessie Fine case, which is how Bob Bauer knew what he knew. If she's chasing this story, even money that Ferdie Platt put her up to it."

"Why would he do that?"

He exhales smoke from his cigarette. "Got me. But I saw him coming and going from her place, which sure as hell isn't in the Northwest, I know that much."

"And what were you doing there?"

The Polack pulls on his beer, doesn't comment. That's the thing about this guy. He's got the soul of a rat, he's a tattletale who's never grown up. He's always keeping score.

"I have to go," he says. "My wife doesn't sleep soundly until I get home."

He leaves me to puzzle over what he's told me. So this little housewife got her big break because she has a cop boyfriend, a colored one at that. I wonder if he put her up to writing those letters to Tessie Fine's killer, told her what to say, if the homicide cops were working her through him. But the cops I know were genuinely upset when the story broke, when the *Star* pointed out the discrepancy between what Corwin told them and what he told her, the thing about the car, the accomplice. Three months later, he's still holding firm with them, insisting it was all a lie, that he just made stuff up to mess with her, but obviously there's an accomplice out there and it's driving them nuts. If they had the accomplice, they could play the two against each other, cinch a death penalty case for one of 'em.

But I'm no tattletale. I won't go running back to the paper and tell folks that this new girl is sleeping with a cop. It's not like she's going to end up covering cops, not for the *Star*.

WHAT DID YOU think when you saw the body? Did I become more real to you? Or less? It was a monstrous thing, I bet, like something from a horror movie. The creature from the park lagoon. I can't bear to call it mine. Can anyone—you, the morgue people, the detectives—still see a person in that thing? I don't blame people for not caring. I don't care. I can't feel anything for that mound of flesh and bone, holding stubbornly to its secrets. Full credit to you for staring it down at all.

I know it sounds silly, but—I was naked, I assume? What happened to my clothes? Obviously, they would be the worse for wear, too, and they couldn't leave them on my body. But are they evidence? Were they examined, then stored somewhere? Cleaned up and thrown away? Every piece told a story, if anyone cared to know it. There was a world of stories in the clothing I picked out that evening.

Because the weather was mild, I chose leopard-print slacks, a light-

weight red car coat, and an emerald-green blouse beneath it, 100 per-cent silk. The combination bothered me because it was too Christmas-y, but there was a man waiting for me, telling me not to dawdle. Time was a-wasting. A scarf tied snug over the hair, straightened just the day before. No jewelry.

The clothes were all gifts from my man, but that doesn't tell you the whole story. Any man can buy a woman a dress, a coat, a scarf. My man was much more cunning. He had to bide his time, then pounce on opportunities that presented themselves. Just like he had pounced on me the second he saw me. Occasionally, alterations were required. He did them himself. He knew my body that well. The idea of him bent over a sewing machine, tailoring those clothes to my frame—let's just say that when I think of that, I know he loved me and I loved him for loving me. He was a king and I could have been his queen, a better one than the one that was forced on him, the one everyone said he had to keep if he wanted to expand his kingdom. I had read a lot of books about Henry VIII and his wives. Anne Boleyn was my favorite. I was, in a sense, trying to play her game, although the rules were a little dif-ferent in 1965 than they were in 1500-whatever.

And the game was so much bigger than I knew. Bigger than me, bigger than him, bigger than all of us.

June 1966

A WOMAN IN a pink housecoat opened the door when Maddie
rang the bell at the psychic's. *Madame Claire has a cold,* Maddie
thought, proud of herself for the literary allusion, then annoyed that
she could no longer remember the name of the psychic in *The Waste
Land*.

The woman in the pink housecoat had a husky, almost froggy
voice, but she did not appear to have so much as a sniffle. Even if
she did, it was more likely to be allergies than a head cold on this
balmy June day.

Maddie had waited until after work to take the bus to Madame
Claire's "studio," an apartment carved out of the ground floor of a
grand old house in Reservoir Hill. Much to her surprise and shame,
she had been scolded for the two-hour trip to the morgue, although
her work had been done and she had those 4.5 hours of comp time.

There was a difference, Maddie was realizing, between being told that she had permission to work on a story and actually working on it. She owed the newspaper eight hours every day. She was good at what she did, efficient and smart. She could do eight hours of work in six. But the time she saved was not hers. Like the miner in the song "Sixteen Tons," she owed, if not her soul, her time to the company store.

When she was a housewife, her speed and her efficiency had accrued to her. She had been her own boss, although she let Milton think certain decisions were his. It was odd, being made to answer to men who were not her husband. It made her feel sullen and rebellious, not unlike Seth. *I did my work,* she wanted to say. *Whose business is it if I take a long lunch to look into the Cleo Sherwood case?* She knew better than to argue, however.

And now she had ridden a bus to a part of the city she wouldn't have dared to drive through not that long ago. If she took a taxi home, would she be allowed to expense the fare? She doubted it. Besides, there were no taxis here.

At least the days were getting longer and it would probably still be light when she left Madame Claire, whose apartment happened to be within walking distance of Milton's synagogue. It wouldn't be there long. Chizuk Amuno had announced that the temple would be leaving the neighborhood for the suburbs in the coming year. After all, that was where their congregants lived. *Where the Jews are.* In her head, on the bus, Maddie had made that into a song to the tune of "Where the Boys Are." *Where the Jews are / No one waits for me.*

Not even a year ago, she had avoided downtown Baltimore, venturing there only for the occasional symphony performance, or dinner at Tio Pepe's or the Prime Rib. She had thought it dirty and dangerous. She wasn't wrong. Yet working at the *Star,* with its proximity to the raucous bars along the harbor, being able to walk to the grand department stores on Howard Street—she felt herself falling in love. Not with the city so much as the possibility of a new start, at an age when she had thought her life would basically be over.

As a child, she used to do the math: Born in 1928, she would be twenty-two at midcentury, seventy-two at the dawn of the twenty-first. She had assumed she would not change, that adulthood was static. Her younger self was not wrong: Maddie's life had been set by the time she was twenty-five. The house they bought that year, their second in Pikesville, might as well have been a mausoleum. An elegant, well-appointed mausoleum, but still a mausoleum. Seth was the only true living thing in that house and he was about to leave. She imagined his departure like a fairy tale, or an episode of *The Twilight Zone*. (A program she didn't really care for, but a favorite of Milton's, so they watched it all the time.) The landscape of their lives would be sere, dead. The emptiness would be revealed.

Did Madame Claire—oh, Claire for *clairvoyant,* too clever by half—intuit any of this as Maddie stood on her doorstep? Maddie didn't believe in psychic powers, but something in the woman's fearsome gaze suggested she could read Maddie's mind if she so desired.

"Do you have an appointment?"

"I assumed you would know I was coming," Maddie said, and immediately regretted it. Why would she use Diller's joke? It wasn't going to endear her to the woman.

"My gift is not always on," Madame Claire said. "It affords me respite as needed. It can be exhausting, my gift." A significant pause. "When I use it, I expect to be paid."

Maddie thought about her purse, the few bills she had with her, her wan hope of taking a taxi home.

"I'm not here as a client. I'm from the *Star.* I want to ask you a few questions about the reading you did when Cleo Sherwood was missing."

"Questions inevitably engage the gift."

"Would three dollars be enough?"

"Let me see the bills." She took them from Maddie and literally sniffed them.

They must have been found acceptable, because she took Maddie into what had once been the house's front parlor. The windows facing the street were draped with shiny red material that hoped to pass for satin, but Maddie could tell that it was a cheap imitation. There was a crystal ball, a deck of regular playing cards. Madame Claire ignored those, asking Maddie to sit opposite her and place her hands, palms up, on the table. She then put her own palms on top, her fingers reaching to Maddie's wrists. She could have taken Maddie's racing pulse if she desired. But she didn't. She didn't do anything.

"So Cleo Sherwood's parents came to you?" Maddie asked, breaking the uneasy silence.

"The mother, not the father. The father believes what I do is the work of the devil." Frowning. "He is a very ignorant man."

"What did you see?"

"I held an object that her mother believed had great meaning to Cleo."

"An object?" *This* was new.

"An *ermine* stole." Her voice caressed the word, drew it out. "A very fine piece of clothing."

"How did Cleo come to have a fur?"

The psychic's look was disdainful. Of course. How did any young, single woman come to have a fur?

"I know what you told the *Afro*. It doesn't seem to have been"—

Maddie had to tread carefully—"it didn't match up with where she was found. Maybe the green, because of the park or her blouse. But not the yellow. Was it from earlier in the evening? This color yellow that you saw?"

Madame Claire nodded. "Yes. I was seeing something from earlier. I think she must have been in a yellow room. Yellow was the last thing she saw."

"You mean—she was killed elsewhere?" Maddie thought back to the morgue, the medical examiner's scenarios. *A dead body is heavy. It would be impossible for a man, even a strong one, to heave it up and into the fountain.*

"Yellow is the last thing she saw," Madame Claire repeated.

Maddie could not believe she had squandered time and money for so little. The detail about the stole was new, but it wasn't enough to make an article. "Do you see anything else?"

She closed her eyes and kept them closed for so long that Maddie began to wonder if she had fallen asleep. Then her eyes flew open with what was clearly practiced flair. "A secret."

"Cleo Sherwood had a secret?"

"No, I think it's yours."

Maddie had to will herself not to snatch her hands back from Madame Claire's rough ones.

"Everyone has secrets," she said.

"Yes, they do. But you have one that's been causing you distress. It's like a tiny pebble in your shoe, yet you keep walking. All you have to do is stop, shake it out, and you'll feel better. But you don't want to. I wonder why that is. It's not a big secret, yet you don't want anyone to know."

Did Madame Claire mean Ferdie, who had just flashed through her mind? *Don't be silly,* she scolded herself. *The woman is a fraud.*

This is all hokum. "Maybe it's not my secret to tell. Or not mine alone."

"No, this happened long ago. But I also see yellow in your aura, although it's slipping away, disappearing, as if the lights are going out very slowly. Is it a streetlight? I don't know. It's gone now."

Maddie put her hands in her lap, breaking the connection, just in case. "Do you ever feel guilty about what you do?"

"Why would I feel guilty?"

"Your reading for Cleo Sherwood's mother gave her hope. But she was almost certainly dead by the time she consulted you. You couldn't give her any real answers."

"I did not ask for the gift and I don't make people come to me. I did not make *you* come to me. And I don't promise answers. People ask me what I see and I tell them. It's not my fault that the other-world is indirect, that the visions don't come with explanations."

"Can you tell me anything about my future? So far, you seem to be looking only at my past."

Madame Claire took a deep breath and held it, staring into Maddie's eyes, her pupils dilating. Maddie felt like a cobra facing a snake charmer. Finally, Madame Claire exhaled.

"Danger," she said. "I see danger."

"I'm in danger?" Her voice was shrill, the walk home on her mind.

"No, you *are* danger. You're going to hurt someone terribly, cause all kinds of trouble."

Oh, she thought, disappointed in spite of herself. That was the past again, Milton. She had hurt him. Seth, too. Sometimes, she wondered if she should have told Milton everything, if exposing her fraud at this late date would make him feel better about her leaving.

Still—yellow, disappearing. The eclipse. That damn eclipse.

She walked home in the June twilight, feeling like a character in

Greek mythology, perhaps Orpheus going into hell to retrieve Eurydice. She held her spine straight, carried her pocketbook with the strap across her chest as women were cautioned to do now. She tried not to walk too quickly, in part because her heels were not made for a fast pace, but also because she wanted to appear as if she feared nothing. But she was such an obvious outsider that the men she passed seemed to fall back, allow her extra room. Did they see danger, too?

That night, she left her window open, a risky thing to do, but the late-spring air was fresh and sweet, perhaps because of the gardens at the cathedral. There were so few natural scents in this part of Baltimore. It was as if the seasons bypassed downtown altogether. She slid into bed, not a stitch on. About two A.M., she heard soft footsteps on the fire escape, listened as the window was pushed wider open. A man's body covered her, possessed her.

"We've talked about this, Maddie," Ferdie said afterward. "Don't leave that window open. Someone other than me could get in."

"Maybe I left it open for someone else."

A pause. The room was dark; she could not see his expression. "Don't be like that."

"Like what?"

"Like, well, some stripper or some lady who goes with anybody."

"Like Cleo Sherwood?"

"You still talking about that?"

"I'm going to write about her. A woman is dead. Maybe I can make people see that they should care about that."

He sighed. "I doubt it."

"Did you know her?"

"Hell no. The Flamingo Club wasn't part of my beat."

"Do you think she had a boyfriend? A secret one?"

hough I usually do more business in the evenings. Most people, pecially churchy ones, prefer to visit me when it's dark. But I am ained. Even the smallest vibration takes a lot out of me.

I am forty-seven years old. I have been married three times, ach time a disaster, but I never talk about it because, again, peo- ple would doubt my abilities. How does a psychic pick such bad husbands? By listening to her heart. The heart knows nothing, sees nothing, but it kicks up a ruckus, throws tantrums to get what it wants. No one understands this thing I do, who I am, how my power works. It's not a machine that can be plugged in and turned on. The gift is sensitive. It prefers dry weather to wet, cold to hot.

Cleo's mother came to me on a good day, cold and bright and dry. When the air has that thin, hard edge, I can feel things I can't on other days. I could see inside Mrs. Sherwood's soul and it was the saddest thing I have ever glimpsed. She loved that girl of hers, she wanted me to see something that would suggest she was alive; maybe that was why I thought it possible. I don't think she loves her husband or her other children as much as she loves this girl, the one who's been so much trouble to her. Some mothers are like that. As I stroked that stole, it almost seemed to come to life, like a cat getting its back scratched. And a scent rose from it, sweet and stale, some kind of perfume. It smelled like—*yearning*. She had wanted something awfully bad, that girl.

I saw yellow, bright, blinding yellow. I saw a woman whose face was turned to the sun, maybe flew too close to it, as that old story goes. We are not meant to fly. We're not meant to see the things I see. I'm a good woman, a churchgoing woman, and there are Sundays when—I would never tell my preacher this—I pray to God to let me see *less*. But God says, *Suzanne*—my real name is Suzanne—*I don't give the gift to people who can't handle it.*

"More than one, no doubt."

He smacked her rump, but lightly, his sign for her to roll over and get on all fours. She had told him once that she had never had sex in anything but the missionary position, that Milton wouldn't hear of it.

That had been true, but also a lie. She and Milton had done it only one way, but Milton was not, despite what he still believed, her only lover, and her first lover had been a bold man who could, alas, convince her to do almost anything. *A green silk sofa. The yellow sliver of a moon during an eclipse.* Ah, but that was Madame Claire's trick, right? Whatever colors she saw, the client filled in the story.

The Medium

IT IS HARD for people who don't have the gift to understand it. Yet maybe necessary, too. If you knew what I see, *how* I see—well, there was a time when they burned women like me, and maybe that was a kindness.

I can tell that the woman who has come to see me today is not a believer. So I decide to throw a little scare into her. She isn't worthy of my gift, she doesn't want to use it for good. I tell her she has a secret, because who doesn't? I did see the aura of yellow around her, though, almost in spite of myself. What I couldn't tell was whether it was connected to her or something that has hung in the air since Cleo Sherwood's mother visited me, asked me to stroke that piece of fur. At the time, I was so sure the girl was still alive. And maybe she was, who knows? Her body could have gone into the lake in late February. But if she was still alive—where was she? Why couldn't I

save her? Was the green the color of the walls in a ro... was kept? Was the yellow I saw a lone bulb in someon... prison?

I was eight when I first realized I had second sight. I ha... In it, my aunt, who was only a teenager, was riding in a c... man, someone she barely knew. He was driving too fast. Sh... him to slow down. The car went out of control. My aunt was... the man died. I woke up that morning and those very thing... happened. My aunt was in the hospital with a broken leg, the... driving the car was dead. I told my mama that I had dreamed... thing. At first, she tried to talk me out of it. She said, "No, ho... you must have heard us talking in the night." Or: "Maybe you h... the dream the next night, but it's jumbled in your head, the ord... of things, because things were so crazy that day after it happened... so many people coming and going, and we were so worried she was going to die."

I believe now that Mama feared for me. She knew the gift would exact a price, and it has. I cannot control it, I cannot summon it. People would think I was a fake if I admitted this part, so I don't mention that. The thing is, anyone who comes to see me gets good advice. They get their money's worth. But not everyone has a true psychic experience. That's not in my control.

Cleo Sherwood's mother—she got the real thing. There was green and yellow, all around. I thought it might be the sun, I thought she was someplace where she couldn't turn her head and was forced to look into the sun. Maybe it was a room, or a ceiling. But her last living, waking minutes were surrounded by yellow, I am confident in that.

After the lady leaves—I don't need my powers to realize she felt dissatisfied—I turn off my light and decide to close up for the day,

That woman, the one who came asking questions about Cleo Sherwood, she was up to no good. I could smell the yearning on her, too, but there was no sweetness to it. She was like a car engine, revving, revving, revving, making noise, sending sparks out into the world. She wants to get somewhere. Trouble is, she doesn't know where she wants to go. That's what makes her dangerous.

I enjoy my supper, a pork chop and string beans, let myself have a little sweet wine, which calms me down. I get ready for bed, for sleep, which I dread. My dreams are a burden because they sometimes come true, but I don't know which ones will come true and which ones won't. Have you ever had the sensation of being stuck in an awful dream and then you wake up, experience relief, because it's not happening? I am denied that release until I can check to make sure that my dreams have not come true. Yes, my vision is a gift, but it's not one I asked for and I long to return it. Take this from me, God, it's not right. Make me ordinary, a woman who can live with a man, put her head on the pillow at night without fearing what might visit her in her dreams, what might still be waiting for her after daybreak, when the dreams and nightmares end for everyone else.

GREEN AND YELLOW, *huh? You get what you pay for, Maddie Schwartz. You know what was green and yellow? The upholstery on the balcony seats in the theater where I sat, two weeks before I died.*

My man had surprised me by taking me to New York, where he had tickets to a musical, Man of La Mancha. They weren't very good seats and we were the only Negroes in the audience, best I could tell. And the music—well, to me, it was kind of trifling, old-people stuff, but it moved him, I could tell. I watched tears slide down his cheeks, only not during the song that everyone knows, the one that's on the radio. (Again, that's only if you listen to old-people radio.) He out-and-out sobbed at the end, when the woman said the dead man in the bed was not the man she knew, that the man she knew and loved still lived somewhere. I thought, in that moment, that he would be mine, that he would choose to be the hero, not the man in the bed. But, no, he was crying because he knew his limitations, knew what he would choose in the end. He was weak.

I watched him watching the show about the show inside the show. It reminded me of that infinity joke we tell each other as kids: I'm painting a picture of myself painting a picture of myself painting a picture. It gets smaller and smaller and smaller until you can't see anything.

So I decided for myself: I'll be the one who lives. Not the old man in the bed up onstage, not the wild, beautiful wives of Henry VIII, Anne Boleyn and Catherine Howard, and not the last one, the nurse, that no one really talks about, who died pretty soon after he did. I'd be Mary Boleyn, Anne's sister, who fooled them all and had a good long life. That's what I would choose.

It was too late. The choice to live had been taken from me and I didn't even know it.

At three A.M. on January 1, I went to my closet and picked clothes for my date, taking time to make sure that none of Latetia's clothes were mixed up with mine. We borrowed one another's clothes, but mine were so much nicer. It wasn't the first time I'd made a late date and I was always alone on holidays, that's how it works. The second shift is how I thought of it. My man was generous, but I always needed more and I didn't make the tips I deserved stuck behind the bar, and whose fault was that? Everybody knew I had late dates. Except him. I hope he never knew, but I'm sure that those who wanted to turn him against me saw to it that he found out.

I pushed that fur far back in my closet, making sure it was in a dry-cleaning bag, as if winter were over. It was for me. Everything was over for me. Mine wasn't the nicest neighborhood, my apartment wasn't that great, even with the view of the park and the lake. I suppose the buildings along Druid Hill were grand once, when white people lived in them, but it had been a while. That was the story of the neighborhood, the story of the world. White people always get out just in time. They have an instinct for when the plumbing's going to go, when the wiring will fray and crackle. Look at you, Madeline Schwartz, leaping from your marriage when you did. You probably thought you were getting out in the nick of time.

I pushed my fur into the back of the closet and went out on my date, dread bubbling up in my stomach. But I had to go. The ending had been written, it was out of my hands.

Six weeks later, when my mama convinced the landlord to open the door for her, she found my fur and recognized it was something I loved. She carried it to the psychic, who buried her face in its pale pink silk lining, stroked the white pelt. It was rabbit, but she pronounced it ermine, which tells you everything you need to know about the woman who claimed she saw my final hours. Green and yellow, indeed. Sure, I wore a green blouse, but the real green was jealousy and there was no yellow—unless you count the cowardice of the man who decreed I had to die but would not deign to do the job himself.

June 1966

"YOU DID *WHAT?*"

Judith Weinstein had been about to sip a spoonful of chicken
soup with kreplach when Maddie told her about the visit to Madame
Claire. As fastidious in her manners as she was in her appearance,
Judith could arrest her spoon's arc without spilling a drop, but she
was gratifyingly amazed by Maddie's recent adventures.

"I went to the morgue, to see Cleo Sherwood's body. Then I visited the psychic that her mother consulted."

"That dead Negro girl? The one who worked in Shell Gordon's
club?"

"She worked at the Flamingo. Is that the place you mean? Who's
Shell Gordon?"

Judith snorted, although it was more like a cat's sneeze, tidy and
contained.

"I *told* you, Maddie. Stewart 'Peanut Shell' Gordon. He's a small-timer trying to be a big-timer, like Willie Adams, whom he idolizes and loathes in equal measure."

"I've never heard of any of these people."

"I told you, you should come to the Stonewall club with me. It's interesting. Although I know most of this stuff from my uncle Donald. Shell Gordon wants to be a powerbroker, like Adams. He puts out a lot of walk-around money on Election Day."

"Walk-around money?"

Judith sipped her soup, a strange choice for such a warm day. The Suburban House's soups were good, but Maddie was treating herself to a full feast—a bagel with lox and cream cheese, accompanied by a Tab. She had walked so much this week. Besides, Ferdie liked her as she was.

"It's how you get your vote out."

"But it's illegal to pay people to vote."

Judith smiled, happy for the chance to be the wise one in their new, tender friendship. "You don't pay people to vote exactly. You pay people to *get out* the vote."

"I'm not sure I see the distinction."

"In the end, there might not be one."

Maddie wasn't interested in a political tutorial. She had sought Judith out because she needed a confidante, someone to listen to her stories from work. Ferdie, she assumed, would be either bored or scandalized by her adventures—going to the morgue, venturing into a Negro neighborhood. Certainly, she could never tell her mother what she was up to. So she had looked for a friend—and realized she had none. She had tried calling Eleanor Rosengren, whom she had not seen since that fateful dinner—really, that was not hyperbole, the dinner had changed her life—with Wallace Wright. But Eleanor had seemed distant, odd. Lines had been drawn up in Pikesville and Maddie realized that her old friends would be on Milton's side, as surely as they lived on the county side of the city-county line. Maddie had abandoned not only Milton but the whole neighborhood. Her new way of life was a rebuke to all of them.

So she returned to Judith, the eager young woman who always jumped when she called. And it was gratifying how happy she was to make this dinner date. She had even suggested that they go to a movie at the Pikes Theater later, volunteering to drive Maddie home in her father's car.

Maddie had assumed their dinner conversation would be about her work exploits, that Judith had no stories to share. To her surprise—and, truthfully, to her annoyance—Judith had a confidence, too.

"Remember those cops, from the day when—" It was hard still, to talk about Tessie Fine, the silvery sole of that shoe, the red hair, the green coat.

"Of course."

"Mine called me."

Maddie took note of the word, *mine*. Had the other cop been hers? He had wanted to walk her to her door, but surely that was just politeness? At any rate, he had not called her or followed up in any way and she felt a tiny shock of jealousy, as if she and Judith were two girls who had gone on a double date, but Judith's date had been successful and hers was not. Silly. She would never date a cop. Oh— she was dating a cop. No, not *dating*. That was not the word for what she and Ferdie did. She blushed, not that Judith seemed to notice.

"What did he want?"

Judith took no offense at the question, borderline rude as it was. "He asked me to go out. I knew my mother would be scandalized, but it was my father who really hit the roof. I don't know if it was the cop part or the Irish part. At any rate, he said there was no way any daughter of his would go out with 'such a man.'"

"A shame," Maddie said, not meaning it. "He was cute." Again, not meaning it. She couldn't recall anything about the man but his vapid chatter.

"He wants to meet up with us tonight," Judith said. "At the theater. If that's okay?"

Maddie felt silly, a little used, although she was the one who had called Judith. She even felt her allegiances shifting toward Judith's parents, to whom she might have been closer in age. If Seth had wanted to date a *shiksa*, a cop's daughter, Maddie would not have approved. But she also would have been careful not to object. That's how her mother had handled her high school relationship with Allan. Pretending not to be worried, inviting his parents over for Passover dinner.

How, Maddie wondered, would her mother have acted if she had known about Maddie's true first love? Somehow, she had managed to hide him from everyone. Perhaps that was her real talent, secret loves. But it was 1966. Being a courtesan was not a career.

Courtesan. She could hear her first love, laughing at her across the years. *Euphemisms are for cowards, Maddie.* He had laughed at her a lot, come to think of it. Mocked her ambition to write, said she would be just another suburban mama.

"Of course, that's okay," she assured Judith.

"And I thought," Judith said, "if you don't mind—we'd give you cab fare to get home. You see, if my parents think that I have to drive you back to the city and home again, that's a good hour of time, and—"

Her turn to blush. Maddie would have been quite jealous now, except that she knew whatever Judith and her date did in their stolen hour could not compare to what she and Ferdie accomplished in that same window of time. But, oh, how lovely it would be to sit in a movie theater, holding hands with someone, anyone. Was this always the choice, passion or respectability?

The movie was *The Sandpiper*. After a carefully staged chance encounter in the lobby, the trio chose seats toward the rear of the theater, then Maddie insisted on moving closer to the front, claiming she had forgotten her glasses. (She didn't wear glasses.) Judith and her cop, Paul something, made faint protests. He was in civilian clothes. He was not especially attractive, not to Maddie. But there was something about the knowledge of this forbidden love (lust) eleven rows back that aroused her. Or maybe it was Richard Burton, so attractive despite his pocked skin. She found herself quite stirred up.

And then she realized that the man next to her had put his hand on her knee.

She picked it up and put it back in his lap, stealing a glance at him. He did not appear depraved. He was not trying to touch himself and his eyes were fixed on the film. She should have been screaming for an usher—and yet. His profile was quite nice. A fine Roman nose, a thick head of hair, long-lashed eyes behind his glasses. There was no dirty raincoat, no unzipped trousers—

It was then that Maddie screamed.

Not because she was scared, not really. Oh, she was terrified, but not by this man. She was horrified by her *lack* of fear, overwhelmed by the thought, however fleeting, that she could lead this man out of the theater and do things to him, let him do things to her. She was becoming depraved, there was no other word for it. This was why she had married as quickly as possible. Because her first love had awakened this terrible lust in her and she knew she had to bottle it, tame it. Now it was out again, loose in the world.

Of course, once she started shouting, Paul and Judith came to her rescue as well, while the man with the Roman nose was never seen again. There was no talk of cab fare, given the fright Maddie had endured. The two drove her home. Maddie almost felt guilty for depriving them of their time together. Then again, they had left the film forty-five minutes in, so they still had at least an hour to spend in each other's company.

Judith reported in the next day, whispering on the line from her brother's jewelry store.

"He wanted to park on Cylburn Avenue," she said. "Near—is that weird?"

"No," Maddie said. *Yes,* she thought. *But not as weird as what I wanted to do last night, so who am I to judge?*

A libertine, she thought after hanging up. *I am becoming a libertine.* Where had she first heard that word? From her first lover, of course. Was he still alive? He had moved away long ago and she had lost track of him. But given the family's Baltimore connections, she assumed there would be an obituary in the local papers if he died. There would definitely be an obituary if his wife died. But he was not old yet, only going on sixty. There was no reason to think he had passed.

She saw herself, not quite eighteen, standing on the sidewalk and watching movers carry furniture into a van.

"Where are they going?" she asked the least intimidating of the men.

"New York," he grunted.

"I know him. Them," she offered. "I was—I went to school with their son."

The moving man was not interested. For months, the gravest fear of Maddie's life had been that someone would discover her secret, what she had done. But now she saw the worst fate was no one's knowing. She had kept their secret too well. All the promises, the whispered words, the vows made in exchange for taking from her something she could never reclaim—there were no witnesses. Only he knew how he had spoken of their running away together, of the visions he had painted, better with words than he ever was with a brush, of a future in which they lived in the Village, true *libertines,* caring about nothing but art and love. She could not prove it had happened, any of it. The most significant event of her young life was being hauled onto that truck, transported to New York of all places, but probably not the Village, never the Village. They probably were going to live on the Upper East Side, in the kind of house and household that he said he despised.

The movers carried a green silk sofa into the van. Maddie had lost her virginity on that sofa the summer she was seventeen. "Can't you stay a little later?" he had asked. "There's going to be an eclipse tonight. That's practically a once-in-a-lifetime event. And I know your parents never worry when you're here with me."

No, they never did. Even at seventeen, Maddie understood how ironic this was.

Two months later, in the fall, she met Milton. Of course he had assumed she was a virgin, and she saw no reason to contradict him. She was and she wasn't. She was someone new, a different Maddie. If anything, she felt more innocent, younger for having been defiled and tricked by an older man, who had no compunction about using words to talk her out of what people claimed was her greatest gift, her singular asset to offer a man, the only dowry that still mattered.

Did Cleo Sherwood have a boyfriend? Everyone said no, but

casual dates didn't give a girl an ermine stole. *Cherchez l'homme.* Maddie was going to find Cleo's lover, this married man, demand answers. It would make up for her lack of nerve when she was seventeen and she failed, again and again, in her resolve to introduce herself to her lover's wife.

Of course, his wife already knew her, but only as her son's classmate, the girl he had dated, asked to the prom, then dumped. The girl whose portrait her husband was painting in his studio. The resulting painting was stiff, absent of her vitality and charm. Absent of all the qualities he said he saw in her, when he put his brushes down and made love to her, again and again and again, the summer she was seventeen.

The Moviegoer

I SWEAR I have never done anything like that in my life. It was not a plan. Okay, yes, it was a plan to *sit* next to her. I have my choice of seats, after all. The theater isn't crowded and I usually don't like to be that close to the screen. It hurts my neck, my eyes. But I see her go in with the couple, almost like their chaperone, then leave them to the back row as she moves down front. I follow, sitting across the aisle, then moving next to her after the cartoon, just as the feature begins.

I am—I don't want to tell you what I do. I'm respectable, trust me on that. I am a good man, a good provider. Yes, I am married, but my wife is cold to me. She has always been cold to me. I don't think she likes me. I ask her sometimes, "Do you like me?" and she says, "I *love* you," as if that's better, as if that should be enough. But it's not. I need her to like me, too, to laugh at my jokes, to seem less put-upon by my general existence. When I come home at the end of the day, my wife seems to find my very presence in the house an imposition. A nice house, that I pay for. It reminds me of the old myth, Cupid and Psyche, only she can't be bothered to try to steal a look at me as I sleep. She'd be fine, being married to the monster, as long as he brought home a paycheck.

So, sometimes, I tell her I have to work late and I go to the movies or stop in somewhere for a drink. But you have to believe me: I have never, ever done anything like what I do tonight. And what I do, is it really that big a deal? I touch a leg, a knee, outside her clothes. Her skirt is short, which is why I make contact with her actual knee. I'm not planning to touch her, I'm not, but then something happens to her breathing. It slows, almost in invitation. It seems sensual to me, although the scene playing out in front of us is not particularly romantic. She smells so good, not of perfume, but of something more organic, some innate essence that is better than perfume or shampoo or soap. It's like walking past a flowering shrub in a neighbor's yard, just over the fence, but maybe a few blossoms are trying to escape. First, you want nothing but to smell it. You lean forward, inhale. It's impossible not to touch it, rub your finger along one silky, velvety petal, release pollen into the air. Then, if the neighbor doesn't come, you cross the line, you actually pluck it and take it with you. Hasn't everyone done this?

I don't go that far. I touch her knee. A friendly touch, a glancing touch, possibly accidental. I wait. For a moment, it seems as if she's considering touching me back. I can feel her thoughts, the way she weighs her options. She puts my hand back in my own lap, but gently, sweetly even.

And then she begins screaming her head off.

Luckily, I know the neighborhood, know the theater. I run out of the fire exit, near the screen, which lets off into an alley. Once outside, I'm too cagey to keep running. They will be looking for someone who is trying to get away. I take out a cigarette, my hands shaking just a little, and light it, leaning against the rear of the Chinese restaurant next door, inhaling more grease than nicotine. I see a man come out, two women behind him, watch them look up and down the alley. I look straight at them, smoking as nonchalantly as possible.

They walk toward the street, but they're less urgent now, not so much looking for the perpetrator but trying to comfort the woman, the couple bookending her, taking her arms as if she's an invalid. I want to yell after them, *All I did was touch her knee.*

I go home. My wife is sitting at the kitchen table, working the Jumble. A kids' game and it takes her almost twenty minutes to do it.

"How was work," she says, not looking up, not even letting her tone go up. It's not a question. It's just something you're supposed to say when your husband comes home. She has less affect in her voice than the robot maid on *The Jetsons.*

"Okay." Her pencil scratches away. She uses a pencil on the Jumble. I do the *New York Times* double acrostic in ink.

"Sheila, do you like me?"

She sighs. "This again. What are you, the road show of *Fiddler on the Roof*? How many times do I have to tell you: I love you."

"I asked if you *liked* me."

"Love is better."

Is it? Is it? Four years ago, I met a woman at a dance. She didn't talk much, which made her seem mysterious and alluring. She was as cagey with her body, her kisses and affections, as she was with her words. I projected so much on those silences, those resistances. Still waters run deep, et cetera et cetera. We were married within three months.

Turns out that even if still waters run deep, there's no current, they can't take you anywhere. All they do, eventually, is close over your head.

June 1966

WHEN MADDIE TURNED on the street where Cleo Sherwood's
parents lived, she realized the block was one she knew. This strip
of Auchentoroly Terrace was not only near the synagogue and the
old Schwartz grocery store, it was also along the route that the
Schwartzes used to take to downtown restaurants and the theater.
Milton liked to go a few blocks out of his way to drive down this
street. He had this odd habit, her not-yet-ex-husband, a tendency
that Maddie privately dubbed Milton's Memory Lane. He was forever checking in with his past, showing Seth its landmarks over and
over again. The house, the grocery, his schoolyard. Nostalgia was
not the point. Milton wanted to remind Seth, and possibly Maddie,
that Milton's young life had been one of hard work and deprivation,
that he was self-made.

"Are these people poor?" Seth had asked when he was seven or eight. It would have been summertime, hot, with people hanging on their porches, kids running up and down the street, maybe even jumping in the spray of an open fire hydrant.

"Yes," Milton would say. "But no poorer than my family was."

This late June afternoon was not particularly hot. Not outside at least. But the air in the stairway up to the Sherwoods' second-floor apartment was heavy and stale, the smell of grease so thick that Maddie felt grimy for ascending through it.

Or maybe the oily sensation on her skin was her own sense of shame, for coming to see the parents of a dead woman, unannounced, and for the questions that she planned to ask them.

Not that she could have called ahead even if she wanted. There was no phone listed for the Sherwood family. But Maddie was learning not to ask for permission. Permission could be denied, whereas if one acted as if one had a right to be somewhere, that very pretense of self-assurance might carry the day. Wasn't that what Mr. Bauer had done to her, not that long ago, although it seemed like years since she had been as naive as that Maddie Schwartz?

She knocked on the door, brisk and ready: "Hello, I'm Madeline Schwartz of the *Star* and I'm here to ask you some questions about Cleo Sherwood."

A younger woman—Cleo's sister?—had answered the door. Even as she turned her head to look back at someone, Maddie simply walked in. Again, she was done waiting for permission. A man, presumably Cleo's father, sat in an easy chair near the front windows, reading the newspaper. The *Star,* Maddie noticed. *Her* newspaper. He did not look up or acknowledge her in any way.

At his feet, two children, boys, were playing with toy trucks on the rug. They must have been Cleo's boys, although they barely

looked like brothers. The older one, perhaps four or five, was thick—
not fat, but stocky and strong looking, with a capacity for immense
concentration. He pushed his yellow truck across the carpet, ab-
sorbed in his own game. The younger one looked remarkably like
Cleo in the one photograph Maddie had seen in the *Afro's* clippings.
He had her pale eyes, delicate features, and a dreamy, self-contained
quality.

Mrs. Sherwood came from the kitchen, her tread heavy, wiping
her hands on a dishcloth. She did not extend her hand to shake,
however. "Is there news?" she asked.

"No, there's no news," Maddie said. "But I want to write about
Cleo in hopes that my story will unearth something, jog someone's
memory and help us find her killer. It would not have been easy"—
her glance shifted to the boys and back—"it would have attracted
attention, I think, whatever happened at the lake that night. An
article might make someone reflect on things that didn't seem important at the time."

That was not her real mission today, but she knew enough not to
go straight to her harder questions.

"The *Afro* wrote plenty about *Eunetta* before," Mrs. Sherwood
said. "No one cared then, so why would anyone care now?"

"I think lots of people care," Maddie said. She disliked lying, but
it wasn't that much of a lie. If the killer were found, especially if it
happened because she refused to let go, then people would care, she
was sure of it. "I just—is there anything I should know? I was very
struck by one detail the psychic shared with me. Madame Claire?"

"*Her.* She didn't help us much."

"The colors yellow and green didn't mean anything to you?"

"No, ma'am."

It was odd, being called ma'am by a woman who was clearly older. But it meant that Maddie had somehow persuaded the Sherwoods that she had authority. Was it the newspaper? Or her whiteness?

"I was struck by the fact that you brought her a fur stole. Is that correct?"

"Yes, ma'am."

"Who gave that stole to—Eunetta?" She had not missed the mother's use of her daughter's given name, the implicit rebuke.

"I'm sure I don't know."

"But it was hers?"

"Yes, ma'am."

"How did you come to have it?"

"Ma'am?"

"She wasn't living here, right? When she disappeared. She kept an apartment with another girl."

"Yes, ma'am. She had a roommate. A girl named Latetia. Skipped town without paying her share of the rent, about a week before Eunetta—" She glanced at the boys on the rug, who seemed to be paying them no mind at all. "Well, back in December, Latetia told Eunetta she was going to go to Florida with a gentleman she had met right before Christmas. A couple weeks later, she cabled that she was getting married. Nice for her, but she should have paid her share of the rent for January. And there was no one there to get her cable, although I guess she couldn't know that. The landlord assumed Eunetta was as flighty as Latetia." She stopped, seeming to think this had answered everything.

"I'm still not sure why you had the stole."

"It was only a matter of time before he changed the locks and put their stuff out. So I went over there and packed up some things, the nicest things. The stole smelled of smoke and gardenias, so I assumed she had worn it pretty recently. That's why I took it to Madame Claire. Because I thought Eunetta had worn it maybe a week or two—before."

"And who gave it to her?"

"How could I know?"

She didn't point out that Mrs. Sherwood had failed to answer the question.

"Can I see it?"

The father rattled his newspaper and cleared his throat, stagelike and unsubtle, but Mrs. Sherwood beckoned Maddie to follow her to the rear of the apartment. She led her to what was once a proper pantry, now a crowded closet, full of clothes and boxes and children's toys. But Mrs. Sherwood seemed to understand whatever order was at work, quickly producing the stole on a hanger, wrapped in plastic. Not the proper way to store a fur, Maddie knew, but she also saw immediately this was not a particularly nice fur. She did not ask permission to remove it from the plastic, just did so, looking for the label. "Fine Furs." That was Tessie's family. How small Baltimore was. She inspected the stole carefully, committing every detail to memory.

"Did she buy this for herself?"

Stiffly, swiftly: "She didn't *steal*. Eunetta was a good girl."

"No, I mean—was it a gift?"

"She made pretty good money. Based on what she gave us for taking care of the boys while she tried to . . . get herself situated."

"Right. She was an accountant? Isn't that what the *Afro* said?"

"Not—precisely. She was a cashier, helped behind the bar at the Flamingo Club on Pennsylvania Avenue. We are not a drinking family, but there's nothing wrong with serving people who do drink. It is legal, after all."

Maddie continued to inspect the stole. No, it was not an expensive fur, but it was nice enough. The pink acetate lining looked like silk. And it was well constructed.

"So she bought this for herself?"

"I couldn't say."

More like won't.

"Do you have any more of her clothes?"

"I wasn't supposed to—the landlord—"

"I won't tell anyone, Mrs. Sherwood. I'm just so—curious. I want to imagine her, to know her. If I could see her clothes—" All she really wanted to do was to prolong the encounter.

After a slight hesitation, Mrs. Sherwood produced outfit after outfit, clearly proud of her daughter's wardrobe. Each item was shrouded in a plastic dry-cleaning bag, but it took Maddie a moment to figure out what else they had in common—they were all a little dated. Not this season, not even last season. A sequined dress that was long by today's standards. One Chanel-inspired suit could have been almost ten years old, while the very tasteful black wool dress with a label from Wanamaker's looked exactly like one Maddie had worn to her father-in-law's funeral. It had been the height of style—two years ago.

Not a single one was yellow or green, Maddie noticed. So much for Madame Claire.

They walked back to the living room, Maddie's mind still on those clothes. Wanamaker's. The Philadelphia department store had never had a Baltimore branch. How did Cleo end up with a little black dress, a good one, from Wanamaker's? And the label had said size 14, but Cleo was almost certainly no larger than a 10.

"Mrs. Sherwood, did—Eunetta have a boyfriend? I know she went on a date that night, with someone new, someone that the cops never found and no one seems to know. But was she seeing someone else? Someone who might have given her that stole, those dresses?"

To her amazement, the question provoked a flood of tears from Mrs. Sherwood, who dropped her face into her hands. "She was a good girl, I don't care what people say or think, she was young and foolish, but she was good and she didn't start anything."

"She was foolish," the father said. "I'll give you that much. She was foolish and spoiled, but that's on you, Merva. You always made excuses for her, never made her take responsibility for anything."

"Are you saying—" Maddie stopped, stunned by the pain of a metal truck that had been hurled at her shins by the oldest boy, shredding her stockings and drawing blood.

"Don't you make my granny cry! Don't you talk about my mother! You get out. Get out get out get out get out get OUT."

The other little boy didn't even pick up his head, just kept pushing his red truck across the carpet as if nothing had happened.

"*Little Man!* You stop that right now, Little Man. What has gotten into you?" The grandmother was appalled, but Mr. Sherwood, while his expression was stern—his face seemed set that way, it was impossible to imagine him smiling—nodded, as if the boy had done his bidding.

Maddie limped out the front door and down the steps, not stopping until she was several blocks away. She caught her breath while sitting on a bus bench, examining the ruins of her stockings. And shins took forever to heal, she knew that. The wounds would keep opening, sticking to her hose, which would then stain as she peeled them off. Her legs were tanned from the sunbaths she took in city parks on these soft summer days, but she could never go bare legged into the office.

Still, the injury, the torn hose, were worth it, she decided. Her hunch was correct. Cleo had had a lover, someone who could afford such gifts—but couldn't afford to be known in the world at large. If the man who picked her up for a date on New Year's Eve was someone no one had ever seen before or again, then who had given Cleo these clothes?

If her date had given her the stole, wouldn't she have worn it that night, warm as it was?

Little Man

THE WOMAN MADE my mama cry. I mean, Granny. I call her by
both names because she is both to me now. When we first came to
live here, I had a mama and a grandmama. Then Mama moved out,
but she came back all the time, almost every week. She told me she
had a job where she had to sleep on the premises, she was working
so that one day we would have a new house here in Baltimore, a
house with a daddy—not my daddy, but a new daddy—and maybe
enough room so that I wouldn't have to share a bedroom with Theodore anymore. At Granny's, we sleep in a room with Aunt Alice,
Theodore and me in a single bed, and he moves a lot in his sleep
and sometimes he falls out. Okay, maybe sometimes I *push* him out,
but it's only because he's kicking and throwing his arms around in
his sleep and I need some space. My mama used to say that when
she lived here. I NEED SOME SPACE! Then she would grab a book

and her coat and run out and I was scared that she would never come back.

Then, one day, that happened. At first, Granny said she was in another city. "Is it Detroit?" I asked. Because Detroit is where my father went to live. My father's in Detroit and Theodore's father was killed in a war, although I don't know where the war is, I don't think there are wars anymore. But my father is alive, he could send for me, although he doesn't. It's probably because of Theodore. "No man wants another man's babies." Granddaddy told Mama that before she went to wherever she went, I think it was Saint Louis, it could be Saint Louis, sometimes she talked about Saint Louis.

Before she went away, she was here in Baltimore and she came to see us every week. She brought us presents. Granny told her that the money she spent on presents could be saved up, put away so we could be together again sooner. Mama laughed and said, "It's not your money, is it?" Her clothes got prettier and prettier. We had the prettiest mother of anyone, always, but after she moved out she began wearing fancy clothes with lots of fur. Fur on her sleeves, fur on her hat, and then, one day, an entire cape of fur. She said she worked for a clothing store and she was allowed to borrow the clothes if she didn't spill anything. I don't know why she had to sleep there, maybe she was the security guard. Anyway, that's why she got upset when Theodore tried to touch the cape, which she called a stole and I asked: "Stole from who?" Granddaddy laughed at that, but it wasn't a nice laugh. "Watch out for Little Man," he said. "Little Man's the smart one." "What am I?" Teddy asked. "The pretty one," our mama said. Who wants to be pretty? Pretty is for girls.

Then a few days after Christmas, Mama came by, she brought us the best gifts ever, Tonka trucks—a yellow tow truck for me, a red pickup truck for Teddy—even though we had just had Christmas. She gave Granny an envelope and her jacket with the fur on the wrists. "Why are you giving me this?" Granny asked. "I saw how you looked at it," she said. Granny said: "I got no place to wear it, you know that." Mama said: "Well, there are always funerals," and Granny told her not to talk like that, it was bad luck.

That was the last time we ever saw her. "When's Mama coming back?" I asked. At first, Granny and Granddaddy said "soon" but I could tell they didn't know. Granny began to cry a lot, when she thought we couldn't hear her. Aunt Alice cried, too, late at night. Then a couple of weeks ago, a man came to the door and everyone in the family cried, but it was a kind of crying I had never seen, more like shouting. It was almost like watching a scary movie, the kind I sometimes sneak with Aunt Alice, there's this one about a man who steals ladies and makes them into statues and when the bad thing happens, when you jump, it feels good in a strange way? It seemed to me that it was like that, that the bad thing had happened and now things might get better.

But Mama's never coming back, not really, and things aren't getting better.

It's summer now. Yesterday, Granny almost laughed again, at something Teddy did or said. Teddy looks exactly like my mama, only he's a boy. Aunt Alice used to dress him up like a girl when he was a baby, as a joke, and people said things like, "What's a boy going to do with those eyes?" "Look at things," I said, and people laughed and laughed, which I liked and didn't like. After Mama went away, I kept trying to say funny things and do funny things, to make people laugh. Everybody's laugh is different now. It used to be so easy for me to make people laugh, but now they rarely do, no matter how hard I try, and when they do laugh, usually at Teddy, they sometimes end up crying.

So when I see that white woman, with her notebook and her schoolteacher voice, making my granny cry, I get up and I hit her with the truck, the last thing my mama ever gave me, I hit her as hard as I can, in the legs. Everybody begins shouting and I'm in a lot of trouble and Granny says I'm going to have to find a way to pay for the lady's stockings, which got tore up where I hit her. But I know I won't have to. Even Granny was secretly happy that I made her go away.

I make people go away. That's what I do. I made my mama go away and now she's gone forever. I used to worry that she was going to come back and take only Teddy with her because Teddy is pretty like her and he belongs in a place where there is fur everywhere. I wasn't sure I would fit in if we moved to a fancy house. Besides, I have a father and Teddy doesn't. They called him and asked if he wanted me to come to Detroit, but he's real busy. Besides, he said, I'd miss Teddy, and maybe I would. Although sometimes, I can almost remember when it was just Mama and me. I think I do.

And even once Teddy was here, I was special, we had things that were just for us. She used to ask me to zip up her dress before she went out. She's the one who named me Little Man. "Give me a hand, Little Man, you're the only man I'll ever need." "What about Teddy?" "He's a sweetheart, but you're my first, baby, and nothing can ever change that. You're the one I count on, Little Man. You're going to steer this family's ship."

I think that means I'm supposed to join the navy because we don't know anybody who has a boat. I know how to swim, though. My mama taught me. She didn't like to swim because of her hair, but she knew how, she was strong and fast and she would take me to the big pool at Droodle Hill, near the zoo, and get her hair wet, just for me. Just for me.

YOU DESERVED EVERY *bit of it, Maddie Schwartz. I wish Little Man had hit you harder. I wish he had bashed your head in with that truck.*

And you weren't done yet, were you? It wasn't enough to make my mama cry and to incite my sweet gentle Lionel to lash out. It wasn't enough to touch that fur, as Madame Claire had done. You had to know where it came from, who gave it to me. You had to pick, pick, pick, prod, prod, prod, never considering what you were kicking up.

Was I even real to you? Was I ever real to you? I don't blame you for not seeing me in the body at the morgue, that faceless monster. But you saw my photographs, you touched my clothes, you invaded my parents' home. You probably would have tried to walk through the rooms where I lived with Latetia if they hadn't been inhabited by new tenants.

You didn't care about my life, only my death. They're not the same things, you know.

July 1966

"**HERE YOU GO**," Bob Bauer said, tossing an envelope onto Maddie's desk.

"Are you delivering paychecks now?" she asked. She liked being pert with Bob Bauer, managing the trick of not quite flirting with him, but also not *not* flirting with him.

"Boss gave me two tickets to the Orioles game tomorrow night. For my work on the Corwin story. I can't use 'em and I figured—"

He did not finish the thought. Maddie wasn't sure he'd even had the thought, that he was capable of admitting that she had traded what was turning into one of the best stories of the year for this little-more-than-clerical job. Bob Bauer had published story after story about the stubbornly silent killer, his still-unknown accomplice, and the equally mysterious experiments at Fort Detrick, where Corwin had been posted after objecting to the draft on religious grounds, as a Seventh-Day Adventist, then dosed with bacteria. Bauer had even interviewed Corwin's mother, who had said sorrowfully that her son never seemed quite right after his time in the army.

Maddie felt like Jack from "Jack and the Beanstalk," only the beans she had received in exchange for her family's cow were just beans. She was not particularly impressed by a pair of baseball tickets, even if they were good ones, four rows behind the Orioles' dugout. But she took them, thinking that she would ask Seth, who would love the outing, might even be impressed that his mother had such good seats. Seth collected baseball cards and spoke about Brooks Robinson as if he were an Old Testament prophet.

"I have plans," Seth said when she called him that night. "I can't go."

"Can they be changed?" Maddie asked. "This seems like such a wonderful opportunity. The team is good this year, right?" She was pretty sure the Orioles were good this year. She didn't follow sports, but the *Star* had a tradition of running a page one cartoon that encapsulated the previous night's game. The pen-and-ink Oriole had been joyous and celebratory more often than not this summer.

"I just saw you last night," Seth said. He had. Another desultory dinner at the Suburban House. He'd chewed with his mouth open. Maddie had drunk coffee. Nothing on the familiar menu had appealed to her. She had begun reading the *New York Times* in the *Star's* library, copying recipes that appeared under a man's name, Craig Claiborne. She was particularly taken by a recent piece on leftovers. It had never occurred to her that one could fry a chicken ahead of time and then eat it cold on purpose. She had thought cold chicken was a default food, something to be eaten in front of the icebox, as Milton always had on the late-night raids that had added pounds to his midsection, which had led him to the tennis club at Cross Keys, which had brought Wally Weiss into her life and led her here. Just last week, she had presented Ferdie cold chicken and broiled tomatoes as a proper meal, and he had been impressed by her chicken. She did not tell him that it was from a newspaper recipe. She sensed he would find that ridiculous, following a recipe for fried chicken.

"Is there a rule that you can't see me two nights in a week?" Maddie had asked.

"I have plans," Seth said.

"A date?"

"Mom." He packed at least three syllables and so much disdain into the word that Maddie didn't have the heart to pursue the matter. She let him go. And when Ferdie came by later that night and they were sated, on steak sandwiches and beer and sex—the same article on leftovers had recommended grilling an extra steak and making sandwiches later, not that Maddie had any business buying steak on her salary—she asked Ferdie: "Do you like baseball?"

NOT QUITE TWENTY-FOUR hours later, they enacted the charade of two strangers, chatting pleasantly after finding themselves seated next to each other at Memorial Stadium. That is, Maddie chatted. Ferdie, it turned out, loved baseball and the Orioles. His eyes seldom left the field. He clapped and cheered with vehemence. Once, when a particular play delighted him—Maddie had been daydreaming, so she wasn't sure what had happened—he jumped to his feet so suddenly that the people around them started. Most Orioles fans tended toward a restrained politeness.

He was the only Negro in their section, Maddie realized. But, of course, they were very good seats. Her eyes traveled the stadium, searching the more affordable bleachers, the upper reaches. Almost all the fans were white. It was entirely possible that there were more Negroes on the field than there were in the stadium's seats. Didn't Negroes like baseball?

She almost touched Ferdie just then, but realized in time that she could not. She had a ticket, he had a ticket. It was happenstance that they were seated together. They chatted as strangers in a stadium might, polite and distant. *Do you like baseball? Yes, I played in Patterson Park when I was young, usually outfield, although I could pitch, too. At Poly, I played center field.* In some ways, she was learning more about him than she ever had in bed.

An Oriole swung, number six, his bat catching the ball and sending it into a backward arc toward them, but it landed a few rows up. Ferdie, his eyes following the trajectory, could have been a teenager; his yearning for it was that pronounced. He watched the lucky man who barehanded it give it to a little boy behind him and nodded, pleased by the man's generosity.

Sex that night was better than ever, which surprised Maddie. She didn't know it could keep getting better. But Ferdie seemed exhilarated—by the Orioles' victory, by the saucy naughtiness of their game, and he kept at Maddie with such enthusiasm that she was worried her little cries could be heard in the street, over the sound of the box fan in her window.

"I don't like that fan," Ferdie said.

"Because it's loud?" She had been grateful for the whap-whap-whap of the old-fashioned blades.

"Because you have to keep the window open when you use it. It's not safe, Maddie."

"You picked this neighborhood for me."

"I know. But—I was thinking of me, really. I needed a place I could come and go, without anyone caring. I thought this was safe enough. In the winter, when I met you, and things—windows—were locked up tight and the only reason I cared about the fire escape was for me to come up and down it before you got a phone. But now—I worry. Remember how we met."

Maddie looked at the African violet, huge and velvety.

"It's worked out okay. It's walking distance to the *Star*. Saves me bus fare. And when I take buses or cabs on assignment, they pay me back."

"Word is that you went to see Cleo Sherwood's parents."

This surprised her. "Word where?"

Ferdie sighed. "You're going to get hurt, going to neighborhoods like that. People are rioting everywhere. It could happen in Baltimore, too."

"It's Negroes getting hurt. Have you seen the news out of Cleveland?" Two black men had been murdered there, several white men arrested.

"There's no *story* in Cleo Sherwood being killed, Maddie. She was just a girl who went out with the wrong man."

"She had a boyfriend. Maybe he got jealous, maybe—"

"The bartender at the Flamingo described the man she left with."

"A man who wasn't her boyfriend." She was proud of how she made this a declaration of fact, how knowing she sounded, but she had no idea if this was true.

"The bartender at the Flamingo isn't anybody's boyfriend," Ferdie said.

"I meant—" She didn't go on. Ferdie knew what she meant. He was being deliberately obtuse.

He placed his hand on Maddie's midsection, a sign that he was done talking. She was embarrassed by her midriff. The current fashion magazines showed girls in bikinis that drooped on knobs of hip bones, their arms and legs skeletal. Maddie had always taken great pride in her slenderness, but she looked bovine when compared to these young girls. Dated, a woman from another era. She wanted to be modern and sleek, a rocket built for missions to the stars.

"I wish—" Ferdie did not finish his sentence right away and in that shining, open moment Maddie felt at once fearful and excited. What did Ferdie want, really?

"I wish," Ferdie repeated, "that I had caught that baseball. I would have given it to a kid, too. But I wish I could have been the one to catch it. Wouldn't that have been something?"

Number Six

BOTTOM OF THE third, I'm facing Lopez and the go-ahead run is on second. Lopez can be wild. He's already hit six batters this season and he wasn't trying to brush them back. He's got no control.

Ball one.

Ball two. It comes close to me. I can feel my teammates tensing in the dugout.

Strike one, looking.

Strike two—it tips off my bat, into the stands.

It's my third season with the Orioles, although I didn't get any real playing time in '64. One at-bat, one strikeout, in the lineup eight times total. Last year, I played a hundred sixteen games, hit .231. Not great, but better than Etchebarren, and my defensive skills can't be faulted. I also got hit by a pitch four times. I don't mind getting hit, but it's not the way I want to get on base.

The next pitch, it's going to curve, it's going to be just in. I swing, I connect, the run comes in, I'm on first. We're up, 2–1.

The Orioles fans are almost too polite, prone to murmuring, not shouting, but then they don't boo that much, either, so I guess it's a push. Still, even in the relative quiet of Memorial Stadium, you can tell the fans know this summer is special. We're magic. Here we are, almost to the All-Star break, and we're 54-25 and I'm hitting close to .300. I won't make the All-Star team. Obviously, that will be Frank, probably Brooks. But one day I'll make it, I bet. The All-Star squad, maybe a Gold Glove or two. I am twenty-two years old and I am making eight thousand dollars a year and I wake up smiling every day.

This is what I've wanted, all my life, since I was eight. Willie Mays was my hero, but when I saw my chance to make the majors, I thought, *I gotta find my own style, can't do that basket catch.* I didn't want anyone to say I was copying Willie. But I can play shallow, like Willie, chase balls in the gap. If I don't catch something, you can bet it's a home run.

After the game, I sit in my car, a '65 Dodge Dart bought for a good price when the '66 models came in, and the kids swarm, asking for autographs. As long as there's a single kid waiting for a signature, I don't leave. The fans are our real bosses, in the end. If they don't show up, we don't have a job. I'll sign cards, balls, scraps of paper, anything. And if a boy asks me if he should try to be a ball player, I'll say yes, dreams come true. I'm proof.

Today, a guy comes up, a little older than me. He doesn't ask me to sign anything. "I'm Ferdie Platt, just want to shake your hand, Mr. Blair. You are living the life." *Mister,* although he's got at least six or seven years on me.

But he's right. This is the life and I am living it.

July 1966

THE FLAMINGO WAS a bit of a disappointment to Maddie, not
because of its lack of grandeur—she had very low expectations for
the second-best club on Pennsylvania Avenue—but because of its
humdrum ordinariness, its very lack of danger. Of course, it was
only six P.M., early for decadence on anyone's clock, but the club
struck her as not that different from the Woodholme Country Club
on a theme night.

She took a seat at the bar, ordered a vermouth. The bartender
was white, a stocky man with dark hair and hooded eyes. Could
this be *the* bartender, the one who had described Cleo Sherwood's
date to police? She hadn't expected a white man in a club owned
by a Negro, which served mainly Negroes. She assumed a white
man would be less hostile to her, but he leaned back, arms folded,
making no move to prepare her drink.

"We prefer," he said, "that our lady customers be accompanied by men. And even then, we don't seat them at the bar. The owner finds that—" He paused, searching for a word. "Disreputable."

"I'm not a customer," Maddie said.

"Good, you catch on fast. Why don't you go hang with the ladies at Hutzler's tearoom? That seems more your style. Or if you really want a drink, the Emerson Hotel."

"I'm a reporter."

Was that amusement in his sleepy eyes? At any rate, he served her, then went to the end of the bar to continue his prep for the evening. She sipped the drink, surprised to find it comparable to the vermouths she'd had in other bars, then realized how silly she was to be surprised. There was not a lot of variety among vermouths. Wines, yes, whiskeys, yes, but vermouth in Maddie's experience ran to sweet or dry. This was a sweet one.

A girl walked in, wearing slacks and a loose blouse, glanced curiously at Maddie, then at the bartender.

"What's your story?" Maddie asked the bartender.

"Don't have one."

"Everybody has a story."

"I don't think that's true. You'd be surprised how many non-stories I hear in a night. What's yours?"

"I told you. I'm a reporter."

"Which rag?"

"The *Star*."

"Never read it."

"Which paper do you prefer?"

"The *Beacon*."

"Why?"

"It's the thickest and I've got a parakeet."

Maddie sipped her drink. Not that long ago she would have been rattled by his hostility, the gamesmanship. She would have started gabbing or maybe even flirting. Now, his attitude just convinced her that she was finally in the right place. The last place that Cleo Sherwood had been seen, heading out with a man no one knew or recognized. According to *this* man.

"I'm working on a story about Cleo Sherwood."

"No story there."

"How can you say that? A young woman has died, under mysterious circumstances. Of course that's a story."

"Maybe I should say, no story *here*. Whatever happened to Cleo—it doesn't have anything to do with the Flamingo."

The young woman who had eyed Maddie earlier returned from the back room, now arrayed in the club's signature costume, fishnet stockings and a leotard with pink feathers at the neckline and around the tailbone. *Oh how sad, how dreary,* Maddie thought. Could anyone find this costume glamorous? She thought of Cleo, the surprisingly fine clothes she owned. Clothes provided by someone, she was sure of that. Find the man who gave her clothes and find—well, something.

"Did you know Cleo?" Asking the girl, not the bartender. Predictably, the girl looked to him for guidance. He met her eyes, nothing more.

"How could I?" she said, putting glasses on a tray. "I took her spot. I wasn't here when she was."

The bartender could convey a lot in a look, give him that.

"Good point." Maddie turned back to the bartender. "But *you* knew her. You worked with her. You described the man she left with that night—early morning—of New Year's Day. Described the man and what she was wearing."

"Yep."

"Tell me."

"It's in the police report, which I'm assuming you've read. You think I'm gonna say something different? I'm not gonna say something different."

She flipped open the narrow steno pad and looked at her notes. *Cleo did not introduce her date, who came into the bar about four* A.M. *She had changed into a green blouse, leopard pants, a red car coat. She wore heels and carried a large green purse. Driving gloves of red leather. The man was a tall, dark-skinned Negro in a black leather coat and turtleneck, maybe in his thirties, with close-cropped hair. Very slender, quite dark.* That fact had been repeated twice in the police report. Was that because the bartender thought it significant or the police did? *It was my impression that she was upset he had come inside. She said: "I told you to wait outside." Maybe she didn't want to be seen with him, but I don't know why. He wasn't anybody to me. I never saw him before and I haven't seen him since.*

"Tell me about her. I mean Cleo herself. What was she like?"

Something went soft in his face. To say he was not a handsome man would be generous. His skin was bad; his hair, while thick, was clearly receding; his nose was bulbous. But he had the bartender's way of inviting confidences, and not just in patrons. It seemed likely that Cleo would have chattered to him. He probably knew more about her than her mother did.

"She was nice," he said. "Smart. Big personality, bubbly. She deserved better than she got in this world. Most people do."

"The man she saw that night—"

"I didn't know him. There's nothing more to say."

"But there has to be. I want to know who *she* was. I want to know what she dreamed about, what she wanted."

"Whatever it was, it died with her."

A thin, feral-looking man, a Negro, entered. Just as the bar-maid had been able to interpret the bartender's look, the bartender seemed to know immediately what was on this man's mind.

"She says she's a reporter, Mr. Gordon. I didn't want to give her the bum's rush."

So this was Shell Gordon.

"Why would a reporter be in my club? Nothing to report on here."

He had directed his question to the bartender, but the bartender didn't answer and Maddie felt bold. "I'm from the *Star*. I'm working on a human-interest piece on Cleo Sherwood."

"Leave that girl be," he said. "Hasn't she done enough harm?"

Maddie did not miss his turn of phrase. What harm had Cleo done? She was dead, after all. Had she caused her parents' grief? Clearly. Had she abandoned her babies? Yes. But no one had come to more harm than she had.

"How much do you pay your girls?"

"You're too old to work here," Mr. Gordon said. "Among other things."

"I ask because Cleo Sherwood had such fine clothes. I'm surprised that she could afford them, working here behind the bar. Cocktail dresses, furs."

Only one fur that she knew about, but *furs* sounded better, more substantial.

Mr. Gordon walked to the bar, took Maddie's glass of vermouth. "On the house," he said. "If you leave *now*. If you stay, you won't be able to afford it. You cannot afford to stay here."

She knew he was a powerful man. But as a white woman, she believed she trumped him, even on his own turf. He wouldn't hurt her. "And if I don't leave?"

Mr. Gordon turned to the bartender. "Spike? Please see her out. *Now.*"

For the first time, the bartender, Spike apparently, seemed discomfited. He had probably escorted many men, even a few women, from the premises. But he did not know how to approach Maddie, how to touch her. Perhaps the expectation was that she would be cowed and leave on her own. If so, then she was proud to call their bluff. Shell Gordon had put her drink back on the bar. She picked it up and sipped it.

Spike sighed, flipped up the pass, and crossed to her side of the bar. He was tall and powerfully built. He could drag her from the stool easily. But he seemed reluctant to put his hands on her. He reminded Maddie of a cartoon dog, maybe one she had seen when Seth watched *Donadio*. Fang, the dog was called, or something like that. Fang had a raspy voice, like this man.

"Miss—"

"Mrs." It seemed more formidable, being married. Besides, technically, she was.

"You have been asked to leave."

"I don't think you have the right to refuse someone service."

"I most certainly do," Shell Gordon said.

"Then call the cops," Maddie said.

"You think I won't?"

"Oh, I think you will. I'd love to know what the complaint is."

"We don't serve unescorted women at the Flamingo. It's not that kind of place."

Maddie laughed, and this seemed to infuriate Shell Gordon more than anything she had said.

"The Flamingo is a club with standards," he said, the color rising in his skin, which wasn't much darker than Maddie's. "It's a place for gentlemen—and gentlewomen. Some of the best acts in America have played the Flamingo. It is my club and I make the rules. You want to come see one of our fine musical acts, you come back with a gentleman. Assuming you know any."

Maddie assessed the situation. She could stage her own sit-in, but to what end? "I'm happy to leave, if Mr.—what was your last name, sir?—will walk me to my car. It's not the safest neighborhood these days.".

"Take her out, Spike."

Outside on Pennsylvania Avenue, the sky still light, the weather warm and sultry, Maddie doubled down on her lie: "It's some blocks away. Sorry."

He grunted. She let a block pass in silence, then said: "Did you *like* her?"

"What?"

"Cleo. Did you like her?"

"Sure. Everybody did."

"Except the man who killed her, obviously."

Silence.

"Would you tell me one thing about her, anything? A detail I can't know from reading things." She waited a beat. "And going to the morgue."

Another long silence, until she despaired that he would ever speak. But then: "She was like a poem."

"What?" She hadn't expected any response, much less an answer that was at once tender and provocative.

"There was a poem they made us memorize when I was in school. I never understood it. But it was about a woman, whose looks went everywhere."

"'My Last Duchess.'"

"That sounds right."

"'She looked on, and her looks went everywhere.'"

He shrugged.

"She had a date the night she disappeared. That's not up for dispute. You told the police that she had a date. You described him, described her, in great detail. But there was another man, right? A man you saw more often, just not that night?"

"Look, you've got it all wrong."

"I wish you'd tell me how."

"You're picking up rocks, but there's nothing under them. The other man she was seeing—he didn't have anything to do with this."

"How can you be so sure?" She figured she had two or three more blocks before she had to confess she didn't have a car. Maybe she could pretend ownership of one on the street, fumble for keys. "Look—when I was young, much younger, I had a secret. There was a man, a married man. He could have ruined my life. He almost did but I got lucky. If her married boyfriend's not part of her story, then that's that. But there is a boyfriend, isn't there? And everyone seems terrified of people knowing that. Why?"

"Just leave her be. Please."

"Tell me one thing that no one knows about her. Just one."

He thought for a moment. "She wouldn't want you to be making trouble for him. She cared about him."

"Was she in love with him?"

"I said what I said. You think about words too much. They're just—words."

Maddie could have said she cared about Milton, still. It wasn't the same as love. It was barely in the same universe.

"I feel like you know more than you're telling me."

"Everyone does."

"You mean, everyone knows more than they say or everyone knows more than I do?"

"Both. You don't have a car, do you?"

"Nope." She felt giddy with deceit.

"I'll hail you a cab and pay the fare if you promise never to come back."

"I'm not going to make any promises."

"Figures. I'll pay the fare anyway."

He found a cab quickly. When she was in the backseat, he leaned in and said: "You're going to hurt people if you don't stop this. Maybe even yourself."

Madame Claire had said much the same thing. But Madame Claire, Maddie reminded herself, was full of shit.

The Bartender

I CAN SPOT trouble. You might say it's what I do for a living, my real job, with the drink-mixing just something to keep my hands busy. I'm here to make sure that if trouble walks in, it walks right back out. Mr. Gordon doesn't have the best rep, but he's been good to me, and I do my best to be loyal to him.

But anyone could tell she was trouble. Even the dim bulb we have on table service figured it out. And Mr. Gordon, he doesn't miss a trick. Anyone who tries to put one over on him is asking for trouble.

I used to work for a guy named Maguire, who did business at the port. Nice fencing operation, nothing too big, but he overreached, decided he wanted to have this retail operation as a legit way to move money. Borrowed to buy a big warehouse in Southwest, was going to sell architectural salvage, got in way over his head. Got to the point where even a bust-out couldn't square what he owed. But

Mr. Gordon is a businessman, his eye always on the almighty dollar. They had a sit-down, talked about what could be done, Mr. Gordon as nice as any bank manager although it was understood that the penalties would be considerably higher if payments were not to his satisfaction. He took the warehouse, everything in it, got the debt down to something Maguire had a shot of making good on. Over the course of the meeting, Mr. Gordon asked if Maguire would give me to him, sort of a marker, until he was paid up. I think it amused Mr. Gordon to buy a white man, in a sense. Or maybe he was trying to say he'd kill me if my boss didn't make his payments.

My boss didn't think twice, said, "Sure, you can have Tommy." Mr. Gordon said, "Tommy's a boy's name, I'm going to call you Spike 'cause you look like a dog I once knew, a spaniel named Spike." Again, I think it amused him, deciding to take me, rename me, compare me to a dog. We all pretended it was only temporary, but I knew that if I was good at my job, Mr. Gordon was going to want to keep me.

And if I wasn't good—well, I didn't want to find out what happened if I ever disappointed Mr. Gordon.

Back then Shell Gordon made most of his money on gambling and running whores, but, yeah, he's moving into drugs. There's just too much cash to be made to ignore it. Yet he loves the Flamingo, wants it to be a really classy joint. It's like he's at war with himself. He wants to be legit, but there's too much money on the other side. And he needs the crooked money to be legit. Maybe in his head, he believes he'll get out of the rackets one day, but it's never going to happen. He has too many secrets. If you're smart, you don't talk about them, ever.

Behind the bar at the Flamingo, I keep the drinks going, but my principal job is to manage the girls, help them find that sweet spot between hosting and serving. It's important to Mr. Gordon that the Flamingo be respectable. He has plenty of other places to run girls, and truth be told, that's how a lot of Flamingo girls end up, but he won't tolerate any of that stuff at the club itself. He knows people say it's a poor imitation of the Phoenix, but then, at this point, almost everything on Pennsylvania Avenue is a poor imitation of what it used to be. The shops, the houses, even the people are droopier, dirtier. If the girls want to date the guests, that's okay, but it has to be on their time, in their own clothes. We're not running a whorehouse. It's a respectable place that books the second-best acts available— the Phoenix gets the best, no reason to pretend otherwise—a place where gentlemen and ladies should feel at home.

Ezekiel "EZ" Taylor is Mr. Gordon's favorite guest. He just loves that guy. A big man, shy, not much for talking. He comes for the music. Hardly ever drinks. Orders a port to keep others company, nurses it all evening, then picks up the tab. He's polite that way. He always wants everyone around him to feel good, be comfortable. That's what Mr. Gordon sees in him, his give-and-take with others. That and his mind for numbers, almost as good as Mr. Gordon's.

I asked him the onct— *What's with the dry cleaners, Mr. Taylor? That doesn't seem like a way to get rich.*

He said, "Think about it, Spike. Who buys clothes that have to be dry cleaned?"

"Rich people," I said. "But—" I was embarrassed to finish my thought.

He smiled. Again, that was his way. He wanted people to feel comfortable, always. "You were going to say, 'Negroes don't have money.'"

"I mean, some do. You do, obviously, Mr. Taylor. And Mr. Gordon."

"Plenty more as well. More than you know and the number's just going to keep going up, up, up. But the thing is, all you need is people who *aspire*. Say there's a lady, she teaches school, saves up for a nice coat, a fur even. Where is she going to take it when it's time to be cleaned and stored? You think she wants to drive out to a store way out north? No, she wants to take it to somewhere in her neighborhood. That's why EZ Kleeners has—"

"'Five convenient locations in the Baltimore metro area. EZ does it!'" It was one of those commercials that everyone in Baltimore knew, up there with "Mommy, call Hampden" or "More Parks sausages, Mom—pleeeeeeeze." Ray Parks was Willie Adams's ticket to respect; Shell Gordon thinks that EZ Taylor can be his.

"People like to keep their money in their neighborhood, when they can. And you know something else, Spike? Names are destiny. I was born Taylor. Taylor—tailor. Get it? I started at Hamburgers, in alterations. But the thing is, a man gets a suit altered only once. He has to get it *cleaned* over and over again. That's all I had, one idea, but it was all I needed. Offer the thing that everybody needs, all the time. Opened the first EZ Kleeners six blocks from here right after the war. What's your one idea, Spike? Maybe it's in your name. Maybe you should be running a knife store or a security company."

I smiled because Spike isn't my name. I'm Thomas Ludlow and I can't figure out what my destiny is. I see myself as a knight, looking for ladies to save, but my name suggests a person who can't rise above his station. Ludlow? Laid low.

Yet who was I to argue with EZ Taylor? He's rich. I'm a kid from Remington who worked for a two-bit criminal who ran up a gambling bill with Shell Gordon, then sold me. Anyway, I liked EZ. Everybody does. Nicest, gentlest guy you ever met. He doesn't deserve to have some reporter digging in his life. He didn't do anything, that's for damn sure. EZ is entitled to coast, not knowing what's going on beneath the surface of things. That's one of the best things about being rich. You get to coast.

I still liked EZ even when he started to fall for Cleo Sherwood. Lots of men took a shine to Cleo. I'm one of them. Not that there was ever anything between us. Cleo required one of two things to be interested in a man—good looks or a healthy wallet. I know I don't have either. Never going to have the first and it's not looking too good for the second.

But that was okay. Then I saw her falling in love with Mr. Taylor, which I didn't expect. I mean, really falling, not just taking him for the gifts he handed out. Oh, she didn't tell me anything, but I could see the shine on her. He took her places she had never been before. Restaurants, trips out of town even. I kept thinking, *This has to be for show, she can't love an older man like that, no matter how much money he has.* Soon, the shine on the two of them was so bright that Mr. Gordon couldn't help noticing. He was not happy.

"That's gotta stop," he said to me. I just nodded. I'm not Cupid. I don't decide who loves who. But we put Cleo behind the bar with me, didn't let her circulate in the club when Mr. Taylor was there.

Mr. Gordon also had a little talking-to with EZ. He said yes, yes, yes, he understood, he needed to be a happily married man if he was going to help Mr. Gordon realize his dreams. Then Mr. Gordon had a sit-down with Cleo and she promised she would break off with him, gentle like. But all Mr. Gordon achieved was to drive them deeper into hiding, which made it more exciting. Now they were going behind everyone's backs, not just Mrs. Taylor's. Cleo's eyes glowed like emeralds. It was a contest and she was sure she was going to win. She couldn't have told you what the prize was if you asked her. I know. I asked her. All she wanted was to win. She talked about going to Mrs. Taylor, telling her everything.

Then a day came when Mr. Gordon asked me to do something terrible. I said I couldn't. He said if I didn't do it, he'd ask someone else, someone who wouldn't care how it was done. Cleo had to go. Didn't care how, didn't care when, but it had to be me. And if I wasn't willing to do it, then maybe I wasn't someone he could depend on. Maybe I needed to go, too. It was crazy, what he wanted. It wasn't even good business. It wasn't business, period.

Do I have to paint you a picture?

After I put the reporter lady in the cab, I don't want to go back to work. My heart is sore and lonely, as it's been every night since December 31. I remember asking Cleo questions about her clothes. "Whatta you call a coat like that, open in the front? What's the point of gloves with holes in them?" Because I knew I had to be able to give a very specific description later.

I miss her. I miss her every day. I might miss her more than anyone else in the world. I didn't mind that she didn't love me.

The other thing—well, I try not to think about the other thing.

OH, TOMMY. I was the only one who called you that, remember? Not Spike, never Spike. Tommy. Spike is a dog's name and you were nobody's pet. Not even mine. I underestimated you, Tommy. But so did everybody else.

But look at me, apologizing to you. Your life might not be much, but it's still yours, you still have it. I don't blame you, but I'm not going to feel sorry for you.

Tommy.

July 1966

"THEY'RE VERY . . . VIBRANT," Judith said, looking at the
fabrics displayed on the counter at the Store.

"I've got my sewing machine back from the house," Maddie said.
"I could run up a summer dress for you, no trouble. That Butterick
pattern I used for this shift I'm wearing—I think it would work for
you, with just a little alteration." Judith was broader through the hips
than Maddie, narrower in the bust, but not by much and the pattern
was a forgiving silhouette.

"I don't wear a lot of prints," Judith said. "Let me think about it."

Maddie was rebuffed. No, she felt as if she *should* feel rebuffed,
then realized that her taste was more modern than her young
friend's. Judith was a conservative young woman in so many ways.
She still wore her hair teased, with a flip at the end, whereas Maddie now wore a chignon to the office, literally letting her hair down

when she was on her own time. And, no, Judith didn't wear a lot of prints. She liked a matchy-matchy style, shoes and purse and dress all the same color. Living at home as she did, she was able to afford quite a wardrobe for a young woman. Today, she was all in yellow— yellow pumps, yellow shift, a pastel yellow linen cardigan cinched at her shoulders with a butterfly clip-chain.

"That's pretty," Maddie said, touching the butterfly's golden head lightly with one finger. Its green eyes glowed.

"Korvette's," Judith said. "Only two ninety-eight."

Maddie widened her eyes, as if amazed by the detail. The clip was pretty in its way and did not look as if it had come from Korvette's. But here, among Betty Cooke's creations, the fake gold butterfly with its green glass eyes seemed almost an affront. She decided to buy a bolt of fabric for herself, all the while glancing longingly at the jewelry. *Oh, to be able to afford these lovely things.* But it would be a rare man who understood how beautiful these items were. Men were so traditional in their idea of what women desired. Cleo Sherwood's mysterious boy- friend, the one Maddie had yet to identify, had bought her clothing, not jewels. That detail still stuck out. A fur stole, not at all surprising. But the other clothes—a Chanel suit. (Well, a copy, but an excellent one.) That striking dress, something one of the Supremes might wear. The perfect little black dress from Wanamaker's. These did not seem like typical gifts to a mistress, if Cleo Sherwood could be called that.

Not that it mattered. Maddie had wasted so much time in look- ing into Cleo Sherwood that no one cared what she had discovered. She had proposed a piece on the psychic, then another one on the grieving parents, only to be told, no, not now. "Maybe a year from now," Cal had said. "On the anniversary."

"Anniversary?" How could such a lovely word be invoked for this circumstance?

"You know, a year to the day she went missing or, better, a year to the day she was found. Rutabaga, rutabaga, rutabaga."

June 1967, maybe January if she was lucky. It felt like a lifetime.

Over lunch at the Village Roost, she brought up her work woes to Judith. She and Judith had an odd way of relating to each other. They shared the conversation, as women are wont to do, but it was as if they were delivering unconnected monologues, cut down to socially acceptable chunks. Maddie talked about her job. Judith hinted, not for the first time, at how she wished she had a private place to "visit" with her boyfriend.

"Doesn't Paul have a place of his own?"

"Not Paul," Judith said. "Someone new. His father is gone, so he lives in the family house with his mother and has a much younger sister—there's no privacy to be had there."

"You have a new boyfriend?"

She blushed. It was possible, Maddie saw, for a woman to blush with pride. "I guess I have two! I don't know how I got myself into this situation, Maddie. This guy, Patrick Monaghan, he totally bird-dogged me after we double-dated at the drive-in two weeks ago. I wouldn't normally dream of going to a drive-in if it wasn't a double date because, well, you know."

Maddie did, although she had never attended a drive-in without Seth in the backseat. How seven-year-old Seth had thrilled to the adventure of going to the movie in his PJs, watching it through the windshield. It was funny about drive-ins. Almost everything about the moviegoing part of the experience was subpar—the sound, the film, the film's appearance, the refreshments, for which one had to trudge such a long way. Yet for a child, novelty trumped everything. How had that little boy, so easily excited by the world around him, ended up surly and monosyllabic? Was he that way with Milton? She wished she could ask.

"Paul knew Patrick from high school and I had seen him around at the Stonewall Democrat meetings. We fixed him up with a girl I know. I swear I didn't plan this."

So you planned it, Maddie thought.

"Anyway, he called me the very next day and there's just something about him. But—Monaghan! My parents would die. And he's not much more respectable than a cop. He works for the state liquor board. But, well, he's cute. The strong, silent type. I think I could really fall for him."

"It sounds—premature to be meeting him somewhere privately."

"We have to be careful! I mean, I'm still seeing Paul and it would hurt the other girl terribly if she knew that Patrick was pursuing me. We're just thinking about others."

Thinking about others while you cheat on them, Maddie thought. Was it cheating, though? The other girl had no claim on this Patrick; Judith had never been serious about Paul. She couldn't be. She had explained to Maddie several times that she had to marry a Jewish man. But then—she couldn't be serious about Patrick, either, in that case.

"Secret loves," Maddie mused. "The world is full of secret loves." She realized she had come too close to revealing her own secrets and added hastily, "I'm thinking of Cleo Sherwood, of course. I'm sure she had a boyfriend, or—a patron. But no one will tell me anything. I went to the Flamingo and they treated me like a leper."

"Shell Gordon's club?" Judith asked.

"Yes, he had me thrown out." A little melodramatic, but essentially true.

"Well, if Shell Gordon is worried, it probably has something to do with Ezekiel Taylor."

Maddie should have been thrilled to hear the name, any name. Yet it was a letdown that the thing she had been seeking fell so casually from the young woman's lips, that it could have been hers long ago if she had just thought to ask Judith more questions when Shell Gordon first came up.

"Where have I heard that name?"

"You probably haven't." Maybe it was Maddie's imagination, but Judith seemed to stress the *you,* as if Maddie's ignorance were specific to her, and anyone else would know. "But you must have heard of EZ Kleeners. 'Whatever you need cleaned, EZ does it!'"

"That's a dry cleaner, right?"

Plastic bags. All the clothes were in plastic bags. She had been looking at the labels, but maybe it was the dry-cleaning receipts that mattered, the paper on the hangers.

"Yes. He's also the man that Shell Gordon is backing to defeat Verda Welcome in the Fourth District."

"And Taylor was Cleo Sherwood's boyfriend?"

"No idea. All I said was that if Shell Gordon was protecting someone, Taylor's the most likely person. They're thick as thieves, and that's not just an expression. Clothes aren't the only thing that get cleaned at EZ Kleeners, or so people say."

"Who says?"

A blithe shrug. "People. My uncle's friends. They also say Shell Gordon is a Baltimore bachelor, for what it's worth."

Maddie turned that phrase over in her head a few times, finally got it. "So Ezekiel Taylor is running for the senate. Obviously, a man running for office can't have a girlfriend."

"Oh, they can *have* them, Maddie. But they have to hide them.

If—and I really don't know anything—but if EZ Taylor was seeing this woman you're so obsessed with, all he had to do was be discreet. Women aren't going to vote for a man who humiliates his wife, especially Negro women, especially when there's a female incumbent in the race. But Taylor plays by the rules, appears in public with Mrs. Taylor, doesn't make waves." She smiled at Maddie's look of wonder. "I told you—the Stonewall Democratic Club is a good place to meet people. And to learn the skinny on stuff. I know so much about how the city works now. I'm making connections for myself, too. One of the state senators that my brother knows thinks he can get me a job at a federal agency, a good one. But I would need some way to commute, it's down in Fort Meade—I've probably said too much already."

"Everyone keeps telling me that the boyfriend doesn't matter because Cleo went out with a different man, someone no one knows, on New Year's Eve," Maddie said, almost to herself. "But what if it was all part of a plan? What if someone sent that man to kill Cleo?"

"Or what if Cleo died while she was with Taylor and they needed to create a story to cover up what happened? As they say, never get caught with a dead girl—or a live boy."

"*Who* says that?"

Judith just laughed. "Anyway, will you think about it?"

"Think about what?"

"Letting me use your apartment when you're not there."

"I'm always there, Judith. Except on Wednesdays, when I have dinner with Seth."

"Even that little window would be enough."

Yes, Maddie knew. It was enough. It could also be too much. "Judith, please be careful."

"I'm always careful."

"With your heart. That's the part they never tell us. They're so busy making sure that we, um, protect our bodies. But bodies are resilient, bodies can withstand a lot of pain. But your *heart*. If the first man you let into your heart isn't a good person, you'll never be the same."

Judith's blush this time was more traditional, the bright red of high embarrassment. "Honestly, Maddie, we're just going to—well, we're not going to do *that*."

"You could meet him at the movies, like you did with Paul."

"But I want to *talk* to this man," Judith said, almost as if surprised by her own desire. "If this were only necking, well, yeah, sure, we could go to the movies. I want to get to know him. He's so quiet. But I could tell, that night at the drive-in, he was looking at me. He wants to get to know me, too. But I can't even linger on the phone with him without my parents' getting suspicious."

Maddie didn't have much experience feeling envy for other women, but she knew a pang of it now. Ferdie was the strong, silent type, too. She had been seeing him for six months and she hardly knew anything about him.

"How do I find this Ezekiel Taylor?"

"Maddie, you should really meet my brother who's in politics."

"Judith, I'm not—I'm happy as I am, I don't need a fix-up."

"My brother's not looking to be fixed up, either. But he *knows* stuff, Maddie. He'll know if you're on the right track. I keep telling you—"

"I know, I know. I should come to meetings of the Stonewall Democratic Club."

The B'hoy

THE SECOND I walk into the bar at the Lord Baltimore, I know which brunette is my brunette, the one my baby sister asked me to see. The woman is quivering like a greyhound, eating pretzels one after another. Judith has assured me that this is not a social meeting. God, I hope so. Judith seems to be the only person in the family who has a sense of who I am, although we never talk about it, of course. She tells people I'm married to my job, too hard-driving for a romantic life, much less marriage and family. That's not untrue. It's truer than most things you could say about me. I wouldn't have time for a family even if I wanted one.

But, oh my God, if I were to choose a bride, my mother would plotz if it could be someone like this Madeline Morgenstern Schwartz, although she wouldn't be happy about the divorcée part. My mom is very hard on other women. Can you blame her? My father—well, let's just say we're lucky that the only public *shanda* in the Weinstein family was the bankruptcy of Weinstein's. Not that I know things. I don't want to know things. That's our specialty in the Weinstein family, not asking questions, leaving the stones unturned.

She sips a martini, eyes demure. Flirtation is her automatic mode, I can tell, natural as breathing. The women I interact with, because of my job, are either flirts or steamrollers. I wonder, sometimes, in which camp Judith will land. Once she hooks a guy, I suspect she'll be more like our mother, trying to control everything, which is the obvious way to be when you control nothing. I don't think Judith has picked up on all the things I've figured out about our parents. She was so young, a baby really, when everything was happening. She's still a baby, in a way, living at home. She thinks she wants out, but I'm not sure why. I'm trying to get her a secretarial gig at NSA, through a guy who knows a guy. I hate calling in favors, don't like to be in anyone's debit column. But I'll do it for Judith, although if she thinks she's going to be allowed to move down to Howard County she really doesn't know our mother. Only marriage is going to get her out of that house. And the guy better be Jewish. Judith has *shaygets* fever. She thinks I don't know, but I do. Redheads, she's forever running around with redheads. She better get that out of her system or she's going to be disowned, not that there's anything to inherit.

"What do you need to know?"

"Why does Shell Gordon want Ezekiel Taylor to get the Democratic nomination for senate?"

I love how she just pulls her big gun out. Experienced reporters palaver, toy with you, waste your time. This one has no idea what she's doing, but at least that means I won't be here long.

"He sees an opportunity, pure and simple. Willie Adams is beefing with Verna Welcome, thinks she's not loyal to him. Jack Pollack, who used to control the Fourth, thinks he can get the seat back. With the field this crowded and two senate seats open, anything could happen. But, hate to burst your bubble, Shell had no reason to get rid of Cleo Sherwood. She made Ezekiel happy and the affair gave Shell even more power over EZ."

I don't tell her that I've heard Shell has been trying to find new girls for EZ, but he's not having it right now. Maybe he's waiting to see how the election turns out, if he's going to have to learn a new level of discretion. He's a long shot and maybe he likes it that way. But Shell isn't going to give up on Taylor. He's almost like a nagging wife trying to force her husband to be ambitious.

The girl frowns. It's a pretty frown. "But if she had gone public, made a fuss, that would have been bad for everyone."

"Girls like that never make a fuss. She knew the score. Besides, she was with another man the night she disappeared. That's an established fact."

"Is it?"

It's hard not to reach over and pat that earnest little head. "Everybody loves a good conspiracy theory. I bet you think the Warren Commission was wrong when it ruled that Lee Harvey Oswald acted alone."

"No—no. It never occurred to me to question that."

"Life is very simple, miss."

"Mrs.," she corrected.

"More often than not, things are pretty much as they seem. Maybe that doesn't make for good movies or page one newspaper articles, but that's how the world works. Okay, sure, this girl they found in the fountain, she dated EZ Taylor. Successful men, rich men—they've always had women on the side. It's no big deal."

"But he wouldn't be able to run for office if people found out."

"No one was going to find out. This happens all the time, *ma'am*." Heh. She doesn't like *ma'am* any better than she liked *miss*. Be careful what you wish for, honey. "All the time, at every level. Men are men. *Presidents* have fooled around—look at Warren Harding. FDR, probably. LBJ, almost definitely. But it's understood if you keep things discreet, keep up appearances, no one talks about it. And Taylor's a long shot, anyway. Shell hasn't built the coalitions he needs to get his own candidate in. Maybe two, four years from now, but not this year."

She looks chastened but not defeated. The set of her jaw—she's going to keep going. Not my problem. I've told her how things work, the way I promised my baby sister I would. Maryland politics 101. It's all about money and organization. The Democratic primary is the real contest, especially in Baltimore city, and it's winner take all, no runoffs. We'll know the winners by the morning of September 14, but we'll pretend it's a contest until November.

I pay for our drinks, or try. She picks up the check, says she'll expense it. Says a newspaper reporter can't have sources buying her anything. I wonder where she heard that one? I pick up checks for reporters all the time, send them whiskey at Christmas, hams at Easter.

We part ways at the corner of Charles and Mulberry. It's close to dusk, but she says she lives only a block away.

"Do you live up this way?" she asks me.

"Oh, I'll just catch the Charles Street bus," I say, not answering her question.

Once I'm on my own, I take a circuitous route, although it's not as if anyone is following me. I'm heading to Leon's, a discreet place on Park Avenue, not even ten blocks from where she lives, but it's a whole different universe.

Once there, I realize all I want is a drink. I don't have the energy for company. A burden lifts the second I walk through the door at Leon's. It's just a relief sometimes to have a drink in a place where I'm allowed to be myself, in total. I can finally be me. Not Donald Weinstein, *macher,* mensch, the hard-driving chief of staff for a guy who could be governor in eight years. I used to be just a muldoon, a foot soldier, but now I'm a b'hoy, calling the shots, making the deals, getting things done. I'll know I've really made it when I have a nickname, like Harry "Soft Shoes" McGuirk, or even Shell Gordon, who's nursing a beer in the corner. I don't care what my nickname is, as long as it isn't *fagalah.*

My life, my preferences—plenty of people know, but no one ever talks about it. I guess people—my boss, my sister—think they're doing me a favor, ignoring the obvious, making jokes about "Baltimore bachelors." I have two friends, Ron and Bill, they share a little house in an out-of-the-way neighborhood up in the Northwest, and everybody seems to think they're just two swinging single guys, on the prowl for women. Ron drives a flashy little sports car, they're both handsome guys. I was over there on Halloween last year and the boy across the street came to the door, trick-or-treating, dressed as a woman. We all had a good laugh at that, gave the kid extra candy. One day, he'll look back, connect the dots, a house full of men at a Halloween party. Heck, maybe one day he'll be one of us. Who knows? I was in my teens before I figured it out, in my twenties before I dared to act on my desires. And I have to be so careful, while the Ezekiel Taylors of the world just have to avoid embarrassing their wives.

An early mentor once told me that the secret to getting by at work was to carry a legal pad and frown; everyone assumes you're doing something important. But I feel as if that's my life, too, that I am charging down the streets of Baltimore with an invisible legal pad always in my hand, brow furrowed in concentration, and no one sees what I'm really up to. "He's married to his job," my mother says, with equal parts pride and exasperation.

It's true. What other option do I have?

July 1966

SHE HAD WORRIED that Judith's brother might insist on walking her to the door, maybe even make a pass. As soon as she was a block west of Charles Street, she hailed a cab.

Men were no help, after all, she had decided. Men kept each other's secrets. Men put men first, in the end. It made no sense for Cleo Sherwood to be killed by some strange man in a turtleneck who was never seen again. Sure, it could have happened. Bad things happened to women all the time. But Maddie was sure that Ezekiel Taylor was the link. And no one cared because no one cared about Cleo. Well, Maddie cared. She cared enough to challenge Mr. Taylor's alibi. And there was only one way to do that, one person.

The cab took her to one of the still-grand blocks near the park. Not that far, her mind registered, from the lake, the fountain. Her own maternal grandparents had lived on this street once; The Park School had started not far from here. It was still relatively early. She was betting that Mr. Taylor was not someone who rushed home. Married men who dallied with young women did not rush home; Maddie knew that about them. She knew more than she wanted to know about married men. It was time to put that knowledge to use. Just as she had drawn on her memories of her old necking spot to find Tessie Fine's body, she would now rely on her regrets to inform her quest into the life of a young woman who had made a similar mistake. Maddie had never confronted her lover's wife. But she would come face-to-face with the woman married to Cleo Sherwood's lover.

The Taylor house was a grande dame among ruffians. Most of the other big old houses had been subdivided; there were telltale signs of a neighborhood losing whatever self-respect it once had. The tiny yards were not being maintained and in the meticulous hedges guarding the Taylor home, someone had left a Zagnut wrapper. The better-off Negroes were beginning to abandon the neighborhood, just as the Jews of Milton's generation had. These beautiful old town houses—not rowhouses, not here, they were too wide, too architecturally distinct—had stood for so much once. For dreams and aspirations. But there would come a day when they were all cut up into makeshift apartments. She was surprised the Taylors had remained.

Once the cab let her out, she stood for several minutes on the sidewalk, knowing how out of place she looked, not caring. She was tired of caring what others thought about her, more tired of how they thwarted her. First and foremost, Shell Gordon and those who worked for him. But also the cops, reporters, even Judith's brother Donald. The world kept telling her to look away, to pay no attention to an age-old system, in which men thrived and inconvenient women disappeared.

Maddie wasn't having it. She set her jaw, squared her shoulders, and marched up to the lovely house with the stained glass features and rang the doorbell.

The Wife

WHEN I GLIMPSE that white woman standing on my porch, bold as brass, I wish for the first time that I had listened to Ezekiel when he suggested we have servants. Of course, we have help—a young girl (not too young), who comes once a week to do the heavy cleaning—but Ezekiel took the notion a few years back that we should have live-in staff. At least, that's how it was presented to me.

I had come downstairs one day to find him at the kitchen table with a young couple, a husband and wife (or so they said, or so I thought, they could have been a brother and a sister, I suppose). They were country and fresh off the bus. I could smell the farm life on them, they had probably done their chores before leaving that morning. They were running away from something, I was sure of that.

But Ezekiel, who always took an interest in young people because, he *said,* we had not been blessed with children of our own, had seen them at that horrible coffee shop near the Greyhound station and brought them into our home. At least he had the good sense not to let them track up our rugs, to bring them through the back door and into the kitchen.

"This is Douglas Frederick," he said, "and Claudia Frederick. They're from Dorchester County." Notice he did not tell me why they shared a surname. So they could have been husband and wife or brother and sister. "They have gotten themselves in a spot of trouble, through no fault of their own, and they felt it was better to leave Cambridge."

"Hmmmm" was all I said, but I knew what was going on in Cambridge in the summer of 1963.

"Family reasons," the man put in. He was slick, I saw that right away, but he wasn't as slick as he thought he was, he was never going to be slick enough to get by Ezekiel Taylor. He had mistaken my husband's kindness for weakness, whereas the truth about Ezekiel was that he could afford to be kind because he had no weaknesses at all. Well, just the one. It's in his blood, he can't help it. When a thing is in your blood, what can you do?

The girl didn't say anything. She looked as if she were used to menfolk speaking for her, around her, about her. She had pale eyes. Not blue, not green, not hazel. Just pale. If I had to put a color to it, I'd say yellow, as faint as yellow can be, the color of urine when you're healthy.

Ezekiel picked up the conversational reins. Some men, when they're trying to get something past you, they talk fast. Not my Ezekiel. He slowed down, let his words roll along, meandering like a stream as if they had no particular place to go. But a stream is busy, a stream has purpose. A stream is full of life and agendas, many of them in conflict. It's a microcosm, a world. In a stream, there is life and death.

"So I see these two, looking overwhelmed, studying the menu, two little rabbits, counting their money, not enough to buy a decent breakfast between the two of them, he was feeding her bites from his plate, and I thought—we could use a couple around the house to help us out."

A *couple of what?* I was thinking.

"A handyman and a live-in girl to do the cooking and the cleaning."

"I'm a good cook, Ezekiel," I said. "You like my cooking."

"I love your cooking, sweetheart. I still want my breakfast to come from your hands, no one else's, but wouldn't it free you up if you didn't have to be the one putting dinner on the table every night?"

Free me up to do what? Free him up to do what?

He can read my mind, my husband, always could. He said: "More time for your church activities and whatever you want to do. I just want to give you the best life I can, Hazel. Let me do this for you."

The girl was looking down at her lap, where her hands twisted like two squirming animals, something newborn and blind, helpless. They were hard-looking hands, dry and cracked, but they weren't hard*working* hands. I can tell the difference. I was country, too, once upon a time, but it was so long ago people tend to forget, even Ezekiel. He forgets that I was young and sweet and slender, with a downcast gaze and a laughably homemade dress, and that he had never wanted anyone like he wanted me. So he got me. Ezekiel Taylor tends to get what he wants.

But not this time, I decided that day. Not under my roof. I had to draw a line. So I said no to Douglas and Claudia. That was three years ago and I hadn't given them a thought until I saw that white lady on my front steps and wished I had someone who could answer the door for me and say, "Go away, Mrs. Taylor is resting now."

I can just not answer the door, I think. *No one can make me open my own door.* But if I can see her aspect through the lace curtain, she can see mine. *Maybe,* I think, *she's selling cosmetics.* And, like a child, I believe my own wishful thought the moment I express it and by the time I open the door I am surprised that this woman does not have a valise. Ding-dong, Avon calling. Not a lot of Avon women are working Reservoir Hill these days.

"I'm Madeline Schwartz," she says, bright as a new penny. She's in her late thirties, a little older than she looked through my etched glass. I'm in my fifties, but I appear much younger than my years. I can pass for my forties, easily. But it was never about being young. Like I said, it's in his blood.

"Yes?" I don't tell her my name. If you're standing on my doorstep, I assume you know who I am, where I stand.

"Is Mr. Taylor home?"

"He is not." I know how, in three words, to say everything I need to say. And she's smart enough to hear what isn't said: *And I wouldn't call him to the door if he was. We do not do business in this house. If you really need to talk to Ezekiel Taylor, you should know that. No business is transacted here, ever, even of the non-financial kind. Not under my roof. You think I let Shell Gordon come to my house? Never. Ezekiel goes to him.*

"My name is Madeline Schwartz," she repeats. "I work for the *Star.* I'd like to talk to you about the night Cleo Sherwood disappeared."

"Who?" I say.

"The young woman whose body was found in the lake."

"Why?"

"She worked at the Flamingo, a place your husband frequents."

"Hundreds of people *frequent* the Flamingo, miss." This woman has not said she is a "miss," but what proper married woman would ever be on my doorstep, asking about my husband?

"Still, I thought—"

"This is not my husband's place of business. It is our home. We believe in—" My words falter and she jumps in:

"A strict separation of church and state?"

I understand the reference. I am a well-educated woman. I was, after all, attending Coppin, studying to be a teacher, when I met Ezekiel. But it hits me wrong, the way she says it, almost as if it's a joke. There is nothing funny about church. Without church, I don't know who I'd be, how I would go from day to day. Church, specifically, not Jesus. Of course I love Jesus, he gives my life meaning, but the church, its schedule and rituals—the church gives my life *shape*. Maybe it sounds funny to some, but I see my days as trees, like in the Tarzan movies. Every morning I get up, grab a vine, and hope it's long enough, my arms powerful enough, to carry me to the next one. I go to church, I change the altar cloths, the seasons pass, the years pass. Christ is born, Christ dies, Christ rises. Again and again and again.

"This is my home," I say, well aware that I have shifted from *our* to *my*. But it's true. I have absolute domain here. Here, things are proper. Here is under my control. Cleo Sherwood and her ilk have never crossed my threshold. A thought streaks across my mind— what if I had allowed Claudia and her "husband" into the house? What if there had been a baby in here, after all? Maybe she would have given it to me, let me have it. A baby could have changed every-thing. EZ wanted babies.

"I came to talk to you. Specifically about what you and your husband did New Year's Eve. Was he here with you? The whole night?"

But I am shutting my door. Slowly, majestically. I want her to glimpse the world behind me, the beautiful rooms, the fine antiques, some of them French. God did not give me children, so I have made our home—our home, Ezekiel, yours and mine, the place you come back to, eventually, every night or early morning—a blessed place, a beautiful place. I keep a fine house, I set a fine table, I make good meals. I listen to the radio, I am up on the news. I have done everything that a man can ask a woman to do, other than give him children. He has forgiven my body's shortcomings, so I forgive his.

That bold piece lingers on my doorstep for a minute or so, rings the bell a second time, as if her first conversation with me was a dress rehearsal. It was not. We are done.

It's not my fault that Cleo Sherwood was a careless young woman who couldn't stay alive. It's not my fault. Ezekiel doesn't even real-ize that I knew she existed. And if I didn't know she was alive—and isn't pretending someone doesn't exist the same as not knowing they're alive?—then how can I know anything about how she died?

Maybe I should have let them stay, Douglas and Claudia. Maybe everything would have been different. She could have been a daugh-ter to me. She was country, poor and rough, but I was country, too, once upon a time. Now look at me. I have beautiful clothes and pearls, a house full of satin and brocade and velvet. Maybe if I had been content to let these things happen under my roof, I could have kept everyone safe.

But I couldn't, I just couldn't. A lady has her limits. That's part of what makes one a lady, knowing her limits, respecting them. Whatever Cleo Sherwood was to my husband, she was not and never could be a lady. She was never going to be his wife, and I don't care what she ran around blabbing to people. She was deluded.

And now she's dead.

YOU WENT TO her door, rang the bell. I am almost impressed in spite of myself, Madeline Schwartz. You did the thing I longed to do, the thing I swore I was going to do. Oh, I talked a good game, that's for sure.

Do you realize that's why I'm dead, Maddie Schwartz? Because I talked about doing that, nothing more. Said I was going to confront her. Promises had been made and I was ready to call them in. Would I have done it? I don't know, but others made sure that I never had the chance to make good on my angry boasts.

Oh, Maddie Schwartz, do you have any idea what you have done?

PART III

"CLEO SHERWOOD WAS seeing Ezekiel Taylor. I'm sure of it."

Bob Bauer, his mouth full, was in no hurry to speak. He had just taken a bite of what appeared to be a Reuben sandwich and he was determined to enjoy it. He was a remarkably neat eater, Maddie noted, and not the type of person to rush his chewing just because someone was waiting for a reply.

"What of it?" he said at last, dabbing the corner of his mouth for a nonexistent drip of coleslaw.

"She was dating a married man, a politician—"

"A *candidate,* and not much of a candidate at that. Name recognition isn't everything. Just because you can get spots out of silk doesn't mean you can be a senator."

"I hear he's playing a long game." She asked for a coffee and, after a brief inward struggle, an order of fries. "He doesn't expect to win this time, but he had to start somewhere."

Bob Bauer smiled as if she had meant to be funny. "You hear things, huh? In the ladies' room at the *Star?* At the hairdresser's?"

"I have my hair ironed in the Fourth District, as a matter of fact." This was true, although the kitchen magician that Ferdie had recommended was silent as the Sphinx, providing commentary on nothing, not even the weather. "So, yes, I do hear things. Although my source on this is a legislative aide."

"And does your source work for another candidate? Or have reason to support another candidate? If he's an aide, chances are he favors the status quo."

"No—I mean, I don't think so. Besides, he didn't tell me about the affair. I put that together on my own, by talking to her mother, some other people."

"So he was having an affair," he said. "You can't write a story about that."

"She worked in Shell Gordon's club and he's backing Taylor for the Fourth District."

"Maddie, have you noticed how many pieces the *Star* has run about the Fourth District senate race?" His index finger and thumb curved until they met. "None. Zip. So Ezekiel Taylor had a girlfriend and she got herself killed. How is that a story?"

"What if she was killed *because* she was Taylor's girlfriend?"

"Do police say he's a suspect?"

Maddie had, after seeking John Diller's permission, asked the homicide detectives assigned to the case if Taylor or Gordon had been considered a suspect in Cleo Sherwood's death. "Just off the record," she had said, feeling very grand. "I have information that she was having an affair with Mr. Taylor, which wasn't good for his political ambitions." The detectives, who seemed to find everything about her mildly hilarious, had shrugged, told her that motives were for Perry Mason. They had reminded her that Cleo Sherwood's death was not, officially, a homicide. And then one of them, the younger one, had asked her out, but she had pretended not to understand the invitation.

"They still believe the bartender," Maddie said. "But if you ask me, his statement is fishy. There's almost too much detail. Why did he pay such attention to the man who picked her up, what he was wearing, what she was wearing? Men don't notice clothes that way. Certainly not a man called Spike."

"Still, the story is that you suspect a prominent Negro was having an affair, and that's it. You can't write that and we won't print it. It's libel, Maddie. It's also nobody's business. It would look as if the paper were peddling gossip provided by another campaign."

"He gave her clothes," Maddie said.

"Well, stop the presses."

"Clothes stolen from his customers," she said. "At least, I'm pretty sure that he took them from his cleaning business. You see, one of the dresses had a Wanamaker's label and it wasn't this season's—"

"You want to cover police or fashion? Seriously, you keep jumping to conclusions you can't support. You saw some clothes. Maybe they were left behind. You know the small print? 'Clothes left for ninety days will become the property, et cetera et cetera.' And even if you were right, what's the lede, Maddie? 'Ezekiel Taylor, candidate for the Fourth District senate seat, helped himself to some clothes from one of his five EZ locations'? Look, it's great that you're trying so hard, but this one's a dead end. A girl died. We don't even know how she died. If she had been found in a car or a bed, you wouldn't even care. The only interesting thing about it is where her body was discovered. Let it go. August is a slow month. Keep your eyes and ears open, volunteer to help out on cityside. You'll find a story you can actually get into the paper."

Disheartened, she headed back to the office. August was slow. In the city, in the newsroom. It felt as if the world had adjusted its pace to suit the long, hot days. The Orioles, in the hunt for the pennant, generated some buzz, as did the upcoming primary, which would decide most races in Baltimore and even the state, given the Democratic party's dominance. George Mahoney, the long-shot Democratic candidate for governor, walked so much as he canvassed that he showed his worn soles to reporters. In August, that was a story, the soles of a politician's shoes. Had it really been so naive to think that she could write about Cleo Sherwood and Ezekiel Taylor?

Even the mail to Mr. Helpline had slowed. The complaints that did arrive were pettier than ever, if such a thing was possible. Traffic-light issues, people who wanted Charles Street to go back to being two-way. Occasionally, there was a misplaced missive seeking advice on love problems. These were forwarded to Dear Abby's Chicago office, but Maddie's heart ached a little for the confused correspondents. One had to be extremely troubled in love to reach out to Mr. Helpline by mistake.

Men don't care about love, she grumbled to herself as she walked. Men thought love didn't matter, it wasn't *news.* Maybe they were right. Men deceiving women in love was the oldest story in the world.

And there, on the sunbaked August pavement, Maddie felt a chill unlike any she had known. Her legs shook so hard that she had to find a bus bench to sit down and catch her breath. Thrust eighteen years back in time—what had taken her there? Why was she thinking about this *now?*

She had been not quite twenty, married to Milton, the honeymoon phase over, money tight, but life pleasant except for the fact that she could not get pregnant. People said it was normal, that she was worrying too much, but Maddie had a specific fear and was terrified to tell her doctor about it. What if she never conceived? If she wasn't a mother, what would she be? She had put all her money— her life, not even two decades of it—on this bet, on being Milton's wife and partner. A homemaker, but one could not make a home for only two people. She watched the carriages multiplying around her modest neighborhood. Once the baby was born, she and Milton would leave the apartment for a house, life would finally begin. She had to have a baby, babies.

It was as she grappled with this fear and anxiety that a friend mentioned she had seen what appeared to be a debutante's portrait, an amazing likeness of Maddie, for sale at a local gallery. Maddie went to see it, and sure enough, there was the portrait Allan Durst Sr. had painted not even three years ago, the summer she was seventeen. It hurt to look at that painting. For one thing, she had to admit to herself that he was a terribly mediocre artist. The brushwork was proficient, nothing more, lacking any spark or wit now that she was not gazing at it through a love-struck haze.

And it hurt to realize that the girl in the painting had ceased to exist when the painting was finished, that she could never be retrieved. The girl that Milton could never have, that no one could have. The prize that Allan Sr. had insisted on having for himself.

Maddie asked the gallery's owner how the painting had come to be in his possession. She might have implied that the provenance was questionable, that it was clearly a portrait of her that had gone missing from her parents' home at some point. "If I could just get in touch with the owner, I'm sure we could straighten this out." She had assumed it would be Allan's wife, forcing him to purge his studio of his trophies. But it was Allan himself, and the address listed was in New York, on the Upper East Side, as she always suspected.

Two weeks later, she took the bus to New York, telling Milton she was going on a B'nai B'rith trip to see *Carousel,* that she would be staying over at a midtown hotel, sharing a room with Eleanor Rosengren. Lie on top of lie on top of lie, and the whole edifice would crumble if Milton ever thought to say anything to Eleanor or her husband. But Maddie knew by then that he would not. He was simply not interested in her day-to-day life. He, too, was anxious for a child and took it personally that Maddie could not get pregnant.

Maddie stood outside the address she had for Allan. It was April, yet it was snowing. She had a book with her, as if that would provide an adequate excuse for standing on a snowy New York corner. Eventually, Allan came out, hatless. He looked his age now, which was forty-four. He had always looked his age, actually—it was just that she couldn't see it when she was seventeen. He was attractive, though. She had not been wrong about that.

She planted herself in his path, ready to exclaim how small the world was. But the moment her eyes met his, she could not pretend. She began to cry, and not in a pretty way. Without a word, he took her by the elbow and led her to his apartment. He fixed her a strong drink, put together a late lunch for her out of things in the icebox, made small talk. She attempted to explain about the painting, tried to recover her pride by claiming she had been contacted by the gallery owner, who was nervous about whether he had the right to sell it. Allan's patient support of her subterfuge made her feel worse in a way. He said that his wife was in Mexico, because she had decided she could not paint in New York in the cold-weather months. Allan Jr., of course, was at college. Yale.

Of course? Oh, yes, he had gone to Yale, too. He had mentioned it often.

"My son is still a boy," he mused. "And yet you, the same age, are every inch a woman." He looked at, but did not comment upon, the gold band on her hand.

"You made me a woman."

"No, darling, you were a woman before I met you. And I wanted you to enjoy, at least once in your life, what it would be like to use that body as it was meant to be used. A woman such as you should be a king's mistress. For a summer, I could give you that experience."

"So you were a king?"

He had laughed at that. "Oh, Maddie, I know I'm a cad. I'm a terrible person. I tried to tell you that all along. You were beautiful, you wanted me, I was helpless. I'm sure it was some Freudian battle with Allan, a desire to displace him, to assert myself as the patriarch. But I won't apologize for any of it. And you, in your heart of hearts, know you should be thankful. Admit it—whatever you have now, it's not the same."

"It's better," she said.

"Don't lie."

"I'm not." She wasn't.

"Look, I'm not saying I have some level of technique in lovemaking that no other man can match. But what we did was sensual, we abandoned ourselves. You can't have that in a marriage."

She wanted to prove him wrong. And strangely, illogically, the only way to do that was to go to bed with him. They defiled his marital bed, lying in sight of his wife's work. (Which was, she saw now, exceptional and accomplished. She wished she could afford it.) The sex was fun, athletic, but Allan seemed pale and wispy after Milton's comforting bulk. She had vanquished him.

The very next night, less than an hour after stepping off the bus, she made love to Milton with a passion and a confidence that so delighted him he suggested she treat herself to more theater trips.

Nine months and two weeks later, Seth was born, an enormous child, almost ten pounds. She never doubted he was Milton's. He looked exactly like his father from the minute he emerged.

Sixteen years later, sitting on a bench in downtown Baltimore, she still had no reason to doubt Seth's paternity. Making love with Allan Durst Sr. had not been a mistake *that* time. She had broken his spell, and that was why she could finally conceive with Milton. Given how easily she had gotten pregnant the summer she was seventeen, she had expected it to be easy at twenty, too. But Seth was to be the first and last pregnancy she carried to term.

It was only now, twenty years later, that she saw how close to disaster she had flown, how easily her life could have been upended, by their affair and even the one-time coupling in New York. Why had she taken such risks? At least Allan was wrong. Her sensuality was not a fleeting thing, a gift he bestowed on her for one brief season. It had always been hers, it was hers now. If she ever did marry again, when she had the luxury of choosing for herself, she would know that kind of passion in marriage. It had to be possible.

She tried never to think about the ghost of a child left behind in the basement office of the doctor that Allan Sr. had found for her the summer she was seventeen, how her heart felt as if it folded in half when anyone said it was a shame that Seth had to grow up an only child. Milton might have forgiven her for being with another man before marriage, but what happened in that doctor's office when she was seventeen would be something he could never accept. Still, she had been punished for her sins, had she not? Only the one son when she had wanted a houseful of children, at least three, at least one daughter. She could have been such a good mother to a daughter.

Even good girls make mistakes when they're in love. But they don't deserve to die for them. Maddie had gotten out alive. Cleo Sherwood hadn't.

August 1966

SHE CALLED IN sick the next day. Her probationary period was over, she was entitled. She was not sure what would happen if it was discovered that she was not, in fact, sick, but she didn't worry about getting caught. No one from the *Star* was going to be lingering on Auchentoroly Terrace, watching to see Mr. Sherwood leave for work. *Waiting for the coast to clear,* she thought, taking her post just before eight A.M. Her mind picked at the origin of the phrase, jumping to the Longfellow poem about Paul Revere she had memorized as a child. She then thought about Edward R. Murrow's sonorous voice—"This is London"—those broadcasts that had led her to the radio club, her decision to join the school newspaper—so many seemingly insignificant moments, yet each one was building toward this life, her real life at last. *Go look for Tessie Fine,* her mother had said. She had and now she was here, sitting at a bus stop in a Negro neighborhood, conspicuous as—she still couldn't find the right comparison. At any rate, she stood out.

She sat on the bus bench on the park side of Auchentoroly Terrace, the sun on her shoulders, marveling at the fact that her mother had gone to school on this very street sixty-some years ago, and Milton's family had lived nearby until his father's death in 1964. The only sure thing was time's passing.

Shortly after eight thirty A.M., Mr. Sherwood left the apartment. She panicked for a moment. What if he were to walk to this very bus stop? She should have planned for that.

Luckily, he headed west. He wore some kind of uniform, a green one-piece. Gas station worker? Janitor? She realized she had no idea what he did.

Even with Mr. Sherwood out of the apartment, she still didn't want to knock on the door. The children would be there, the boys, possibly Cleo's sister and brothers. *Eunetta,* she reminded herself. *Don't call her Cleo.*

Summer would be over soon. It was almost eight months since she had left Milton, and they had made little progress in the divorce. She had thought he would accept the inevitability of their marriage's end when she found this job and it appeared she no longer needed his money. Only she did need his money. She couldn't live like this forever, scraping by week after week. How long would this drag on? Would it drag on like this summer day, waiting to see if Mrs. Sherwood would leave her apartment?

A marriage can drag on forever, she thought, *but it's a rare day when a mother with small children doesn't have to leave her home, if only to maintain her sanity. Little boys drink a lot of milk, eat a lot of food.*

She was right. Slightly before lunchtime, Mrs. Sherwood emerged, headed south. Maddie gave her a head start of a block, then trailed behind her, hanging back when she entered the corner grocery. When she came out holding a single bulging bag, Maddie was waiting.

"Can I help you with that?" she asked. She knew she would be refused, but it seemed nice to ask.

"I'm fine," Mrs. Sherwood said, shifting the bag in her arms, shifting her glance to the sidewalk.

Maddie fell in step beside her.

"Did Eunetta confide in you?"

"I'm not sure what you mean." Eyes still down, as if she were playing the old game. *Step on a crack, break a mother's back.*

"Did she tell you she was in love? Did she talk about him?"

"Which time? My daughter fell in love a lot, ma'am. Those two boys, my grandsons—that was love, too."

Too.

"So she had fallen in love again. Did she talk about him?"

"Not with me, no."

"But you must have known. That she was with Ezekiel Taylor. A mother always knows."

Maddie did not believe a word of what she was saying. Her mother had never had the slightest inkling about Allan Sr. If she had—well, her family would have found whatever the Jewish equivalent was to a convent and locked Maddie away.

"I'm not a stupid woman, Miz Schwartz. I know what those clothes had in common."

Maddie didn't. Did that make her a stupid woman?

"He gave them to her?"

"They all fit her perfectly, even though the sizes on the labels didn't match. Fit her like a glove."

Maddie thought of the shape of the woman she had seen behind the lace curtain. Imploring her—commanding her—to leave. Tall. Not fat, but broader than slinky Cleo. She wondered if Taylor had gone so far as to pilfer some of his wife's clothes and have them altered to fit Cleo.

"Was it serious between them?"

"He has a wife. How serious could it have been?"

"What do *you* think?"

"My daughter's dead. That's serious. That's as serious as it gets."

She had managed the trick of falling back a few paces, so she did not appear to be walking with Maddie. *Mrs. Sherwood doesn't want to be seen with me,* Maddie thought in wonder. Was she afraid word would get back to her husband? Or was Maddie simply an embarrassment? Were there tears in her eyes? *Step on a crack, break a mother's heart.* She had a block left to get this woman to open up, to trust her, to let her in. Not back into the apartment, she knew she was forever barred from there. But to let her into their lives, let her know the story of Cleo.

"Tell me about the last time you saw Eunetta. Please? I'm a mother too. I understand."

Mrs. Sherwood sighed, shifting the bag to her hip.

"She brought the boys toys, which made no sense. It wasn't even a week after Christmas and there she was, with two new trucks. She spoiled them so. Brought them things, when all they wanted was her. My husband says I spoiled her, but I didn't. She was blazing to do something, be someone. All I tried to do was not get in the way."

"Is it possible she knew she was in trouble? That she knew someone wanted her dead?"

Mrs. Sherwood stumbled on the raised lip between two squares of pavement. *Step on a crack.*

"No," she said. "She said she might take a trip, but she'd let me know if she did. When a little time went by and I didn't hear from her—I didn't worry at first. She was careless that way. Then I got to thinking—she gave me a jacket of hers that I always liked." A pause. "I said, 'There's no way that's going to fit me, your arms are so long.' But it fit me. So she'd had it altered, just for me. Said it was a late Christmas gift."

"Mrs. Sherwood—why would someone kill Eunetta?"

"Doesn't have to be a why, does there? Or if there is a why, it started so long ago, before any of us could know, or see where things were headed. She wasn't a bad girl. But she spoke her mind. When you are very, very pretty, you start to think you can get away with so much. But I guess you knew that, too."

Knew? There was something a little barbed about how quickly Mrs. Sherwood had anointed Maddie with the power of beauty, only to imply it was past.

"Did you ever meet him? Ezekiel Taylor?"

"No. There was no reason. I wasn't going to be his mother-in-law, no matter what Eunetta thought." She snorted. "That would have been something, to have a son-in-law older 'n me."

So there it was. Ezekiel Taylor was Cleo's boyfriend, her mother said so, and Cleo had believed he might become her husband. Would that scuttle his political ambitions? No, because as Maddie now knew, it was not considered news if a man running for office had a young girlfriend on the side.

But what if the girlfriend would not be silenced, what if she threatened to make a fuss?

The status quo relied on women's playing by the rules of a game they could never win. Cleo Sherwood's own mother said the only thing to do when Cleo wanted something was to get out of her way.

Could Cleo Sherwood truly have wanted Ezekiel Taylor, older than her own parents? She might, at the very least, have wanted the life of a rich man's wife, or a state senator's wife.

As they reached the steps of the Sherwood apartment, the sister, Alice, was waiting outside.

"Mama, I told you I needed to go to work—" She broke off, stared angrily at Maddie. "What do *you* want?"

"Nothing," Maddie said.

August 1966

SHE BIDED HER time. She was serenely, bizarrely confident that the world would provide her the opportunity she needed. She felt full of energy, even when nights with Ferdie meant she got only four, five hours' sleep. Pushing back against August's doldrums, she worked harder than ever, wrapping up her work by three, then dropping by the city desk to tell Cal Weeks she was available if he needed help.

"I'm not authorized to pay you overtime," he told her, ever suspicious.

"Not looking for OT," she said. "Mr. Heath is on vacation for the next two weeks and filed his column ahead of time, so there's only so much I can do."

He gave her press releases to rewrite. Maddie found that even Cal Weeks had a few things to teach her, such as words to avoid.

"Be careful with terms like *first* and *only* because they're often in-accurate. And the word *unique* never takes a modifier." He also had insights into the city around them, who the real players were. And he liked her. Men always did, if Maddie wanted them to. So when she saw that Ezekiel Taylor was going to be opening his sixth dry cleaners, on Gwynn Oak Avenue, she offered to cover it.

"I don't know, Maddie. He's one of eight candidates in the Fourth. Might look like favoritism."

She had prepared for his objections. "It's at four o'clock today. I skipped lunch, so I'll be off the clock, more or less. What if I go by and see if he makes news? Like a policy position? Or something about Senator Welcome?"

Weeks snorted. "Your time, your dime."

She would not expense the cab she took to Gwynn Oak.

Maddie knew the signs that indicated a neighborhood was about to tip from white to black. The newest location of EZ Kleeners was next to a beauty shop in a neighborhood that was just beginning to change. The "Under Contract" and "SOLD" signs swinging beneath the original "For Sale" signs were covert code for *Get out now*. She couldn't understand why whites in the city didn't want to live next to black people, but they didn't. The mass hysteria over the issue meant that values plummeted rapidly. Was it bigotry to want to live among one's own? The Christian neighborhoods hadn't wanted the Jews. Still didn't, really. The white women walking into Pietro's to get their hair cut and styled would be happy for the convenience of a dry cleaners in the neighborhood, but they wouldn't want Mr. Taylor as their neighbor.

She had arrived in time for the ribbon-cutting, which she knew from Cal Weeks could never be considered news. But that was all there was—a ribbon-cutting, with a photographer from the *Afro* dutifully recording it. The *Afro* had different standards from the city's dailies, apparently.

Mr. Taylor had that charisma that some successful men have, a way of making you think that you'd find him attractive even if he weren't successful. Bulky, he moved slowly, spoke slowly and softly, but his eyes were sharp and watchful. Maddie could feel him assessing her quickly as she approached, reporter pad in hand.

"Madeline Schwartz from the *Star*," she said.

He smiled, but it was a smile that showed no teeth. "Glad to know the *Star* thinks this is news."

"Well, you are running for state senate. Although I suppose if you win, you'll leave the dry-cleaning business behind."

"Maryland has a part-time legislature, miss, as I'm sure you know. It would be an honor to represent my district, but I still need my job."

She did not, in fact, know that Maryland's legislature was considered a part-time office. It had never occurred to her to think about it. But she did not intend to dwell on politics. She had other topics to discuss with Ezekiel Taylor.

"One thing I did want to ask you—did you know a young woman, Eunetta Sherwood?"

"Eunetta—" His brow furrowed.

"Most people knew her as Cleo, but her parents preferred her given name, Eunetta." She wanted to remind him that Cleo was someone's daughter. "She worked at the Flamingo. You know, Shell Gordon's place over on—"

"I am familiar with Mr. Gordon and the Flamingo. The young woman, however—"

"After she went missing, her mother found clothing from your dry cleaners in her apartment. Lots of clothing. Even a fur."

"Obviously, I don't know all my customers."

"Obviously. But Mrs. Sherwood, Cleo's mother—she told me that Cleo said she was going to marry you one day."

There was a split second of hesitation—and then he laughed and Maddie was impressed. This was not an easy man to rattle. "The stories girls tell their mothers. I am married, Miss—"

"Mrs.," she said. "Schwartz."

"I do go to the Flamingo when they have musical acts to my liking. I tip well. Who knows what kind of story a young girl could build on top of a little folding money left on a table for a job well done. I'm sure Cleo Sherwood knew who I was. And I'm sure I saw her a time or two behind the bar. Now, if you'll excuse me . . ."

He walked to his car with an unhurried, unconcerned gait. Why should he be concerned? He had absolutely checkmated her. Or maybe the better metaphor was poker. Maddie had been so sure of her winning hand that it never occurred to her that she could be bluffed, stonewalled. The men made the rules, broke the rules, and tossed the girls away.

What had she expected? That he would sweat and stammer? That he would confess to her that, yes, Cleo Sherwood had been killed because she threatened his ambition, his livelihood?

She watched a *Perry Mason* rerun that night, an episode clearly modeled on *Oliver Twist,* only the Fagin character, played by Victor Buono, was killed. Mason defended the accused boy, one of the gang members. He sensed something good in him.

The next day, Cal Weeks said: "So, no news out of the ribbon-cutting?"

"Nope," Maddie said.

"Not even in August could a dog-and-pony show like that make news."

Who was the dog? Who was the pony?

September 1966

LABOR DAY. *WHERE was I a year ago?* Maddie wondered. At
the club, the straps of her gingham checked one-piece pushed down,
burnishing her tan so it might last a few more weeks. Her mother
had always said that Maddie shouldn't sunbathe because she tanned
too easily. Such an odd idea, that anything achieved with ease was
to be avoided, but that was Tattie Morgenstern's worldview in a nut-
shell.

This summer, Maddie was not her usual pecan hue, but even if
she had been, she would have still seemed pale alongside, beneath,
Ferdie. She was under him for much of the holiday, not minding
the heat, the pooling sweat. They made love until the sheets were
slushy, until it felt as if they were underwater, then they took cool
showers together, changed the sheets, ready for a second turn. It
was a luxury, having that second set of sheets at the ready, but she

had found a cheap laundry on North Liberty Street. She could drop off her linens on the way to work tomorrow. She didn't have to be ashamed in front of the woman who took her bundle of soiled sheets, who spoke no English. Understood, perhaps, but didn't speak, and it was what others said about you that could hurt, not what they thought.

But on this particular night, a holiday even for lowly clerks and patrolmen, at least this lowly clerk and patrolman, they did not resume making love after the shower. Ferdie pulled her to him, stroked her hair, and murmured the last thing she ever expected him to say.

"I think I have a story for you."

"A story?"

"For the newspaper. It's going to happen tomorrow."

"How can you know what's going to happen tomorrow?"

"Because it's happening now, actually. Started to happen. But the guy won't be arraigned until tomorrow. What time is your deadline?"

"They go all day, right up until three." Could Ferdie really have a valid tip for her? He had known the inside details about Tessie Fine, after all. "But it's best to have it in all editions, and update throughout the day."

"It's supposed to happen tonight. I got a tip. I mean—the man who told me, he didn't realize it was a tip. To him, it was gossip. He likes being in the know. Makes him feel big. He liked telling me about police business, telling me my business, to show how plugged in he is. Cock of the walk and all. Didn't occur to him that I know anyone at the papers."

"Ferdie, *what* is it?" As urgent as she felt, she also was sure it would be nothing, an anticlimax. She had been wrong so many times about what might be news. How could Ferdie's judgment be any better?

"A man's going to walk into headquarters tonight and confess to the murder of Cleo Sherwood."

Not an anticlimax.

"Who?"

"The bartender from the Flamingo."

"The white guy? Spike?"

"That's the one. Tommy something. It was all made up, everything he told the police. He killed her. He told her he was in love with her, she laughed at him, and he killed her. But he can't be arraigned until the courts open back up tomorrow. So he'll be in lockup tonight."

"How do I get the story?"

"If you trust me, you got it. The guy who works overnight at your paper, no one's going to tell him, right? It's a holiday, they probably got the second string on. This is solid, Maddie. Look, call Homicide right now. Tell them you're from the *Star*, that you have a tip. They'll deny it. But then you say, 'I'm going with it if you don't tell me I'm wrong. You don't have to confirm or deny it, you don't have to say anything.' Reporters do it all the time." A pause. "That's what I'm told."

Would that work? It seemed a dangerous game to play. Diller would be angry, being usurped on his beat, but what would it matter if the tip was right?

She stared at her phone, scarlet and inert, indifferent to its role in changing her life. "What's the number?"

Ferdie rattled it off, then said, "But don't call from here. Wait another hour, take a cab to the office, make the call from there, okay?"

She kept the promise to wait but broke the others, calling from home, not bothering to go to the office. After she hung up with the homicide detective, whose silence confirmed that Thomas Ludlow had arrived without an attorney to confess to the murder of Eunetta "Cleo" Sherwood, she dialed the city desk and said, as if she had said it a thousand times before: "Cal, this is Maddie Schwartz. Please put me through to rewrite. I've gotten a big break on the Cleo Sherwood story."

Cal quizzed her, of course. But she had it cold, and she had won him over, doing all those thankless tasks in the dog days of August.

And by ten o'clock the next morning, most of the city knew it: a white man had killed Cleo Sherwood for the very everyday crime of not loving him. It was not a page one story and Maddie understood the calculus that determined that: the dead woman was a Negro, she was killed for love, or for lack of love more accurately. But it was a story good enough for the metro page, the ending to the tantalizing tale of the Lady in the Lake.

Mr. Heath was back from his vacation and she went about her usual tasks with her usual efficiency, waiting for the moment she would be summoned to the boss's office. She understood and accepted that she would not continue to report the story—that Tommy's arraignment would be covered by someone on courts or cops, that Diller would look for a folo out of the cop shop. That was fine. She didn't want to be a cop reporter.

After the final deadline, Bob Bauer stopped by her desk.

"Hey, Scoop Schwartz."

She blushed in spite of herself.

"So you have sources, huh?"

"I do."

"Who are they?"

She hesitated. He leaned in, his voice low and serious. "You don't tell anyone who your sources are. Not other reporters, not the bosses. Not the law, if it comes to that. Whatever you do, protect your sources."

It seemed an odd comment, but she realized that Bob, plugged in as ever, must have known what was coming for her. Because when she was summoned to the city editor's office not even an hour later, it was not for an "attagirl." It was because a furious John Diller wanted her reprimanded for poaching from his beat.

THIRTY MINUTES LATER, a shaken but dry-eyed Maddie walked out of the office and into the ladies' room, where she splashed water on her face, then gripped the sink with trembling hands.

"You okay?" asked Edna, sitting there with her three C's—coffee, cig, and copy.

"I think so."

"Saw your byline. Nice work. Diller's pissed, isn't he?"

"You could say that."

"He's terrified someone's going to dethrone him at cop shop. As if anyone wants to be the dean of that bunch. Cop shop's a place to pass through. No one good stays there."

"He—he wanted me to tell my source. He claims to know who it is. I don't understand why that should matter."

"Like I said, he's scared."

The man had appeared more malevolent than scared to Maddie. He had fumed and sputtered like Rumpelstiltskin, on the verge of tearing himself apart. "I know who told you about the confession. That's no *source*. You risked the paper's integrity trusting him."

"Except I was right. Tommy Ludlow did confess."

The city editor had treated them like two squabbling schoolchildren. "It was a holiday weekend, John. She had a tip, she ran with it, and it's good. It's not a big deal."

"It's not the way we do business around here. It was sloppy, it was amateurish, it was—"

"What are you implying, Mr. Diller?" Maddie was investing so much willpower into not crying that her voice screeched a little.

"You don't know what you're doing. You got lucky this time, going with a one-source story—and *that* source at that. Stay away from the cop shop."

"You knew I was trying to write about Cleo Sherwood. And you didn't mind when I filed the story on 'Lady Law.' That was fine by you."

"Because it was barely a story. It was press-release pap."

"I'm just trying to become a reporter. Is that so wrong?"

When Diller left, muttering all the way, the city editor sighed. "It was a good story, Maddie. But I don't want you to pin your hopes on a reporting job. It's a young person's game. If we were to hire a rookie, I'd want it to be someone with a long future ahead of him."

Him.

Now, in the bathroom, she stared at her own reflection, ashen in the mirror. If Diller really did know the identity of her source, what would that mean for her, for Ferdie? Would he get in trouble? She wished she could call him, be comforted. But she could never call him. She didn't have his number, didn't know where he lived. If she wanted to find Ferdie, her only hope was to head up to Northwest and walk down the street, screaming her head off, which was how she had found him nine months ago. Otherwise, she waited for him to come to her.

She decided to take a walk up to the New Orleans Diner, grab a coffee before closing. She sat at the counter while the waitress she remembered from her lunch there with Bob Bauer leaned on her elbows, reading the newspaper. Reading Maddie's story.

"I wrote that," she said. Technically untrue; the rewrite, Ettlin, had written it from her notes. But she couldn't help herself.

"So you're"—the waitress looked from the byline to Maddie, back to the byline—"Madeline Schwartz?"

"Yes."

"I knew her. Cleo. Back at Werner's." She seemed at once shy and excited. Maddie noticed for the first time how young she was, younger than Maddie, with freckles on her nose and the bit of chest she let show in her pink uniform.

"What was she like?"

The waitress took so long to answer that Maddie assumed she hadn't been heard. But then: "Hungry. She wanted things. She just didn't know what they were."

Tell me about it, Maddie thought. Except—she knew what she wanted. She was going to be a reporter. Not just any reporter. She was going to be like Bob Bauer one day. A columnist, someone who got to pick and choose her stories.

Oh, it wouldn't be the same. It would be harder. And while she could see the goal, shining, shimmering, she couldn't see the path. It seemed ridiculous. She had just been told she couldn't even be the night cop reporter, that the paper would never hire her. And yet— she was not unlike Cleo Sherwood. If she really wanted something, she got it. She had wanted Allan Durst, had seduced him as much as he had seduced her. She had wanted Milton, the cloak of re- spectability he promised when Durst left her, deflowered and almost ruined. She had wanted to have a child. Then she had wanted her freedom. Thirty-seven might have been old or late to do such things, but it was not impossible. After all, there was . . . well, Grandma Moses. Oh lord, there must be someone other than Grandma Moses.

WHEN SHE RETURNED to the newsroom, the fifth floor had that extra charge, unusual with the final deadline past. "What's happening?" she asked one of the copyboys.

"Shooting at the courthouse," he said. "At the arraignment for that guy who confessed to the Lady in the Lake killing."

She had used that phrase this morning, in her story, and now here it was, set, immortalized. Maddie had sincerely forgotten that she had stolen it from the medical examiner.

"What happened?"

"Guy took a shot at him when they took him out of the wagon at the side entrance."

"Is he dead?" She felt a weird throb of sympathy for the man who had walked her to her car, had compared Cleo Sherwood to a poem.

Then she remembered he had killed her.

"In surgery at Mercy. No condition report yet."

"And who shot him?"

"Cleo Sherwood's father."

Maddie didn't even bother to ask. She grabbed a notebook and went to Auchentoroly Terrace. There, a stunned Mrs. Sherwood let her inside, sobbing. In the span of less than twelve hours, she had seen her daughter's death resolved, only to have her husband make this ill-conceived stab at vengeance. Her daughter was dead and now her husband was going to be in jail, possibly for murder.

Maddie approached Cal Weeks about eight P.M., knowing he would have eaten dinner by then.

"Has anyone talked to the mother?"

"The who?"

"Merva Sherwood. She was the mother of Cleo Sherwood." Cal looked confused. "Her husband—Cleo's father—was arrested for trying to shoot Cleo's killer today." She added: "Her parents preferred to call her by her given name, Eunetta."

"No one was home by the time a reporter got there. They're probably in hiding at a relative's."

"I talked to her. I had been to the apartment before—on my own time. I was so interested in Cleo's death. I just kept thinking there had to be an answer. And now, I guess, there is."

"Did you take notes?"

"Yes."

"Feed 'em to rewrite."

"But I'm right here and the first deadline isn't until—"

"Feed 'em to rewrite. Don't worry, you'll get a trib line."

"I'm not worried about that. I told her mother I would write the story. If you want my notes, you have to let me write it."

While she could not put everything she knew about Cleo Sherwood in the paper, she could tell the story of her mother. Of a woman who had lost a daughter and would now lose a husband. A woman who had a closet full of beautiful clothes and had no idea how her child had come to own them. She could tell about the psychic, the still-baffling visions of green and yellow. The waitress who knew her back at Werner's. They had to cut quite a bit—"It's only a sidebar, for Christ's sake"—but she fought to keep the detail about all those altered clothes, hung on the paper-shrouded wire hangers from EZ Kleeners. She wanted Ezekiel Taylor to know that someone knew his secrets.

September 1966

NO MATTER HOW hot the weather—and it was very hot in 1966—September will always be the beginning of fall and fall will always be the true start of the year. Maddie's mother assumed her prodigal daughter would return to the Morgenstern household for Rosh Hashanah and Yom Kippur. Maddie remembered, wryly, how she had struggled for years to wrest the holiday dinners from her mother, how insistent she had been on creating her own traditions, how she had scandalized her mother with her recipe for *haroset* at last year's Passover, made with figs and dates. It all seemed so trivial now.

The primary fell two days before Rosh Hashanah and Maddie volunteered to take results. It was an inglorious job, but no more inglorious than the job she continued to do every day, despite her "scoop" on the Sherwood story. She typed the vote tallies in the city legislative districts, her swift fingers stopping for a second when it came time to enter the numbers for the senate seat in the Fourth District. A newcomer, Clarence Mitchell III, was the top vote-getter, but Verda Welcome was second. Ezekiel Taylor was a distant fourth.

How silly she had been to think that any of this had anything to do with Cleo. Hindsight, they called it. Well, in hindsight, Maddie saw the world for what it was, where women belonged in it. Men were entitled to have their girls on the side, as long as they were discreet. Men, some men, felt entitled to kill the women who did not return their affections. Cleo Sherwood did not matter enough; she could not have swayed this election. She had never mattered at all.

Here was Ezekiel Taylor, his reputation intact, his campaign underwritten by Shell Gordon's dirty money. How silly Maddie had been. Cleo's death had been more interesting as a mystery. Solved, it was dull. Her father's crazed, desperate act outside the courthouse had drawn more attention than his daughter's murder. It was one thing for a white man to kill a Negro woman, crazed with love for her. But for that woman's father to start shooting outside the courthouse, in a crowd, grazing a young police officer—he was expected to spend as long in prison as his daughter's killer, if not longer.

Maddie became aware, as she kept taking calls and updating numbers, of a sensation sweeping through the newsroom. There was a surprise, something unexpected in the results. Even jaded Edna, here to write a color story on whatever patterns emerged from the statewide races, looked caught off guard.

"What's up?" Maddie asked Bob Bauer, who had just pulled his column from his typewriter. But instead of calling "copy," he crumpled it and inserted a fresh sheet.

"Damn thing's too close to call. With all the precincts in, Mahoney's got the lead by less than a hundred fifty votes. There's going to be a recount. Clarence Mitchell the Third is already saying he'll organize Negroes for Agnew if Mahoney is the candidate."

"How could Mahoney win?" Maddie had followed the governor's race in the papers all summer. Mahoney was a six-time loser in state politics.

"Sickles and Finan split the base. And Mahoney had a message that resonated, 'Your home is your castle.'"

"But wasn't that racist?"

"Maybe to you. To some guy who's watching the value of his home plummet because his neighborhood is changing, it's different. You can't mess with a man's home. It defines him." He looked at the paper in his typewriter. "That's it, that's it. You can't mess with a man's home. I've got my lede, Maddie, so if you'll excuse me . . ."

It rained all day the next day. It rained almost four inches, a record. It was not a cleansing rain, the kind that left a city refreshed. Humidity lingered and Maddie's straightened hair seemed to shrink as her natural waves returned. Everyone at the paper was tired and cranky, working on too little sleep and too much coffee.

On Thursday, she went to her mother's house, carrying a dish of homemade chicken liver with pistachios.

"Is this from Seven Locks?" her mother asked.

"Actually, I made it myself." She had, a laborious job that involved pushing the chicken livers through a sieve. "It's kosher."

Her father picked the nuts out—"They're bad for my bowels," he said—but her mother's inability to criticize the dish was a kind of validation. Unfortunately, it also freed her to move on to Maddie's personal life.

She began: "Yom Kippur is coming."

"Of course."

"So, are you going to go back home? If you ask Milton to take you back, he would probably consider it. After all, part of atoning is to forgive others."

"I have nothing to atone for," Maddie said sharply. "And nothing for which I need to be forgiven."

"Are you dating?" There was something sly about her mother's question, a hint of things unsaid, but Maddie's mother had no way of knowing what happened at the corner of Mulberry and Cathedral.

"No." It wasn't a lie. Maddie reasoned it wasn't a date if all you did was have sex in your own apartment. She thought about the night at the ballpark, how thrilling it was simply to sit by him, shoulder to shoulder.

Then she thought about John Diller, eyes narrowed, saying, *"That source."*

Her mother said: "Really, Maddie, I understand, believe me. The summer before your senior year in high school, I went a little crazy. It's natural. You spend your life raising a child, then it's time for the child to move on. It happens to every woman I know. Debbie Wasserman got caught shoplifting at the Giant over on Ingleside. She drove all the way over there to steal a Sara Lee swirl cake."

Maddie slathered some chicken liver on a piece of toast. It really was excellent. She was a better cook in her galley kitchen with the two-burner stove than she had been in Pikesville, with a freezer full of Hutzler's cheese bread and all her little tricks for making dinner parties seem homey and homemade.

"I don't think that's my situation. I have a brain. It almost atrophied from lack of use and now I want to use it."

"At a newspaper. And the *Star*, of all places." The Morgenstern household took the *Beacon* in the morning, the *Light* in the afternoon, and was suspicious of those who didn't follow suit. Her mother had never even seen Maddie's work. "Look, I'm just telling you, Madeline. I *know*."

Her mother leveled her gaze at Maddie and suddenly she was sixteen again, but only for a moment. She wondered what her mother did know. Did she suspect that Maddie was not a virgin before she married, that she had visited an abortionist on lower Park Heights? It seemed impossible that she would figure out that Maddie had sought Allan out, made love to him again, then come home and conceived a child with Milton. More impossible still that she could have heard any whispers about Maddie and Ferdie. (How silly their names sounded together, she realized, and yet how right.) And if Diller knew about them—well, so what? It wasn't as if her mother was going to run into the *Star*'s cop reporter, or even his wife, at the Seven Locks market.

"You could be home by October first," her mother said now. "Every marriage has its bumps." She glanced at her husband, who had made a neat pile of pistachios on his plate. He had been chosen for her, Tattie's parents designating him as the only acceptable suitor for their oldest daughter, not that different from a *shidduch* or the *Fiddler on the Roof* days. Her mother's German Jew parents would be horrified by such a comparison, even in the privacy of Maddie's mind, but it was apt enough. Her father wasn't even first generation; he had been born on the boat en route to the United States. Nineteen oh six. Sixty years ago. How could 1906 and 1966 be part of the same century? In 1906, there had been no world wars, most people didn't have telephones and cars. In 1906, women couldn't vote and black men could by law, but not in practice.

Her parents seemed impossibly distant from her. She seemed distant from herself. Maddie couldn't believe that she was related to the woman who used to sit in this same chair, eating this same Rosh

Hashanah meal, minus her fancy chopped liver. She felt a chill, almost as if a ghost passed through her, but it was the ghost of who she used to be. Forget 1906 and 1966. Maddie couldn't believe that 1965 and 1966 were part of the same century. She was different. Couldn't her mother see how different she was?

A week later, on Yom Kippur, she didn't attend synagogue, although she fasted until sundown out of habit. She then ordered too much food at Paul Cheng's with Seth, taking home the leftovers, confident that Ferdie would drop by.

He did.

October 1966

"WHEN'S YOUR BIRTHDAY?"

Ferdie and Maddie were in a tangle of limbs, enjoying that first truly chilly night of fall, the night when quilts return to the bed and one leaves the window open a scant two inches. Even here, above the traffic and dirt of Mulberry Street, the air smelled fresh and new.

"Why do you ask?"

"Why wouldn't I ask? We've been seeing each other almost a year and you haven't had a birthday yet, not that I know of."

"Only nine months," Maddie said.

"That's almost a year, isn't it?" Amused, but also with a tinge of hurt, as if she were downplaying whatever they had.

"November," she said. "November tenth."

"And you'll be thirty-eight."

Her turn to be hurt. She didn't think she looked her age. Ferdie must have realized his gaffe because he added: "I asked for your driver's license the day we met. I remembered the year but not the date. What do you want for your birthday?"

"Oh, I don't need a gift."

"Maybe I need to give you one, have you ever thought about that?"

It was almost instinctive, almost, to begin kissing him, to move her body down the length of his, past that lean torso, that knot of a belly button, down, down, down. It was only later that Maddie realized how many times she had done just this to avoid certain conversations. When Ferdie said anything that sounded romantic, partnerlike, she distracted him with sex. Distracted herself, too. She liked pleasing him because he always pleased her back. Her pleasure had seemed secondary to the other men she had known. Sometimes she enjoyed it, sometimes she faked it, and Milton couldn't tell the difference. Allan had loved seduction, the buildup. She wondered now, for the first time, if Allan preferred taking virgins because they had nothing to which to compare the experience. As someone's first lover, one is inevitably the best.

"Thirty-eight is such a stupid age," she said later. "It's not forty, yet it's not *not* forty." A beat. "How old are you? When is your birthday?"

"December. December twenty-fifth."

He didn't give his age, though.

"Ah, so you probably never have much of a birthday. But December twenty-fifth means nothing to me. We can do what the Jews do, eat Chinese food." She didn't add, *and go to a movie,* although a matinee, then Chinese food, had been the tradition in the Schwartz household.

"In bed." He seemed glum.

"That's the old joke. Take your fortune cookie, read the fortune, and add the words *in bed*. It always works." He didn't laugh. "We can do whatever you like on your birthday."

"I would like—" Her heart almost stopped, terrified that he would ask for something she could never give him. Instead, he buried his face between her breasts, but he wasn't trying to distract her. "I would like to give you the world, Maddie."

"I don't need the world," she said. "You've given me more than I could ever imagine."

With that, she slipped on a robe and went to fix a tray. The second feature on channel 2 was *Devil's Harbor,* some kind of a crime film, while the Moonlight Movie on 11 was *Her Master's Voice,* which seemed to be a comedy—mismatched lovers, Shakespeare's favorite story, but executed at a much lower level. Maddie let Ferdie choose and was surprised when he picked the comedy, already thirty minutes in.

She would be exhausted at work tomorrow, keeping such late hours. But who cared? She didn't need to be fresh to open mail, answer phones, and fetch Mr. Helpline's lunch.

"I'm going to get you the best gift," Ferdie said suddenly, his hand on her thigh. She thought he wanted to make love again, but he continued to watch the movie. At some point, she fell asleep, and when her alarm sounded at six thirty, only the tray with the empty plate and two drained glasses proved that he had ever been there.

October 1966

MILTON WANTED TO meet. For lunch, he said, making the
phone call himself instead of relying on Seth to transmit the message. Just the two of them, he said. He suggested Danny's, an old
favorite, and Maddie had to explain that she had an hour for lunch,
at most, and she almost always ate at her desk. By the time she made
her way to Danny's, she'd have only enough time to order a drink,
bolt it, and return to work.

"Dinner, then. Tio Pepe's?"

No, that was too grand. She countered with Maison Marconi's,
within walking distance of her apartment. She would have time to
get home, change, and meet him there for dinner at a very respectable six thirty. Plus, although the food was delicious, Marconi's was
overlit, not the least bit romantic.

Still, the request worried her. There had been phone calls before, some angry, some benign, some both. But they had not been alone, face-to-face, since January. He had continued to send a little money to her, but never on a predictable schedule and never the same amount twice. Seth would hand her an envelope of cash at their weekly meetings. "To cover dinner, Dad says." Inside would be far more money than required by dinner at the Suburban House or Paul Cheng's Cantonese, but also less than her monthly rent. An odd gesture, one that could be seen as hostile or well-intentioned. Maddie had decided to take the more generous view. She had broken the man's heart. And for what? It probably would have been much easier on Milton if she had left him for a richer, more successful man—say, Wallace Wright. If she had left him for anyone or anything tangible. From where he sat, it must have seemed insulting for his wife to leave only to work as a newspaper clerk, one with little hope of advancement. (She had not had a byline proper since the story on the Sherwoods. Her achievements kept being written off as flukes, feats she could not repeat.) He had never seen her apartment, of course, but he must have had some inkling of it. The whole thing could have fit into their living room in Pikesville.

Yes, how baffling this whole adventure must have been to Milton. How baffling it was to Maddie.

She dressed carefully, trying to find a middle ground between her old and new selves. One of her longer dresses, slightly below the knee. High heels instead of the boots she now preferred. She put her hair up, back-combing it just a little. Her only jewelry was a pin she had found in a secondhand store in Fells Point, a cursive M of sterling silver. She wondered often about the woman who had given it up, what her M had stood for. She remembered how delighted she had been to realize, upon marriage, that her monogram would be two small M's—Madeline Morgenstern—on either side of an S, for *Schwartz*. It was so beautifully symmetrical, those two M's bracketing the S. How she had doted on the embroidered pieces of her trousseau.

But now it seemed to her that those two M's dwarfed by the S had predicted all too well what her life would be. A handmaiden first to Milton, then to Seth.

She applied a pale lipstick, one of the newer shades.

In the bright lights of Marconi's, Milton looked nervous. Oh dear. He leaned in, seemingly to kiss her on the cheek, then apparently thought better of it and offered her a comically firm handshake. Hail, fellow, well met.

They talked about Seth until the chopped salad arrived, then about work—Milton's, not Maddie's—while they waited for their entrees. (Dover sole for Milton, sweetbreads for Maddie. She really wanted the lobster cardinale but felt it would be gauche to order the most expensive thing on the menu. And she still held on to the habit of not eating shellfish in front of observant Milton.) The conversation was pleasant, but throughout there was a sense that Milton was postponing what he really wanted to say.

Over the ice cream with the famous chocolate sauce, he blurted out: "You don't wear your rings anymore."

"They were—" She had almost forgotten the story. "They were stolen. From the first apartment. That's part of the reason I moved."

"I'm not sure you picked a safer part of town."

"I live not even two blocks from here. If it's safe enough to drive down for dinner, how bad can it be?"

She regretted telling him that her apartment was nearby. He would probably insist on taking her to her door. What if he tried to kiss her? She had loved Milton, she really had. If it hadn't been for Wally Weiss, she might never have realized she had fallen out of love with him. She remembered fondly his broad, fuzzy chest, how safe she had felt with him.

She didn't need to feel safe anymore.

"I'm sorry I haven't done anything about the divorce. But it's almost a year now. I've been advised I can file on grounds of abandonment."

Strangely, she almost wanted to defend herself. *Abandonment*. She hadn't abandoned anyone. She had been saving her own life.

"Would I receive alimony?"

"Do you need it?"

Ah, that question hurt because the answer was yes, she did. But she could not bring herself to say that. "I'm merely curious about how the law works, in general. We were together almost twenty years."

"I'll probably sell the house. Seth wants to go to Penn." A non sequitur. Or was it?

"There's money enough for that, isn't there? Without selling the house?"

"Money's not the issue. Maddie—I've met someone."

Of course. *Of course*.

"And she doesn't want to live in 'my' house."

"She hasn't said as much. But with Seth going away—she's quite young."

"What's young?"

"Twenty-five."

Of course.

"So I'm not quite old enough to be her mother, but you could have been her father."

Milton looked disappointed in her. It was the first time he had ever looked at Maddie like that, as if to say: *Maddie, this is beneath you*. It was. It wasn't even accurate. Technically, Milton could have conceived a child at sixteen, but it seemed unlikely. He had not been precocious in that way. Between the store and his studies, he hadn't had time for girls.

"What's her name?"

"Ali."

"Is that short for something?"

"I—I don't know!" Bemused at his own besottedness, the fact that he was unsure of his true love's name.

What else should Maddie ask? It was a one-of-a-kind conversation, one she had never had before and would never have again, discussing her husband's new love. She didn't feel dog-in-the-mangerish, not quite. She didn't want Milton. She didn't want the life he was about to create with this Ali, which was going to be essentially a do-over of his life with her. *Oh, Milton,* she wanted to say. *You're still young. There's so much to do and see in this world. Don't go back to diapers and Donadio the Clown.*

"You should grow sideburns," she blurted out.

"What?"

"I just think they would look good on you." She did. He had kept his hair, so far. It was thick and had almost no gray. She wondered what Ali looked like. She was going to either look exactly like Maddie or be as opposite as possible. Maddie would find it more flattering if he had chosen her opposite number. Another blue-eyed brunette would indicate that she was just a type, whereas a wispy blonde would suggest that he would never quite get over her, that she would be with him forever, sort of like chicken pox.

He did insist on walking her home and she toyed with the idea of taking him upstairs, of showing him what her body had learned over the last few months. The temptation to mark him as hers was strong. But also, she knew, unfair and petty.

"You'll need a lawyer," he said. "I'll cover the costs. And it will be simple, I promise. I'll do right by you."

Of course you will. Ali is eager to get married. The advantage is mine.

But she would not abuse her power. She gave him a polite kiss on the cheek, realizing that they would be going forward as an odd triangle. Maybe eventually a quadrangle, and it made her smile to imagine Milton and Ali, Maddie and Ferdie, showing up for Seth's milestones. High school graduation, senior prom, too. College graduation, his marriage, grandchildren. All those things were to be. Of course, Ferdie would not be with her. Eventually, another man might, if that was what she wanted. What did she want?

She was going to have money now. Not a lot, but enough. She could find a better apartment, maybe try to find a job where she would have an opportunity to advance.

As Milton said good night, his old look, the worshipful one, returned for a moment. But she also saw confusion in his gaze. He did not know her anymore. Fair enough. She didn't know herself, either.

October 1966

IT WAS HALLOWEEN, of all things, that broke her. A Halloween with no trick-or-treaters. At the corner of Mulberry and Cathedral, it could have been just another Monday night. The only bright
spot was Ferdie, tired from the day's petty assaults on law and order,
but also fired up.

"I talked to Pomerleau today. Just in passing. He visited the
district."

"The new commissioner?" There was a time when Maddie would
not have recognized the name. But she read the paper now, front
to back. Read the competition, too. Her mind was stuffed with the
news of the day.

"He announced that the department ended up with a net gain in
men this month. That reverses a trend of more than a year, in which
the resignations and retirements outnumbered the new recruits.

Now that morale is improving he's going to start promoting Negro cops. Things are going to change, Maddie. I could make detective, and *fast*. Maybe even homicide. I've been cultivating one of the guys there. He trusts me. He tells me stuff."

"That's nice," she said absentmindedly. This conversation was beginning to remind her of how she and Milton spoke to one another. And that was not a good thing.

But the sex that followed was very good, so she decided not to worry. In fact, something about Ferdie's professional dreams seemed to make the sex even better, as if he were a different man, in his own mind, and therefore she was new to him and he was new to her.

"Detective," she purred at one point, and it excited him. His eyes grew wide, and without bothering to ask if it was what she wanted, he flipped her on her stomach, then used the belt from her bathrobe to tie her hands behind her.

"You've been warned about shoplifting, miss," he said. "I have to take you in."

There had always been a sense of play for them in the bedroom, probably because this was outside of life, proper. They could afford to be silly, to expose parts of themselves that no one else had seen.

"I'll do anything," she said. "Anything."

And she did. This was the one part of her life where things continued to grow, change, where she could meet her potential. The night was cool, but they needed a shower when they were done. They crowded together into the ridiculously small stall, started over again, needed a shower from the shower. It was almost two A.M. when they finally began to fall asleep. At least, she was falling asleep. Ferdie was wide awake, stroking her hair.

"My friend in Homicide, he told me something about Tessie Fine."

"What?"

"They're pretty sure they finally know the accomplice. The woman who came and got him."

"Woman?"

"His mom, Maddie. They think he called his mom and she came to get him. But all the detectives can prove is that he called his mother from the store. They both agree that he was calling only to say he would be late that night. They're rock solid on that. The detectives have been pushing him hard and now he's willing to plead, but only to manslaughter. Of course, there can't be a plea."

She sat up in bed. "That's a huge story."

Ferdie grabbed her arm as if she might bolt for the door. "No, Maddie. No. You can't write about this. They'll know it was me."

"You gave me the tip about Ludlow."

"That was different."

"How?"

His gaze slid away from hers. "A dozen people could have told you about that. And no one knows about us."

Maddie thought about Diller's staring at her malevolently in the city editor's office.

"If no one knew about us then, then no one knows about us now. That hasn't changed. This is sensational stuff. The mother covering up her son's crime."

"She's not trying to cover up for anybody. She's trying to save her own neck. And the son's going along with it, so far."

"Could I say that police have identified the long-elusive accomplice?" She was already writing the story in her head.

"No, Maddie." His voice was sharp, almost a shout. "This information has been held very close. They'll know it was me. You cannot write about this."

"But—Tessie Fine was my murder. I found her."

He got up, began to dress. He usually waited until she was asleep to go.

"I don't know what it is about you and dead people, Maddie, but it's getting out of hand. Can't you find another way to get ahead?"

"Can't you? You're the one who wants to be a homicide detective, after all."

"Do you even see how much this means to me? I joined the department almost ten years ago. There's no place for me to go, not really. Or there wasn't until Pomerleau started a month ago. It's going to change, Maddie. It's been dirty, a place where Negroes can't advance. I know you know what it feels like to have a dream. I'd never do anything to get between you and yours. You cannot take this information out of this room."

"It's in my head now. It's not like I can forget it. It goes where I go."

"You know what I mean. You can't tell anyone. Look, if I find out there's a break, if they're on the verge of arresting her, something like that—I'll tell you. Until then, you cannot write about this."

She said carefully, "I won't write anything about the police developments."

"Don't be cute, Maddie."

"I'm not," she said. "I promise you—I won't write anything that could be linked to you."

Not even eighteen hours later, she knocked on another mother's door.

November 1966

WHAT WERE YOU *thinking?* Maddie was asked frequently in the
weeks that followed her visit to the home of Angela Corwin on the
afternoon of November 1. Is that question ever really asked in an
open-minded, non-accusatory way? Is one ever asked, *What were
you thinking?* as a prelude to a compliment? Maddie thought not.
Still, she told the truth, more or less:

"I thought Mrs. Corwin might talk to me, mother to mother, in a
way she had not talked to police detectives."

It was true. True enough. She had rationalized that if she could
get Mrs. Corwin to confess to her, or at least make a little slip, then
she had not violated Ferdie's confidence. She wasn't really sure that
Ferdie would see it that way, but she believed she could persuade
him this was so, eventually. The son had spoken to her. Why not the
mother? Maddie had found the body of Tessie Fine. She had gotten

the killer to tell her a detail he had omitted in the police interview, the very detail that had led to the hunt for his accomplice. People kept stealing her story—stories. This one would be hers.

And, at first, it seemed to be going so well. Mrs. Corwin was a tiny woman with lovely manners. "Oh, yes, I remember your name," she said. She invited Maddie in, asked her if she wanted tea or coffee. She brought out a plate of cookies, bakery cookies. "From Bauhof's in Woodlawn," she said. "They make Silber's look like trash." Maddie helped herself to one, a pink-and-white refrigerator cookie. It was outstanding. If she lived closer to Woodlawn and still entertained, she would have served them to guests and pretended they were homemade.

"I love my son," Mrs. Corwin said, "but you know he's quite mad. Insane. But they won't let him enter an insanity plea. They don't want the information to get out."

"The information?"

"About the experiments at Fort Detrick."

"Ah, yes, Bob Bauer wrote about that. Operation Whitecoat." She didn't point out that this meant that information had gotten out, that the world now knew—and didn't care—about the germ experiments.

"He was a conscientious objector. We're Seventh-Day Adventists." She sipped her tea. "We don't mind Jews, though."

Maddie could not tell if that assurance was meant for her, Tessie Fine, or both of them.

"So there's no doubt in your mind that your son did kill her."

"I wouldn't want to gossip about Stephen with a stranger."

"In his letters to me, he didn't admit guilt. I hear now he's trying to plead to manslaughter and they won't have it because he hid the body."

"Well of course not. They're determined to make a liar out of him, if you ask me. They rejected the insanity plea, said he doesn't meet the standard, when he's clearly crazy. So he keeps saying what they want to hear, but it's never good enough. I hate to say it, but—he was never very bright, my Stephen. It was such a disappointment to me. I went to Woodlawn High School and made straight A's."

Maddie widened her eyes as if this were a singular achievement.

"His father's genes were—not what I thought they would be. Not at all. Then he left us. It was almost a relief. But I see him every time I look at Stephen. How odd to have married a redhead when I don't care for them at all. I think it was because I was scratched by a ginger tabby when I was small. My family was very well-to-do."

Maddie let the woman talk and talk and talk, although she quickly despaired of the idea that Mrs. Corwin would ever say anything relevant. Her voice was bizarrely hypnotic—squeaky, yet low in volume. It was like trying to listen to a mouse. A garrulous mouse.

After a very confusing story about her father's golfing at Forest Park—"We could afford a private club, but he was very egalitarian, when you are truly to the manor born, you don't worry about such things"—Maddie tried to jump in.

"You know, they still think your son had an accomplice. If they could find that person, it would give your son leverage. Or the accomplice would have leverage. That's how it was explained to me."

"Stephen didn't even have friends, I find it hard to believe he could find anyone to help him."

"He called here, right? The afternoon of Tessie Fine's murder?"

The woman pursed her lips. All her life, Maddie had heard the phrase and failed to understand it, but she saw it now, the way Mrs. Corwin's thin lips snapped together.

"How did you come by this information? Have the police been telling their tales?"

Maddie remembered she must be careful about referencing the police. "A little bird told me. A little bird from C & P." Then, gently, almost as if she were offering an apology: "It was you, wasn't it, Mrs. Corwin? Who helped Stephen?"

"Does my boy talk to you?"

"What? No, never. I mean, he wrote me a couple of letters last spring but stopped speaking to me after they were published."

"Yes, he wrote to you. And that's why he's in this fix. There was no accomplice. He had the car that day. I don't know why he keeps lying about that. He did something very bad and he has to face up to it. It's not really his fault. The experiments—"

"At Fort Detrick."

"Yes." She looked at the plate. "I'm going to get you some cookies to take home, Miss Schwartz."

"Mrs." Maddie wondered if she still was that, or would continue to be. She was going to be divorced soon. What did people call divorced ladies? At any rate, there would be a new Mrs. Milton Schwartz. Ali, whatever that was short for. It had to be short for something.

Mrs. Corwin returned from the kitchen with a white cardboard bakery box, tied with red-and-white string. "Oh, I couldn't take so many—" Maddie was saying as she brought a hand up in protest, only to have Mrs. Corwin insistently thrust the box toward her. It felt almost as if the woman had tried to punch her in the midsection with the box, only to drop it. Why was the box red now? How had paint gotten on the box?

A steak knife, she saw it now in Mrs. Corwin's tiny fist. It was

not large, but it was large enough. The woman made a second inef-
fectual pass, this one at Maddie's chest. She managed to block her
hand, to grab her wrist and twist it, so the knife clattered to the
floor. Mrs. Corwin screamed in pain. *Why are you screaming when
I'm the one who's stabbed?* Maddie thought. She was experiencing
a sensation wholly new to her—a supercharged energy, a clarity of
thought. She was aware that she should be in pain, but there was no
actual pain.

Beneath the screams were words, sputtered, hissing words. "Stupid, stupid, stupid. I was being kind, helping him put that girl out of
her misery. I'm trying to be kind to you."

Oh lord, the mother had *instructed* him. Was it possible that she
had even—

"Just like the chickens on Auntie's farm, just like the chickens on
Auntie's farm, what was the big deal? Easier than the chickens because the chickens run from you, before and after."

Given enough time, the woman would kill her, Maddie did not
doubt it. She had to get away, but how? Could she run? She felt as
if she could. She felt as if she could run, climb mountains, do whatever she had to do to survive.

To her amazement, the first thing she chose was to box the woman's ears and shout in her face: "Naughty!" Where was the phone?
Was there a phone? Of course there was a phone, Stephen Corwin
had called his mother from the fish store that day.

She pushed the older woman away with tremendous force, hard
enough to knock her flat on her back, and bolted for the kitchen,
where she shoved a chair beneath the doorknob and dialed 0.

"Send the police, send police," she panted. "A woman is trying
to kill me." They asked for the address and she went blank, then
remembered it. Even as she spoke, she was rummaging through the

drawers, looking for a knife of her own. "A knife," she told the operator. "She stabbed me with a knife."

Outside, she heard a car starting. She peered through the window, saw Mrs. Corwin behind the wheel of an older-looking car, comically small. Was Maddie safe? She was probably safe. By the time police arrived—seconds, minutes, hours later, she couldn't tell—the burst of adrenaline that had saved her was long gone. She pressed a kitchen towel to her middle, watching the blood seep out. She was going to be okay, she thought. She was almost certainly going to be okay.

Then: *She did it. She all but confessed she did it. Even if Stephen twisted the girl's neck, it was because she told him to. Tessie Fine was alive when his mother got there.*

The police would talk to her at the hospital. She would have to tell them what had happened, what Mrs. Corwin had said to her. Then what? Should she call the *Star,* tell them what she had learned?

No, she thought. They'd just make her talk to rewrite.

November 1966

THEY TOOK HER to Sinai, the same hospital where she had
given birth. Milton insisted they keep her overnight, and Maddie
was almost weepily grateful to him for being there, taking charge.
Later, she learned that he knew having her spend even a night in
the Pikesville house would mean resetting the clock on their legal
separation, which would slow down his marriage to Ali Whoever.
But she didn't mind even when she understood. She didn't want to
be in the Pikesville house, either, but she was too tender, in body
and mind, to be alone in her apartment.

She was given a private room with her own television and
watched through the evening as the story unfolded. Mrs. Corwin
had not gotten very far; she had crashed her car on Northern Parkway. She was in custody for stabbing Maddie and was expected to

be arraigned for her role in the murder of Tessie Fine. She was her son's accomplice and she had stabbed Maddie because she believed he had told her as much.

It was very satisfying, hearing her name in Wallace Wright's mouth. He described her as a reporter on assignment. Not accurate, but who cared. She had assigned herself. She had not broken her promise to Ferdie. The paper's top editor called her, ever so solicitous, making it clear that he expected Maddie, once recovered, would give the *Star* the scoop.

"We'd have you write it in the first person," he said. "Face-to-face with a killer. I could put you on with rewrite now, or in the morning if you need to sleep—"

But Maddie was an old hand at not making promises to men and she glided through the call with her usual grace. "I'll call when I feel up to it," she said.

She was exhausted, sincerely, yet had trouble sleeping. It was almost midnight when she closed her eyes. A few hours later, she woke disoriented from a thankfully dreamless sleep. Where was she? What was going on? She was in the hospital. She had been stabbed. She had helped police find the accomplice—perhaps the perpetrator. With the two of them charged, police could then press one to cooperate, ensuring the death penalty for the other. Surely, that mother happily would see her son dead, would make that deal in a heartbeat if it meant a better outcome for her. How unnatural she was, but then—what is natural? People might call Maddie unnatural, too, if Seth were to screw up one day. *What do you expect when his mother up and left when he was just sixteen?*

While she had required stitches, Mrs. Corwin was an inept assailant. The scar would not be pretty—Maddie thought of Ferdie and his bumpy navel—but it would seldom be seen by anyone. Maddie, eight days away from her thirty-eighth birthday, was past the time for two-piece bathing suits, never mind bikinis.

Someone was in the room. A nurse? No, this was a Negro woman, fiddling with the trash. How inconsiderate, Maddie thought. Surely the trash could wait until tomorrow.

The woman turned and said to her: "What have you done now, Madeline Schwartz?"

"Maddie," she corrected, automatically, stupidly. "Only my mother calls me Madeline. Do I know you?"

"No, but not for lack of trying." The woman sat in the Formica chair for visitors, the one where Milton had sat not even six hours ago. Even in the dim light, Maddie could see that the drab uniform was baggy on the woman's slender frame, that her bone structure was striking, her eyes pale beneath dark lashes.

"Who are you?"

"I was Cleo Sherwood."

Maddie was hallucinating. Or dreaming. She gave herself a small pinch near the base of her elbow. But the woman didn't disappear; quite the opposite. As Maddie's eyes adjusted to the light, her face came into sharper focus.

"Cleo Sherwood is dead."

"Yes, she is, always will be. But, man, you couldn't let her be, could you?"

"I don't—"

"No, you don't. You don't understand anything and you never will."

"I just wanted to know who killed you, how you came to be in the fountain. When I realized whom you were dating—"

"*Whom.*" The repeated word felt like an accusation. But what, exactly, was the charge?

"Who killed you?"

"Shell Gordon ordered me killed. Because it was the only way to keep me from becoming the second Mrs. Taylor. That was going to happen. Ezekiel—not EZ, never EZ, not to me—didn't care about the state senate. He didn't care about Shell, and that was the real problem. One thing to be married to Hazel and to tomcat around Baltimore with any old piece. But to find love? To know happiness? That ate Shell up inside. Ezekiel was going to choose life with me and there was no job, no woman that Shell could dangle in front of him that would get him to change his mind."

Maddie remembered Judith's tossed-off words, *They also say Shell Gordon is a Baltimore bachelor, for what it's worth.*

"He told Tommy to kill you. So who did Tommy kill? Whose body was in the fountain?"

"My roommate, Latetia. But Tommy didn't kill her. She overdosed two days after Christmas. So we dressed her in my clothes, although not my favorites, did what had to be done, put her someplace where she wouldn't be found for a while."

Even in her haze, Maddie found the story not quite right. If Thomas Ludlow had been ordered by Shell Gordon to kill Cleo, why not just say he had and let her go? Why did there have to be a body at all?

"Who are you, really?"

"Why, I'm Latetia Tompkins. I eloped over the holidays, sent my roommate a telegram from Elkton. I've been living in Philly. Close enough so I could sneak down from time to time, just look at the people I left behind. I thought, maybe one day, that I could tell them. But, no. It's gone too far. Now my father's in jail, probably going to die there. Nice to know he loved me, after all, but it was a hell of a way to find out." A pause. "I blame you."

"All I did was write the story. Someone was going to write it."

"That's true. But you had already kicked up so much dust. Going to see the psychic. Talking to my parents, in front of my boys."

Maddie still felt as if she were in a dream. But one can, at times, be sharp in a dream.

"Tommy wouldn't know that. About your parents. And there's no doubt that they think you're dead. But someone else knows. Your sister, the one who lives at home?"

"You should have let me be. That's all I ever wanted. You can't leave anything be. Who was I to you? The Lady in the Lake? Well, I wasn't a lady and I was never in no lake. Everything you wrote was a lie, whether you know it or not. At least you're haunting other folks now. Leave me be, Maddie Schwartz. I'm warning you."

"Why did you need a body? Why couldn't Tommy just tell Shell Gordon that you were gone for good, buried somewhere you'd never be found?"

"I didn't say we needed one. I said we had one, and we used it."

Maddie pondered the serendipitous death of Latetia, the girl who wouldn't be missed. Perhaps Thomas Ludlow did, in fact, have something to confess to. Maybe he had loved Cleo enough to do whatever he thought was necessary.

Or had Cleo killed Latetia without thinking things through, then called Tommy in a panic? It still seemed impossible for even two people to drag an inert body up and over the fence, across the lake, up and into the fountain. But—a double date, a seemingly spontaneous dare. *Let's row over to the fountain, climb up, look at the city lights from there.* Maybe Cleo had gone out that night with the man Thomas Ludlow had described to police, but maybe she had fixed Ludlow up with Latetia. Maybe it had just been the three of them.

"But—"

"Goodbye, Maddie Schwartz."

Maddie watched almost in wonder as the woman stood, allowed her long, lovely body to droop into the defeated posture of a janitress, and shuffle out into the hall. Maddie would have been within her rights to wonder, come the morning, if it all had been a dream. But it was true. Cleo Sherwood was alive and Maddie could never tell anyone.

As she fell back asleep, she realized that the hospital walls were a pale institutional green, while the Formica chair was yellow.

November 1966

MADDIE WAS HOME before her thirty-eighth birthday. She expected a visit from Ferdie, curious about the gift he had promised, but he didn't show up. Perhaps he didn't realize she had returned to the apartment.

Thanksgiving came and went, disturbingly warm, sixty-six degrees. In New York, the unseasonable temperatures created a bizarre smog event, blanketing the city with dense, blackish air until a cold front dispelled it. By the last Sunday of November, the weather had returned to normal, late-fall temperatures. But Maddie's apartment on the third floor was always warm, so she continued to sleep with her window cracked. At least, that's what she told herself.

She was not asleep when she heard the window being raised—it wasn't quite ten o'clock—but she pretended to be.

Only Ferdie did not slide into bed, as was his usual practice. After a minute or two of playing possum, she opened her eyes. There he was, out of uniform. He wore slacks and a V-neck sweater with a collared shirt. His hair was getting longer—well, fuller. It grew out and up, not down. It looked good. He looked, Maddie realized, like a boxer whose photo had been in the papers earlier this month, frugging in London with a striking actress.

"I've told you and told you about that window, Maddie."

"It just gets so hot up here." She pushed away the covers, glad she'd had the foresight to wear a pretty gown.

"You've been a busy girl."

"Yes, I suppose so." Laughing, uninterested in talking. She held out her arms to him. But he stayed by the window.

"You promised me, Maddie. You promised not to write anything."

"I promised not to write anything based on what *you* told me. And I didn't."

"Yeah, maybe people who read the papers believe you went to talk to her—what did you say, mother to mother? No one in my shop was fooled. They knew someone had to have told you. They realized right away it was me." A pause. "That we were together."

"But how—"

"Some other cop saw me leaving here once, in a patrol car. That's what they got me on. Not talking to you, but unauthorized use of a vehicle. Got me and my friend in the garage, who would let me borrow patrol cars at night, using them for a few hours before they were to be put back into service the next day. Did you ever wonder how I got here at night, Maddie? Do you know where I live, how far it is from here, how buses don't run in the middle of the night?"

"You never wanted to talk about yourself."

"Maybe I was waiting to be asked."

She had tried to ask him questions, she was sure of it. He had always deflected them. Hadn't he?

"I thought you were married."

"I'm not."

"That you had other women."

"I won't lie to you. I did. At first. But then—Maddie, I love you."

She had nothing to say to that.

"I guess that's my answer. You don't love me."

"I do, Ferdie. But you have to know it's impossible."

"Because I'm black."

Yes and no, she thought. It was illegal because he was black. But it was impossible because he was younger. Because he was a cop and she was Madeline Morgenstern Schwartz and she wasn't going to be a newspaper clerk forever. She could go out in public with—her mind groped to think of a black man of stature—Sidney Poitier. Andrew Young. Harry Belafonte Jr. But Ferdinand Platt was impossible on many levels, and race was only one of them. Wasn't it?

"That's really not it."

"You know my happiest day of the past year? Going to that ball game with you. Even if I couldn't hold your hand or put my hand at the small of your back as we moved through the crowd. Some people knew we were together. I could tell, by their looks. We fooled most people, but we couldn't fool everyone. I was so proud to be with you. I love you, Maddie."

She still could not say the words back, even though it would be so easy, so true. She would not be bound by them, and yet she could not say them, even in past tense. "I don't think I want to be anyone's wife again, Ferdie. I don't want to lose you, but I don't want to lose myself, either."

"Well, I've lost my job," he said.

"For using a patrol car off hours?"

"They let me resign. I could have stayed, but I wasn't going to go anywhere. I put our business out on the street. Almost got a civilian killed."

It took Maddie a beat to realize she was the civilian. She lifted her nightgown, showed him the bumpy loop of a scar, then lifted the gown off her head.

"Maddie—"

"I'm so sorry for everything. I'm sorry about the job. I'm sorry—" She could not tell him her other regrets. She was sorry for Thomas Ludlow and sorry for Cleo's father. Sorry that Cleo's mother could never know that her daughter was alive. She was even sorry for Shell Gordon, trapped inside so many identities, never allowed to express what he really yearned for, small and mean enough to want others to be denied what he could not have. She was sorry for Latetia, dead and unmourned, fixed in history as a careless girl who eloped and was never heard from again. She was sorry for Mrs. Taylor, living in her beautiful house with a man who loved another. She was sorry for Cleo's children.

Most of all, she was sorry for herself. Because, like Ezekiel Taylor, she was so close to having a second chance at real love and she wasn't brave enough to take it.

"We shouldn't," he said. "We never should have started in the first place."

"My ring wasn't stolen," she said. "I did that to get the insurance money."

"I know," he said. "I told you about Tommy Ludlow because we thought it would make you stop. Shell told Tommy he had to confess, to make you stop."

"I know," she said. She hadn't.

He came to bed. For one last time, he came to her bed, and for the first time ever he stayed until the sun rose. Maddie walked him downstairs and kissed him goodbye at the front door, in full sight of the cathedral and whoever was walking down Mulberry Street at seven A.M.

And then she went to work.

The Woman's Club of Roland Park,
October 1985

"AND NOW, OUR speaker. Madeline Schwartz has worked at the *Beacon* since 1966, where her career began with a harrowing first-person account of her near death at the hands of Angela Corwin, who was eventually convicted of the first-degree murder of Tessie Fine, a young Jewish girl killed in the tropical fish store where Corwin's son worked. Stephen Corwin was given the death penalty for his role in the crime, but that was changed to life after a US Supreme Court decision struck down most of the nation's death penalty laws in 1972. Schwartz started at the *Beacon* as a general assignment reporter, went on to cover city hall and the legislature, but is best known for her work in the Living section, first as a reporter of human-interest stories, now as a columnist. In 1979, she was a finalist for the Pulitzer Prize in feature writing."

Maddie edited her introduction in her head. This was not the copy she had provided, she was sure of that. Close, but embellished here and there. Although, yes, she was the one who had written the *Star* out of her official history. She had taken her first-person near-death story about Angela Corwin, parlayed it into a job at the *Beacon,* and never looked back. The *Beacon* was a little stuffy and dull after the *Star,* but it was willing to give her a chance as a reporter.

"Good afternoon," she said. "And 'finalist for the Pulitzer' is a very grand way of saying that one *lost* the Pulitzer."

Audiences like a little gentle self-deprecation, but she was always of two minds about publicizing her bridesmaid status. It bugged her that she hadn't won that year, the first time that the prize for feature writing was given. More galling, it had gone to a colleague on the *Light,* the *Beacon*'s less mannerly sister paper. He had written about brain surgery, while her story had centered on a child with a rare heart condition. "Brains trump heart, I guess," Bob Bauer had said when they met up for drinks later that week. The remark had been tinged with envy; Bauer had won all the state prizes and some national ones, but had never come anywhere close to a Pulitzer.

Maddie had won almost everything, too, and she still had plenty of years in her.

As a high-profile columnist, she was much in demand on the ladies'-luncheon circuit. The *Beacon* had a speaker's bureau and actually paid its reporters to make these presentations; the paper considered it a good community-relations ploy. Maddie had learned how to appear to talk off the cuff, to vary her stories just enough so she couldn't be accused of being canned or rote.

"I'm often asked"—a lie, she was never asked—"what, exactly, is human interest? What makes a person interesting? Well, I believe all people are intrinsically interesting if you know the right questions to ask, if you take time. I think a good reporter should be able to open a phone book, stab a name with a pencil, call up the person, and find a story. Sometimes, I do just that."

(Also a lie, she had never done that.)

She told of her latest triumph, an exclusive interview with the parents of a child who was kidnapped from the Sinai Hospital maternity ward by a woman disguised as a nurse, caught several days later when she tried to con another hospital into giving her a birth certificate. The parents still expressed wonder at how easily someone had slipped into Sinai Hospital. Maddie did not tell them she knew it was, in fact, quite easy. A uniform and a defeated posture could do the trick.

"The law required the parents to take a paternity test," she told her rapt audience. "But the judge looked from that round-cheeked baby to his father and said, 'I think we all know what the results are going to tell us.'"

Her talk was so familiar to her that she could almost disengage, hover above the proceedings like a ghost. Even as she told the stories about the stories that had made her a local treasure—the spiky newsstand owner, the last local hatmaker, the piano prodigy—she was thinking about the stories never written, the people never profiled. Ezekiel "EZ" Taylor, for example, who sold his dry-cleaning chain abruptly in 1968, blaming the riots and the weather. He said he was asthmatic, that he had been advised to move west for his health, New Mexico to be precise, but his wife preferred to stay in Baltimore because of her church activities. Did EZ go in search of Cleo, after all? One thing was for sure: there was no listed phone number for Ezekiel Taylor anywhere in New Mexico. Maddie had checked, repeatedly.

"I got my job at the *Beacon* by being brash, insisting on being the reporter instead of the subject. It was a gamble on both sides, but the editor, Peter Forrester, said he saw something in me. I think it was my willingness to start at the lowest possible salary."

There were days when Maddie was convinced that it's all a coincidence, that EZ went west for his health and Shell Gordon, still bent with grudge over a woman he saw as a rival, found a more trustworthy assassin to finish the job Thomas Ludlow failed to do.

And there were days when she believed this mismatched couple was somewhere, maybe the Land of Enchantment, maybe not, delighted that they beat the odds. Not the odds of Cleo's death, but the odds against finding love, a real love that can sustain you, a love that's worth giving up everything.

"One of the biggest breaks I ever got as a reporter happened because I got terribly lost, lost in my own hometown . . ."

She had tried to find out if Cleo's sons were still with their grandmother, but the family had moved not long after Maddie joined the *Beacon*. To the county, one neighbor said. To the country, another neighbor said. She couldn't find the mother anywhere and Alice Sherwood, Cleo's sister, had shut the door in her face the one time she tried to talk to her.

"Of course, we always remember the ones that got away. Every year, I write a certain Baltimore novelist and beg her for an interview. And every year, she sends me a polite refusal."

Ferdie had ended up rich. Rich and fat, which amazed her. He left the police department and started his own home security business. His timing was good; crime and safety were on everyone's mind. He made lots of money, married, had three children, and ended up having far more influence over local politics than either Shell Gordon or EZ Taylor ever had. Maddie had seen him once, across a room at a big political fund-raiser where she was shadowing the candidate. Even with an extra fifty pounds on him, he was magnetic. If he had given her so much as a glance, she would have slipped into a back room with him. But his wife kept him close, well aware of her prize. If Maddie could have glimpsed the future, seen what he would become—but *no*. She was right about herself. She did not want to be anyone's wife. She loved her life. And she sensed a sadness in Ferdie, over what he never became, never could be. All he'd wanted to be was a detective and Maddie had cost him that.

". . . and that was the second time in my career I was on the receiving end of an unexpected confession. He looked up at me with these big brown eyes and said, 'I told Jimmy not to do it.'"

Maddie was a grandmother now, not atypical for a woman about to turn fifty-seven, but it was not vanity to think that she still looked good. Wallace Wright, of all people, recently out of marriage number two, had asked her for a date not long ago. She had turned him down, saying she was seeing someone. She was. He was forty and, lord help her, a gardener, but not *her* gardener, so it wasn't totally Lady Chatterley. You couldn't call what they did dating, not really. He came to her apartment, fucked her silly, and left. It was, in fact, very much like the arrangement she'd had with Ferdie, but with different drinks and snacks. Only now she had a daytime arrangement as well. There was a pompous old judge, almost certainly gay, who required a presentable companion at times, so that worked well for both of them.

"When I was given the column at the *Beacon,* I was one of its first female columnists with license to write about the world at large. My column may be in the features section, but no topic is off-limits. One day, I might be talking about Reagan, the next day, the insanity of the Rotunda parking lot."

Knowing laughter, at least about the parking lot at the nearby shopping center.

Cleo Sherwood had said that Maddie ruined lives. Did she? Ferdie may never have become a homicide detective, but he had prospered. She had rather lost track of Judith Weinstein, who had married Patrick Monaghan after all. Thomas Ludlow had been released from prison eight years ago and now ran his own bar on Franklintown Road, although with another man's name on the liquor license, given that he was a convicted felon. Cleo Sherwood's father had died in prison. But none of this was Maddie's fault. Cleo was the one who had faked her death, with Ludlow's help. Ludlow was the one who had chosen to confess after Maddie dared to confront Hazel Taylor. Ferdie was the one who had brought her that "tip," courtesy of Shell Gordon. Men. They tried to close the circle, only to bust everything wide open.

What about Latetia, the true Lady in the Lake? Who was she, how did she die? The likely suspect had confessed, a sentence had been meted out, justice of a sort achieved. Did it really matter whose body was in the fountain? Did it matter if the right person had gone to jail?

Yet—Maddie imagined three people, maybe four. *It's so warm. Let's climb the fence at the zoo, I know where they keep the boats. We can toast the New Year from the lake. Or maybe even climb the fountain.* Three people, maybe four, sitting on the lip of the fountain, tossing back drinks. Two roommates, sharing each other's clothes. How easy it would be for one to fall, to be pushed.

How could everything be Maddie's fault?

When these thoughts invaded, the only thing to do was go to the computer and write a cheery seven hundred fifty words about her latest adventure in the Rotunda parking lot. Or dig into her past—

that time she was fondled at the Pikes Theater was good for a laugh. A man's hand on one's leg seemed so innocent now. She also revisited the Tessie Fine story, her role in it, at suitable intervals. This was what she did, this was her life, a life of her choosing. She wrote about herself. She told herself it was because she had done her time, writing about others, but in her heart, she knew she was always writing about herself, that the only story she could ever know was her own.

And maybe not even that one.

"This erudite group will recognize that 'Only connect' is from E. M. Forster's *Howards End*. But do you know the rest of it? 'Only connect the prose and the passion, and both will be exalted, and human love will be seen at its height. Live in fragments no longer.' My column embraces all aspects of life, it celebrates all people. This group will also know, no doubt, that the Ouija board was invented here in Baltimore; I wrote about the heirs to the fortune last year. I see myself as the planchette, that little plastic piece on which you balance your fingers and, perhaps subconsciously, then guide across the board toward the answers you desire. I am telling you the stories *you* want to hear, answering your questions. I am your instrument. Without my readers, I have no purpose."

She sat down to thunderous applause, took a sip of wine. That was the best thing about talking to Presbyterians. They served alcohol at lunch.

WHERE AM I, Maddie Schwartz? Where are you? Why am I still talking to you in my head, all these years later? I guess it's because you're the last person who saw me, the actual me, Eunetta "Cleo" Sherwood, alive. Not Tommy on New Year's Eve, although that will always remain the official story. It was you, in your hospital bed, ten months later, and you were too groggy and overwhelmed by your own drama to pay close attention to mine. I was dead and you had made a good run at it. Did your life flash before your eyes? Mine played out so slowly, continues to play out every day. Where would Cleo be right now? What would her life look like? I walked out of that hospital and said goodbye to Cleo Sherwood forever. Said goodbye to my parents, my babies, to Baltimore.

But I didn't say goodbye to life, or to love. My life has been a rich one, a full one. A happy one. I sacrificed a lot, so I don't feel guilty about being happy now. My boys might not have had me, but they both went to McDonogh, growing into fine men, then on to college. My sister told my mama they got scholarships and she decided to believe her because she didn't have the luxury of looking too closely at good fortune. Knowing my fate, the way I've been able to care for those I love, I wouldn't do anything differently. Can you say the same thing?

Did I tell you everything? No. I wasn't about to trust you with my secrets, Maddie Schwartz. Who could blame me? You were careless with my life and my death. Thank God you found another dead girl to pursue. I'm happy, I got what I wanted.

I saw you once, Maddie Schwartz, before any of this began. You had a man you didn't want. I ended up wanting a man everyone said I could never have. I saw you, saw you seeing me seeing you. It's like that joke you tell when you're a kid: I'm painting a picture of myself painting a picture of myself painting a picture of myself. The picture goes on and on, the words go on and on, until they make no sense, until the picture is so tiny that you can't see anything at all.

AUTHOR'S NOTE

WHEN I STARTED this book in February 2017, I had no idea that it was going to become a newspaper novel; in some ways, Maddie Schwartz surprised me as much as she surprised her longtime husband. I had no desire to write a newspaper novel, but I soon found myself caught up in trying to imagine and re-create the world my father had known when he took a job in 1965 at what was then called the *Sun*. Many, many colleagues, his and mine, helped me with this. They include: G. Jefferson Price III, David Michael Ettlin, and Joan Jacobson.

The book's small details are largely factual, except when they're not. The two murders at its center are clearly inspired by two cases from 1969, but my versions are not steeped in fact, although I am eternally grateful to Jonathan Hayes for helping me with the theoretical postmortem on "the lady of the lake." The gubernatorial race in Maryland in 1966 is represented accurately, down to the weather on the day after the primary, a detail gleaned from *Time* magazine. Two real-life people—Violet Wilson Whyte (Lady Law) and Paul Blair, the Orioles center fielder—"speak" in these pages; I read interviews with them and, in the case of Blair, watched videos, hoping to approximate their real voices. I could never establish that Whyte had, in fact, appeared on *To Tell the Truth,* but I heeded the age-old advice from *The Man Who Shot Liberty Valance*: print the legend.

The first draft of this book was submitted on June 27, 2018. The next day, I headed to my mother's home on the Delaware shore with my young daughter, stopping about an hour into the trip to tell her we had eaten lunch and should be there within the next two hours. She asked me if I had run into traffic near Annapolis. No, I said, why would I? "There was a shooting." When I learned that it was at the newspaper, I knew it was all too likely that my friend Rob Hiaasen was one of the victims. So while I usually take time here to thank everyone who helped me, I hope my friends and the people in my publishing life will understand that I want this book to end with a roll call of names of people who died that day. This one is for Rob Hiaasen, Gerald Fischman, John McNamara, Rebecca Smith, and Wendi Winters, and their loved ones.

About the author

Read on

Insights,
Interviews
& More . . .

Meet Laura Lippman

Leslie Unruh

Since LAURA LIPPMAN's debut, she has won multiple awards and critical acclaim for provocative, timely crime novels set in her beloved hometown of Baltimore. Laura has been nominated for more than fifty awards for crime fiction and won almost twenty, including the Edgar. Her books have been translated into over twenty languages. Now a perennial *New York Times* bestselling author, she lives in Baltimore and New Orleans with her family.

Excerpt from *Dream Girl* by Laura Lippman

Keep reading for a sneak peek at
Laura Lippman's next thrilling read,
Dream Girl
Coming Fall 2021

**Excerpt from *Dream Girl* by
Laura Lippman** (*continued*)

Prologue

Gerry dreams.

   In a rented hospital bed, high above
the city, higher than he ever thought
possible in stodgy, low-slung Baltimore,
Gerry is asleep more than he's awake.
He floats, he wakes, he drifts, he dreams.
He tosses, but he cannot turn. He is
Wynken, Blynken, and Nod, casting
his net over the glittering lights of
downtown, deceptively beautiful at
night, a city where someone might
choose to live, no longer a city where
one gets stuck, not at night, not in his
dreams.

   There is no clear demarcation
between Gerry's dreams and his
fantasies, his not-quite-sleep and
his not-really-awake. His brain chugs,
stuck in a single gear, focused on one
thought or one image. Tonight, he feels
he is revolving, ever so slowly, like the
old restaurant on top of the Holiday Inn.
Then he finds himself slipping from the
minute hand of the clock in the Bromo
Seltzer Tower, a Charm City Harold
Lloyd, slipping, slipping, slipping.

   Someone is waiting on the sidewalk
below, arms outstretched. It's a woman,
but he can't see her face. He lets go
and—he wakes up.

   Or does he? Was he really asleep, is he
ever really awake these days? He spends

almost all his time in this bed, except for the supervised visits to the bathroom, where a nurse attends to him with more cheer and finesse than he would have thought possible for someone who makes a living wiping adult bottoms.

Is it the medication? It must be the medication. His sleep has never been like this before. Maybe he shouldn't take the medication. Does he need the medication? Is he at risk of getting hooked on the medication? Museums are stripping the names of opioid heirs from their buildings, yet here is Gerry, late to every trend as usual. Just like his hometown.

From downstairs, he can hear the faint hum of the nurse's television show. It weaves itself into his thoughts, a soothing murmur. Tonight's program appears to be a talk show. It sounds like Johnny Carson. It cannot be Johnny Carson. Except—there is some weird channel, something called MeTV, a jumble of older programs from Gerry's youth. Is the nurse watching MeTV? Is her TV—HerTV—different from HisTV? If it were really MeTV, wouldn't it be tailored to his specific preferences? Johnny Carson, *Mannix, Columbo, Banacek*. That would be Gerry's MeTV, which was really his mother's TV. MomTV.

He will ask the nurse tomorrow about his pain meds, what exactly he's taking, what he's risking. After the surgery— there had been no time to brief him ▸

**Excerpt from *Dream Girl* by
Laura Lippman** *(continued)*

before, given the nature of his injury—
he had been given a pamphlet in the
hospital titled, "Your role in pain
control." The unwitting couplet is
stuck in his head.

    Your role
In pain control
Your *role*
In pain control
Your role
In pain *control*

    The words, said over and over,
become ridiculous, as all words
eventually do. What is Gerry's role in
pain control? Isn't the human condition
a cradle-to-grave attempt to gauge one's
role in pain control? To whom has Gerry
caused pain and to what extent did he
control it? He makes a list.

    His first wife, Sarah, but if she hadn't
been so jealous, things might have been
different.

    His third wife, Lisa.
Not his second wife, Gretchen.
Not Margot, no matter how she pouts.
His mother? He hopes not.
His father? Who cares?
Carrie, Wade?
I've got a little list. Nixon had a list.
Are people really nostalgic for Nixon
now? That seems a bridge too far.
His mother hated Nixon. He remembers
his mother screaming out in the night.
What happened, Mama? Someone shot
Robert F. Kennedy. *No, mama, they shot
JFK.* It's happening again, it's happening
again, her voice rising in hysteria.

Everything is happening again.

There was a letter, Gerry tells himself. There was definitely a letter. That was the indirect cause of the accident, a letter, a letter from a person who can't possibly exist. Only no one can find the letter now. No one knows anything about the letter.

He's pretty sure there was a letter.

"Mr. Andersen, you need another pill."

The nurse, Aileen, looms over him, glass of water, pill in hand. By day, when he is lucid—well, relatively more lucid—he has checked the label: she is following the dosage meticulously. Still, he's skeptical of the medicine. But what is his role in pain control? Should he ask for less? Does he want less? How would he rate his pain on a scale from one to ten, as the pamphlet encouraged him to do? He feels as if he's in a lot of pain, but he's never really been in that much pain before, so it's hard to rate what he's feeling now.

A seven. Gerry gives himself a seven.

Is that the pain in his leg or his heart? Is pain the problem or does it mask the problems he doesn't want to face, the problems that haunt his dreams, the fear and regret, the people he let down. The dead—his mother, Wade—are kind to him, at least. The living, however. He feels as if the living are enjoying his current discomfort way too much. The living have been waiting a long time for Gerald Andersen to have a ▶

comeuppance, although this is more of
a comedownance.

"Your pills, Mr. Andersen. It's very
important that you take your pills."

He has no choice. He swallows.

Chapter 1

Gerry Andersen's new apartment is a topsy-turvy affair—living area on top, bedrooms below. The brochure—it is the kind of apartment that had its own brochure when it was on the market— boasted of 360-degree views, but surely that was just another marketing lie. PH 2502 is the middle unit between two other duplex penthouses. The three two-story apartments share a common area, a most uncommon common area, a hallway with a distressed concrete floor, available only to those who have a key that allows them to press "PH" on the elevator. But not even the corner units have 360-degree views. Nothing means anything anymore, Gerry has decided. No one uses words correctly and if you call them on it, they claim that meaning is fungible, that it's oppressive and prissy not to let words mean whatever the speaker wishes them to mean.

Take the name of this building, The Vue at Locust Point. What is a "vue"? And isn't the view what one sees from the building, not the building itself? The Vue is the view for people on the other side of the harbor, where, Gerry is told, there is a $12 million apartment on top of the Four Seasons ▶

**Excerpt from *Dream Girl* by
Laura Lippman** *(continued)*

Hotel. *A $12 million apartment in
Baltimore.* Nothing makes sense
anymore.

This apartment cost $1.75 million,
which is about what Gerry cleared when
he sold his place in New York City, a
dated two-bedroom he bought in the
fall of 2001. How real estate agents had
shaken their sleek blond heads over his
kitchen, his bathrooms, as if his failure
to update them was indicative of a great
moral failing. Yet his apartment sold
for almost $3 million last fall and, as
he understood the current tax laws,
he needed to put the capital gains in
a new residence before the end of the
calendar year. Money goes a long way
in Baltimore, and it was a struggle to
find a place that could eat up all that
capital without being nightmarishly
large. So here he is at The Vue, where
money seems to be equated with cold,
hard things—marble in the kitchen,
distressed concrete floors, big metal
light fixtures.

"Impressive," his literary agent,
Thiru Vignarajah, says as he stands in
the foyer, or what might be called a foyer
in a more traditional apartment with
walls. "But did they mention it was in
Baltimore, Gerry?"

"Very funny, Thiru. You know why
I bought down here."

Eight months ago, Gerry had been
assured by doctors that his mother had
less than two months to live. Her only
desire was to die in her home, Gerry's

"boyhood" home. Gerry, ever the dutiful son, figured he could grant that wish. Two months passed. Then three. At month four, the doctors admitted they were fallible and that his mother might live for years, although not necessarily at home, but she could remain there for the foreseeable future. (Which, of course, is an oxymoron; the future cannot be seen.) Hounded by his New York co-op board over what it believed to be an illegal sublet but was really just an unruly, almost–ex-girlfriend causing her usual chaos, Gerry decided that buying an apartment in Baltimore would solve all his problems. His New York apartment sold quickly, despite the kitchen and bathrooms, and he snapped up this place, fully furnished, from the CFO of some smoke-and-mirrors tech company who was going through a bad divorce.

His mother died on December 31, the day after he closed on the Baltimore apartment. Maybe she couldn't bear the idea that they would no longer be under their old roof together.

Now two weeks later, Thiru, always the full-service agent, is here for what he insists on calling the memorial service, which consisted of picking up Gerry's mother's ashes and taking them to Petit Louis for lunch. Not that his mother ever ate at Petit Louis, but back in the 1960s and '70s she chose the old restaurant in this location, Morgan Millard, for every milestone occasion. ▶

**Excerpt from *Dream Girl* by
Laura Lippman** *(continued)*

Gerry's graduation from middle school,
Gerry's scholarship to Gilman, Gerry's
acceptance to Princeton. Her birthdays.
Once, only once, Gerry had persuaded
her to breach her loyalty to Morgan
Millard, insisting that they dine in
New York on the day his second novel
was published. He had taken her to
Michael's, she had seen a famous
anchorwoman, then she had pressed
him to get up and ask her to feature
him on her show. Gerry had declined.

At Petit Louis, a perfectly respectable
French bistro, he could not help
wondering if Thiru was judging it.
Gerry actually prefers this restaurant
to its New York counterparts, bistros
like Odeon and Pastis. It's not so much
of a *scene*. He prefers quite a few things
in Baltimore, or maybe it's just that it
seems important now to keep a running
list in his head of things that are better
in Baltimore. *Movies*: it's almost unheard
of to encounter a sold-out movie here.
Weather: the winters are a tad milder,
shorter. *Grocery stores?* The Whole Foods
on Smith Avenue is just as awful as the
one on the Upper West Side, albeit in
different ways.

Thiru proclaims himself charmed by
Petit Louis, by all of North Baltimore.
He seems less charmed as they approach
Gerry's new home in Locust Point,
a working-class neighborhood that
is allegedly gentrifying, with Gerry's
new home as Exhibit A. Thiru is
uncharacteristically silent as they pull

into the garage, leave the Zipcar in its designated space, and take the elevator to the main floor, where Gerry picks up the mail from Phylloh at the front desk. Thiru does brighten at the sight of Phylloh, a curvy girl whose ethnicity is a mystery to Gerry, although he knows enough to know that he must never inquire how she has come by those eyes, that skin, that hair. Would Thiru be allowed to ask? Is it wrong to wonder if Thiru would be allowed to inquire? The modern world is killing Gerry.

The button for his floor is marked "PH," although Gerry will never call his apartment a penthouse, never.

Thiru's bright eyes continue to appraise everything. It's almost like being present for the unbearably long periods that Thiru has one of Gerry's new manuscripts.

"Can you imagine what an apartment like this would cost in New York?" Gerry asks. Tacky to talk about money, of course, but Thiru is his agent; he knows to the penny how much money Gerry has earned. He had to certify Gerry's net worth when he bought the New York co-op.

"Yes," Thiru says. "But—then it would be in New York, Gerry."

"I'll be back," Gerry says. "I just need to stay here a year or two so I don't lose too much money. And then I'll downsize, maybe try another neighborhood. I was getting tired of the Upper West Side." ▶

**Excerpt from *Dream Girl* by
Laura Lippman** *(continued)*

"Is real estate appreciating here, then?
I thought the city had been rather, um,
challenged in recent years. There were
those riots? And the murder rate is
rather high? I feel as if I just read a piece
in the *Times* about it."

"Millennials are drawn to Baltimore,"
Gerry says, parroting something he
heard, although he can't remember
from whom. "It's the most affordable
city in the Northeast right now. Real
estate has been a little soft since, um,
Freddie Gray."

He does not add that it's a fraught
choice in Baltimore, whether to refer
to the events of 2015 as the "riots" or the
"uprising." Gerry can't bring himself to
use either term.

"Hmmmm." Thiru begins pacing
the top floor, not bothering to ask if
he can look around. He is a tiny man
with an enormous head, only eight
years older than Gerry. But the two
men have been together for forty years,
since Thiru read one of Gerry's stories
in the *Georgia Review,* and the age gap
still seems significant to Gerry. He has
longish hair that he wears in a brushed-
back leonine mane. The once blue-black
hair is silvery now, the peak has receded,
but there is still quite a bit of it, thick
and shiny. His suits are bespoke; they
probably have to be, given his height.
He still terrifies Gerry on some level,
although their relationship has outlasted
seven wives (three for Gerry, four for
Thiru).

"Are you working on something, Gerry?"

"You know I don't talk about my work-in-progress."

"Fiction."

For a second, Gerry assumes this is an accusation, not a question, but that's probably because it *is* a fiction that he is working on. He hasn't written for months. Reasonable, he thinks, under the circumstances, although he was able to work through every other difficult period of his life.

"Of course. What else? You know I have little patience for literary criticism right now. Most American writers bore me."

"I thought with your mother gone, you might consider that memoir we talked about."

"*You* talked about. The memoir is a debased form."

"But it's such a good story, the thing with your father."

"No, Thiru. It's sad and banal. And I used it for my second novel. I have no desire to revisit that material."

"It's just that your publisher would like you to sign a new contract."

"And when I have finished a new book—the new book—we shall. I don't like advances, Thiru. That's what undercut my early work, that's what made *Dream Girl*, and everything that followed, different. I won't take money upfront for an unwritten book. I can't—" ▶

**Excerpt from *Dream Girl* by
Laura Lippman** *(continued)*

He stops, fearful that he is about to
say the thing he doesn't want to say out
loud: *I can't write anymore.* It's not true.
It can't be true. But given the
circumstances of his mother's death,
how can he not worry about receiving a
similar diagnosis one day? This thing
runs in families.

Over the past eight months, he
has become a detective of sorts,
searching the past to determine when
the signs of his mother's dementia first
manifested. She was only eighty-two
when she died and her illness had been
obvious for three years, but now Gerry
believes the signs were there earlier,
if only anyone had cared to notice.
Those odd lies she told about his father
visiting her, despite being remarried—
he thought she manufactured those
stories to shore up her self-esteem.
Now he believes they were delusions,
which would be consistent with the
illness's progression.

How many years does he have?
Enough for one book, two? What if he
is already slipping? How will he know?
Who will save him from publishing
gibberish that will undo his reputation?
He thinks about a recent book by one
of the previous generation's greatest
writers. Utter trash, but no one would
say so. Don't writers realize that the
words are all you leave, that there's no
percentage in achieving a status in which
one is no longer criticized? People think
that Gerry is thin-skinned because he

can be cranky about the melee of social media, its sudden and simplistic judgments. But Gerry appreciates the young women—and they are all young women—who want to debate and deconstruct his work. It's proof that he's still vital, that he matters. They can say whatever they want, as long as they continue to talk about him, his *ideas*. The end of the mockery will be the canary in the coal mine.

How many years does he have?

"Well, the view is really something," Thiru says, his admiration sincere.

"In fact, I'm not sure I could work with such a panorama spread out before me. I like the fact that you can see the working part of the harbor, not just the fancy parts."

"This used to be a grain silo," Gerry says. "The site of the building, I mean."

"Well, good thing you're not gluten intolerant."

"Ha ha, funny Thiru." Gerry gives him 15 percent of a smile.

His agent peers down the staircase to the darker rooms below—Gerry's office, Gerry's study, Gerry's bedroom. He has set up the three-bedroom apartment so that guests are almost unthinkable, with one extra bedroom used as his study and the third, smallest one, dedicated to the overflow of books that didn't fit in the study or on the upstairs shelves. If Margot should propose visiting—doubtful, someone like Margot would never be drawn to Baltimore—he will ▶

Excerpt from *Dream Girl* by Laura Lippman *(continued)*

be able to tell her there is no spare bedroom, and she is no longer welcome in his.

"That's . . . interesting."

"It's called a floating staircase."

"Oh, I'm familiar with the *concept*. But wouldn't it make more sense in an open space, where it could be seen? Rather wasted here. It's like staring down a mouth. A mouth with big gaps between the teeth."

"I didn't design the apartment," Gerry says. "I needed something in move-in condition. Most of the furniture was part of the staging and I asked to keep it. The only things I brought from New York were my Herman Miller chair, my books, and the dining room set."

Thiru's eyebrows, thick and furry, make a perfect inverted V on his forehead, then quickly relax. Gerry decides that Thiru's teasing is a form of envy. It's a beautiful apartment and Baltimore, which he fought so hard to escape, feels serene after New York. Maybe this is all he needs to get back to work, a change of scene. A change of scene, no more Margot drama, no more suspense over the quality of his mother's end-of-life. He will be able to write again. Soon.

"Anyway, I've brought some things that came to the agency—the usual fan mail"—Thiru grins because Gerry's mail runs more to anti-fans—"and speaking requests, some for quite good money."

Thiru hands Gerry a manila folder of

envelopes. Glancing through it,
Gerry notices that one is addressed in
cursive, an undeniably feminine hand,
so perfect that he suspects it's a machine
posing as a person. But it has a Baltimore
postmark and the return address seems
vaguely familiar, an address he should
know. Fait Avenue. He's filled with
warmth and then—his mind goes
blank; he cannot remember the person,
someone who provokes nothing but
affection, who lived on Fait Avenue.
He knows, technically, what has
happened. His frontal cortex has seized
up and will not be able to provide the
information he wants, not now. Later,
when he's relaxed, it will come to him
easily. But for now, the memory is locked
away, like a phone on which one has
tried a series of incorrect passwords.
This is not a sign of dementia. It's not,
it's not.

Thiru insists on taking an Uber to
the train station as Gerry's new assistant,
Victoria, has yet to return from her
errands. Gerry doesn't own a car—
although his mother's long moribund
Mercedes is parked in his deeded
parking spot, he has decided to make
do with Zipcars, Ubers, and the
occasional water taxi.

"I look forward to seeing what
you're working on," Thiru says. Again,
a perfectly normal thing to say, especially
given that Gerry, for almost forty years
now, has always been working on
something. He's not the most prolific ▶

writer—only seven books total—but
thanks to *Dream Girl*, he doesn't have
to be.

He has, however, always been a
disciplined writer, working every day,
from eight to twelve and three to six.
Lately, he can't write at all and it's not
the view's fault; his office is downstairs
and he keeps the blinds drawn to avoid
glare. He writes on a computer with a
special display, one that resembles an
actual page. It's amazing to Gerry how
many writers fail to grasp the visual
context of their books, but then, with
people reading novels one paragraph at
a time on their phones, maybe he is the
one who's out of step. He has a perfect
chair and a perfect desk and he keeps
his assistant out of the apartment as
much as possible, having learned that
he cannot stand to have a breathing
human in his space when he's writing.

Still, nothing's coming.

When Thiru leaves, he goes dutifully
to his office, taking the envelope full
of mail with him and sorting it—one
pile for recycling, one pile for bills,
one pile for personal and professional
correspondence—but he can't find
the energy to open any of it. Should
he entrust Victoria to do that as well?
She's an eager beaver, about thirty or so,
but with no defined ambition. She won
the job when she told him that she loved
to read but had no desire to write. The
worst assistants are the little vampires

who try to turn an essentially menial job into a mentorship.

Now that he thinks about it, maybe Victoria was the one who told him that Baltimore was popular with millennials, although she arrived here as a college student and seems to have stayed out of sheer inertia. They eventually figured out that she had been at Goucher the year he was the visiting professor in Creative Writing, back when the century was relatively new, but she had switched her major to biology by then so their paths never crossed. She has no idea why she studied biology, no idea what she really wants to do. This is baffling to Gerry, who has known since he was thirteen that he wanted to be a writer, fought with an indifferent world to make it so, and was almost forty when it was acknowledged he had the goods. He's not one for millennial-bashing—as a tail-end boomer, he resents the stereotypes heaped on his generation, which have almost nothing to do with him. But he is suspicious of this current mania for happiness. Anyone can be happy.

He forces himself to turn on his computer and a few words trickle out. He is trying to write a novel about Berlin in the early 1980s. *A memoir!* How could Thiru suggest that yet again? It wasn't out of respect for his mother that Gerry has avoided writing about his father; it's been out of respect for his own ▶

**Excerpt from *Dream Girl* by
Laura Lippman** *(continued)*

imagination. He has nothing to say
about his father, a stultifyingly ordinary
man who did one extraordinarily
despicable thing. Gerry wouldn't give
him the satisfaction of taking up the
mental real estate that even a slender
memoir would require. Not that his
father would know; he's been dead for
almost two decades.

Gerry gives up on his own writing and
reads for the rest of the afternoon until
he hears Victoria entering the apartment
above, bringing his dinner. Gerry does
not cook and has no patience with all
the attention heaped on food nowadays.
Food is fuel. Part of Victoria's job is to
bring him something ready-made, from
Whole Foods or Harris Teeter, for dinner
every evening. He can handle breakfast
on his own—oatmeal warmed in the
microwave, fruit, and yogurt. Lunch is
a turkey sandwich, maybe with some
carrots. As a result, Gerry remains
quite lean and fit, requiring no exercise
beyond walking and a rowing machine.
He wouldn't even have the rowing
machine, but it was part of the
apartment's staging and the company
assumed he wanted that as well when he
asked if the furniture could be included.
So, sometimes he puts on gym shorts
and a T-shirt and he rows, twenty-five
floors above the water, feeling like he's
in some goddamn ad, although an ad
for a rowing machine would feature a
younger man, he supposes.

He eats his dinner, watching the

sunset. The city is beautiful at night. Flaws disappear, lights glow. He finds himself wondering if he is obligated to get in touch with his father's heirs about his mother's death. He has not been able to establish that his parents ever divorced, but her lawyer was adamant that his father's second family cannot make any claims on his mother's estate. Everything goes to Gerry.

The problem is that "everything" is the house, which has three mortgages and an overwhelming amount of stuff. He's going to put Victoria in charge of emptying it, but he can't completely hand off the responsibility. His mother, it turns out, saved *everything*, including his juvenilia. The University of Texas, which outbid Princeton for his papers, wants a complete accounting. He'll have to go through every carton and crate, just to be sure. He supposes he should set up a system for all his mail, too, archiving emails and filing the regular mail—

The mail. Fait Avenue. How could he have forgotten who lived on Fait Avenue? Actually "lived," given she exists only in a book, his book. Fait Avenue was Aubrey's address in *Dream Girl*. An inside joke, a little homage, to Nabokov and his Aubrey McFate in *Lolita*, a bit of cleverness that went unnoticed by virtually everyone, given that Fait Avenue is a very real place in Baltimore. He had placed Aubrey in the heart of Greektown, within hearing ▶

**Excerpt from *Dream Girl* by
Laura Lippman** *(continued)*

distance of the expressway, walking
distance to Samos. Fait and Ponca.
But the address was fake: there was
no 4999½ Fait Avenue, no basement
apartment where a beautiful woman,
following her own mysterious agenda,
seduced a slightly older man in despair
over his life. Had that been the address
on the letter? 4999? That should have
jumped out at him, but he's so distracted
these days. No, he thinks there was no
number, just the street name. He would
have noticed the number. Fait Avenue,
Baltimore, MD.

He has to know. He jumps up,
bumping his knee hard on the underside
of the table, then stumbles, tripping
over the rowing machine that sits
near the terrace's sliding glass doors,
staggering and sliding across the slick
floor. His foot lands unsteadily on the
first step of the floating staircase landing
and he slips, his arms windmilling,
finding nothing because there is nothing
to find, tumbling ass over teakettle,
as his mother used to say—*why did his
mother say that, what does it even mean,
a teakettle doesn't have an ass*—until he
lands, a crooked, broken thing, in a heap
at the bottom. He tries to get up, but
his right leg isn't having it and there is
nothing within reach that will allow him
to pull himself up and hop. He tries to
drag himself across the floor, but his leg
hurts so much it seems ill-advised. What
if he aggravates the injury by moving?
He tries to find a comfortable resting

position—fuck, distressed concrete—
and waits until morning, when Victoria
finally arrives.

"Call 911," he says with as much
authority as he can muster, positioning
his arms to hide the stain from where
he relieved himself at some point during
the long, miserable night.

* * *

1968

His mother was always slow to call the
doctor. Not for fear of bills; not even
later, when money was tight, did they
ever worry about doctors' bills. Even as
a boy, Gerry was aware of what caused
his mother financial anxiety (extras at
school, broken things, the amount of
milk that a growing boy can drink)
and what did not, which was pretty
much doctors' bills and holiday gifts.

But doctors, in his mother's view,
were for surgery and bones, maybe
the occasional prescription. It was
a weakness to call them. So, when
appendicitis began making its claim on
Gerry's body, she treated each symptom
as it came, never seeing them as parts to
a possibly deadly whole. His father was
away—his father, a traveling salesman,
was usually away—so there was no adult
to second-guess his mother. Vomiting?
Put the boy to bed with flat ginger ale.
Fever? Baby aspirin. Abdominal pain?
She draped a heating pad, something ▶

**Excerpt from *Dream Girl* by
Laura Lippman** *(continued)*

Gerry normally loved, over his
midsection. Olive green, with three
color-coded buttons—yellow, orange,
red.

It was the heating pad, the doctors
later said, that caused his appendix to
burst.

He ended up at GBMC. His father was
not there when he came out of surgery,
but he made it back to Maryland the
next day. Gerry woke from a nap to
his parents by his bedside, hissing at
each other. He fluttered his eyelids and
pretended to slumber. His parents never
fought in front of him, never. He wanted
to hear the words they said to each other
when they thought he wasn't listening.

"It's not my fault I wasn't here," his
father was saying. "It's my job."

"Your job," his mother repeated.

"Yes, my job," his father said,
responding to some tone that Gerry
hadn't heard. It was as if the word "job"
didn't mean "job." Then what did it
mean?

Gerald Andersen sold school
furniture. He had a suitcase that
Gerry had doted on as a child, until
another neighborhood boy had accused
him of playing with dolls, rather ruining
it for him. His father's sample case had
desks (for students and teachers), chairs,
cunning little chalkboards. Gerry still
sometimes unpacked the case when
his father was home, marveling at the
miniatures, the specially designed case
where each piece fit, almost like a jigsaw

puzzle. His father's territory was Ohio, Illinois, and Indiana, one of the better regions. The 1960s were a good time to sell school furniture. The population was soaring, new schools were being built, old ones upgraded. Gerry remembered the stunning headline in his *Weekly Reader* when he was in third grade, prophesizing that the United States would hit 200 million people by the time he was in fourth grade. Now here they were, in the biggest and best country in the world, even if Nixon had just been elected president, a profound disappointment to his mother.

He wasn't so sure how his father felt about the election. "A man's vote is confidential, buddy," he had said in October, patting his breast pocket, as if all his secrets resided there.

"But we're supposed to talk about current events at home," Gerry said. "We pick one story in the news and we talk about it at home, then bring in articles and make a presentation at school."

"We don't have to say who we're for, though. It's enough to know their positions, right? Okay, tell me what Humphrey is going to do."

Years later, Gerry would sometimes wonder if his father had voted for George Wallace. He never said anything that was outright racist, but he was a man given to nostalgia and that nostalgia was for whiteness. He loved the small Ohio towns he saw on his travels. He called ▶

them the "real America." And when
Gerry asked why Baltimore wasn't real,
his father waved a hand in front of his
face and said there were just too many
people here, and no respect for the "old
ways." But he never clarified what the
old ways were.

Gerry was having trouble keeping his
eyes closed without scrunching them
tight, so he tried to roll onto his side.
But he was tender from the surgery and
the effort made him yelp.

"Hey, buddy," his father said.

"How are you feeling?" his mother
asked.

"Better. When do I get to go home?"

"Tomorrow. They just want to make
sure there's no risk of infection," his
mother said.

"You can tell everyone at school that
you almost died—and your mother gave
you baby aspirin."

His mother defended herself. "How
was I to know?"

The question hung in the air,
unanswered. How was she to know
that this stomach pain was something
more? Fair enough. How was she to
know what her husband did on his
endless trips to Ohio, Illinois, and
Indiana? He called home late at night,
when the rates went down, reversing
the charges. He described his day,
complained about the motels, the food.
Gerry was asleep, or supposed to be,
when he called. His mother didn't
realize how late he stayed up, listening

to Johnny Carson from the top of the stairs. Surely, if she knew, she would have muffled her tears after these calls.

Once, when Gerry pulled the furniture from his father's case, a strand of long blond hair came out with the miniature desk, the one for children, but a seven-year-old boy had no context for such a discovery. He uncoiled the hair from the desk leg, even as the memory coiled itself inside his mind, waiting to spring back one day. *Another child has been playing with these things.* That seemed ordinary enough. If he had bothered to investigate the idea further, he would have imagined a school superintendent's child being distracted by the objects during his father's sales pitch. Or maybe the items had been taken out during a school board meeting and a bored board member had fiddled with one.

A long blond hair means nothing to a child. ❧